LAWLESS ELEMENTS

A Novel

Greg Bascom

This book is a work of fiction. The characters, incidents and dialogue are drawn from the author's imagination and are not to be construed as real. Any resemblance to actual persons, living or dead, is entirely coincidental.

No part of this book may be used or reproduced in any manner whatsoever without written permission from the author except in the case of brief quotations embodied in critical articles and reviews. For information go to:
www.gregbascom.com

FOR BEATRIZ,

MY SECOND WIFE,

THE ONE WHO TAUGHT ME HOW

TO LAUGH

Acknowledgements

I thank my daughters, Michelle and Cynthia and their Mom for their encouragement and helpful comments. I am deeply indebted to the members of our writer's group, Dr. Lenny Karpman, Carol Marujo, Jo Stuart, Robin Kazmier and Mike Crump for their good ideas, and for talking me out of some terrible ones. All of the many reviewers of the opening chapters at YouWriteOn.com and Authonomy.com were helpful, especially author Rosalind Winter and the anonymous Patty who nailed the problem with the first two chapters. And special thanks to author Elizabeth Ridley for reviewing my manuscripts over the years and lathering me well before shaving.

Like other struggling novelists, I am indebted to The Mary Freeman Wisdom Foundation, The Faulkner Society, their donors and volunteers and especially Rosemary James, that dauntless warrior who has carried the society's banner through devastating hurricanes and the worst recession in seven decades.

Tropical islands charm. They hale from afar migrants, preachers, explorers, conquistadors, missionaries, imperialists, adventurers and romantics. Islands conceal peril. They harbor pirates, revolutionaries, insurgents, subversives and lawless elements.

Moroland

The clans that migrated to the Philippines did not comprehend individual land ownership. They staked out tribal territory for their community of 30 to 100 families headed by a chieftain called a *datu*. The *datu* awarded legal rights to families to use parcels of the clan's land. That changed in the 15th century after Malay preachers converted the tribes of the Sulu and Mindanao Islands to Islam. For the Moros, the predominately-Muslim tribes of the southern Philippines, the land belongs to Allah.

Ancestral domain is all the natural wealth—land, rivers, game—in communally bounded territory, continuously occupied since time immemorial by a homogenous society differentiated from the majority by common language, customs and traditions. Ancestral domain is the clan's turf, or Allah's realm.

The Spanish recognized indigenous concepts of ownership and their right to ancestral domains. The American colonial government declared that lands not belonging to individuals were public property and in 1902 required persons to register their land. Eleven months later, they declared unregistered land public property subject to homesteading. Since individual land ownership was contrary to Moro traditions and beliefs, the majority did not register their parcel of ancestral domain.

In 1909, a unanimous decision by the U.S. Supreme Court, written by Oliver Wendell Homes, overruled the contention that unregistered ancestral lands were public property and restored indigenous ownership. The

American colonial government ignored that decision. To dilute the perceived Moro threat, they encouraged landless peasants from Luzon and the Visayas to resettle in the south. They allowed Christians up to 24 hectares, but non-Christians no more than ten.

In 1936, during the Philippine transition from an American colony to independence, Commonwealth Act No. 141 adjudged ancestral domains public land. For the next sixty years, migrants from the north and domestic and foreign corporations acquired rights to exploit tracks of ancestral land. In 1996, after decades of Moro insurgency, the Philippine government began to recognize indigenous rights and issue certificates of ancestral domain, but by then the Moros had lost over seventy-five percent of their land.

What remains of Moro ancestral domain is in Central Mindanao. The 2007-RAND study, *Ungoverned Territories,* considers Central Mindanao an area of contested governance between the Moro Islamic Liberation Front (MILF) and the Philippine government. This ungoverned territory includes the vast and resource rich Liguasan Marsh, where a few lawless elements hide amongst hundreds of thousands of peaceful people.

This story about the violent conflict over Moro ancestral domain revolves around actual events in February 2003.

CHAPTER I

Davao, Philippines, Sunday afternoon, February 2, 2003

Steve bounded up the outside stairs, unlocked his kitchen door and faced Julius hunched in front of the refrigerator glowering like an angry wife. Meooow! When he bent to scoop him up, Julius scampered through the dining room and stopped at the top of the inside stairs. He glared at Steve's lumbering feet with impatience. Julius wanted him downstairs.

The dining room air conditioner kicked on and blew cool air across Steve's damp swim briefs, but intuition chilled him more. Things happened upstairs. Pots boiled over. Cooking oil smoked. Lavatories flooded. Human lapses did not happen downstairs, yet something down there required his attention, a varmint too big for Julius to handle on his own.

Julius waited until Steve came within arm's length before scurrying down the stairs. He stopped at the bottom and stared through the open door to the maid's room, a room appended to the rear of the house. Steve's maid did not live in. After his employer allowed him to work from his home, he used the room for his office. Amina did too.

Steve stood at the threshold. The office looked normal, yet it was not. Something—sunlight, aroma, humidity, vapors—felt corrupted. Then he saw it. One of the windows peeped open a crack. Neither he nor Amina opened them, had never unlocked them. Someone had entered their space. As he listened and waited, he prepared to pounce, braced to slam the heel of his hand under the intruder's nose a few millimeters short of fatal, because killing someone upsets tranquility. Prepare, watch, listen and wait, wait for the scumbag to come out of hiding.

The art of waiting is a struggle against the fear that nothing will happen. Disappointment crept up. Steve stepped inside and saw the bathroom door ajar. They kept it closed because with a cracked sewer pipe the toilet sometimes stank. He planted his left foot and kicked the door's upper panel with his right. The wood split. Half the panel fell when the door slammed against the wall and rebounded. Julius scurried up the stairs.

Steve flipped on the bathroom light and whipped aside the shower curtain. His improvised darkroom—he still shot film occasionally—appeared undisturbed.

"Shit," he hissed, "my cameras."

He strode out, yanked open the wardrobe and looked over six thousand dollars worth of photo gear. It seemed untouched, everything in its place, his pistol too, mummified in its oily rag. A greater fear displaced the rush of gratitude. Breaking and entering without looting, a more sinister motive—something worth more than six grand.

Inspecting the windowsill and the floor beneath, Steve flushed with anger—no broken glass. He raised the bamboo blind. A swirl of paint flecks surrounded the unlocked latch. The burglar had had inside help. Then he smiled, thinking the window had jammed and foiled the treachery—the reason nothing had been stolen. To be sure, he slipped his fingers into the crack and lifted.

The window opened.

He spun around and eyed his desk. The disarray of papers did not alarm him. With Amina out of town, he had labored until late the night before on his Apex fertilizer solicitation. Afterwards, he had spent an hour or so scribbling ideas on how they might persuade Amina's family to accept their relationship. He stared at the yellow legal tablet with his scrawled notes. A translucent stain splotched the top sheet. He felt it. It was dry, not damp, oily, or sticky. He had not done that. Someone had gotten in. He peered through the office door and listened but could hear nothing over the whir of the room air conditioners.

Looking over his desk again, he saw that his laptop appeared lopsided. When he lifted it, he spotted an access plate lying on the desk. He turned over the computer and cussed. The hard drive was missing.

With clenched teeth, he eased open the desk drawer, first exposing pens and pencils in the tray, then the clutter beyond—homeless parts, a 9 mm short cartridge, mementos and leftovers—the jumble of stuff he rifled through from time to time. It was impossible to determine if the thief had. He pulled on the drawer and smiled at the stack of diskettes. Fearful that his old laptop would crash and burn, as Amina's had, he backed it up every Friday night, updated its last will and testament. The diskettes contained all his work except for the analysis of the fertilizer bids, and they had all of Amina's files, her "homework," huge databases he could not know about because Apex threatened to terminate him if he got involved in Filipino politics. Even so, he had let Amina use his computer until they got around to buying her a new one, and had procrastinated. He poked the diskettes. Some contained a mixture of Amina's stuff and his. *What's in your files, Amina? Who's after you?* The burglar knew. Steve supposed the thief had long gone, but he had to make certain.

He went out onto the stairwell. The wood creaked. The sound pinged off the barren tile floor of the huge living room, unfurnished except for the sofa at the rear where they watched CNN, and his photographs hanging on the walls. The room looked bleak, like a photo gallery without customers. He peered across the empty expanse to the sliding-glass front door. The latch was horizontal. The burglar had not gone out the front in plain view of the guard at the gate, no surprise there. Racing upstairs, he checked the two unused bedrooms, then the master bedroom and bath before yanking aside the blind beside their bed. The compound looked empty as far as he could see.

He went outside to search the compound that Apex leased for its expatriate employees. A twelve-foot high concrete wall with a solid steel gate surrounded them. Steve and Amina lived in the second of four houses in a row, flanked by the Van Der Zees nearest the gate and Brenda on the other side. The fourth house, the guesthouse, had been vacant for a while. An armed guard manned the gate, feminized it perhaps. The Only

Ladies Security Agency, a group of thirty-something petite women, had kept delinquents out—until now.

Outside the compound, shacks squatted amidst bushes under towering coconut trees, but the plot inside had been bulldozed level—no trees, mounds or gullies, the few shrubs scrawny—no place to hide. Their row of homes with white roofs and outsized eaves to provide shade from the blistering Philippine sun looked like gigantic mushrooms that had spawned on an oasis of grass.

Naked but for his swim briefs, the heat felt good after the canned air inside, although without a breeze, the humidity clutched his skin. Except for the room air-conditioners buzzing and groaning, the houses seemed to be dozing between chores, waiting for their occupants to return. That was typical for Sundays if the weather was nice. The thief had chosen the perfect time, but he had not come through the gate. The guards allowed no one into the compound unless a resident approved their visit.

Looking around for anything strange, Steve ambled to the rear of his house. Underneath the office window he saw gouges in the grass and the impression of a boot heel. Cracked paint around the window sash evidenced the burglar's struggle to pry it open. Steve felt ill with a sour stomach and clammy skin, as if some diseased son-of-a-bitch had given him the flu. He walked toward the rear of the compound, inspecting the wall, shrubbery and grass. In the back corner by the guesthouse, he found a trampled bush, scuffmarks on the wall and deep scratches near the top where the bastard came over with a grapple.

Steve trudged back to his house under the weight of certain trouble. Apex lawyers enjoined its foreign employees from getting involved in Filipino politics, yet he slept with a dissident who worked for the Moro Islamic Liberation Front. As if that weren't joining enough, some of his backup diskettes had both his and Amina's files. He had to report the theft to Apex Davao. Haradji, chief of security, would come. The bald-headed snoop would take his backup for critical executive review because with nothing else taken it appeared the thief had come for Apex's secrets. And when the critical executives discovered an MILF subversive had been using a company computer, there would be no more enjoining, no more job, no company house, company paid utilities or company truck. That would end his dumb procrastinating. It had been near three months since Amina's computer had crashed. It was not someone's flu; his dilly-dallying had made him sick.

If Julius had not alarmed him, he would have had a beer and a shower before going to the office and that's what he would do, act as if he had nothing to hide. He needed time. He had to wait for Gerrit Van Der Zee to come home and use his computer to scrub his backup clean of dissidence. *What dissidence*, he wondered. Amina prepared legal documents for the MILF negotiators seeking autonomy over Moro ancestral lands. And she campaigned to get Moro women a role in the peace talks. She did not need huge databases for those tasks.

While he showered, Steve tried to figure the theft. Someone had paid his maid to unlock the window, and if not her, one of the guards. The thief intended to copy files, not his, he held no secrets, but he had to take the hard drive because the old laptop used diskettes, not CDs. *He came for Amina's files, her personal stuff; he violated her.*

Steve thought of Rita, violated, raped, sodomized. Blood surged from his toes to brain. His head throbbed. He thrust his fist at the shower wall but snapped back his arm as his knuckles pecked the tile. Nearly two decades had passed since he near killed Rita's stepfather. They had sent him to the Benedictine military school for that. The monks made him pray for his own deliverance and the salvation of assholes. That quenched his anger. He perfected the art of not connecting, celebrated life at arm's length, always stopping a millimeter short of getting involved in someone else's issues—his chicken soup recipe for serenity. Now someone spilled his soup and he had forgotten how to pray. He might never get the lid back on the pot.

Steve looked out the window at the Van Der Zee's carport. Gerrit's truck was still not there, but he phoned anyway hoping Isabela might be home.

"*Casa* Gerrit."

Steve sighed. "Hi, *Profesora*. Is Gerrit around? I need a favor."

"Gerrit went downtown but he'll be back soon. Come on over."

Steve sorted through his backup and put several diskettes in his pocket along with some blanks. He tore off the first several pages from the yellow legal pad, stuffed them into a manila envelope and filed it with his personal papers. No matter the mysterious splotch on his notes might be DNA-laden drool. He did not want the company to know about his troubles with his lover's family. Then he called security at Apex Davao and reported the burglary to the duty clerk.

Through the front doors, Steve saw Isabela sprawled on the living room carpet reading a book. Margreet, her eighteen-month old daughter, slept on a blanket beside her. He tapped on the glass. Isabela got up and slid the door open.

"*Hola,*" she whispered. "Come on in." She put her finger to her lips. "Margreet's napping. You want a beer."

"Sure, thanks."

As Isabela climbed the stairs to the kitchen, Steve wrestled his eyes away from the curves of her perfect behind to look elsewhere. The four houses had identical floor plans, but unlike Steve's bleak living room, the Van Der Zee's looked like a library. Gerrit, a Dutch agronomist, had row upon row of tomes about bugs and plant diseases. Isabela, a Moche Indian from Northern Peru and a professor of history, had scores of texts about the colonization of indigenous peoples, her specialty. When Apex moved Gerrit from Peru to the Philippines, Isabela began to study the Moro-Spanish wars that lasted more than three centuries. She joined Amina's campaign for the Moro cause. Listening to Isabela and Amina discuss history, Steve felt as if he was taking a graduate course in discontent, but he did not get involved.

Isabela returned with a bottle of San Miguel and a glass of *chicha*, her homemade Peruvian concoction of fermented corn, a somewhat sour joy-juice. She handed the beer to Steve and sat on the floor. Steve sat close by so they could talk without disturbing Margreet,

"How is Amina doing at the MILF conference?"

"She can't call me until tomorrow when she gets to Manila."

"What's she going to do in Manila?"

"On Tuesday, the Islamic Studies Institute has a symposium on women. She's giving a presentation about Moro women as the traditional negotiators in settling blood feuds and her arguments for their being involved in the peace talks."

"She's a determined woman."

"Yep. Hey, do you know how to interrogate a cat?"

Isabela smiled. "What's Julius done this time?"

"Someone broke into my house. Julius is the only witness."

"Que!" Isabela straightened and glanced at Margreet. "When? How'd he get in?"

Steve shrugged. "Sometime between ten and four while I was swimming at the Insular Hotel. He came over the back wall by the guesthouse."

Isabela looked at her daughter again, leaned close to Steve and whispered. "How'd he get in the house?"

"He climbed through my office window. Someone unlocked it."

"Do you think Posey did it?"

Steve did not want to accuse his maid, although she had been acting skittish lately. "Can't tell how long it's been unlocked, could be someone else, a workman maybe or one—"

His cell phone vibrated. He plucked it from his shirt pocket. "Steve here…Hi Haradji…Yeah, came over the back wall and took my hard drive, nothing else. He ignored a fortune in camera equipment." Steve waited. "Well, he could have swiped a beer, but I don't think he left my office….Okay, I'll tell the guard to wait." Steve clicked off and worried that he had called security too soon. If Haradji arrived before Gerrit returned, there would be bad problems.

"What's Haradji going to do?"

"He'll be over to interrogate the guard after he has a chat with Stillwell."

"What's the general manager got to do with this?"

"Stillwell is going to think that one of the company's competitors is behind the burglary." He shook his head. "I don't think so." He frowned and gazed at Isabela.

"What's the matter?"

"Haradji will be questioning you and Gerrit. You know Amina uses my computer. I don't want Haradji to know that. Let's keep Amina out of this."

"No problem," she whispered. "I know nothing. I've nothing to tell Haradji, and neither does Gerrit. Gerrit doesn't like him."

Margreet stirred as they heard the guard opening the gate. Isabela picked up her daughter and they went to look out the front door. When a pickup truck pulled inside, Steve exhaled. "Good, it's Gerrit. I need to use his computer."

Gerrit watched Steve transfer files and delete the originals. "Those are Amina's files, aren't they?"

Steve nodded.

"What's in them?"

"I don't know." He turned and looked at Gerrit. "I didn't want to know for fear I'd be getting involved in the insurgency."

"*Now* you're involved, I'd say."

CHAPTER 2

The compound, Sunday evening, February 2

Gerrit with a Heineken, Steve with a San Miguel, sat on the Van Der Zee's front porch not many yards from the guardhouse and called out reassurances to "Toots," that it was not her fault, that they would support her—men aiding a pretty woman in distress.

"She's cute," Steve said. "She has to be innocent."

"Certainly is. They're our girls. Gave 'em jolly good names, we did."

Filipinos acquire jovial nicknames. Local news stories featured Rody the mayor discussing thorny issues, Beds, the thief, nabbed by Ting-Ting, the policeman, and orphans coddled by Sin-Sin, the Catholic priest. During an impromptu picnic after Apex hired The Only Ladies Security Agency, the tipsy residents renamed their regular guards Toots, Boots and Oops, who tended to drop things. Their job consisted of opening the gate, relaying messages and being cheerful.

Toots wiped the palms of her hands on her dark blue uniform and tried to smile but it waned before it had a chance. Toot's relief, Boots, the heftiest of the female guards, arrived shortly before six. At a glance,

Boots knew the dreaded had happened—a theft—and that before the sun went down Haradji might snap his fingers and fire The Only Ladies Security Agency. Toots and Boots huddled, whispering.

A horn blared outside. Her body heaving at a forty-five degree angle, Boots slid open the heavy gate with one hand, the other holding the agency's pistol and holster firm against her thigh, which was too beefy for the rawhide strap to go around. Toots stood stiff beside the little guard shack. A pick-up truck rolled forward and stopped. Both women snapped to attention and saluted. Haradji spoke to Toots. She sagged, recovered, and then saluted again, although with a little wobble.

"She's pissin' in her knickers," Gerrit said.

Reputed to be progeny of a near-extinct Moro clan of goliaths, Haradji loomed over Filipinos. Sturdy yet spry, a man who valued exercise and vegetables, he appeared younger than his advanced years. Reportedly fluent in Tagalog, Visayan, English and several Moro languages, Haradji spoke with an intimidating, prayer-like monotone. He had ugly sloe-eyes—jet-black pupils set in membranes fractured with red veins—and after decades working with the NBI, the Philippine FBI, they said he could frighten the crap out of a water buffalo with a level stare.

He opened his passenger door and signaled to Steve to get in. They drove the short distance to the guesthouse's carport.

"Someone took your computer. What else?"

"Not the computer, the hard drive, the memory where files are stored."

"Damn it." Haradji pushed the bridge of his sunglasses up his nose. "I don't need a fuckin' lesson on computers. Tell me what else was taken."

"Nothing else is missing."

"What about damage? Things messed up; drawers opened?"

"No, he didn't disturb anything outside my office."

"How do you know he's a he?"

"You'll see. He wears a size ten boot."

"What makes you think this person came over the wall?"

"I'll show you."

After Haradji inspected the marks on the wall, he removed his sunglasses and focused on Steve. "What did you have in your computer besides company information?"

"I had two dozen bids on a fertilizer tender. I suspect that's what the thief wanted."

"Anything else?"

"My financial records and some letters, that's all."

"Does Miss Taiba use your computer?"

Steve shrugged. "Amina used it for email sometimes." He tossed his hand. "I think they took it for the fertilizer data, but we need to check my Apex files. I backed up Friday night."

Haradji brightened. "Good, I'll take your backup." Something stirred behind the vile eyes. "Do they contain *everything*?"

"Sure…I mean the diskettes were in the drawer where I left them. I'll need them returned as soon as possible so I can work."

Haradji nodded and then examined the bushes and wall again. He checked the rear windows of the guesthouse and ambled toward Steve's home, inspecting Brenda's house on the way.

"Where's Miss Brenda?"

"She went over to Samal Island yesterday. She should be back soon."

"What about the Van Der Zees?"

"Isabela has been home all day, but she told me she didn't see or hear anything."

When they reached the back of Steve's house, Haradji studied the window and stooped to scrutinize the footprints before taking pictures. Then he stepped back and considered the row of houses. The builder had set them at an angle to the driveway and perimeter wall. Haradji mused aloud that the rear of Steve's home was visible from Brenda's house, but not from the Van Der Zee's.

"Where's Miss Taiba?"

"Up on Luzon for a few days."

Haradji gave Steve a wry look. "Now that's handy. Miss Brenda in Samal, your friend up north, you at the Insular and your backside window unlocked."

"Yeah, rotten apple in the barrel."

"Have any of the guards been in your house?"

"No, but when I go to Brenda's or the Van Der Zee's, I don't bother to lock up."

Haradji looked around. "With all the blinds down against the sun and these noisy air conditioners, a guard could sneak in, especially after dark."

Steve nodded.

"Okay. Mr. Stillwell wants a briefing at noon tomorrow. We'll meet at the guesthouse in the morning, seven sharp. When Miss Brenda returns, please tell her to join us. What time does your maid get here?"

"At seven."

"When does Miss Taiba return?"

Steve did not want Haradji interrogating Amina before she knew more than he did. "Friday," he lied. He studied his reflection on Haradji's sunglasses and imagined a crapping carabao. *Great picture,* he thought.

Haradji stared back at him. "I'll have a chat with her then."

Haradji pulled out his cell phone and made two calls. Steve understood the first conversation; he had learned Tagalog. Haradji asked one of his NBI contacts a phone number. For the second call, Haradji spoke Visayan.

Haradji pocketed the phone. "Okay, Mr. Jake Severino will be here in about an hour to dust for prints. He'll take your fingerprints for comparison. He can get Miss Taiba's from her personal items. Let's go inside."

Before going to the office, Haradji patrolled the other rooms wearing a surgical glove on his right hand, although he did not touch anything except doorknobs. Aside from the disheveled bed and a pile of dirty dishes, the house appeared tidy and spartan, uncluttered by knick-knacks. Amina decorated with Steve's photographs. Haradji paused to look at each one. He studied the picture of the raging water buffalo hanging in the dining room.

"Is that the carabao that gored you?"

Steve nodded.

Haradji examined the photograph up close. "You shook the camera a little."

"Like hell. The camera shook, not me."

Haradji stepped back, still studying the photograph. "Mr. Bryce, you are a lucky son-of-a-bitch." He pointed. "That bull has murder in his eyes."

Shortly before eight o'clock, Steve saw Brenda's pick up coming through the gate. Brenda, blonde, unattached and overweight, had come from the home office three months earlier to monitor Apex's expansion projects in Southeast Asia. In her early thirties like Steve and Amina, they had become friends but not confidants. Steve had spent an anxious hour preparing for the delicate conversation with Brenda. He could not ask her if she knew Amina used his computer, but Haradji would. He rushed out to greet her as she was unloading her truck.

"I see you enjoyed Samal. That's a lovely sunburn."

"How do you do it, Steve—blond, blue-eyed *and* tanned? You look toasted to perfection."

"Gradually," he said, raising his finger, "by swimming forty laps every day, eighty on weekends." He eased back her blonde forelocks and winced at the crimson below her pallid hairline. "Girl, you cannot bake in the sun. Christ, didn't you use suntan lotion?"

"I slept off a hangover by the pool today."

Steve hoisted Brenda's ice chest onto one shoulder, slung her tote bag over the other and followed her up the outside steps to her kitchen.

"We have a meeting at the guesthouse first thing in the morning."

"What's going on?"

"Someone broke into my office today and swiped the hard drive from my laptop."

Brenda glanced at her family/dining room. "Did he break in here?"

"No, and he didn't touch my cameras. Nothing's missing but my hard drive."

"Oh shit, espionage. What did you have on it?"

"I don't think my Apex data was worth stealing. No doubt they were after the fertilizer bids."

"Did you have anything on the expansion projects?"

"My materials estimates include the expansion, but there are too many variables to back them out of the total. But the fertilizer bids have detailed prices for the bulk material, bagging and transportation, a great deal of very specific information."

"Is the bidding still open?"

"No, it closed Friday. But with bids from over twenty suppliers, I have perhaps the most comprehensive review ever of the fertilizer business in Southeast Asia. There are over twenty suspects."

"Are you sure you didn't have useful information on the expansions?"

Steve crinkled his brow, thinking Brenda's fixation on the expansions a good thing. "No, I'm not sure. I have some databases that could have sensitive information. Haradji has my back up from last Friday. You better go through my files and see for yourself. Stillwell wants a report by noon."

"Great, you have a current backup. We'll go through it in the morning. Thanks again for hauling up my stuff." She smiled. "I'm burned out. See you at the meeting."

As Steve walked to his house, he felt he had implicated the fertilizer data without overdoing it, and Brenda would be anxious to look at his backup. She had not considered Amina might be involved. Still, he worried what Brenda might tell Haradji. If she saw Amina using his computer, he hoped his email explanation would prevail.

CHAPTER 3

The Compound, Monday morning, February 3

Steve was brewing his second mug of espresso when he heard a car pull into his carport and then footfalls on the outside stairs. He opened the door to Bipsy, information technology manager at Apex Davao, fellow photo enthusiast and good friend. He handed Steve a carton and grinned.

"Whoa," Steve said, stepping backwards. "Good morning, Bipsy. Come in." He put the box on the kitchen counter and opened the flaps. "You're kidding. It's new."

Bipsy pulled at his goatee. "Let's see, you have 512 megabits of RAM, a 60 gig hard drive and a CD burner. There's a couple of CDs in there with your backup."

"Wow! You want some coffee?"

"No thanks, your espresso drain cleaner dissolves intestines. I'll take some juice, whatever you have."

After giving Bipsy mango juice, Steve took out the new laptop and placed it on the dining room table. "What did I do to deserve this?"

"Hah, you hired an assassin to brutally dismember that turd of crap you had and left me no choice. We can't get parts for that antique. Besides, I'm in love with your blue eyes and cheerful demeanor. It should have most of the software you need. Let me know if you want anything else."

"Thank you, thank you."

"What happened, Blue Eyes? I want sordid details."

The sound of vehicles coming into the compound interrupted Steve's recount of the burglary. He pulled the bamboo blind aside.

"Oh, shit! It's an invasion." Haradji had put one of his men at the gate. The three Only Ladies Security guards walked in a huddle to the guesthouse. Jake, the fingerprint guy and Haradji's assistant stood beside Slick Guzman, Apex Davao's controller and Haradji's boss. Slick also served as Steve's administrative supervisor, the person who approved or disapproved his benefits and privileges, such as working from his house rather than the Apex office complex. Gerrit and Isabela cradling Margreet joined the crowd. Steve's eyes darted from one disgruntled face to another. "They're going to lynch me for disturbing the peace."

The guard opened the door beside the gate. Posey, Steve's maid, stepped inside and froze. She gawked at the commotion and tried to bolt. The guard grabbed her arm, pointed to the guesthouse and growled. She trudged after the others.

"Your noose is loosed, Blue Eyes. The butler did it. She goes to the gallows."

"She unlocked the window, but for whom. I hope Haradji finds out."

"Do not fret, Blue Eyes. This is the Philippines. Posey will spill the beans. Let us haste pronto. Torture excites me."

The part-time caretaker for the guesthouse had made coffee and laid out an array of sliced fruit on a table in the living room. Steve walked over to Gerrit, who was filling a plate.

"Where's Posey?"

Gerrit jabbed a fork in the air. "She's upstairs with the guards. I think they're getting fingerprinted."

"Yeah, Haradji's fingerprint guy lifted a clear thumbprint from the window lock. It matches several others he found around the house."

"Posey's?"

"No doubt. Listen," Steve whispered, "Amina's returning Wednesday, but I told Haradji she's coming back Friday."

Gerrit smiled and looked over his shoulder. "Not to worry, my friend. I wouldn't tell Haradji where the loo is. Let him shit his britches, I would."

Brenda pushed open the sliding glass door and greeted them. She spied the fruit and picked up a plate.

Haradji came downstairs and ordered everyone to quiet down. Standing with one hand on his hip while giving the floor a condescending stare, he demanded someone tell him who knew the compound would be vacant except for Mrs. Van Der Zee.

"Everyone," Gerrit snapped. "Our friends, the neighborhood, the guards and even you should know. If the sun is out on Sunday, so are we. My wife being home yesterday was unusual."

"Where were the maids?"

"My maid doesn't work Sundays," Steve said, puzzled. He thought Haradji knew that. "None of us has a live-in maid."

"I do." Gerrit raised his hand. "I sleep with her."

Isabela had been feeding Margreet a piece of mango. She flipped it across the room and hit her husband between the eyes. Everyone laughed except Haradji.

"Haradji, please sit down," Slick said in a tone that told him to shut up too.

After an awkward silence, Slick asked how often the guards patrolled the compound. Gerrit told him they walked around at night, but not often during the day. Steve admitted the residents sometimes became irritated if they had to wait for the guard to open the gate, so they did not stray too far.

"We will wait," Isabela said. Her eyes locked on Haradji. "Make them patrol like soldiers." She hefted Margreet, who stared at Haradji's sunglasses.

They talked about ways to improve security for the compound and agreed that installing electrified concertina wire on top of the wall would discourage intruders. Slick told Haradji to submit a work order for his approval.

Slick excused Gerrit. Isabela and Margreet left with him.

"Okay," Slick said, turning to Steve. "What did you have on that hard drive?"

"The bids on the fertilizer tender—prices from every producer and importer in Southeast Asia. That's my top pick. Anyone in the fertilizer business would love to get their hands on that information."

Haradji's assistant thundered down the stairs and whispered to his boss. Haradji excused himself and went upstairs with his deputy. Someone was crying; Steve recognized Posey's screechy sobs. A few minutes later Haradji came back down. He looked at Steve.

"Your maid confessed. She unlocked the window for her new boyfriend. Claims he said he was curious and wanted to look around the house."

Steve scoffed. "Sure, right, she's not *that* stupid. Who is he?"

"He gave her an alias, but from her description of him, ah…her intimate description, I know who he is. He's an American, an ex-Special Forces soldier supposedly looking for the gold the Japanese hid here during the war. But the NBI suspects that's a cover. They think he might be a mercenary. They want to talk to him, but they can't find him. He uses aliases and disguises. They're not even sure what he looks like."

"Then how do you know it's him?" Brenda asked.

"He's known for a peculiar sexual fetish involving jalapeno peppers, and he's hung like a mule." Haradji looked at Steve. "Your maid provided positive identification."

"Yes, Posey's been wearing a gratified grin lately," Brenda said. "I've been envious."

Steve frowned. "Who does this guy work for? What's his name?"

"Could be anyone. He's for hire. The NBI believes he works alone. He's reclusive and antisocial with no known associates. That's another reason he's hard to find. His name is Marty Santana."

CHAPTER 4

Steve's house, Monday night, February 3

Steve was sitting at the dining room table rebuilding his analysis of the fertilizer bids when his landline rang. He smiled. Amina did not trust the new cell phone service. In four strides, he reached the phone at the far side of the room.

"Steve here."

"Is this the home for wayward infidels?"

"Yes, chief infidel speaking. Would you like to talk to the lonely one?"

"Please."

"One moment, he is procuring a beverage."

Steve dashed to the kitchen and grabbed a cold beer before plopping into his overstuffed reading chair.

"Hi there," he said. "We need to talk about a problem. First, tell me, how did the conference go?"

"Fine. What's the problem?"

He gulped some beer. "Someone broke into the house yesterday and stole the computer's hard drive. Nothing else was taken."

After an interminable pause, she said, "Shit!"

His gut tightened. Amina had picked up the "shit" expression from him. She used it precisely. It meant grave and foreboding circumstance replete with dire and dread.

"Listen, I backed up Friday night. I've got all your homework."

He waited, listening to heavy breathing not of the erotic kind. He set down his beer and whispered, "Tigress, what do you have in those files?"

"Not over the phone. Tell me what happened."

He recounted the burglary and then picked up his beer, took a sip and waited.

"Did you report this to the police?"

"Haradji is handling it. This morning he put the squeeze on Posey. She confessed to unlatching the window for some American adventurer by the name of Santana. You ever hear of Marty Santana?"

After a few moments of silence, "Who's he working for?"

"No one knows. Haradji says he's a loner for hire. He was on Luzon for several years and then came to Mindanao a while back, supposedly to look for the Japanese gold. When the NBI got interested in him, he dropped out of sight. He's short and dark, speaks Tagalog and can pose as a Filipino. That's all that Haradji would tell me. Maybe some of your friends in the MILF can find him."

"What's Apex doing about this?"

"Brenda and I spent the morning going through my files. I didn't have anything significant. She thinks the thief came for the fertilizer bids."

"Does Apex have my homework?"

"No. It's all here, on separate diskettes."

"But it's on the hard drive."

"Haradji wants to talk to you. I told him you would be returning Friday, not Wednesday. We won't let the guards know you're back until Apex loses interest in the burglary."

"No, Sweet Steve. I'm not going to play hide and seek. I am not an Apex employee. I have no obligation to speak with Haradji or anyone else from the company. I understand that can be a problem. It might cause us difficulties with Stillwell if I do not cooperate. But I will not allow that degenerate Haradji to question me. I will stay here with Nashita until you can assure me Stillwell has lost interest."

He sighed. "Okay. We'll wait until this quiets down. The subsidiary managers are flying in for meetings on Wednesday and Thursday. On Wednesday, I present my proposal for the fertilizer contract. They'll discuss the theft then. I'll know the situation Wednesday night, Thursday at the latest."

"Okay, I'll be calling every night. I miss you. Think about me."

"For sure, I'll be thinking."

"See you soon, *Insha Allah*."

"God willing," he echoed.

Steve cradled the phone and slouched in the armchair with his beer. Just a few days separation was hard. He imagined the terrible pain when he lost her forever.

Nineteen months earlier, shortly after Steve moved into the compound, he was washing his pick up in swim trunks when a young woman came to the gate. He saw her pretty face when she greeted the guard, who knew her. As she walked to the Van Der Zee's house, eyes on the ground, Steve stared. The woman wore jeans, a long sleeve blouse and a scarf. When Isabela came out to welcome her guest, she called out to Steve and waved. The young woman did not glance his way. Steve waved back and watched them go into the house. He gazed at the door long after it closed, visualizing the body under all those clothes. The next day, Steve asked Isabela about her visitor. She invited him to dinner to meet Amina, adding with a mischievous smile that *she* had asked about *him*.

As Isabela introduced them, Amina pulled off her scarf and examined Steve's blue eyes. The glitter in her onyx eyes bewitched him. He stared. Amina held his gaze. Isabela said later that he had licked his lips and panted.

The dinner conversation about conquistadors, Moros, ancestral lands and religion fascinated Steve. He asked questions, mostly of Amina, their glances ripe with another curiosity. After desert, Isabela abruptly stood and gathered some dirty dishes. "Steve, you should take Amina for a stroll and show her your favorite place." Amina lifted her scarf to cover her hair. They stepped into the cool night and went out through the gate.

The compound, just north of the city, abutted a dirt road between the highway and the Gulf of Davao. Aside from warehouses along the highway, a tired coconut grove spanned the area, the owner waiting for lucrative offers from developers as the city expanded. Beneath the trees, families at the margin had built homes with sticks, fronds, scrap lumber and pre-owned nails. They too awaited the developers, although with anxiety.

As they strolled toward the gulf, Amina lagged a step or two behind, her head bowed, walking not by his side but not quite following him. A couple greeted Steve. A little farther on, an old man bid him well in Tagalog.

"These people know you," Amina said. She sounded surprised.

The dirt road dead-ended at a dilapidated fishermen's dock. It was Steve's favorite place. Here, by slanting, evening light, he photographed weathered wood, wrinkled elders and students absorbed in their books. Amina let Steve guide her onto the old dock. They sat down. Another couple not far away drifted off. Moonlight glanced across the water.

"I like it here," Steve said. "Out here, I feel I'm in the Philippines." He pointed. "See there, that light, it's a *banca* boat. I caught the faint put-put of its engine a moment ago. You don't see outriggers like that in the States. For you, it is nothing. For me, that sound is a souvenir."

Amina laughed. "You are a silly romantic, Sweet Steve. That is what I will call you, 'Sweet Steve.'"

The put-put of the motor grew loud before Steve heard it again. "Okay," he said, "but men are not supposed to be sweet. I'll think up an embarrassing name for you."

They giggled. Their shoulders touched. The *banca* boat drew near and then receded, its wake sloshing against the pier.

"You are wrong," Amina said. "Sounds over the water carry strong feelings to me. I am Maranao, which means people of the lake. I was born in a little village on the shores of Lake Lanao. Do you know where that is?"

"It's a huge lake in Central Mindanao but I've not been there, not yet. I'd like to see your village."

"It's gone. They destroyed it."

He jerked at the fierceness in her voice. Her words reverberated in their space and silenced the night sounds.

"Who?" He whispered.

"Hypocor, that's the Philippine Hydropower Corporation." She spoke the name with abject bitterness, but then continued as if she were describing her private universe. "Lake Lanao empties into the Agus River. They have several hydroelectric plants on the river. They built a dam at the mouth of the river to control the flow of water to their plants. When the rains were strong, they closed the dam and flooded our villages. When the rains were weak, they opened it and drained our rice paddies and fish farms." Her hand rose and fell. The rancor returned. "We had to abandon our homes."

"Didn't they help you relocate your village?"

She laughed. "Sweet Steve, this is the Philippines. We are Moros, the mostly-Muslim tribes in a mostly-Catholic country. Imperial Manila has bigger guns."

Steve knew that bigger guns in the Philippines did not mean better lawyers. He turned to her. "So what happened? What did you do?" She gazed over the Gulf of Davao, but he sensed her mind looking back at Lake Lanao.

"I was ten. I cried. And then I was hungry." She looked at him. The moonlight gleamed on her pupils.

"We moved to Marawi City and gathered strength. I have six older brothers. They all went to the university. I'm the only girl, I went too."

Her eyes smiled with victory but still burned with the fierceness that had startled him moments before. "And Hypocor?"

"They will pay."

He saw not anger, but a cunning determination. She had let him see something personal, more private than her body. "Tigress, I will call you 'Tigress.'"

Their first kiss ignited a frenzy of hungry mouthing, caressing, fondling, and groping, without hesitation, without boundaries. They began to sweat and the smell of their heat excited them more. The dilapidated pier creaked.

In the days that followed, they discussed the complications of a relationship between an indigenous Filipina raised Muslim and a lapsed Catholic American. They tried to be objective, but lust vanquished their concerns. Amina Taiba moved into the compound to sleep with an infidel. God shrugged. Allah shrugged. Two guardian angels groaned.

Steve sat up and drained the last of his now warm beer. He felt Amina's warmth, smelled her scent, saw her. Except for Moro occasions, she wore "Christian clothes"—layers of them, all buttoned up. Her face she exposed—wide nose, high cheekbones, smooth, unblemished skin. But she always wore a shawl over her head at the ready to cover her expression and become inscrutable. She often rolled up her sleeves when she worked, exposing her only jewelry, single-strands of cheap little-girl beads, one on each wrist. He saw her hand—fingers thickened by toil, trimmed, unpainted nails—holding a long pencil. She gripped it up high when she wrote her Arabic squiggles, as if the pencil were a paintbrush. And when she paused, he could discern her mood from its angle. She walked with her head bowed. She appeared submissive and prudish, subservient and dull, until she looked at him. Her glittering onyx eyes caught light not available to others. They sparkled with a magic potion. He knew why she walked with a tilt. She watched the earth for him. She kept it rotating.

"Shit," she had said. Her files harbored secrets, private things. Santana had gotten his dirty paws on them. Steve cursed himself for not knowing, not getting involved, for letting Apex's lawyers enjoin him. He sprang from the chair and paced. He rubbed his distorted knuckles and thought of Rita's stepfather lying in a coma for days.

Don't get involved in someone else's problems. Don't stick your nose in someone else's arse—my chicken shit guide for tranquility.

He studied his photograph of the carabao charging, two bared teeth, battle-scarred horns, bits of drool splaying from his chin and the eyes, glazed, crazed, demented eyes. Three hooves firm on the bottom of the frame, the fourth bounding up, shoulders heaving, momentum full forward, decisive moment.

I got the shot, but he got me. Lower the fucking camera and get the picture.

CHAPTER 5

Davao City, noontime Tuesday, February 4

Sweating in a cheap hotel without air conditioning, Marty Santana sat on the edge of the rumpled bed, glanced at his watch and eyed the three geckos on the ceiling. In Nam, he had made a bet he could snatch and disable two dozen geckos in a minute and had won. He was twenty-five then. Now, at nearly fifty-nine, he wondered if he could nab three. He questioned why he should try. Nadine would be calling in two minutes and it was too hot for games, yet he could not resist the challenge.

He looked at the second hand on his watch. At one minute to noon, he flexed his fingers, leapt onto the chair and grabbed two geckos, one in each hand. The third skittered to the base of the ceiling fan, which whirred at full speed. "Smartass," he growled. He bit off the heads of the two geckos and hurled their corpses at the third. It fell. The fan splattered it against the wall. As its carcass fell behind the bed, the phone rang. He checked his watch. *Not bad, nine seconds.* He jumped down, spit out the heads and grabbed his cell phone.

"Hello."

"Are mosquitoes biting?"

"I don't fish for mosquitoes."

Any response other than "yes" or "no" meant he was alone and okay. "No" indicated he could not speak freely and would have to call her later. "Yes" meant Mayday, a call for the cavalry to whisk him to safety. In over thirty years working for Nadine, and being her bottom on occasion, he had never cried "uncle." He figured they might shoot him, although that would be better than hanging.

"Whip, you're fifty-one seconds early," Marty said.

"Buy new watch, Leash. Let's talk."

He pressed a three-key combination on his cell phone, the equivalent of a crypto key, and waited. Although his mobile looked like a bulky, outdated phone, Nadine had assured him that only the NSA could crack its encryption algorithm. After the third ping signaled a successful diagnostic, they had a secure line.

"Did the hard drive get to Manila okay?" He asked.

"Yes, what was problem?"

"It was an old laptop. I didn't have diskettes. Anyway, the break in was already obvious. I had to jimmy the window. The maid can ID me."

"That does not matter. You are leaving Davao. Go to Talisay City on Cebu Island. Get room at Pasigan Beach Resort."

"Resort," he groaned, imagining beach chairs, cocktails with umbrellas, butt-licking waiters and pretentious tourists.

"Do not worry. It is recreational facility for locals and budget-minded tourists. It features swimming pools with kiddy-slides, restaurant with Formica tables and bare-cement dance floor. Filipinos go for day. They have dozen rooms in separate building, each with bed, bible and cold shower. Foreign guests are Aussies, few Americans, usually unaccompanied males under forty. You can have all female guests you like, but no screwing in pool before midnight."

As Nadine talked, Marty stood and ambled to the window. He looked down at the street without seeing. He knew about Talisay City. At the end of WWII, the Japanese and American troops had left the beaches and jungle littered with abandoned ordinance, which fostered a cottage industry that fabricated illegal percussion bombs for blast fishermen. The manufacture of illicit explosives persisted. Adventurers looking for Japanese gold sometimes needed explosives. That could be his cover.

"What's the job?"

"Resort's owner is Ferran Yuchengco de la Cruz. They call him Zorro. He is also owner of FerMar, company licensed to trade in explosives. FerMar has two registered explosive magazines on property adjacent to resort. Authorities believe Zorro sells bomb materials to delinquents. Firearms and Explosives inspectors cannot find discrepancies in logbooks for registered magazines. They think he has another magazine. They tried undercover agent to spy on Zorro, but cops tipped Zorro off. He pays police for protection."

"But he won't suspect an old gringo fortune hunter at his hotel."

"Old gringo okay, but not your gold-adventurer story. You do not want Zorro thinking you know something about explosives. When you find magazine, inventory it and take pictures. Do not leave traces."

"No dead sentries, huh."

"Do not trample grass. But if you are spotted, blow up magazine—make it look accidental."

He moaned, "Oh, Whip, you're a beast. I'm getting a hard-on."

"Listen to me, Leash boy." Nadine's tone toughened. "Stakes are more than that magazine, much more."

He sat on the edge of the bed. His grin faded. "I'm listening."

"Zorro's wife is Moro. One of her nephews is Abu Sayyaf. Jemaah Islamiah trained him in explosives. That is worrisome considering his relationship with Zorro. Another worry, Zorro converted to Islam some years ago. He has had phone conversations with suspected member of RSM. Have you heard of RSM?"

"Some new movement that scares the shit out of Manila."

"Rajah Solaiman Movement—some Christians that converted to Islam and turned radical. They are dangerous because they live and work within Christian community, tough to identify, and they have resources. Zorro is too old for them, they are young Turks, but he is likely source for them to get explosives. It appears Zorro is preparing to supply large quantity of bomb materials to someone, whether Abu Sayyaf or RSM or MILF is unknown."

Marty plucked a jalapeno pepper out of the jar on the night table and popped it into his mouth. He positioned it with his tongue and bit off the stem, being careful not to let the juice burn his lips. He swung the cell phone aside to avoid dribbling on it.

"So why don't I just blow the magazine and liquidate Zorro—end of problem."

"No, Leash, something major is brewing and they want to know who is involved. Phone chatter has surged. Never problem in Cebu, but kettle is bubbling there. Muslim population on Cebu is small, yet substantial monies from suspicious Saudi charity went to Cebu City and disappeared."

"Sorry, Whip. I can't keep track of the money in my own accounts."

"Agencies are working money trail. Zorro is only suspect in explosives business on Cebu they know about. Philippine authorities are certain he sold some materials to bomber in Mindanao. Zorro got away because bomber blew himself up. Now they have this burst of chatter on Cebu, and no one knows of Abu Sayyaf or RSM cells there."

"So what do you want me to do?"

"Zorro does all his business at resort where he feels safe. They want to know who his friends are. You be tourist. Take pictures, anyone who talks to Zorro. Put names to faces when you can."

Marty stared at the wall. He saw a lecherous old fart with fistfuls of cash and grubby fingernails, a tequila bottle, a couple of whores in bikinis and a particular camera, a digital with eightX optical zoom. He started working out a scheme so that the girls would be taking most of the pictures.

"Leash, are you there?"

"Ah…I can't leave for a few days. I doubt they have the camera I need in Davao. I'll have to wait for them to get it from Manila. And then I need a room in Cebu City, someplace safe to stash the phone, laptop, passports and stuff."

"Leash, get moving. Our client is certain bad guys are mobilizing. Get your ass to the resort and Beep Beacon as soon as you are checked in."

"When will I hear from you again?"

"Noon, your time, on fifth day after you check in. Ring Beacon if you find something urgent before then. Ciao."

"Ciao."

Marty lay back. He had to do it again, reinvent himself and create a new deceit. The Philippines fit him like old boots, but he had worn them too long. Soon, he would bump into someone from an old job and he would not remember who he had been. It gave him the jitters. He felt old; felt he should quit.

Ever since Nadine Novak broke him, he had taken orders from her. The Cong could not break him. Withstanding pain made him smug and courageous. He did not fear pain. Torture toughened him. But he needed someone to tell him what to do. Nadine the twisted psychiatrist understood that. The sadistic bitch was schizier than he was.

Thirty years ago, the army had deprived him of sleep, had forced him to hike across Fort Bragg in full gear, exhausted him until he could not think, and then sent him to Nadine the shrink who grilled him about the shit he had done in Vietnam. Accusations had piled up but the Cong caught him before the army did. The army gave him a medal for escaping the Cong and overlooked the other stuff, but they did not know what he had done in the jungle prison. Nadine, the ugly amazon with a Slavic accent, she knew.

She knew stuff he had forgotten, had the names of his foster parents, had the old complaints about what he had done to their bratty kids and mangy pets. She had the names of Vietnamese whores abused and sodomized, Vietcong prisoners tortured and liquidated. And when she mentioned the name of the ratty lieutenant he had killed in that jungle prison, he pissed his trousers. He faced life in the pen at best, more likely hanging. Frightened and rattled, he had failed to wonder why a shrink was interrogating him and not the provost marshal.

"I'm gonna kick your schizy ass out of the Army," she growled. Then, whispering, "But don't you worry Marty boy. Nadine is going to take care of you, and you are going to do whatever Nadine wants you to do." She bound his wrists, drove him to a seedy motel, tipped the desk clerk twenty bucks and told him to ignore the screams.

He chose the word "uncle." She molested, humiliated and tortured him—literally strung him up by the balls. He did not cry uncle, though. He did not want the other hanging. He swore he would do whatever she asked.

They gave him a medical discharge citing an unspecified neurological condition and Nadine took over. Back in Nam, doing jobs that years later would be considered atrocities, he thought he was still working for the Army. When the military pulled out, he figured he was an adjunct CIA operative. Later, while in the jungles of Colombia blowing up cocaine laboratories, he supposed he was working for the DEA. After odd jobs like hijacking a truck in Wyoming, breaking into the San Francisco mayor's office and blowing up a computer in Honduras, he learned he worked for "The House." Back then, The House did dirty tricks for government agencies, although Nadine never told him which agencies or which governments. Now, with oversight committees scrutinizing intelligence outsourcing, he figured The House did contract work for the outsourcing companies. The House sold deniability. The House did not exist.

Marty sat up. It was a nice arrangement. The House's clients, whomever they were, paid well. With an expense account, hefty retainer and "performance bonuses," he had enough tucked away in numbered accounts to buy whores, tequila and jalapeno peppers until the end of his time. *And then what?* He wondered. *Nothing to leave behind.* He shrugged. He had gnarled genes that should wither unnoticed. The House did not exist, and neither would he.

CHAPTER 6

In flight, Davao to Cebu, midday Friday, February 7

The aircraft keeled and rebounded through heavy rain and dark clouds sporadically brightened by lightning flashes. The engines roared, or so it seemed, because the passengers were silent except for those murmuring prayers. It felt like a funeral service. The lone steward strapped in his jump seat faced aft and gazed at the passengers. He looked scared. A middle-aged man in a business suit beckoned him, pulled him close and spoke to his ear. The steward hesitated with a questioning expression and then popped open an overhead compartment. Nearby passengers groaned.

Marty, sitting in an aisle seat near the rear, watched the baby-faced steward stagger towards him. He opened another overhead exposing an inflatable life raft. The woman sitting next to Marty screeched and clutched her purse. The steward glanced at her with beady eyes and grinned at Marty, a greenish grin as if he had farted in church. Marty unsnapped his seatbelt and lunged. As the steward shied backwards, the plane heaved and dumped him to the floor. Marty grabbed his collar and yanked him to his feet.

"Better buckle up, sonny."

The kid opened his mouth to protest, looked at Marty and decided not to. Marty watched him stumble away, slammed the overhead door shut and sat down. He felt trapped. Cooped up in the crowded plane rife with the stench of fear reminded him of jungle prisons. By the time the plane landed, his mood was fouler than the weather.

Cebu International, the second largest airport in the Philippines, is on Mactan Island northeast of Cebu City. Display boards in the terminal advertised hotels, resorts and a fancy bed and breakfast lodging. None appealed to Marty. He trudged outside lugging his bags to see if a taxi driver knew of a room he could rent for a month. At five foot four with dark complexion and graying black hair, speaking fluent Tagalog and passable Visayan, he seemed Filipino. Tippy, a cabbie in his mid-fifties, said his daughter recently moved out and he would rent her room. Marty tossed his bags into the rear of Tippy's taxi and introduced himself as Juanito Ramos.

Marty had six solid identities—two American, one Colombian and three Filipino—with passports, driver's licenses, bank accounts and credit cards for each. Two of his identities had gun permits, one authentic. He rarely used the charge cards except for ATM withdrawals and never had cause to show his permit to carry. Marty also had a couple of altered Philippine driver's licenses. These might not hold up if scrutinized by the police, but were good enough should Tippy ask for an ID.

Although decorated in hip dainty, the room, in a secure home on a well-lit street, pleased Marty, even more when he spotted an internet connection. He told

Tippy he was a freelance writer and would be traveling a lot to gather information for articles; he did not expect to use the room often—just needed a secure place to store his gear and write on occasion. Tippy wanted to know what a freelance writer did. "He writes," Marty said, and gestured Tippy out of the room.

Marty lay on the bed and thought about the turbulent plane ride and his rage. It did have an eerie similarity to Cong prisons—people bound together in isolation, threatened by a force they could not battle and without hope of assistance. They had no one but themselves. Marty never had friends but he understood comradeship in confrontation. Whenever challenged, bickering orphans became fiercely loyal to one another. The baby-faced steward had reminded him of the baby-faced lieutenant, both of them green and scared. The lieutenant had been blabbering to the Cong, endangering the group. Marty garroted him.

He heaved up and sat on the edge of the bed. He supposed thinking about the past was a consequence of aging, like cheese contemplating its mold.

He had killed the lieutenant in rage and with instinctive deceit; the Cong never suspected him. He did not want to understand how his mind worked. He had felt rage because the steward had frightened already scared passengers and had grinned, whether from stupidity or malice did not matter. Marty accepted his bursts of rage as abnormal, a touch of insanity perhaps, yet he could control them. Instinct stopped him if the time were not right. He imagined his rage and deceit were a package deal and did not try to understand either. Does the cheese wonder why it is moldy?

When the rain stopped, Marty put on his running shoes and went outside to reconnoiter the neighborhood. He ran for a couple of hours and then wandered around, stopping at a tiny restaurant for supper before returning to the safehouse. But thoughts of the jungle still haunted him. In the murk of early Saturday morning, he assembled his Beretta. The ritual quieted the jitters and he slept.

CHAPTER 7

The guesthouse, Friday night, February 7

The gods of good fortune conspired to declare Friday night party time—the perfect storm party. Forecast as torrential rain blowing in from the Celebes Sea, the tempest howled like a typhoon raging up the Gulf of Davao a mere hundred yards from the compound. The visiting Apex managers had left during the morning, leaving behind booze and snacks, leftovers from what the company had stocked for them, which the caretaker would not inventory until Monday, and Gerrit had a purloined key to the guesthouse. Perfect. And the residents had good reasons to celebrate. The meetings and presentations had gone well for Gerrit and Brenda, and Steve in particular. The managers concluded the theft of his hard drive had been for the fertilizer bids and Stillwell told Haradji to forget about the burglary. Steve gave Amina the good news and she booked a flight for Friday afternoon, perfect timing for the party. Then the huge disappointment. As Steve waited for Amina at the Davao airport, the bad weather turned violent and forced her flight to return to Manila.

Cozy in the guesthouse, Gerrit and Margreet watched Isabela trying to coax Brenda's behind into a Latin beat. Steve sat on the sofa staring at the bottle of San Miguel in his hands. The music stopped. He looked up and saw Brenda headed his way with a grin, her hips still searching for the rhythm. She sat on the sofa next to Steve.

"Why so somber, Amina will be here tomorrow."

"Jiriki is coming."

She glanced into space. "Uhmm, Jiriki, that's Amina's brother. I'd like to meet him. So he's coming. What's the problem?"

"It's complicated," he said. His eyes asked if Brenda were in the mood to listen.

She scooted to the end of the sofa and settled her back against the armrest. "Tell me about it."

He thought for a few moments. "Amina has loyalties to family and clan, deep-seated loyalties that are hard for us to understand. It's rooted in the struggles of indigenous peoples, I suppose." Steve looked across the room. "Isabela has it, although maybe not as fiercely as Amina does."

"I know what you mean. It's something in their blood." Brenda chuckled. "It's like Isabela's dancing. I can't quite get her beat."

Steve appeared disappointed.

Brenda raised a hand. "Okay, okay, it's not like dancing. I get it. It's spiritual. It transcends individuality."

Steve brightened. "Wow, I like that—*transcends individuality*. That's exactly the problem. It's like a trump card. No matter what feelings Amina has for me, this thing voids them. It's not something new. Amina and I understand we're temporary. I've known the ending since the beginning. That seemed fine for a time, but not now."

"You got hooked in the middle."

He groaned. "More like impaled."

Steve took a swig of beer. "Jiriki is coming here to tell me something about Amina, something she didn't know around three this afternoon when I talked with her. The airline rebooked her on the nine o'clock flight in the morning. Ten minutes ago, Jiriki called and told me he needs to talk to me about Amina's return, but not over the phone. He was gloating. He's found some way to take Amina away from me. I tried calling her from my cell, but the number doesn't ring.

"What's his problem with you and Amina?"

"Oh, he's had a problem with us from the start. Two years ago, he moved from Marawi City to take a journalist position here. At the time, Amina was ten years a widow and sick of the strict lifestyle imposed by her family and the Muslim Capital. Her mother let her go because she would be living with her eldest brother. Six months later, Amina chose to live with me. Jiriki tried to stop her, but he couldn't. Their mother was furious, she still is. The entire Taiba clan blamed Jiriki. He's been trying to get Amina out of my house since the day she moved in. I'm afraid he's succeeded."

"She's thirty-three and single like me. She can do whatever she pleases."

"It's different here." Steve leaned back against the sofa. "You and I have goals, Amina has destiny. The Moros are fighting for their land and culture. If Jiriki convinces Amina she better serves the cause elsewhere, she will go. It's her duty. Duty is her fate or her destiny, something like that. Like you said, it transcends individuality." He shook his head. "We're not wired to understand this stuff." Steve breathed deeply and sighed. "And there's her subversive stuff." *It's about her files*, Steve thought, but he could not talk to Brenda about that. "There's another trump card."

Brenda wiggled. "Oh, my, I want to hear about this, something subversive."

"Maybe subversive. I like to imagine there's someone clandestine under the covers." He grinned. "Sex feels dangerous when you're sleeping with an insurgent. It's the ultimate aphrodisiac."

Brenda sighed. "That makes it hard for a good girl to compete."

"It's more like revenge than subversion, I suppose. Amina has a deep-seated bitterness that goes back to when she was a young girl. It's about hunger, starving hunger." He bit his lip. "She taught me that the pain of hunger is something you never forget. Before Amina eats a meal, she pauses and looks at her plate. That look gives meaning to the word grace. Sometimes I see remembered pain but most often I see a craving for vengeance against Hypocor. Whenever she mentions Hypocor, the walls shudder."

"Jesus, who's Hypocor?"

"They supply power to the entire island from hydroelectric plants in Central Mindanao. The Taiba clan once lived in a village on the shores of Lake Lanao. Without compensation or even an apology, Hypocor built a dam that forced the clan to abandon their homes.

Suffice to say, they were angry and predisposed to be militant."

"They became insurgents?"

"For awhile. Amina married an insurgent. He died in a skirmish with the government when she was twenty-one, but she accepted that. In war, shit happens. Time passed and they have a ceasefire agreement. It's been twenty-five years or so since Hypocor destroyed their homes. Amina's family moved to Marawi City and prospered. Amina graduated from the University and became a legal aide. Jiriki's an influential journalist. Her other brothers in Marawi do well, I think. You could say they are better off for Hypocor having disrupted their subsistence livelihood, but don't make that argument around Amina. As a young girl, she starved. She wants revenge."

"So you think this is about Hypocor?"

"It could be. At three o'clock, Amina and I were okay. Hypocor is the mother of all trump cards. I'm hoping that it's something else, something Jiriki has to negotiate."

"I've seen your work, Steve. If it's a negotiation, you can handle Jiriki."

Steve drained his beer and frowned. "The rules of negotiation are never to underestimate your opponent, do your research and know your position. The presumption is you know what you're haggling about. That's my first problem. I've another problem. It's personal. When it's personal, you don't *have* a position. You keep digging trenches until you bury yourself."

Brenda sat up. "I'm thirsty. Can I get you another beer?"

"Thanks, you're a pal."

Brenda, holding Steve's beer in one hand and eyeing a too-full glass of wine in the other, paused every few steps for the ripples in her glass to settle. She made it to the sofa. Proud of her dexterity, she looked up and smiled at Steve but her eyes focused behind him. He followed her gaze to the sliding-glass door. A trim figure in black trousers and black shirt, rainwater dribbling from his matted hair, jabbed the doorbell that did not work.

While toweling his face and hair, Jiriki exchanged greetings. Steve introduced Brenda. Jiriki smiled.

Brenda frowned. "You will not take Amina away from us."

Steve muffled a chuckle in his throat. Although an agnostic from New Jersey, Brenda had the blunt toughness of a New York City Jew. What Brenda wanted, Brenda got. Jiriki tightened his jowls, glared contempt and turned his back to her. *He lost his cool,* Steve thought, *because that's precisely what he intends to do. He's going to take Amina.* Steve drooped without air to speak or traction to move.

Isabela ignored the comment. "What can I get you to drink, Jiriki?"

Jiriki eyed the pitcher of *chicha* on the bar and smiled. "I'd enjoy a glass of that."

Jiriki's clichéd social speak irritated Steve. Whenever Jiriki said, "It's soo good to see you again," as sincere as hound greeting hare, Steve just gritted his teeth. But at this moment, "enjoy" nauseated him. He pulled a little pouch from his pocket and wiggled it.

"I'm going upstairs to roll a joint."

Isabela nodded. After she stopped breast-feeding, she had started smoking marijuana again, but made it clear she did not want the stuff near Margreet.

Steve was twisting the ends of the joint when Gerrit and Isabela came up. He looked at Gerrit. "How are Brenda and Jiriki getting along?"

"White flags on spears, I'd say. With Margreet in her arms, Brenda's practicing motherhood. They're talking about Jiriki's kids."

Steve lit the joint and passed it to Isabela. "Did he say anything about Amina?"

Isabela shook her head. "What's going on?"

"He's here to talk to me about Amina. He's either found an excuse to break us up or it's about her files."

"Could be the files," Gerrit said. He took the joint from Isabela, filled his lungs without his lips touching the reefer and then scavenged the wisp of smoke from the tip. "At the meeting yesterday, Haradji questioned me again as to why you were at our house when he came to investigate the burglary. He had asked us that on the day of the theft after he noticed my desktop has a diskette drive. I gave him my stupid question look and told him again that you came over to have a beer and talk about the break in. He gave me his I-don't-believe-you-look. We stared at each other for a minute and then he asks me when Amina is coming back."

"What'd you tell him?"

"Nothing. Gave him my don't know, don't give a crap face." Gerrit jutted his chin, puckered his lips and shrugged.

"Maybe he questioned Jiriki about Amina's files. Jiriki wouldn't want that creep interrogating his sister."

"You stay here," Isabela said. We'll get Jiriki to talk about Amina and send Brenda up with whatever we learn before he talks to you."

Steve beamed. "Great idea, *Profesora*."

Gerrit got up and reeled a bit. "Hey, that's good dope."

"It's my reserve for special occasions."

"What's the occasion?"

"I expect Jiriki will take a hit."

Gerrit grinned.

Steve busied himself cleaning his little stash of high-octane grass and began rolling another joint. He kept stopping to wonder why Haradji was so interested in Amina. He began to suspect there was more to Haradji's inquisitiveness than the missing hard drive. He was working through some possibilities when Brenda came up the stairs.

"What's happening down there?"

She pointed to the half-joint in the ashtray. "That must be good stuff. Gerrit's telling stories about grave robbers in Northern Peru and won't shut up."

"Did Jiriki say anything about Amina?"

"Only that she wouldn't be coming back," she raised her hand, "for a while."

Steve sagged in his chair. "I've been wondering if Stillwell is behind this."

"Stillwell!" Brenda sat down and plucked the joint from the ashtray. "What's Stillwell got to do with this?"

He passed her the matches and tapped the table. "We are in someone else's country, a country that has issues. Apex doesn't want even the appearance of its foreign employees getting involved in Philippine squabbles, which could jeopardize its concessions. Okay. I get the hots for a Filipina and she moves into the compound. We're not married. Apex doesn't care. She's a Moro. So what? Apex employs Moros. She's with the MILF. Now *that's* worrisome. Ever since she moved in, Haradji would ask me about Amina whenever we met, just being polite I thought. Then after the hard drive is stolen, he asks if Amina used my computer. If Santana stole Gerrit's computer, do you think Haradji would ask if Isabela used it? Maybe Haradji convinced Stillwell the theft has something to do with Amina's activism."

"But she's a women's rights advocate. That's not an issue."

"Maybe not in New Jersey, but this ain't New Jersey. She's a *Moro* rights advocate. Stillwell decides he doesn't want her on his turf."

"Okay, so what's that got to do with Jiriki?"

"Maybe Stillwell figured Jiriki loaned Amina to me so he telephones Jiriki and tells him to call in the loan."

Brenda scowled. "Lousy metaphor, Bryce. Loan is demeaning, as if she were some chattel."

"Christ, loosen up your feminist girdle." Steve pointed to himself. "I'm a loan, here for a specific job. I consolidate purchasing, cut inventories, teach the Filipinos some tricks and then Apex sends me to Timbuktu. Can you see Amina going with me?"

"You're in love, Steve. Stay with her."

"Oh, right." He flipped his hand as if Brenda were in la-la land. "My house, furniture, pick-up truck, computer, even the goddam dishes belong to the company. My work permit and residency depend on Apex. The company does my taxes, renews my permits, keeps me legal and up to date. Shit, I'm an indentured worker."

"You can do it, Steve. You live like a Filipino, eat their food, speak their language. Become a photographer here. Your photographs, my god... I'm here, I walk around, I look but I don't see. You *see*. Your pictures grip. They shake me up and say, 'Look at what you missed.' You capture playfulness, determination, courage and defiance. You make me see a people rich without wealth."

Steve laughed. "We need a tape recorder. You're eloquent when stoned. Look, I take pictures so someday I can impress my grandchildren with my adventurous life, but really, we're outsiders here." He swept his arm in a broad semi-circle. "This is interesting, fascinating. There's history, culture and revolution, but I'm just an observer." He rubbed his brow. "Shit, we're just a notch above tourists."

She chortled. "Yep, we're transients, hoboes with expense accounts."

"Hoboes on expense account, that's hilarious. Shut off the recorder. Silence the truth."

Isabela called up from the bottom of the stairs, "Brenda, let's dance."

Brenda stood. "That's my cue. Jiriki's getting impatient to talk to you."

The storm was cyclical, subsiding and resuming. A little high, Steve listened to its rhythms, imagining a symphony. The footsteps on the stairs kept its beat. A sense of presence caught his attention. The graying black hair appeared and then the solid black shirt and pants. Jiriki carried himself well, jowls firm, lips tight, like the President poised to assure the nation that he's gonna do the right thing.

Another gust slammed against the windows so hard the bamboo shades shivered. Jiriki stopped at the top of the stairs. "Despicable weather, it's more furious up here."

"Sit down and take a couple of hits. If you're stoned, the storm sounds like Rachmaninoff." He picked up the fresh joint and offered it.

Jiriki sat down and accepted the reefer. "You mean it plays all the elements of darkness." He took two hits and held it for Steve.

"No thanks, I'm high enough for now." This was true. He had just enough of a buzz to dampen his anxieties.

Jiriki put out the joint, keeping his eyes on the tip until he had squished the last ember. Even then, he continued to stare at the ashtray.

Checking weapons before battle, Steve thought.

Steve embarked on a soliloquy of metaphorical gibberish about the weather and its cyclical relevance to the rhythms of the soul until he could suffer himself no longer and then he slid seamlessly into apologetic excess for the doorbell not working. He pretended to be stoned until certain his adversary was—chemical warfare.

When Jiriki's condescending glare clouded over, Steve figured the marijuana had kicked in.

"Soo good to see you again, Jiriki. I feared you might not brave this storm."

Jiriki fiddled with the ashtray and examined the joint. "Amina won't be able to return here," he said to the ashtray. He looked at Steve. "Not for a while."

Steve's head swirled with questions, but he could not think of one that would do him any good. He kept his mouth shut and waited.

"Something has come up, a project, an important project."

Steve counted backwards from one-thousand to muddle his facial expression. Jiriki gazed at Steve and then studied the ashtray. Discomforted by Steve's silence, he fidgeted and squirmed, and then toyed with the joint.

"This will likely be a long project."

"Long project, is it?"

Jiriki looked hard at Steve. "Family concern, ticklish."

Steve admired the precision: "Project," ambiguous and indefinite, "family concern," not Steve's concern, and "ticklish"—meaning too delicate to discuss. He started counting backwards again.

After another long silence, "I've come to get Amina's things."

I've got hostages Steve thought. "Oh, I'll send Amina whatever she needs."

"We don't want to bother you. I'll send her everything."

If he wanted everything, then "a while" meant forever. Steve leaned forward and spoke without intonation. "I'll send Amina whatever she needs."

"Let's keep this simple," Jiriki snapped. "I'll send her all her things." And then with a phony sweetness, "We don't want to burden you, Steve."

"Oh," Steve waved his hand, "No burden at all. I'll call Amina and find out what stuff she wants for this *ticklish* family concern." He stood. "Let's go get a drink."

"I'll be down in a minute. Your smoke has me a bit dizzy."

Steve thumped down the stairs, the insouciant beat of his heels intent on telling Jiriki nothing had changed, but Steve knew it had.

When Jiriki came down, he excused himself, saying he had another commitment. Before he opened the sliding glass door, he paused to scan the room and its foreign contents, as if he were checking a file before sending it to the archives.

As soon as Jiriki left the compound, Steve dashed out of the guesthouse, raced through the downpour and thundered up his outside steps two at a time. Fumbling with his key, he cursed himself for having locked the door. He left it open and grabbed the phone. Although his landline had a dial tone, the number he called did not ring.

Throughout the night, alternately trying his cell phone and the landline, he called Nashita's apartment where Amina was staying, but the storm had disrupted communications. When he finally connected around nine in the morning, he got a recording. The number was no longer in service.

CHAPTER 8

Davao City, early Saturday morning, February 8

Gretchen's Club for Girls, a windowless loft on the third floor of a dry-goods warehouse, is not a girl's club. The girls there, the exotic dancers and escorts, are for the boys, the old boys. Except for bodyguards, those who have not lived in Davao for ten years or so would not be comfortable for long in Gretchen's. The clientele are shady businessmen, tainted politicians, ex cons, thugs and similar ilk. Haradji goes to Gretchen's sometimes to talk with the Patek twins and Benjie. Benjie owns the club. Only he knows whom Gretchen is, or was.

The Pateks manage the club except to hire and fire the girls. Benjie, a dapper gentleman with white hair and cane, does that. When necessary, Benjie sends one of the Pateks out to pick up a few ladies for him to interview. He checks them thoroughly. First, he feels them, with special attention to their behinds. Benjie has to feel the girls because he is blind. If a tush feels good, excites him, he evaluates the girl's talents as an escort. He does not test other skills. Gretchen's Club for Girls is not renowned for exotic dancers. The performers tend to wiggle rather than bump and grind, although they do the shag well. The ladies at Gretchen's are renowned for their extraordinary butts and giving good head.

Benjie sits at a table at the rear of his club. His regular customers come over to swap information—gossip, spin, rumor, innuendo, truthiness and facts. Benjie filters what he is told and what he tells, that's understood, but he knows what happens in Davao.

The stairs from the street up to the club are narrow and steep. Haradji climbed them and paused on the stairhead. He coughed on the dank stench of stale smoke and spilt liquor. He peered over the top of his sunglasses. At two in the morning, there was not much left to see. On the grand central stage surrounded by the bar, a tired stripper worked a huddle of four drunkards and five ladies hoping to score. The bartender, leaning over the opposite end of the oval bar, talked with two wrinkled codgers. Benjie relaxed at his table. A dark-haired girl rubbed his shoulders. When she spotted Haradji, she bent and spoke to Benjie's ear and left to sit alone at the far side of the bar.

The bartender stopped talking, stood erect and watched Haradji. When Haradji nodded, the bartender picked up two glasses and filled them with cola; neither Haradji nor Benjie drank alcohol. Haradji went to Benjie's table. They chatted until the bartender brought their drinks and left.

Haradji adjusted his sunglasses. "Have you heard anything about Santana lately?"

Benjie chuckled. "Old Long Dong's one of my favorite characters."

"But have you heard anything?"

"He could be bonking Tuk's wife. She meets her boyfriend at a bar over in barrio Ingles. The bar owner thinks the guy could be Santana."

"It's him alright…was him. He dumped her. I owe Tuk a favor. I need to find Santana."

Benjie took a tiny sip of his drink, sat back and thought for a minute. "Haradji, I heard someone swiped a computer from one of Apex's managers. Tuk's wife worked for him, and now she doesn't. Then you come around asking about Santana. Don't tell me you owe Tuk a favor. Tell me what was on that computer."

Haradji leaned over the table. "Fertilizer bids; it had a ton of information about the fertilizer business. I have to find out who paid Santana to take it. Who is he working for?"

Benjie shook his head. "Rumor has it he's CIA. Rumor has it *I'm* CIA. That's why he's one of my favorite characters—no one can figure what he's doing. But he wouldn't work for some manure peddler. If Santana took that computer, it had something more interesting on it than the price of bat shit."

"That's what I'm thinking, but without any ifs. I *know* he took it and I need to know why. Do you know where he's staying or what he looks like?"

Benjie laughed. "You're asking *me* what he looks like? He's in his late fifties, short, looks like a Filipino but isn't and he likes jalapeno peppers. A couple years ago, he took out one of my girls. It took her a week to heal. He's as strong as a gorilla and just as rough. I could tell you how he fucks, but that won't help you. Oh, he has old scars on his back, big nasty scars I was told.

That's all I know." Benjie pointed to the bar. "He could be sitting there listening to us."

Haradji looked around. He turned back to Benjie and whispered. "That computer was taken from the house where Amina Taiba stays."

"Ah, now I see. There's another curious character, baby sister of Jiriki, our dauntless commentator on lawless elements. So little sister has been taking notes. If Santana swiped that computer, she had something of interest to *powerful* elements."

Haradji spoke through clenched teeth. "I *know* he took it. I know who sold the scoop on when and how to steal it."

Benjie laughed, "Oh, that sarcastic, bitter tone. You didn't know it was for Santana. You sold too cheap."

"Tell powerful elements there's a copy of Taiba's files floating around. I'll get it. In Santana's business, there's more than one customer."

"Fifteen percent, agreed?"

"Depends, Benjie; depends on what's in those files, and what they want to do about it." Haradji gulped the rest of his cola. "If you hear anything about Santana, I'm interested."

Benjie nodded. "Be seeing you, Haradji."

Haradji went into the back office and talked with the Patek twins as if they were old friends. The Pateks don't look like Haradji, but they are his brothers. No one knows that, not even Benjie.

CHAPTER 9

Steve's house, Saturday, February 8

Steve needed sleep but he could not even sit, just slouched for a few moments before bouncing up, pacing, flipping open his mobile, picking up the landline receiver, checking that they worked, struggling against the fear that neither would ring.

Phone numbers have addresses, but the bitch won't give up the address. Operator, can you give me the number for Sloppy Joes? Of course sir, is that Sloppy Joes on 21st Street or Sloppy Joes on 9th Avenue?

They've got addresses, damn dissident operators with one-way names and wrong-way numbers. Why didn't I ask Jiriki where she was, where she was going, whom she would be with, where she would be staying?

But he knew why. He had no reason to think he could not talk to Amina. And he knew better than to ask an adversary a question if he did not already know the answer.

Who's Nashita? Nashita Sarip or Sarid... no listing for Nashita Sarip, no Sarid either. Must be more to her name than that—and a nickname, a codename.

Subversives have codenames. That telephone bitch won't tell me anything about the disconnected number I have, except that I have a number disconnected, temporarily disconnected. How long is temporary—until they fix the line, pay the bill, return from Timbuktu, renounce the insurgency? Miss Unlisted Nashita, Nashita...Nashita sounds Japanese. Why hadn't I asked Amina about that? Steve Bryce, famous freelance photographer for the insurgency, can't even get the nationalities straight. Can't remember names, can't spell them if I could, can't speak Maranao, can't read street signs, not in ciphered logograms, squiggly Arabic thingies.

Every few minutes he refreshed his email, looking for a reply to his urgent message to Amina.

The stolen files compromised her, endangered her. "Shit"—grave and foreboding circumstance replete with dire and dread.

He went through Amina's things but could not find her address book. He scoured her papers, jotted down names, looked up phone numbers and called every one, everyone but Jiriki. They scoffed, ignored his pleas for assistance, said they did not know whom he was speaking of, and if they did, said they had not heard from her, did not know her whereabouts either. No one knew Nashita.

Subversives don't tell, rude and uncooperative people that they are. Call Bipsy, he can bust into her email... and her password-protected files. Why don't I have her password? Because I didn't want to get involved.

He inventoried her clothes, tried to figure out what she might be wearing. For a symposium on Moro affairs, she'd have packed Moro clothes. What did she wear to the airport? Christian clothes and her bracelets, always wears her little-girl beads. He diagramed ideas and scribbled notes until he knew what he had to do. Starting with the University, he would search the city, scour metro Manila, population one zillion. He rummaged through his desk for Photoshop and loaded it into his new computer. He made twenty glossy prints of his best portrait of Amina and wrote his name and mobile number on the back of each. He would show them around.

In the morning, he would email Slick saying that he had some work to do in Manila and that he would be taking a few days vacation afterward. An early Sunday morning email and then take the first available flight, gone before Slick could disapprove. *Find Amina. Apex can wait until I do.* Before leaving though, he had to burn Amina's files to CDs, duplicate them, carry one and hide the other. He had to be careful, cautious, clandestine, subversive.

Having decided on a plan, he went to bed, but only to toss, turn and squirm, worried for her and angry with himself. He got up, sat at the dining room table and drank screwdrivers with double shots of vodka until his mind went numb. Then he slept alone with his nightmares.

CHAPTER 10

Talisay City, Cebu Island, Saturday evening, February 8

Late Saturday afternoon, Marty took a cab to the Pasigan Beach Resort, which he discovered was in an isolated area south of Talisay City. He told the cab to wait and checked in as Samuel Fuentes Mora, laying his Colombian passport on the counter. When asked for a credit card, he pulled out a wad of bills and growled, "I pay cash." The receptionist, who was also one of the waitresses, smiled as she flipped off the deposit for a week's stay as if it were petty cash. He could see her profiling him—Colombian, all cash, gruff and tough. *Never fails,* he thought. *She'll be telling Zorro I'm a drug dealer.* In fact, Samuel Fuentes Mora was a Colombian narcotics boss, current whereabouts unknown to anyone but Marty, who had buried him.

His hotel room had three double beds and no bible, but otherwise fit Nadine's description. With a plywood plank ceiling, bare cement floor and incandescent light bulbs without fixtures, there was no clever place to hide stuff. He duck-taped two flying knives behind the lavatory in the severe white, no frills bathroom, and stuffed his Maglite, a lock pick, a couple condoms and a foldable filet knife into his cargo pants. The Beretta he had left at the safehouse. Carrying his new camera, extra cash and passport to store in the resort's safe, he sealed the door of the room with a filament of airplane glue. After depositing his valuables at reception, he took the still-waiting cab to an internet café in Talisay City.

Marty sent a text-less email from leash@zoomail.com to whip@beacon.net. The "sent" line, February 8, 7:16 PM, told Nadine that he had checked into the Pasigan. At noon Thursday, she would call his cell. He would have to interrupt his Zorro watch and hustle back to the safehouse sometime that morning.

The Pasigan Beach Resort had a different atmosphere than he had expected. Located well off the highway in the boondocks south of the city, it was not a place where someone happened to go. It was a destination, a premeditated address, not some random joint for the wandering crowd. It had water slides for kiddies. Nadine told him they did birthday parties and did not allow screwing in the pool before midnight. Although cheap, raunchy perhaps, it was more family orientated than the lover's playground he had imagined. He could not play the debauched, horny drunkard rollicking with a couple of rowdy hookers. That would attract unwanted attention. He needed to appear jaded enough for Zorro to dismiss him as a thug, but not so repulsive as to be told to leave.

After reconnoitering a variety of sleazy bars and joints, Marty's cab driver suggested the Talisay Monarch Hotel, which had a restaurant and lounge in a building detached from the guest rooms. The cabbie described the hotel as catering to traveling businessmen and "whorists," single male tourists who weren't interested in museums. The lounge attracted moonlighting secretaries and other "uppity" ladies of the night. "They won't rent you a room for an hour or two. You have to pay for the whole night," he said.

The Monarch lounge had subdued lighting and mahogany tables. Swinging doors next to the bar led to the restaurant. The smell of broiled seafood spiced with garlic stirred Marty's stomach. He stood in the shadows near the entry and surveyed the room. The patrons were foreign males with Filipinas. The ladies did not look like short-order hookers, but single mothers and day laborers, or unemployed. They would be all-night escorts if the guy were generous and not obnoxious—okay companions for the Pasigan.

Two of the women had engaged a couple of Japanese businessmen, four more were hustling some noisy Australians at the bar. Three ladies sitting at a table nursing their drinks looked interesting. One, much older than the other two, spotted Marty. She smiled, flashing a gold tooth. He went to their table.

"Do you mind if I join you," he said in English.

The girl in the simple blue dress on his left observed him as if it was not for her to decide. The hot-looking one on the right said, "Please," and pushed the empty chair out from underneath the table. The forty-something lady with the gold tooth eyed him with congenial interest.

"I'm Sammy," he said, reaching across the table.

"Tata," she said, dropping the second syllable as if she were tired of it. She clutched his hand. Hers had been toughened by hard work. She was not even a part

time hooker. He imagined her in ample shorts and a
halter by the Pasigan pool. She would fit in. He
wondered what she was doing at the Monarch with two
good-looking girls in their early twenties.

The girl in the blue dress introduced herself as
Perla. She sat erect with her legs crossed, her hands
resting on her lap. She did not appear to be a hooker
either—too prim. The other girl with long black hair and
bright red lipstick scooted her chair close, leaned
forward enough for her blouse to droop and said she was
Lilibeth. When he glanced down from her eyes, she
dipped lower to flash firm breasts without a bra and
placed her hand on his knee. He did not doubt her trade.
The waiter cleared his throat.

"Order whatever you like, ladies. Let's party."

Perla asked for cola. Tata ordered a scotch on the
rocks and Lilibeth said she would have whatever Sammy
was drinking. She seemed disappointed when he asked
for a beer. After their drinks arrived, he raised his bottle
and said, "Here's to a good time." He pressed his bottle
against Tata's glass for a long moment before tapping
Perla's. He turned to Lilibeth. She glanced at the
entrance.

"Are you all alone, Sammy?"

He shrugged, "Yep, I'm a lonely loner."

Lilibeth leaned forward and put her hand on his
knee again. "We want to have a good time, all *three* of
us, *together*."

He had thought Perla and Lilibeth would be
delighted to lose Tata. He hesitated before touching
Lilibeth's glass, and then slid her hand from his knee to
his crotch. "Is this enough for three?"

Lilibeth, her hand hidden under the table, fondled him with inquisitive fingers. Her jaw dropped and eyes widened. "Plenty enough," she beamed. She looked at Tata and said in Visayan, "He's immense." Tata reacted as if she were a little girl just offered a triple-scoop ice-cream cone.

He sipped his beer. With casual questions, he tried to sort out the relationship amongst the three women. Lilibeth did most of the talking. Tata's English was meager and Perla preferred to observe.

Tata owned a small boarding house. Perla and Lilibeth shared a room there. Tata was lonely, *very lonely*. The poor woman suffered from the long absences of her husband, who worked on a cruise ship. Lilibeth and Perla had invited Tata to come with them to the Monarch. "She's horny," Lilibeth said, nodding at Tata. Marty suspected the young ladies wanted their landlord to get laid, but they were not going to leave her alone with some ruffian who might slap her around and sodomize her—precisely what Marty had in mind.

When they ordered the second round of drinks, Perla switched from cola to rum and cola with lime. She relaxed and stopped tugging at the stubborn blue dress, which insisted on creeping up over her knee. She worked at a department store, afternoons and evenings during the week, but she had the day shift on Saturdays. Lilibeth was a regular at the Monarch. Perla often came along on Saturday and Sunday nights.

Lilibeth leaned close to him. She nodded at the table where the two Japanese businessmen were huddled, now with three young ladies. "Some men like to watch girls doing each other. Perla and I are bisexual."

He looked at Perla. She flipped her eyebrows up and smiled. He doubted she was bisexual. Perla did not appear to be a woman who could not make up her mind. He sensed she might be difficult to handle, yet he liked her cool attitude.

Lilibeth pitched herself as the party girl, a lady of pleasure who considered respectable employment loathsome. "My career is sex," she said. "I'm a nympho. I love sex, every kind of sex, whenever and wherever, like now." She closed her eyes and began fondling Marty underneath the table. Tata giggled. Soon Lilibeth's breathing became audible, her face crinkled and flushed. She pressed her thighs tight together and looked at Marty. "See, I come easy."

Marty smiled. "We are going to have fun, aren't we," he said, gesturing to include all three women. Looking at Lilibeth he added, "For a week or more, full time."

"I can stay with you day and night. Tata has to work at the boarding house from early morning until just after lunch. I'm sure she wants to play in the afternoon and evenings." She had glanced at Perla a couple of times, but Perla said nothing.

Marty let them assume he was staying at the Monarch Hotel until he had flashed wads of cash and established his generosity with four plates of lobster from the restaurant. When he told them he was staying at the Pasigan Beach Resort and that they would party there, Lilibeth frowned and suggested he stay at the Monarch, much nicer she assured him.

"I prefer the Pasigan," he said, waving away the suggestion.

"I've been there. They don't have hot water. I like warm showers. We want to stay here," Lilibeth said.

He guessed her protest had nothing to do with water temperature. The hustler in charge was not going to get her and her friends stranded in the boondocks with a tough looking stranger. He did not have time to argue. If Lilibeth insisted on staying at the Monarch, he would cut his losses and look elsewhere. He patted the pocket of his cargo pants—the pocket that Lilibeth knew held a large bundle of Philippine pesos and looked hard at her. "Listen, I already have a room at the Pasigan, a room with three beds. If you want to party with me, we're going to the Pasigan, now." He tapped his finger on the table.

Tata grabbed Lilibeth's arm and in rapid Visayan asked for an explanation. She did not understand what was going on, but it seemed her prospects for a lusty night were fading. Pretending not to understand the language, Marty surveyed the lounge as if he were looking for better prospects. Tata's voice turned shrill and her eyes pleaded with Lilibeth as might a child's on the verge of a tantrum.

He had guessed correctly; hot water was not the issue. Lilibeth told Tata that the Pasigan Beach Resort was in the middle of nowhere, and if something went wrong, they could not get a jeepney or taxi in the middle of the night to escape. She had stayed there once. The place was spooky. After the restaurant closed, all the employees went home. Only a decrepit old night watchman remained, and he did not come around to the hotel building, which was a long way from the restaurant and pool area. They would be vulnerable there. But the Monarch had a desk clerk on call throughout the night. They could get help if there were trouble.

Tata could not understand what Lilibeth feared. Sammy seemed like a nice man to her. If his room had three beds, they would all be together—three against one. She very much wanted to party with Sammy. The debate continued, but Marty could see that Tata would prevail.

Perla, sipping her drink, disregarded the discussion. It seemed she too knew how it would end, and she looked comfortable with going to the boondocks, confident that she could take care of herself. He smiled at her. She returned a knowing smile, her eyes saying that she knew he was listening to the conversation when he pretended to look elsewhere. His gut warned him that Perla was no fool, yet he still wanted her at the Pasigan, although he had to wonder why.

"Okay, okay," Lilibeth said in English, patting Tata's hand. She glanced at Perla and then looked at Marty. "We'll go to the Pasigan."

They talked it over and agreed that all three would stay the night. In the morning, Tata had to go to the boarding house, but not for long. Lilibeth would go with her to get her bikini and things. In return for a generous allowance, she would live at the Pasigan for a week. Tata had to leave Sunday night. Except for Sundays, she worked at the boarding house through lunchtime, but she would spend her afternoons and evenings at the resort.

He looked at Perla. "Will you stay with us, for the week?"

"I'll go with Tata and Lilibeth in the morning to get my swimsuit. I would like to hang out at the pool tomorrow—it's my day off. I work during the week, remember, the department store…"

"What are your hours?"

"Two to ten on weekdays, nine to six on Saturdays." She tilted her head slightly to the side and waited.

"So you can come to the Pasigan after work and stay for an early lunch."

She leaned back and picked up her rum and cola. "We might be able to arrange something. Let's see how things go tonight." She smiled over the rim of her glass. "Tomorrow we can decide how much I'm worth."

His gut warned him again. It appeared Perla thought he was up to something more than partying. Party guys do not make commitments for a week, certainly not with a gold-toothed matron. Perla seemed adventurous but also suspicious and cautious. He admired that. He wanted Perla around, but not for sex.

CHAPTER II

Pasigan Beach Resort, Saturday night, February 8

They rode out of Talisay City in silence. Tata had wanted to sit next to Sammy, but he commandeered the passengers' seat and had his ladies sit in the back of the taxi. When the driver attempted conversation, Sammy told him to stop the jabbering and pay attention to his driving.

Amused, Perla observed her companions and their "date." Pouting, Tata stared out the window. Lilibeth cringed. Sammy sat alone with his thoughts. Perla wondered about his thoughts. He would not be sitting solitary and somber if he wanted to party. He looked as if he were plotting, positioning his three girls like pawns on a chessboard. Perla could not see herself as a pawn. If King Sammy wanted her to play, he would have to crown her queen.

Lilibeth sat with her arms between her knees pressing her mini-skirt tight against her groin as if she feared she might pee. She frowned with worry. Her nervousness increased as the city receded. Perla knew Lilibeth felt safe only in the city. Even then, unless a lusting male hovered nearby to protect her and light spilled into the dark corners, the night spooked her.

Perla stared at the back of Sammy's head as if she might read his thoughts. Morons might show off a wad of bills and wimps might squander them in hopes of getting some nooky, but Sammy did not fit either category. He was not after the thing that Tata pouted about, or the one that Lilibeth squished beneath her mini-skirt. Perla felt excited. She liked intrigue.

When they turned off the highway onto the gravel access road to the resort, Tata cheered at the sign pointing to Pasigan Beach even though it was eerie black outside, no lights anywhere. The taxi's headlights pierced the darkness. Jungle loomed on both sides, but beyond the gully on their right a chain-link fence topped with concertina wire stretched for a couple hundred yards. Perla scrutinized it. A boring fence without a gate or posters cordoned off the jungle, the barbed wire more compelling than no trespassing signs. Then the fence abruptly turned in. So did their taxi.

They stopped beside an oversized jeepney fashioned from a truck with "Pasigan Beach Resort" painted on the sides. There were two dilapidated mini-buses and a couple of cars. Perla's gaze followed the fence. It cut an L-shape around the parking lot before abutting the back of a building—the resort's restaurant-bar, Sammy told her. In the rear of the lot, the fence had a gate and a sign with the weathered letters "FerMar." Beyond the gate, bleak lights glowed.

Marty paid the taxi driver and looked over his companions. "Follow me," he said, beckoning his arm like a squad leader.

From the parking lot, a broad walkway or perhaps narrow driveway sloped down between a chain-link fence entwined with bougainvillea on the left and the windowless side of the restaurant on the right. The walkway and fence continued past the end of a gigantic swimming pool to the ocean. Marty turned right and walked between the restaurant and pool. The ladies followed. There were a dozen or so patio tables with umbrellas and white plastic chairs. All were empty. The patrons were inside the restaurant or dancing on the cement slab in the open-walled structure next to it. Marty chose a table that had an unobstructed view of the restaurant.

The terrace did not have lamps. The pool lights and glow from the restaurant provided sufficient illumination without disturbing hanky-panky in the shadows. The front of the restaurant-bar had large rectangular windows without glass. Instead, they had wooden shutters hinged at the top, which were propped open with long poles. Marty saw four men and a woman—from their accents, Aussies—partying. There were two or three large families of Filipinos, at least three generations, celebrating an occasion. Off to the left of the restaurant, teenagers crowded the dance floor. A mirrored globe reflected a strobe light to highlight their gyrations. No one inside or out fit Zorro's description.

He gave Perla and Lilibeth a fistful of cash, told them to get what they wanted, a beer for him and a Scotch on the rocks for Tata.

Perla pointed to Tata, lax and drooping in her chair, ogling Marty's crotch. "She's ready. She doesn't need another drink."

"What, you her mother or something? Bring her a *bottle* of scotch and a *bucket* of ice," he ordered, waving them away.

Tata cooed, wobbled out of her chair and crouched beside Marty. "You're nice," she said, wiggling her fingers over his pecs and down the side of his torso. Her kiss surprised him—her tongue demanded and her mouth of oiled satin undulated in unison with the fingers caressing his crotch. Gasping for air, she nuzzled into his neck. "My god, you *really* big." She stood up and tried to straddle him.

"Not here," he snapped.

She groaned. "Okay, we go room."

"Later. We'll have a drink here first. Sit down."

Sulking, she slid her chair next to his and cautiously began working her hand up his inner thigh. She babbled with delight when he unzipped his fly.

He looked over the restaurant again. Earlier, the receptionist had described Zorro as about his age and height. "Black hair with gray streaks, not peppery like yours," she had said, eyeing Marty's silver trim. "His teeth are crooked. He looks eight months pregnant." She chortled, curving her hand over her stomach in a profound arc. No one in the restaurant fit that description. Zorro might be in the kitchen, or perhaps in the little reception office.

Perla and Lilibeth returned with the drinks. Perla spotted Tata burrowing into Sammy's pants. She peeked. "Whoopee!"

"Perla, do me a favor. I need to know if the owner is here." He wagged his finger. "I do *not* want to talk to him, just want to know if he's here. He's old and graying like me, but with a big belly. Check the kitchen and that reception office." He pointed.

Perla looked at the open door at the back of the restaurant. "What's his name?"

"Don't ask for him. Just look for someone who acts like he owns the place."

"Okay," she said, but instead of leaving, she watched Tata play in Marty's entertainment center.

He flipped his hand. "Vamoose."

He admired Perla's jaunty stroll in beat with the hip-hop music blaring from the dance floor, her shoulder-length hair jiggling. At first, he guessed her age as early twenties, but her mature demeanor soon made him think she had to be older. Her spirited bounce made her look early twenties again. When she entered the restaurant, one of the Aussies stood and spoke to her. She gave him the universal sign for "Just a minute," peeked in reception and then looked through the window of one of the swinging doors to the kitchen. She came out of the restaurant towing the Aussie by the wrist, paused to shake her head at Marty, and skipped on to the dance floor. He admired her playfulness, an odd reaction. Usually youngsters irritated him.

"Hey, take a break," Lilibeth said. She pulled Tata's hand away and wrapped it around a glass of Scotch.

Marty stared at the blue dress flittering in the light of the strobe. "Your girl's got some nice moves."

Lilibeth, looking at the dance floor, sighed. "Not my girl. More like I'm her toy…seems you like her too."

He groaned and muttered. "Christ, I'm going gaga. Never thought about having a kid before."

"Com'on Sammy, let's go." Tata grasped the nape of his neck. Her silky mouth fed him a chunk of ice. She swirled it with her tongue. He smiled and nodded to her glass.

"Finish your drink and we'll take a walk."

Tata gulped her drink and stood.

"Put on your shoes," he said, happy to see they were sturdy-looking flats.

Beyond the main pool, they passed the first of three small pools. Each had a three-sided lean-to with picnic tables. He led Tata along the dimly lit walkway between the pools and shelters. It led to a few steps and then went on to the hotel.

"We goin' to room, Sammy?"

"Nah, it's too stuffy."

Just before the steps, he stopped and glanced around. "Let's get in here out of the light." He pushed Tata to the rear of the shelter, feeling his way along the wall of unpainted planks. The rough, porous wood had soaked up the musty odors of wet bathing suits, spilt beer and furtive sex.

"Okay," he said, sitting on top of the rearmost picnic table. "You sit here, between my legs." He wound his fingers into her hair and twisted. "Suck my cock real good, swallow every drop and lick it squeaky clean. I hope I don't have to teach you how."

The restaurant, dance floor and shelters backed against a hummock. Marty had hoped to climb onto it from the rear of the shelter, but as his eyes adjusted to the darkness, it did not look promising. Through the wide gaps in the planks that boarded up the back, he could discern a crude wall that held back the hummock. Even if he could squeeze through the narrow space between the shelter and the wall, he would have to do it alone. He wanted Tata with him.

He could not concentrate on plan B. Tata did not need lessons. She wiggled and babbled yummy sounds as she teased him up to the brink and eased him back down again and again until he yearned to lose control. She finished him, squeezing, sucking, licking and would not let go.

He pushed her away and groaned. "Where did you learn to do that?"

"You like?"

He did, so much so it worried him. He could not afford distractions until he finished the job.

"You wait. I'll be back."

After checking for pedestrians, he started up the steps to the walkway leading to the hotel building and then jumped onto the abutment that angled up from the steps to the hummock. Coiled concertina wire stretched across the top of the retaining wall to the rear corner of the shelter. He pulled out his Maglite. Rusted baling wire tied the end of the coil to two eyebolts screwed into the corner of the shelter. He jammed the handle of his filet knife into the eye of the lower bolt, braced his feet and twisted with both hands. Working the bolt back and forth, he stressed the baling wire until it ruptured and released the bottom of the coil. It took several minutes to loosen the upper bolt and break the concertina wire free. It whooshed away, slapped and scraped against the wall and then crackled into the scrub before snagging, not thunderous noises but certainly curious ones. He darted into the shelter.

Tata peered through a gap between the planks. "What you do, Sammy?"

"I'm gonna bugger you up there." Someone chattered. He shoved Tata against the rear wall, yanked up her skirt and fingered the crotch of her panty. The voices, closer now, sounded like a couple talking with a young girl. He jerked aside the panty and probed until after they passed and the night quieted except for the music from the dance floor.

Without the concertina wire, they had an easy climb onto the hummock. He crawled through the scrub. Tata crept along behind him. He stopped every few yards to look around and listen. When they reached the crest, he peered over the bushes to check out the layout of FerMar. On the dirt road below, forty yards away, he spotted two guards talking underneath a light. Both cradled shotguns. Fifty yards farther on, where the road ended, a similar light illuminated the door to another magazine. Marty doubted they had a roving sentry, but if they did, his reason for being on the hummock would be obvious. He put on a condom, shoved Tata onto her hands and knees, pressed her head to the ground and flipped up her skirt. With one hand clamped over her mouth, he tore her underpants aside and prodded between her cheeks with one finger, and then two. "Be quiet," he whispered. While she whimpered into the palm of his hand, he took in the lay of the land.

As they rested, Marty puzzled over what he had seen. The dirt road into FerMar from the back of the resort's parking lot ended in a turnaround in front of the farther magazine. The jungle might hide a third, but he doubted it. A path from the road into the jungle or another gate in the perimeter fence would be too obvious. He sat up and looked over the terrain again. It seemed odd how the hummock dipped between the two magazines and then swept upwards behind the shelters and dance floor, terminating against the side of the restaurant.

He considered the two guards. Although he could not see insignia, he guessed from their bearing and their manner of patrolling that they were military—young, bored army recruits. *Outsiders, perhaps arbitrarily assigned at the whim of their commander.* If Zorro had no control over the guards, then he had to have a scheme to handle contraband explosives in their presence.

It did not take Marty long to imagine what Zorro had done. The natural slope of the hummock dropped below the roofs of the magazines. They had had to plow up earth to cover the roofs—standard procedure to contain an accidental blast—but building up the hummock behind the shelters and dance floor seemed unnecessary. He figured he and Tata were sitting on top of a third magazine built perpendicular to the first one and then buried. They probably accessed it through a hidden entrance inside the first magazine. Zorro's men could handle the illegal explosives without the guards outside knowing.

Marty stared at the young soldiers. Not for the first time, he realized how much he had changed since Vietnam where even ten-year olds could be dangerous. There he had learned never to hesitate. He wished these guards to stay out of his way.

CHAPTER 12

Pasigan Beach Resort, Sunday morning, February 9

Marty woke to the sound of rain and Tata snoring. She had whimpered and pouted when he told her to sleep alone in the middle bed. A blowjob while listening to the rain appealed to him, but the dim shapes of Perla and Lilibeth in the third bed spoiled his libido. He got up and went out onto the balcony.

Backed against the hummock, the three-story hotel had twelve windowless rooms, each with a wide balcony overlooking about thirty yards of wasteland that sloped down to a sliver of sandy beach and then the sea. As Marty looked over the terrain, he realized that to construct the pool area they had had to excavate the slope, no doubt piling the dirt onto the hummock. Perhaps the odd hill behind the shelters did not hide the third magazine after all.

The rainstorm merged with the ocean, obscuring the horizon. The clouds were a thick blanket, the sky dull. The pool area looked murky and forlorn. It appeared the storm would last through the morning if not all day. *Perfect weather*, Marty thought. After hustling the women off to the boarding house for their clothes and things, he would find out if Zorro had buried secrets. Listening to the rain, he wondered where the FerMar guards found shelter. There had to be a guard shack, probably tucked into the hummock not far from the gate.

He began his morning calisthenics with some hand stands to loosen up. His right arm felt sore and cramped from struggling with the eyebolts for the concertina wire. He flexed it while he ran in place, pumping his knees to the horizontal. After running for a half-hour, he did a hundred two-handed push-ups before trying with one hand. His arm felt okay.

He showered, pulled on cargo pants, and went to Perla and Lilibeth's bed. Perla was sleeping on top of the sheet wearing only panties. He had given them T-shirts to wear. She must have pulled hers off during the night, or maybe Lilibeth had. He shook her shoulder. She opened one eye and studied him. Rolling onto her back, she glanced at Lilibeth still asleep by her side and then looked at Marty again.

"What, is it my turn to fuck you? May I pee first?"

Marty chuckled, picked up the T-shirt from the floor and draped it across her small breasts. "Go pee and meet me on the balcony. I'd like you to do me a favor."

Perla flicked her eyebrows, the Filipino affirmative gesture.

While Perla rousted Lilibeth and Tata, Marty went down to the first floor and picked the lock on the maid's closet. He found large, black trash bags and took several. When he got back to the room, Perla and Lilibeth were showering together. Tata sat on the bed sulking.

"You don't visit me in night, Sammy. You not want me anymore?"

He grabbed her bare buttocks. "Get your ass back here at noontime. If it's still raining, I'll bugger you until it stops."

She smiled. "I pray for rain."

Marty handed her four trash bags. "Here, spread these out on the floor. I'm going to make ponchos." With his filet knife, he cut head holes in the bottoms of the bags. "Okay, these will keep you dry. Have a big breakfast at the restaurant and then take a taxi to get your things. Perla has the money to pay."

After they left, Marty donned a trash bag and went outside with another to cut a sack full of branches from the scrub at the base of the hummock. Back in the room, he took a lightweight rain poncho and baseball cap from his luggage and sewed foliage on them. After an hour and several critical examinations in the mirror, his camouflage satisfied him.

He strapped the sheaths with his flying knives to his calves upside down so that the handle rested against the side of his boot. A Velcro safety strap kept the knife from jarring out of the sheath while he hiked, but when stalking, he undid it so he could tug the knife free in an instant. Marty preferred flying knives when he could not use the Beretta, like in a magazine where a stray projectile might trigger an explosion. Unlike throwing knives that rotate haft over tip, a flying knife spins around its axis like a spear. Within a range of fifteen yards, he could hurl the knife into a man's throat with deadly accuracy, although perhaps not in a blinding rainstorm.

His pocketsize digital camera would be good enough for taking pictures inside the magazine, but the flash took a long time to recharge. He considered going to reception for his new camera, but decided it too bulky. After checking his gear, he stuffed the camouflage poncho and ball cap into a plastic bag and went outside.

Head down against the rain, he trotted along the gravel sidewalk to the shelter where he had taken Tata the night before. He glanced around—no one in sight—and scrambled up the wall onto the hummock. After crawling through the scrub to the crest, he donned the baseball cap, elevated his head and inspected the road in front of the magazines. The sentries had taken refuge from the rain. From the gate to the first magazine, a wall of gabions filled with rocks held back the hummock. He spotted a lintel interrupting the wall, sneaked close to it and heard the faint murmur of voices below.

Back on the crest, he put on his camouflage and crept along the curve of hummock past the first magazine until he could see the entrance to the guard's shelter. He waited to see how often the sentries would patrol in the rain. Forty minutes later, the guards still had not ventured outside. He cussed for having missed an opportunity. The downpour had eased and the sky had brightened. Creeping to the side of the magazine out of sight of the guardhouse, he studied the door. It had two padlocks in hasps with the straps on the doors and the staples on the frame. He guessed five minutes max to get into the magazine, but he could not disguise the breach. If the guards inspected the door while he was inside, he might have to kill them and blow the magazine. He had not thought to get baling wire to reattach the concertina wire, an essential task if the explosion were to look like an accident. He considered aborting, but then the rain picked up. He was starting to take off his camouflage when a guard stepped out onto the road.

Marty hunched back into the poncho and peeped through its foliage. The guard looked down the road, glanced at the magazines and then scurried back inside. From where the guard had stood, he could see the door to the magazine but the framing would obscure his view of the locks.

Marty stashed his camouflage at the side of the magazine and scooted to the door. It took him less than a minute to pick the first lock. The second one, more complex and of a different type, took him nearly five. The two-lock system made Marty wonder if the Firearms and Explosives Department controlled one of the locks. Zorro would have to bribe someone there to get the key.

The contents of the first magazine warranted no more than a glance: prilled explosive grade ammonium nitrate, TNT, detonators, blasting caps and coils of detonator cord—reasonable quantities in good condition and neatly arranged. With his Maglite, he examined the storage shelves and the concrete block wall. There did not appear to be anything hidden. In the rear corner, a bin on the floor half-filled with drill bits, hand picks and other mining tools rested on a metal pallet. He tugged on the bin but it would not budge. Feeling under the open end of the pallet, he found a lever and pulled on it. The pallet and bin rose nearly an inch. He tugged on the bin again. It rolled aside, exposing a pit with a ladder. After climbing down and crouching through a short tunnel, he entered the third magazine.

Marty swept his light around the small room. The sacks of ammonium nitrate near the entrance had different markings than those in the first magazine. The prilled explosive grade came from France, the fertilizer grade from China. An array of items, a few of each, littered shelves. He counted five different styles of blasting caps, product from the Talisay City cottage industry, two landmines made from mortar shells that appeared old, not well made and defused. He inventoried and photographed a rifle grenade, a couple hand grenades, some dynamite and a variety of ordinance useful in fabricating small bombs. Dust covered everything except the ammonium nitrate. Nothing seemed worthy of Saudi funding and suspicious phone chatter. Then Marty spotted two chests tucked under the shelves. He pulled them out and opened the lids.

"Holy shit!"

The chests contained enough C4 to demolish a palace. There were two types. One he recognized as U.S. army issue, the other he guessed Australian. He counted thirty-two kilos of C4, twenty detonators and a half-dozen timing devices, all in excellent condition. At black market prices, Zorro had a small fortune.

After finishing the inventory list Marty checked his pictures. The shots of the grenades were too dark but they were not important. He had been inside for forty-five minutes and worried the rain might have stopped. He hustled out to the first magazine and replaced the tool bin. Before opening the door, he pressed his ear to it and cussed at the silence. He pushed the door open a few inches to listen. The hinges creaked, but he did not hear the guards. The wind blew mist in his face as he eased the door open enough to peek past the doorframe and then farther to look around. He slipped out, snapped the padlocks closed and scrambled up the side of the hummock. In the distance, he heard one of the guards shout.

Marty grabbed his camouflage and scrambled as far as he could up the slope and still remain hidden by the mound of dirt covering the magazine. He slipped into the poncho, put on the cap and inched upwards until he saw the guard standing in the road halfway between the gate and the first magazine. The guard scanned the hummock, spoke to the second guard who Marty could not see, and then trotted back toward the guardhouse. Keeping an eye on the road, Marty managed to move up another five yards into the denser scrub before the guard reappeared with his companion, both carrying shotguns.

The guard who had called out, a teenager, marched toward the first magazine. The other one, older, ambled along the road looking at the hummock. The recruit moved out of Marty's sight, but from the noise, it sounded as if he had yanked on the padlocks. He came around the side of the magazine and clambered up onto the grassy slope. Marty smiled. The kid had just trampled his tracks.

The older guard stood on the far side of the road where he had a panoramic view of the hummock. The other walked into the scrub. Being careful not to move his poncho, Marty undid the Velcro and eased a flying knife out of its sheath. Even if he had damaged his camouflage, the recruit would be within striking distance before he became suspicious.

With a little luck, Marty figured he could slash the kid's arm, grab his gun and escape. The guy on the road would be to far away to hit him with the type of short-range shotgun used by magazine guards. These soldiers were outsiders, not party to Zorro's business with the C4. They would not even have the keys. No one would believe an accidental explosion. They had no volatile materials, no picric acid or nitroglycerin, not even sweating dynamite. Only a klutz building a bomb inside the magazine could trigger an explosion. The House would understand if he had to screw up the job, but Marty knew he would need a heap of luck to get out of the resort before someone caught him.

He hunkered down between bushes and listened to the recruit stalk through the scrub. He stopped. Marty guessed him to be about eight yards off to his right. He hoped the other guard did not come onto the hummock.

"I don't see anything," the recruit shouted in Visayan.

"Me neither."

The guard moved closer. Marty expected the kid to poke him with the shotgun.

"Must have been a *bayawak*."

"What?"

"Nothing," he shouted. "I'm coming down."

Marty felt relieved to be mistaken for a monitor lizard.

But the kid did not go down. He moved closer and stopped no more than two yards away. Marty guessed the guard had spotted him and had shouted about the lizard so as not to alert his prey. He tightened his grip on the shaft of the knife and shifted his weight so he could spring the instant he heard the kid snap off the safety. It was going to be tough to stab him and get his weapon without shucking the camouflage. He inhaled, let half the air out and waited.

The kid stomped down the hummock. "Must have been a *bayawak*," he shouted. "In the rain, it looked like someone's legs."

Marty exhaled. He heard them walking on the road but he resisted the urge to peek. They would no doubt watch the hummock for a while. It was nearly eleven. The ladies would soon return. Now that he had finished the tricky part of the job, Marty hoped the sun would come out. He could watch girls in bikinis while sipping a drink and keeping an eye on Zorro.

CHAPTER 13

Steve's house, Sunday morning, February 9

Steve's head felt clogged with fuzziness, vodka residues no doubt. He glanced at the clock and sprang out of bed. It was past nine already. He had slept longer than intended and perhaps deeper too despite his nightmares. *Had Amina called and I hadn't heard the phone?* He checked. Both phones worked, but no messages on his voice mail. He fired up his laptop. It seemed slower than his wits. The hourglass blinked as useless programs opened up. *A dozen wastes of time to uninstall.* At last, his email opened. For once, the you-got-mail guy did not irritate him. He had received three new messages in the night. "Shit." He checked the names of the senders again and trudged to the kitchen.

The sleep had helped his appetite. He needed food, but espresso more. After the first mug, he fried three eggs and broiled a chunk of steak. While he ate, he pondered what little he knew.

No call, yet phones have been working for over twenty-four hours. Why doesn't she answer my email? No computer of her own, but Nashita surely has one.

Idiot! With her phone disconnected, they probably don't have internet. But the university has computers.

By the time he finished breakfast, he had worked out a scenario.

They are not near the university. She and Nashita are on the move and expect to be away for a while. Why else disconnect the phone. For sure, Amina asked Jiriki to tell me where they were going, but he came to the guesthouse in the storm to get Amina's things, came to take her away, not to tell me where she is.

Julius jumped onto the table. Steve cut the gristle into small pieces, fed them to Julius and watched him lick the greasy plate clean.

Haradji convinced Stillwell he has a subversive in the compound. Whatever happened, ticklish or not, Jiriki solved Stillwell's problem...unless I go looking for Amina. Stillwell will disapprove my request for vacation. Get out of town before they tell me that if I leave I'm out of a job. Really, no reason to think Stillwell involved except for Haradji's persistent curiosity. Stillwell tells Haradji to forget about the theft, yet Haradji still asks questions. He seems certain Amina used my computer and I copied her files.

"Enough supposing," he said aloud.

After checking his email, Steve punched the numbers for Bipsy's cell phone.

"Hey, Bipsy, I need your help if you've a little time."

"Oh, good morning, Blue Eyes. It so pleases and entertains me that you should call on this fine Sunday morning to inquire about my health and happiness. You coddle me so."

"Sorry, Bipsy, I'm having a spastic attack. I'm in a rush to get to Manila."

"Ah, suddenness traveling, what might I do for you?"

"I've some diskettes I need to burn."

Steve listened to several moments of silence.

"Ah, hidden files have escaped the searing light of public scrutiny and indignation, and your silver-coated megabyte beauty is missing a diskette drive."

"Just some personal files."

"A pronto job?"

"If you can, Bipsy. If it's inconvenient, I'll find someplace in Manila."

"When you return from this caper, you will share your adventures and several bottles of San Miguel?"

"That would please and entertain me."

"Meet me at IT in thirty minutes."

"Thanks, Bipsy," Steve said, but Bipsy had already snapped off his phone.

Steve forwarded his landline to his cell. As he drove to Apex-Davao's offices, he called Gerrit's house. Isabela answered.

"Hi, Isabela. How you guys doin'?"

"We're doing well. Have you heard from Amina?"

"Nothing yet, which is why I called. I'll be flying to Manila, no calls while on the plane. Are you and Gerrit going out?"

"You bet. It's our anniversary. Gerrit's at the office, but he'll be back soon. The thrifty Dutchman promised me a fabulous meal, dancing, and after that, romance."

"Oh, darn. I want to forward my calls to you in case Amina phones. You could quiz her about what's going on."

"Steve, *aniversario*—flowers, food, music, dancing, romance—*Comprende!*"

"Okay, sorry. I'll check my voice mail once I get to Manila."

"When do you get there?"

"Justa sec." He slowed at the guardhouse for the Apex Davao compound and returned the guard's salute. "I don't know yet. I'm hoping to catch the one-fifteen flight." He checked his watch. "Christ, it's almost eleven and I've not packed yet. I'll work something out."

"Okay. We'll take care of Julius."

"Oh god, thank you, thanks. I'm in such a state I forgot about him."

He parked beside Bipsy's old Toyota coupe. Apex provided foreign managers with pick-up trucks, and maintained them, but local managers were on their own. It seemed unfair, but Steve understood. Foreigners are temporary, hoboes with expense accounts. He looked over the Toyota and peeked through the window. Bipsy took care of his things. The car looked in perfect shape. Steve wondered how much a reliable vehicle would cost him.

As he swiped his access card to unlock the door, he realized a computer was recording the moment he entered the IT building. He wished he had not called Bipsy. He might well be putting his friend in an uncomfortable position. The guard's log would show that Bipsy and Steve entered the Apex compound at about the same time on a Sunday morning—unusual for

Bipsy, perhaps, but unprecedented for Steve. Noticing the anomaly, Haradji would check the building access records and see that Bryce had need for computer work before dashing off to Manila. In the morning, Haradji would be inquiring as to what services Bryce required.

Steve strode through the silent IT office, an array of cubicles for systems analysts and technicians, to Bipsy's private office. Bipsy had already booted up his desktop computer. A bevy of provocative nymphs danced, crawled and somersaulted across the twenty-inch LCD monitor—a distraction for heterosexual visitors perhaps, but not for Bipsy. Steve glanced at shelves laden with software boxes, one no doubt with a program to circumvent Amina's passwords.

"Thanks, Bipsy, I really appreciate this." He held up the diskettes, wagging them. "Personal files, do you mind if I make the copies?"

"Ah, Blue Eyes, you may, but not until I check your children for contagious infections and intestinal parasites." Bipsy pointed to one of two CPU's on the floor. "Please insert the first diskette." He swiveled to his keyboard.

Steve watched Bipsy pull up virus scan software, select the diskette drive and start the program. A list of files appeared with the words "password protected" next to every one of them. After a few keystrokes, Bipsy asked for another diskette, scanned it and found more password-protected files. He swiveled around.

"Okay, Blue Eyes. You have some rather large files, all password protected. I need the passwords to check for lurking desperados."

"I don't have them."

Bipsy turned and looked at the file names for a few moments. They were not in English or Tagalog, leaving no doubt as to whom the files belonged.

"Ah, I see the glimmer of darkness."

"Forget it, Bipsy. I'm sorry to have dragged you out here for nothing." He stooped to retrieve the diskette.

"Do not fret, Blue Eyes, we'll use Grandma. She's not in the loop. Come along."

Bipsy led him to a cluttered workshop where technicians cleaned and repaired hardware. Bipsy fired up a tired-looking computer with a bulky CRT monitor.

"Grandma is old and slow but she is not connected to the network. She can't bite a bit. She can bake your cookies without you giving up the recipe."

While Bipsy hooked a CD burner to Grandma, Steve copied Amina's files into her memory.

Steve made a second set of diskettes and two copies on CDs. Grandma *was* slow. He abandoned hope of catching the one-fifteen flight. While they waited, he and Bipsy chatted about photography, their common interest, which distracted Steve from his concerns. At noon, as he followed Bipsy's coupe out of the office complex, he realized he had not deleted Amina's files from Grandma's memory. He thought to call Bipsy and ask if they could go back, but he had been nuisance enough for this Sunday.

When he got home, he checked his email and sighed. He opened Amina's message and read it rapidly. He thanked Grandma for making him miss the flight to Manila and felt grateful for not having told Slick he had to go there. His plans had changed. Seeing that Amina appeared safe, he reread her email.

Sweet Steve,

I can not understand why Jiriki did not tell you that Nashita and I were leaving Manila and so let you worry, but I like that you worry about me. I told Jiriki when he gave me this job that I would need Christian clothes, but I could not then make arrangements. He had no right or need to ask for all my things. It seems curious if not strange. You were correct not to comply. I will discuss with my brother when I return.

Please inquire about sending a package to the address below. If possible, we want to avoid going back out to Mactan airport to pick it up. I need both of my jeans, the beach shorts, six shirts or blouses, the walking shoes, leather sandals and housework shoes. Send a couple of shawls too.

I am at an internet café. They will close early on Sunday. I will try to call you tonight. If I cannot, I will check email tomorrow around lunchtime, or perhaps a little later because of errands to do in the morning.

This matter may take many days. This is one of those times we must negotiate and wait. Insha Allah, we will succeed.

I miss you sweet Steve. The food does not taste good unless I am eating with you. I am starving.

Your Tigress

He smiled at her code. She never wore shoes in the house. "Housework shoes" meant homework, her password-protected files. Maybe whatever she was working on had come to fruition. He smiled at the other code. "I am starving," meant she was *really* horny.

He leaned back in his office chair and stared at the address. She seemed safe. He was glad he had not made a fool of himself by running off to Manila.

Instead of emailing Slick, he called him. Grumpy over being disturbed on a Sunday afternoon, Slick was in no mood to approve anything. Steve negotiated. He promised to handle any residual details on the fertilizer deal by email. He had seven weeks of accrued vacation. He convinced Slick to approve a two-week leave. He would take more if necessary. And then he would take the rest of his life. He had felt the pain, the agony of losing Amina. Brenda had been right. He was in love. Only love could explain his frenzy over losing Amina and this joyous relief after finding her. Neither Apex nor Jiriki could separate them now.

Hang on Amina. I'm coming. I'm in. No more chicken soup.

He logged on to the Philippine Airlines website and bought a ticket for eleven-forty the following day, the only direct flight from Davao to Cebu City. He had never been to Cebu Island. He was going on vacation, a romantic holiday, *Insha Allah.*

CHAPTER 14

Pasigan Resort, Sunday afternoon, February 9

Lilibeth and Perla sat out on the balcony while Marty "visited" with Tata as he had promised to do if it were still raining. The girls were listening to make sure their landlady did not suffer any more cuts and bruises. He screwed around until Tata seemed satisfied. He could not perform with Perla listening, maybe peeking.

They went to the restaurant. Tata and Lilibeth played cards while Perla watched Marty tinker with his new camera. He took pictures of her. As they examined the results, Perla snuggled close and whispered.

"Tata told us where you took her last night. She has scratches on her arms and legs. Her knees are purple. You could have taken her to the beach and buggered her on the sand. Why cut through the wire to screw in the bushes?"

He fiddled with the camera. "Because it's more exciting to do it someplace where you're not supposed to be. It's the thrill of maybe getting caught."

"Uh-huh," she muttered with a smirk. Then she pressed against his arm and toyed with his hair. "You want to watch Lilibeth and me?"

His brow furrowed as he shook his head.

"We put on a good show. Lilibeth wants to entertain you. She loves threesomes."

"No." He glanced at Lilibeth. "I'll do her when you're not around."

"You don't want to screw me?"

He tried to imagine it and guessed sticking a gun in his mouth would be easier. "Maybe not."

She pulled away and snapped. "Then what am I doing here?"

Be nice and they bust your balls. He looked out at the pool. The rain had subsided to occasional light showers, but it looked gloomy. "I had hoped we could party by the pool and I'd take pictures of your cute fanny in a bikini."

"Do you want me to come back Tuesday morning?"

His mind fluttered. It was Sunday. She did not have to go to work until Monday afternoon. She had decided to stay the night. That was news. Tata would leave soon, but return the next afternoon. Two ladies would provide enough cover while he watched Zorro. He did not need Perla, yet he wanted to keep her around if he could.

"Yes, please," he said. "Please come Tuesday morning for breakfast."

"Why?"

His gut tightened as he imagined her accumulated suspicions. Why the Pasigan Beach Resort? Why three women? Why send her to look for the owner he did not want to talk to? Why take Tata to the hummock? He set the camera down and stroked wayward strands of hair away from her eyes.

"You are pretty, sexy and smart. I like having you around." He kissed her lightly on the forehead. "So you're staying tonight?"

"Yes. I'm hoping for sun in the morning. I brought my uniform so I can stay for early lunch and go straight to the department store."

"Great. Will you come back for breakfast Tuesday?

"Hmmm, do you mind if I hang out with Christopher, the guy I was dancing with last night?"

He grinned. "Of course not, that would be great. Invite him to join us. Tell me whenever you want to use the room. I'll clear everyone out...unless you want Lilibeth too."

Perla laughed. "You keep her. That girl is hornier than a hooker on holiday. If it weren't for Tata, she'd jump your bones."

He looked at Lilibeth and then the rain. He had good reason to celebrate if Perla could get Christopher and the other Aussies to join them. Zorro would never make him. Tata would be his woman, but he would be cheating with the hot hussy Lilibeth, which made him think of a mattress on the balcony and listening to the pitter-patter of rain on the roof while he romped with the supposed nymphomaniac.

"Good idea," he said. "You hustle Tata on her way. Then send Lilibeth up with a bottle of whatever she wants and a bucket of ice. I'll hang a towel over the balcony rail. He tapped her shoulder. "You do not go near that room until the towel comes down. *Comprende?*"

She smiled and flicked her eyebrows. "Please wear her out. I'm really not into girls."

"I figured." He peeled off several bills. "Here, this is for expenses. Keep the change. Go find Christopher and have some fun."

"Thank you," she said, counting the money. "Thanks a lot."

He went to the bar, bought a bottle of tequila and started to leave, but stopped and went back to feel Perla's bicep.

"Listen, if the owner comes in, they call him Zorro, throw a bottle of soda pop onto the balcony—a *plastic* bottle, empty."

Perla smiled.

CHAPTER 15

Pasigan Resort, Monday morning, February 10

The blood, the faceless recruit, a barrage of fireworks bursting in the sky and he could not hide from the light. The blood he could not wash off, only change its color—crimson, scarlet, mahogany, black.

Marty jerked awake, sat for a moment and then stumbled to the balcony gasping for air. The chill of sweat evaporating felt good. He had not killed the recruit.

He relaxed by doing push ups and thought about thirty-two kilos of C4, with detonators and timing devices—dangerous stuff. The Philippine media had never mentioned C4 being used in bombings as far as he could recall. Maybe they had used a pound or two, but thirty-two kilos in the right places could demolish a shopping mall. He considered dashing to the safehouse to tell Nadine the situation was as serious as they had suspected, but he might miss Zorro conspiring with his connections. He had to sit on the C4 and Zorro. Already he had made a mistake. *Toss a soda pop bottle if Zorro comes. Perla knows I'm here to watch Zorro.*

Marty realized the girls had not yet had an opportunity to snoop through his gear, but Perla would at first chance. He had to finish off the jar of jalapeno peppers and check his stuff for any other personalized quirk. He cut short his calisthenics, took a shower and went through his luggage. Besides the jalapenos, he had the explosives inventory and his old camera. He stuffed them in this pocket. While devouring the peppers on the balcony, he remembered the flying knives taped behind the sink. He had to keep Perla from snooping until he took them to the safehouse. When the first morning light promised a beautiful day, he roused Lilibeth and Perla for an early breakfast.

While Marty ate, he glanced at Zorro reading a newspaper by the open window. His front corner table had a triangular wooden block declaring it reserved in case a customer failed to notice his cell phone, black zippered notebook, coffee mug and the stinking cigar smoldering in the ashtray. Smoking a cigar for breakfast was reason enough to kill him.

From his corner, Zorro could monitor both the pool area and the restaurant. He had plenty of light to read his paper, and to have his picture taken along with whoever might sit at his table.

Three Filipinas arrived with a bunch of noisy kids, paid their pool fees and received plasticized wristbands. Marty spotted the patio table he wanted to commandeer before someone else did. The Pasigan probably did a good business on sunny days. The resort's jeepney would soon bring in another load.

"Okay ladies, bikini time."

"I'm going to get something to read," Perla said. She went to the rack of left-behind books near Zorro's table and browsed the paperback novels.

"Bring me some magazines," Lilibeth said.

While Lilibeth and Perla took off their T-shirts and shorts, Marty moved the chairs so that sitting with his back to the pool he had a clear view of anyone talking to Zorro. He had Lilibeth sit across from him in her skimpy Brazilian bikini. Posing her in various positions, he took pictures of her, and with minor adjustments of angle and zoom, portraits of Zorro framed in the window. After reviewing his shots, he consulted the instruction manual, tinkered with the camera and repeated the test until he had perfect photographs of Zorro reading his newspaper.

The Aussies came down from the hotel carrying a ball. Christopher strolled over, greeted them and invited Perla for a game of volleyball in the pool. Perla looked at Marty.

"Go ahead, but if I ask, please come back quick."

"Can I play too?" Lilibeth asked Christopher.

"No, you sit right where you are," Marty said.

Lilibeth smiled. "Oh, Sammy, are you jealous?"

"You can go when Perla comes back. I'm not going to sit here by myself."

Lilibeth went to him and ran her fingers into his hair. "No, Sammy, I won't leave you alone." She kissed him and pressed her crotch against his arm. "I'm ready whenever you are," she whispered.

"Later."

"Before Tata comes, I want to."

He laughed. "Go sit down and do it yourself. I'll take your picture."

Marty amused himself by taking pictures and exploring the features of the camera. He learned that in continuous mode, the camera took three frames every two seconds if he held the shutter button down. After the first two frames, the viewfinder blacked out, but he continued to shoot blind and use the review mode to see if he had captured a Kodak-moment. He practiced by taking pictures of Perla and the Aussies in the pool. When employees came to Zorro's table—the waitress to see if he wanted something, the cook to get his signature—he took their photographs to make sure he had the correct focus and exposure.

Lilibeth, an unabashed exhibitionist, delighted in having her picture taken. He was posing her for provocative shots of her behind when two women came around the corner of the restaurant from the entrance path. They stopped when they saw the pool area, as if they might have come to the wrong place, and it seemed they had. They were Moros, dressed in *malongs*, versatile tubular garments with batik patterns. One wore the *malong* as a dress and had tied it to bare one shoulder. She was young and chic. The other woman, older looking, used the *malong* as a full-length skirt. She had a long-sleeved blouse and a scarf draped over her hair. Many of the bathers quieted and stared.

"Sit down, Lilibeth." Marty pointed to the chair.

Marty shifted to place the Moros in Lilibeth's background, zoomed in, held the shutter down and panned them as they walked into the restaurant.

Lilibeth looked over her shoulder. "You takin' pictures of the Muslim girls?"

"Yeah, their dresses are picturesque."

The woman with the scarf went directly to Zorro's table. The chic girl followed. Zorro had been standing since they passed his window. He looked puzzled. He surely had not expected this visit. He signaled to the waitress to bring chairs and the Moros sat down. Marty tried to take a portrait of the woman with the scarf but she did not turn her head and the damn scarf masked her profile. He reviewed his blind shots. He had the younger woman—she had looked around—but scarf-lady had kept her eyes on the ground. She wore a bracelet of colored beads on her left wrist. He changed the camera back to picture mode and pointed it at Lilibeth while watching and waiting for Scarf to turn her head. She did not. But when she raised her right arm, he saw she had the same type of beaded bracelet on the other wrist.

He signaled to Perla. She came and toweled dry.

"We're going into the restaurant for a while. Leave your stuff here to save our table."

Perla glanced at Zorro's window, looked at Marty for a few seconds and then back at the restaurant. Her expression stoic, she picked up the novel she had taken from the rack of left behind books and said, "Okay." He took his camera but they left their clothes and towels. Lilibeth left her magazine.

Besides Zorro and his visitors, only a Filipina and two children were in the restaurant. Perla pointed to a table and spoke clearly. "Hey, Sammy, can we sit by the window? I want to read."

"Sure."

Marty took the chair to position his back to Zorro and the Moro ladies, one empty table between them. He sent Lilibeth to the bar for three ice-cold beers.

Perla read. Marty stared out the window while he listened to the conversation at Zorro's table. When he gave Perla a puzzled look, she got up, spoke to the waitress and returned with a pen and piece of paper. Ignoring him, she appeared to copy something from her book and then continued reading. He glanced at the paper.

Maranao language
Understand a little

When Lilibeth came back juggling three paper cups of beer, he turned Perla's notepaper face down. Lilibeth started to whine about wanting to go to the room before Tata came.

"Go seduce the two loose Aussies. Don't touch Christopher. Be naughty. I'll take your picture."

Lilibeth beamed. "Really, I can do them?"

"Have a great threesome. Vamoose. Perla wants to read."

She grabbed her beer, sashayed to the pool and soon had the men posing with her. Marty took their pictures while he eavesdropped on the conversation behind him. Perla turned pages at regular intervals and jotted down a few words from time to time.

At midday, bathers started spilling into the restaurant. Their noise drowned out the conversation at Zorro's table. It did not matter. They had finished their business and were chatting over lunch. Two mothers and their kids took the empty table between theirs and Zorro's, but they needed more space. Marty and Perla moved back outside. Perla sat across from him with her back to Zorro and glanced at her notes.

"Surprise, Zorro speaks Maranao pretty well."

Marty leaned forward. "His wife is Moro. She must be Maranao. Where did you learn the language?"

Perla looked at her hands and smiled. "Not to speak it, but I remember words." She looked at Marty. "When I was a young girl an old Maranao woman took care of me. She often told me stories from an ancient epic poem about her people. She chanted the stories in her language, full of expressions and gestures with her face and hands, beautiful and melodic, and then she would explain the stories to me." Perla looked at her hands again, moved them lyrically and hummed. "Those were wonderful years." She brushed a tear away, opened her book and looked at her notes.

"Okay, I understood some of the Maranao, but Zorro also used a lot of Tagalog. The woman with the bracelets does not speak Visayan. She was bartering for cakes. They used the Tagalog word *keyk*, which we use for the western type, not traditional Filipino cakes. Zorro has thirty-two cakes to sell in two different sizes. Apparently these cakes are very expensive." She paused and then looked at Marty. "I think you caught that much of the conversation and you know what these cakes are."

He jerked back and gawked at her. "You're scaring the shit out of me." He had guessed they were talking about the C4, but Perla with younger ears and knowing some Maranao had understood more. What frightened him was she had seen that he knew the subject of the conversation. If she noticed that, so might have Zorro.

"You amaze me. You're a sharp soldier. What else did you learn?" He reached for her notes.

Perla pulled them back and wagged her finger. "Oh no, Mr. Sammy, that was a free sample. You have to buy the rest."

He smiled. "How much?"

"One-hundred bucks."

He nodded. "Alright, go ahead."

"Hmmm, should have asked for more." She shifted and leaned closer to Marty. "Okay, this might not be important, but Zorro and Bracelets are related. They used some words in Maranao that are a bit vague, but it seems Zorro is her uncle. Also, she mentioned a man named Kule in the beginning of the conversation. Zorro called him Bedz or Badz. Then they both referred to him using a Maranao word that means cousin or nephew or…I don't know…a blood relative. Anyway, Kule Bedz or Badz and 'cousin,' are the same person and he's in their family.

"Now, here's the interesting part. It seems Zorro and this cousin person already had a deal for the cakes. Then Bracelets suddenly shows up to renegotiate the arrangement because something vague happened to Cousin. And I don't mean vague to me. Bracelets wouldn't tell Zorro what happened to him. Zorro kept asking about Cousin and Bracelets kept avoiding the question. It seems Zorro got the cakes for Cousin, and if Cousin doesn't buy them, Zorro has a problem. Bracelets is offering to take them for a discount, but I didn't hear any mention of price. If they discussed price, I didn't catch it. Up to the time we left, they hadn't come to an agreement. I think Zorro is not going to bargain until he finds out what happened to Cousin."

Perla paused to check her notes. Marty watched Zorro and the two women eating lunch. Their body language told him they were not talking business, but he agreed with Perla. Their business was not finished.

"One other thing," Perla said. "Bracelets doesn't live around here. She's from either Davao or Marawi City; she mentioned both places." Perla folded her notes and stuck them in the book.

"Interesting," he said, feeling strange. Perla had grasped his intention to eavesdrop and collaborated without comment. See recognized an opportunity and cashed in without asking questions. He felt proud of her, as if she were his. Weird, but it felt good.

"Well, Mr. Sammy?"

"We better go order lunch or you'll be late for work." He nodded at her book. "I won't pay you the hundred bucks for your bookmark until the morning. I want to make sure you come back."

She grinned. "You needn't worry as long as Christopher is around."

"When are the Aussies leaving?"

"Saturday morning, early."

"Good. Before you go, invite Christopher to have breakfast with us." He glanced at Lilibeth working the two Australians. "Looks like Lilibeth has those two hooked. We should mix in with the Aussies."

Perla looked at her roommate nuzzling one man, her hand on the other guy's thigh. "Gotcha," she said.

The Moro women were leaving. Marty watched their body language. It seemed they intended to meet again. He wondered when and where.

By the time Perla left for work, Tata had arrived, Christopher and the Australian couple, Patricia and Peter, were sitting at Marty's table, and Lilibeth was in the hotel screwing the other two Aussies. Marty thought he should go to the safehouse and send what he had to Beacon, but he was too amused to leave. He watched Zorro chomping on his cigar as he made phone calls, each one agitating him more than the previous. Marty smiled. Bracelets, it seemed, had Zorro by the balls.

CHAPTER 16

Room 702, Cebu Midway Hotel, Monday, February 10

Alone after tipping the bellhop, Steve admired the king-size bed. He had never owned one. He did not think Amina had ever slept in one. Soon she would. He imagined them romping, using all that extra space. As regional materials manager for Apex Fruits International, he could afford a king-sized bed. As a freelance photographer for the insurgency, he would be lucky to have a cot. He thought of the story about soldiers in Vietnam, about the things they carried, measured in pounds with decimals and ounces. Amina had brought only a little bag when she first moved into his house. "When one ventures into the unknown, Sweet Steve, one prepares for hasty retreat," she had explained. He had to decide what to carry and what to shuck.

He unpacked, connected his laptop to the internet and loaded Amina's secret files. He took a hot shower, donned the hotel's white terrycloth bathrobe, opened the mini-bar, selected an ice-cold San Miguel and looked out the double-paned window at the panoramic view of the city. His vantage point seemed odd. He realized he was on the tenth floor, not the seventh, because the hotel sat on top of a supermarket and department store; quite convenient those, guests need not step outside into all that humidity. The hotel was good value at fifty bucks a night. They had cable television, offered erotic movies, room service, waiters and maids in starched uniforms and central air conditioning. *Enjoy while you can,* he thought.

The phone rang. Steve leapt for it. "Room 702," he said. Two minutes later, he opened the door at the first knock. Amina rushed in.

"Had a great morning," she said.

He closed the door, flipped the dead bolt and attached the safety chain. When he turned around, she tossed her blouse at him. "I'm glad," he said.

Steve lay on his back with his arms folded behind his head and let Amina toy with his blond hair. "Okay, Tigress. What do you have in those files?"

She pushed up and sat on the bed facing him. "Some are lists, notes and plans about women as negotiators—my public project. The others deal with a sensitive issue. Just a second...I'll explain."

She went to the mini-bar, opened a bottle of juice and sat in the armchair. She drank some and gazed at Steve for a while. "I'm not sure where to begin." After taking another sip, she contemplated the bottle, turning it back and forth, as if she were looking for a cue line. At length, she shifted in the chair and began.

"Back in 1972, the Moro *National* Liberation Front started the fight for what was left of our ancestral lands. Four years later, they signed a peace agreement with Marcos in return for an autonomous region. It was a lousy agreement." She stared at the window for several moments.

"Around 1978, when I was eight years old, dissidents split from the MNLF and formed the MILF. For twenty-five years, we fought for Moro rights and became strong. Now we are 12,500. We have the government at the negotiating table again. With international support from Libya, Malaysia and Indonesia, we can get a workable agreement for a new autonomous region. But we have a problem."

She got out of the chair and went to the window. "We have no idea how many radicals are in the 12,500. Some have relatives in the Abu Sayyaf and Jemaah Islamiah. We do not know how many. We have commanders who let men from those groups train in our camps. We do not know how many. When a bomb goes off, they blame it on us. We deny it, but we do not know." She smirked. "We do not know who our renegades are until the army catches them red-handed. We have soldiers we cannot control."

"That's an uncomfortable negotiating position."

She shook her head. "Oh, it is far more serious than that. The Americans want military bases on Mindanao. Already you have soldiers here because your President of the World declared the Abu Sayyaf a terrorist organization." She flipped her hand in a gesture of exasperation or perhaps disgust. "A group of one or two hundred bandits kidnaps two American missionaries so he declares them terrorists and sends in the troops. He wants to declare the MILF a terrorist organization too, because he will need bases to deal with 12,500. If these radicals and renegades give him an excuse to declare us terrorists, we won't have a negotiating position at all. They don't negotiate with terrorists.

"Now, Steve," she said as she strode two paces and stood over him. "Tell me what you do when you are struggling for your livelihood, and after thirty years you think you're on the threshold of a deal, and then the door slams shut in your face—forever?"

"Fight. Fight desperately, violently, recklessly."

"Give it a name. What would I call it?"

He saw it burning in her onyx eyes. "Jihad."

"Yes. If we have nothing to gain, we have nothing to lose. We join the global jihad. We *become* terrorists."

"He declares you terrorists and he's right. It's a self-proving assertion."

Amina snickered. "And he gets away with it because the Americans don't care about the issues here. But there are consequences."

"Chicken fucking soup," he muttered.

"What?"

He shook his head. "Sorry, it's an old American expression."

She drained the last drops from the bottle of juice. "This is making me thirsty." She looked in the mini bar and took out a bottle of water.

"Okay, so what's in the files?"

She went to the desk and tapped his computer. "I'm compiling a database of suspects—renegades, radicals, rascals, mercenaries, possible CIA agents, *anyone* with experience in handling explosives, whether they are MILF, army, NBI or whatever. They're all going into the database because we are certain someone besides a few MILF renegades are behind these bombings."

She smiled and sat in the armchair again. Her tone changed from somber to enthusiastic. "We're getting all kinds of information on these people—where they live, where they have lived and when, their resources, their close associates. I'm building another database on past incidents—date, place, type, skills required, materials used. We will try to match people and bombings. And when a bomb goes off, we can sort through the database for likely suspects. We have to stop those who plant bombs and blame us."

"That's a big project." He jumped off the bed and began to pace. He had helped her structure the databases, but as templates without her data. Her files were no longer samples with Jane Doe and John Smith, XYZ characteristics and nice round numbers. He could visualize data. Matching would be a bitch—so many variables. "How do you collect the information? Is it reliable? We need to develop some sort of reliability algorithm."

She shrugged. "Others supply the data. My job is to build the databases." She smiled. "You, Sweet Steve, have been very helpful is in that regard."

He raised his beer bottle and grinned. "All for the cause of peace and tranquility."

She slipped out of her chair and hugged him. He grasped her shoulders and looked into her eyes. He loved how they always sparkled. "What's the ticklish family concern?"

She pulled away and sat down again. "We have a renegade commander in the family."

"Jiriki?"

"No, no," she said, shaking her head. "Jiriki has him under house arrest."

"Tigress, why are you in Cebu?"

She smiled. "I'm having a romantic holiday." Her grin faded. "Trust me, you don't want to know anything about this. It's *very* ticklish. You don't want to get involved."

"But what if I do?" He turned away to avoid his own question and opened the mini-bar. "We need more beer."

"No, *you,*" she pointed, "*want* more beer."

"You're right, I'll get some at the supermarket downstairs. Let's go out for dinner. Are you hungry?"

"Whoopee, the infidel has a heart!" She leapt out of the chair and kissed him on the cheek. Going through the clothes he had brought her, she chucked jeans, a three-quarter sleeve blouse, a pale blue camisole and a scarf onto the bed. She opened drawers. "Ooh, I forgot to tell you to bring underwear. I'm going to wear my jeans."

"We'll buy some after dinner."

They strolled in the dusk, he lumbering at half-stride, she walking by his side but seeming to follow along, bent in her distinctive tilt, as if she were too timid to confront the world. They stopped, conferred in soft voices and entered a Chinese restaurant. After they ordered beverages, she took off her scarf to study the menu.

"I'll have steamed fish and white rice," she said. "Get some egg rolls. I'll smother them with Chinese mustard. I like the way that stuff burns my nose—makes me feel like a dragon. I'll *ravish* you."

He admired her eyes. After eighteen months, she was still an enigma, a mystical puzzle with pieces that did not seem to fit the pattern. She was Maranao, the people from the lake—enchanting that. What happens when you solve the puzzle, put all the pieces together and see the whole picture? Is the enchantment then gone? You take a photograph and know it's wonderful until you start to print it and see defects—the focus isn't right, the perspective is off, you missed the decisive moment—the image you captured is not the one you imagined.

She swept her hand in front of his eyes. "You in a trance, having an out of body experience?"

He looked at his menu. "I'll get mixed vegetables and meats on rice, and lace it with that." He pointed to the dish of fiery chili sauce. "That stuff is for slaying horny mustard dragons."

After they finished the main course, she asked for a sherbet. He ordered another beer. When the waitress left, he leaned forward. "They stole my hard drive to get your database. Who knew about it?"

She flipped her hands. "Lots of people. About fifteen persons send me information and I don't know how many more are funneling stuff through Jiriki."

"Who would want your database?"

She chuckled, set down her spoon and counted on her fingers. "Let's see. Imperial Manila, the NBI, FBI, CIA, NSA…all those rascals with a stake in the war on terror would like to know who is behind the bombings for their agendas, whatever their agendas may be." Her hands and fingers punched and prodded as she ticked off the outlaws. "And then there are those who *are* behind the bombings, big business and the power elite, those who want your President of the World to declare us terrorists so they can take our land. They want to destroy my files before we find out who they are. Others want our land, including your military." Her face flushed.

"If we get a truly autonomous region in Lanao where the Americans…" she shot her finger at him, "where *you* want to put bases, we can authorize them independent of the Philippine constitution, and I will personally negotiate what we want in return. Go tell that to your bleeping President of the World."

He admired her fierceness. She was on her steed, lopping off heads. He began to zoom out, to see the whole picture and search for his place. Where did he fit in? What would be his role? He had to get involved, get into the picture. His sitting on the sidelines dickering with a database seemed a boring image not worth printing.

"Excuse me, sir. Would you like something else?"

"No, just the check, please."

He watched Amina finish her sherbet, spooning out the melt and checking to make certain the dish was squeaky clean. She took her cup of green tea, sucked out the last drops and lapped up the dregs.

"So one of these many now have your files."

She shrugged. "They're not finished. We still have a lot of data to collect and I need your help with the matching. I had something else on your computer, though. It scares me to think about it. They didn't steal the hard drive for that document. Only Nashita knew I had it. But if it gets into the wrong hands…" She sighed and stared into her empty cup. "I wish I knew who has it."

"Did you find out anything about Santana, the jalapeno pepper guy?"

"Nothing new. Some say he works for imperial Manila. Others think he's CIA. No one really knows. I hope CIA."

Steve glanced at his watch. "Enough subversive stuff. Let's go buy you some panties."

He bought beer at the supermarket and they went up to the department store. She pointed to the bench for smokers near the entrance. "Sit there," she whispered. "I'm buying *underwear*."

He shook his head. "No, you sit. You'll buy those plain ole chastity belt things. I'll pick out the ones I like, the skimpy, sexy, peek-a-boo kind."

She smiled and sat down. At the checkout counter just inside the glass doors, the salesclerk eyed her like a meerkat on sentry duty.

Steve selected seven panties. One by one, he held them up between his thumbs and index fingers and wiggled them for Amina's approval. Her head bowed, she appeared to ignore him, oblivious, but she was smiling. He took them to the register.

"Will that be all?" The girl asked.

"What? Ain't this enough? You got a minimum panty purchase rule?"

"No sir," she said, smiling. "Do you have a Midway frequent customer card?"

"No, I'm just visiting."

"Oh, where're you from?"

"Well, I was raised in San Francisco, but that was a long time ago. Now I live in Davao. You're pretty."

"So is your wife." She tilted her head toward the bench where Amina sat.

"I wish, I mean that she were my wife."

The salesclerk, having removed the price tags, began tallying his purchase. She glanced at Amina. "She's blushing."

"Or pissed," he said. "Can't tell the difference if you can't see her hands."

"Nice selection," the girl said as she slowly folded each panty into tissue paper and placed them into a cutesy bag with pink flowers. "Where are you staying while you're in Cebu?"

"Up there," he said, pointing with his finger. "You take Visa I hope?"

"Sure, but I'll need your phone number and ID."

He gave her his driver's license and cell phone number. She wrote the numbers on the voucher and he signed it. He was looking at Amina and did not notice that the clerk dropped the sales ticket in the bag, but not his credit card receipt.

Perla watched them leave, Bracelets tagging along, head bowed, looking timid and submissive, oblivious of her surroundings. *Like a stalking cougar*, Perla thought. *She caught me gawking like a schoolgirl. She recognized me, but she didn't twitch.*

Shortly after ten that night, Perla approached the reception desk at the Cebu Midway Hotel. She held an envelope with the logo of the Midway Department Store containing a Visa receipt. It was addressed to Mr. Steve Bryce.

"Excuse me," she said, "Mr. Bryce ordered things for tomorrow, but they won't arrive until the day after. I don't want to disturb him. Can you tell me how long he'll be staying?"

The desk clerk glanced at the woman in the department store uniform and tapped keys on the hotel's computer. "No problem," he said. "He is booked for ten days."

"Great," she said. "Please give him this note so he'll be aware of the delay."

Perla looked at a brochure on the counter until the desk clerk stuck the envelope in the cubbyhole for room 702.

CHAPTER 17

Pasigan Beach Resort, Tuesday morning, February 11

Marty leaned over the balcony railing and listened to the night creatures prepare to doze through the day. He decided to go to the safehouse after breakfast. Perla could take pictures if someone visited Zorro before he got back. His gut had told him to involve her and she had overheard crucial information he would have missed. But she was a risk. They had never caught him because he had never trusted anyone, because he always worked alone. She would likely go through his stuff. With his job in FerMar done, he could take the flying knives to the safehouse along with his old camera and the inventory of the third magazine.

He had been lucky and too much luck gave him the jitters. Imagining what might have happened on the hummock scared him. He could have snared himself in his poncho; the recruit could have blown his head off from two yards away. After Tata had left and Lilibeth went to sleep, he had finally retied the concertina wire. For three days, no one had noticed the breech—more luck. And Perla, how lucky can you get? Something too good to be true was usually not.

He exercised and showered. He was to meet the Aussies for breakfast at eight. After checking his watch, he yanked the sheet off Lilibeth.

Patricia, Peter and Christopher were already at the restaurant. Lilibeth's playmates, Peter and Tom, were no doubt recharging batteries. Marty ordered only coffee. He was looking at Zorro reading his newspaper when Perla walked past his window. He liked to watch her jaunty stride, liked the way her hair jolted. She seemed extra chipper this morning.

"Cheery good morning everyone," she said. She signaled to the waitress and sat next to Christopher. Perla wiggled with excitement as she ate with gusto. As soon as she finished she grinned at Marty. "Sammy, Tata asked me to explain something to you. Can we take a walk on the beach?"

"Sure."

Marty followed Perla past the pool area to the beach. They sat on a cement piling half-buried in the sand.

Perla watched the waves roll in. "Would you like to know where Bracelets is staying and who she's staying with?"

He chortled, releasing short bursts of air through his nose. "You're amazing." He rubbed his forehead. She had not left the Pasigan until an hour or so after Bracelets had. Perla could not have followed her, although he had thought of asking her to. "Okay, how much?"

"Hmmm, I've got a hundred coming, right?"

He patted his pocket. "Right here, if you want pesos."

"I'll take three hundred more?"

"You're dreaming. It's not worth it."

"You're right, Sammy. It's worth a lot more. FerMar stores explosives. The cakes are expensive illegal explosives of some kind. You have spent a couple thousand dollars already trying to figure what Zorro is doing with them. All you know is Cousin is out of the picture, Bracelets is in, but you don't know who she is. Don't waste my time, Mr. Sammy. Price is now five hundred."

"Three-fifty."

"Four hundred, final offer."

"You want it in pesos or dollars?"

She poked her hand into the pocket of her shorts. "Depends on your exchange rate." Still watching the waves, she handed him a folded slip of paper.

He opened it. "Shit!" His hand shook. He wanted to kill Nadine.

"Oh, you know this guy." She slapped her knee. "Damn it, it's worth more than five hundred, already."

Marty stared at the note.

> Bracelets with Steve Bryce
> Cebu Midway Hotel, room 702
> Tel. (63 32) 232-7666 x702
> Has booked room until Feb 20
> Raised in San Francisco
> Visiting from Davao
> Blond hair, blue eyes, about 6 feet, 180 lbs
> Tanned, muscular, good looking

Not married to Bracelets
Bought seven panties for pesos 1,893
DOB 11 Nov 1970
Cell phone (63 82) 463-2987
Driver's license C02-07-014037
Credit card number on bargain sale today

"You know this guy, don't you?"

"Fifty-four pesos to the dollar,"

"Hmmm, I'll take pesos, then."

Marty tugged at the Velcro flap on his pants pocket and pulled out an envelope. "Here's ten thousand. I'll have the rest before lunch." He smiled and kissed her on the forehead. "See ya," he said.

She pointed to the camera slung around his neck. "Want me to keep that in case someone visits Zorro?"

As he started to slip the camera off his shoulder, he changed his mind. "No, you stay away from that cigar smoking bastard. Don't even look at him. Promise me."

She regarded him for a moment before flicking her eyebrows.

CHAPTER 18

Apex Davao, Tuesday morning, February 11

When Bipsy went into the IT office Tuesday morning his secretary flipped her thumb at his office and mouthed, "Haradji." As Bipsy opened the door, he saw Haradji sitting in his swivel chair. Bipsy spotted his computer monitor flicker to a game of solitaire.

"Good morning, Haradji. And how is it that the Minister of Defenses honors me with a visit?"

"Thought I'd drop in and talk about access cards."

"Ah, yes." Bipsy said, thinking of Steve's visit. "Let me pull up the roster."

As Haradji got up, his back turned, Bipsy held down the "Alt" key and tapped the "Tab" key twice. He glimpsed Windows Explorer. He opened the software that managed the Security Access Control System for the Apex Davao offices. Each employee received a magnetic card to open doors within the complex. The system controlled which employees had access to which areas. The Human Resources Department was supposed to notify IT when an employee left the company, or went on extended vacation, travel or sick leave. IT then decommissioned access privileges or suspended them until the employee returned.

"Here's the active list," Bipsy said.

As Bipsy scrolled through the names, Haradji commented on two employees Apex had recently dismissed. Bipsy called his secretary on the intercom. She confirmed she had their access cards, but had not gotten around to archiving their names. Bipsy continued to scroll.

"Bryce took two weeks vacation," Haradji said.

"Ah, that rascal, he told me it was an urgent journey."

"I noticed you and he were here on Sunday. What did he need from IT?"

"We didn't load all the software he needed in his new computer."

"Why would he need his computer if he's on vacation?"

"You don't know? That bourgeois capitalist plays the stock market like some play solitaire." Bipsy smiled.

Haradji stiffened. "I'll have Human Resources send you a memo to suspend his card," he said, and left.

Nonsense, Bipsy thought.

Human Resources never suspended a card for an absence of fewer than thirty days, and then only if the employee had left the Philippines. Haradji's visit had nothing to do with access cards. From the moment his secretary told him Haradji was in his office, Bipsy figured he would ask about Steve's Sunday visit. Haradji seldom bothered with IT other than to check the access cards two or three times a year, and he had checked them a month or so previous.

Bipsy checked Windows Explorer. Haradji had been snooping through the detail lists of his files. Bipsy had to give Haradji credit; he had changed the sort sequence to show the most recent date modified first. At a glance, he could spot new files. Bipsy got up, grabbed his password-recovery software and went to visit Grandma to see what Amina had in her files.

CHAPTER 19

Cebu Island, Tuesday, February 11

Marty took a taxi to the Philippine National Bank in uptown Cebu, withdrew 100,000 Pesos and took another taxi to the safehouse. Tippy's wife greeted him and said she had put an electric fan in his room. He noted the broken airplane glue on his door but neither his laptop nor his suitcase had been touched. After booting up the computer, he looked up the name of Steve Bryce's lady friend. Then he sent an encrypted email to Beacon with the inventory of the third magazine, and what he knew of Amina Taiba's conversation with Zorro about "cousin" Kule Bedz or Badz and the C4. At the end of the message, he added an angry comment that he had been compromised because he was not told about the connection between Amina Taiba and Zorro, but he did not mention Perla.

The snails-pace internet connection made transmission of photos exasperating. He sent only the pictures of the C4, Bracelets and her companion. After transferring the pictures of Zorro and his visitors to the computer, he deleted them from the camera but kept his touristy photos. While he waited for the files to upload, he considered searching room 702 at the Cebu Midway, but decided to get back to the Pasigan to keep an eye on Zorro. Before locking his suitcase, he slipped a miniature voice recorder into his pocket.

Again using two taxis, Marty got back to the Pasigan shortly after eleven. Perla and Christopher were talking in the pool near Zorro's window, but Zorro was not there. Perla climbed out of the pool.

"Where's Zorro?"

"He went into the kitchen a little while ago."

"Uh-huh, I told you to ignore him."

"I kinda did until two policemen came around and leered at me. Christopher glared at them and they went inside to talk to Zorro. Zorro slipped one of them an envelope."

Marty nodded. "Any other visitors?"

"Nope."

Marty saw Tom and Peter lounging by the pool. "Where's Lilibeth?"

"She went back to the room to take a nap. You dragged her out of bed too early. She usually sleeps 'till noon."

"Anything else going on?"

"Someone fixed the barb wire, although I didn't see any maintenance men." She smiled.

He nodded. He imagined her going to the room to change into her bikini and glancing at the concertina wire. While in the room, she would have looked through his things. He wondered if Lilibeth had helped.

During lunch, Marty looked for a place to plant the voice recorder near Zorro. Taping it to the underside of his table would be ideal, but the restaurant did not use tablecloths. Anyone stooping down might spot it. The shelves with left-behind books and magazines were about five feet from Zorro's chair, too far away to activate the recorder if he talked softly. But the bookshelves had an advantage. He could retrieve and replace the recorder at any time without drawing suspicion, or better yet, Perla could do it. While Perla and Christopher chatted, Marty browsed for an appropriate book. It did not take long to find it. On the top shelf, he found a dusty hardback about Philippine politics. Notwithstanding the dust and its age, twelve years since published, the binding was stiff. No one had touched it in years, and it had the advantage of being over an inch thick.

When he returned to the table, Christopher looked at the title. "I see you're going to do some serious reading, Mate."

"Not really. I plan to take a nap. Figure I'll be sound asleep by page two."

When Lilibeth came into the restaurant with Tom and Peter, Marty pecked Perla on the forehead and said he would see her at breakfast. He went to the room, bolted the door and saw that someone had gone through his things. Whether Lilibeth, Perla, or both, he could not be sure, although for the neatness of the search he guessed Perla had worked alone. Except for duct tape and his heavy-duty sewing kit, she had found nothing strange, but he imagined her snickering at his oversized condoms.

He prepared the book for his miniature recorder. It did not take long to cut out the center of the pages, but perforating the cover with his sewing needle was tedious. After an hour of piercing and testing, adding more holes did not seem to improve reception. He quit. When talking at a normal volume in the room, his recorded voice was muffled but understandable. Depending on the noise level in the restaurant, he could capture at least some of the conversation at Zorro's table. If necessary, The House could separate voice from the background noise. For now, it was the best he could do. He lightly sealed the covers and pages with airplane glue, returned to the restaurant and stood the book upright at the end of the middle shelf.

After Marty had left that morning, Perla had grabbed the same patio table they had used the day before. She had hung out with Christopher, Lilibeth, Peter and Tom. Later, Patricia and Peter joined them. In the afternoon, Marty lounged with the Aussies. Tata sat by his side pining to go to the room. He sipped beer and snapped pictures like a photo enthusiast on vacation. Marty felt comfortable staking out Zorro in plain sight. With the Aussies on board, his cover seemed impeccable.

The uneventful afternoon passed with Christopher talking ad nauseam with the Patricia and Peter about student programs at some university in Australia. Around five, Marty, was about to announce that he and Tata needed a nap when two men rounded the corner of the restaurant. Marty blinked and nuzzled into Tata's shoulder.

The young Filipino strutted with the arrogance of wealth. He wore a too small silk jersey and black leather trousers, tailored to show off his tight ass. It looked like he had a rolled up sock in his crotch. Marty did not know him but he knew his Chinese companion. Chopsticks, as they called him, wore cargo shorts and a flowery aloha shirt that could conceal his Glock, but not his disfigured neck. Marty regretted having left his Beretta at the safehouse.

CHAPTER 20

Pasigan Resort, Tuesday evening, February 11

Marty shifted his chair to place Tata between him and the restaurant. He huddled with her, as if in confidential conversation, while he peered over her shoulder. The young Filipino strutted directly to Zorro's table. Zorro smiled. This visitor, he had expected. Chopsticks stood by the door, surveyed the restaurant and took an empty table in the rear where he could keep an eye on the door, the clientele and his client. He could also see Marty's table.

Once the bodyguard for an arms dealer selling weapons in Luzon, Chopsticks looked like a sad shadow of his former self. Back then, he had been vibrant, with the brawny torso and bull neck of a weight lifter. Now his body sagged, perhaps in deference to his cockeyed neck. With droopy jowls and puffy eyes, he seemed weak, tired and ill. All good reasons, Marty knew, for Chopsticks to yank out his Glock and shoot the instant he recognized him, witnesses be damned.

Marty started to take off his T-shirt. "Tata, take the camera and follow me." He stood, pulling his T-shirt over his head as he ambled toward the blind side of the restaurant and parking lot.

"Where we goin', Sammy?"

"Let's take a little walk and then maybe we'll go dirty the sheets."

Tata smiled, her gold tooth glimmering in the glancing light from the setting sun.

Most people came to the Pasigan by jeepney, motor-tricycle or taxi, but Marty figured Chopsticks and the kid had their own transportation. Sure enough, the shiny green Toyota sedan had a warm hood. Marty peered into the interior and noted the newspaper on the rear seat. "Nice car," he said, smiling at his mental image of Chopsticks having to drive a rich kid around for a living; bodyguards don't do well after their boss is killed. He took the camera from Tata and snapped a few pictures while he considered what to do. He had the filet knife and the advantage of surprise.

Stride into the restaurant, walk toward Chopsticks, he pulls out the Glock, finish off his throat, hotwire the Toyota, go to the safehouse and get out of town. Make a mess, screaming people, dozen witnesses, blow my cover, screw up the job and leave the Philippines forever on the next jet out.

He had no choice but to hide in the room until Chopsticks left the resort. But if he walked past the open windows of the restaurant, he would likely get his head blown into the swimming pool.

He looked down the walkway toward the beach where he and Perla had talked that morning. From there, they could walk along the shore to the hotel. Chopsticks could not see the beach from where he was sitting, but he might spot him walking past the end of the pool. He could not go outside the perimeter fence with Tata. She might panic over his dragging her through scrub again. Besides, the fence extended into the surf. They would have to swim around it. He had to take her down the walkway inside the resort to get to the beach.

Marty strolled next to the fence with his right hand on Tata's shoulder. As they passed the end of the pool, he moved slightly ahead so Tata would block his profile from Chopsticks' line of sight. For once, Marty was content with his height; he was only a couple of inches taller than Tata was. If Lilibeth or the Aussies called out, he would squeeze the nape of Tata's neck and ignore them. He listened for the scrape of a chair, but heard nothing out of the ordinary.

When they reached the beach, he sat down on the half-buried piling and turned to make certain that Chopsticks could not see them if he walked outside. Tata sat close beside him. He stopped her from digging into his trousers, pointing to some kids cavorting in the surf. The sun was setting behind them. It would be better to wait for dusk before walking along the beach to the hotel.

"Let's go to room, Sammy."

He thought about that. "Yeah, let's have a party."

He dug into his pocket and peeled off several bills. "First, go get Lilibeth away from those Aussies. Buy a bottle of tequila, a bottle of scotch for you and Lilibeth…and get a bucket of ice. Now listen. There's an ugly Chinaman in the restaurant. I saw him leering at Lilibeth. Ask her if she knows him. You buy the bottles. Tell Lilibeth to go straight to the room. Here, here's the key. I don't want any trouble. Do you understand what I'm saying?"

Tata gave him a worried look and nodded her head. He made her repeat his instructions. "Okay, go on now. I'll see you ladies in the room." He watched her hurry out of sight and chuckled, imagining how she would scowl at Chopsticks while she waited for the booze.

After sneaking along the beach and up to the room, Marty rested on his bed. As the women became tipsy, they nagged and teased him. They wanted to play. He complained about not feeling well, went out onto the balcony and closed the door. The light breeze carrying in the scent of the sea pleased him. He sat with his feet propped on the railing. *Nothing to do but wait.* He thought of the little recorder doing its job, sucking up the conversation. He dozed off.

A door slammed. The sound of laughter drifted up from the pool area but no music—a slow night at the Pasigan. He strained to sort out the sounds—the chatter quieting down, people leaving, an engine starting in the distance—too far away to determine the type of vehicle. He heard the Aussies coming to the hotel, all five of them. He ducked below the railing and listened. They had two adjacent rooms on the second floor, one right below his. After they entered their rooms, he heard them opening doors and dragging chairs out onto their balconies.

Marty looked at his watch. It was almost eleven. He had not dozed; he had slept. Except for Friday and Saturday, the restaurant closed at eleven, but reception remained open until midnight while the employees cleaned up and Zorro tallied the day's receipts. Marty realized he had better get the recorder. He went inside the room.

"Tata, it's late. Go get us some ice and tell reception to call you a taxi." He handed her a couple of bills. She wobbled and crumpled them into her pocket.

"Send Lilibeth." She burped. "I'll get you blowjob."

"I told you I wasn't feeling well. Besides, you're drunk. Take the ice bucket and go see if the Chinese guy is still there. Vamoose."

After she staggered out, Lilibeth asked. "If yous too tired for me, cans I go see Aussies?" She burped.

"Jesus, are you girls soused. Go shower your drunken ass and get in bed. You're staying right here." She stared at him with her mouth open. "Move it," he snapped. She jerked back. "Now!" She, swayed, stumbled into the bathroom and slammed the door. He heard her puking as he looked around the room. They had near emptied a liter bottle of scotch. He remembered that they had not eaten dinner.

Tata returned with the ice. She was out of breath, as if she had been running.

"Is the Chinaman still there?"

At first she nodded, then shook her head. "He jes left with boy and cigar man. My taxi, already."

"Go then. Don't fall down the stairs."

As she wobbled out the door, he checked on Lilibeth. She was slumped over the toilet bowl, moaning. He shut the door on her and went to the balcony. Tata was doing fine, taking long strides and swinging her arms for momentum, or perhaps balance. He slipped out of the room and crept into the night, staying in the shadows so the Aussies would not spot him.

The kid was either Cousin or someone from the RSM group that Zorro knew. Whichever, he suspected they were closing a deal. If Chopsticks and the kid had hung around this long, they were waiting for the resort to empty before going into FerMar.

Marty stood by the dance floor until he heard Tata's taxi leave. As he walked into the restaurant, he heard another car engine start. A waitress and the resort's jeepney driver were cleaning up. The night watchman sat drinking a cup of coffee. Otherwise, the place seemed empty. Marty glanced into the kitchen and reception—no one.

When he retrieved the book, he heard noises behind the restaurant. He bid the employees goodnight and started walking toward the hotel. It would be safe there. He considered listening to the recording on the balcony while sipping a glass of tequila, but he knew he should not sit around and let the C4 get away. Once out of sight of the restaurant, he snuck around the far side of the pool, thankful that they had turned off the pool lights. As he started up the walkway to the parking lot, he could see Zorro's pickup truck and the resort's jeepney, but not the Toyota. He froze when he heard squeaky noises and then a metallic clang. He waited, prepared to stroll back to the restaurant, but the footfalls receded.

He moved forward enough to spot a guard walking back inside FerMar after closing the gate, but he had not locked it. Marty crept to the fence and listened. In the guardhouse not ten yards away, he heard two soldiers deciding to play chess. When they quieted, he could hear noises farther inside FerMar. He crawled in far enough to glimpse the Toyota parked in front of the first magazine and retreated.

Hiding in the jungle across the road from the parking lot, Marty yanked open the book. He started listening to the recording. They had spoken in Tagalog. If the kid were Cousin, he would be listening to Maranao. The shutters for the restaurant windows banged shut as he strained to hear Zorro's voice on the tape, but the arrogant kid spoke loud enough. He rewound and listened to the crucial part several times until he had no doubt. They had made a deal for twenty kilos of C4.

Marty heard the waitress and jeepney driver coming up the walkway. He hunkered down and pressed the recorder back into the book. A bug buzzed near his ear. He resisted the urge to swat it. The cool breeze on his balcony beckoned him. He could hear the tinkle of ice in his glass, but he could not stop thinking about the destruction they might do with twenty-kilos of C4. The jeepney engine started and he listened to it leave.

Kicking up gravel, Marty raced down the access road. The first blind curve would have been perfect if it were not so close to the resort. He remembered another not far from the highway. He hoped it adequate. When he reached the bend in the road, he plunged into the jungle on the north side. With his Maglite, he spotted a rotting log that he could use as a last resort. Logs don't rot in the middle of the road. Chopsticks would pull the Glock the instant he saw it. He wanted a hefty limb that looked like it had fallen naturally but without a hatchet, he doubted he would get one.

Time chased him. How much time could he spend? Should he waste time to find the perfect prop and risk losing the opportunity, or use the log and risk getting his head blown off? He did not like having to pick from lousy choices. Already he had gone so far into the jungle that even if he found what he was looking for it would take too long to wrestle it through the underbrush to the road. He grabbed several branches, dragged them out through the scrub and arranged them to appear as one. Listening for an engine, he cut green twigs with the filet knife and spliced them into the branches.

When he finished the barricade, he dashed back beyond the beginning of the curve. Using his Maglite as if it were a headlight, he imagined Chopsticks coming around and seeing the barrier. He would have fewer than seventy feet to decide, a matter of seconds, and would have no reason to expect trouble. Marty hoped the arrogant kid in the backseat of his shiny car would go berserk if Chopsticks scratched it. Chopsticks' instinct would tell him to plow over the roadblock, but it looked solid enough to make him pause and worry about disabling the car. The kid would be screaming for him to stop.

Chopsticks will hit the brakes. How hard? Where will he stop?

Marty's arms burned. He had scratched them while tussling with the branches. That worried him, but he did not have time to dream up an alibi for scratches. Besides, in a few minutes he might suffer grave wounds. His eyes darted about looking for a rock of the right size. He found one, and tossed it into the ditch by the perimeter fence. It landed with a soggy thud. Holding his filet knife, he squirmed into the mucky gully, pulled up grasses to hide his bulk and waited.

As he listened to the car in the distance, he felt as if something were missing. He patted his pockets. He had the Maglite, but not the book and recorder—he had left them on the far side of the road. He judged the distance of the car and scrambled out of the gully. "Here bookie, bookie," he whispered. He had to risk it. He cupped his hand around the head of the Maglite and swept the narrow beam along the edge of the road. His heart ticked like a time bomb. The car was too close. He doused the light and darted back to the gully, kicking the damn book as he did. It was on the side of the road a few feet from his hiding place. He grabbed it as he dove back into the ditch.

Marty smiled. After two baths in the sour, smelly slime in the bottom of the gully, he probably looked and stunk like a fiend from the depths of a Stephen King novel. With a beastly growl, he might scare Chopsticks to death.

As the Toyota slowed, Marty set his feet and listened to the crackle of tires on gravel. He heard Chopsticks ease down on the brake and feared he had miscalculated the spot where the car would stop. If Chopsticks stopped short, he would see him dashing to the car and have time to react. He could wait until Chopsticks got out to clear the road. No, he thought, Chopsticks would look around a put a slug in the suspicious lump of muck in the ditch.

The car rolled on, the slowing crackle on the gravel music to Marty's ears. He leapt up, growling with his left arm cocked ready to hurl the rock, but he did not need it. Chopsticks drove with his window open. He had been leaning forward to peer at the branch when Marty popped up. Now he looked at Marty; the dash lights glancing upward over his mutilated neck did not flatter him.

Chopsticks did not lurch with fright. He gave Marty a look, first of recognition and then of resignation. Marty felt it too. Like old pals, men of honor meeting for the last time.

Three seconds full of momentum. Neither had time to avert the inevitable. Chopsticks raised his hands, the tired hands of a man who recognized his impending death. He did not shout or speak; his eyes did not plead. Marty stopped his stupid growling, yanked Chopsticks arm aside and slit his throat. The screaming kid scrambled out the back door and ran into the jungle.

Chopsticks flailed and the car jerked forward. Trotting along side, Marty thrust the knife into the dying man's neck and wrestled the keys out of the ignition. As the car rolled to a stop against the barrier, he yanked off his muddy T-shirt and wiped the blood from his hands and arms. He tossed it into the car.

Marty smiled when he opened the trunk. They had bought time-delay detonators along with the C4. While he waited for his respiration and heartbeat to subside, he retrieved the book and recorder from the ditch, slipped the recorder into his pocket and dumped the book into the trunk. He checked his pockets and tossed in the lock pick too. When he felt calm enough, he held the Maglite in his mouth, put the C4 into three stacks and rigged each with a timer. He wanted to be damn sure it blew.

When he finished, he stared into the trunk and imagined the havoc. Zorro had fenced off his property and the magazines were outside the range of the secondary blast—no one to harm on the south side or the resort. Marty supposed the kid had not gone far, but he would have no regrets if he killed an arrogant, rich twerp dealing in explosives to blow up god knows how many. Were there squatter shacks hidden in the jungle? Would the blast reach the highway? What if a car happened by at precisely the wrong time? Lousy choices all around.

He stooped to examine his work. With steady hands and heedful eyes, he checked the wiring and started the timers. Straightening up, he swept the Maglite around the trunk and something curious in the back caught his eye. He swung the light back. The thing did not belong there. He had a ridiculous urge to grab it, to save it. He stared at the rangy thing.

"Who do you belong to?"

He waited.

No one answered.

He slammed the trunk shut and raced down the road toward the resort. He would be sick, and he would get over it. He had been through this before. Soon enough, Chopsticks eyes would merge into the collective face of the others. But that doll would haunt him. He had an insane desire to go back and save Raggedy Ann.

When he neared the parking lot, he saw that Zorro had closed the gate to the walkway into the resort and imagined him inside reception gloating over his outmaneuvering Bracelets. Marty smiled. Zorro would not be going home tonight.

Marty crept through the scrub outside the resort, grateful for the clear night. He did not need to risk using the Maglite. When he reached the beach, he eased into the surf and slipped around the end of the perimeter fence while looking for the night watchman. Once on the beach inside the resort he knelt and retched as quietly as possible. In a moment of fuzzy dementia he rolled into the surf thinking that if he had saved the doll and given it to Perla she would have clutched it to her little breasts and suckled it to life like a good mother should.

When the dizziness stopped, he crawled into waist deep water, dunked his head and scrubbed his hair, face, arms and chest, scooping up sand and scouring his flesh, indifferent to the scratches on his arms. His ablutions finished, he walked along the beach like a stupid drunk who went for a dip with his pants and running shoes on, but he did not see the watchman. The three Aussie boys were still on their balcony. He hoped they did not notice him.

Light shone from the space under the door to the room. He eased it open. Lilibeth was not in any bed. He opened the bathroom door and saw her passed out on the floor. Grinning, he dug a prophylactic out of his pocket and went out onto the balcony to strip off his wet clothes and put it on.

Naked except for the condom, he lifted Lilibeth, carried her to his bed and rolled her onto her stomach. She groaned but did not wake. He pulled up her dress and straddled her behind. Looking at his watch, he caressed her crotch and his hard-on until eleven minutes before midnight. He eased her panty aside and pressed his cock between her cheeks. She stirred. Sweat beaded on his forehead, a few drops falling on Lilibeth's buttocks as he leaned forward. His breathing quickened to short gasps. A minute went by and then another. His erection began to soften as the moments passed and became limp when he realized something had gone wrong.

Marty collapsed next to Lilibeth in a stupor and cussed himself for underestimating the kid. He had disregarded him as an arrogant, rich faggot and had imagined him hiding in the jungle, pissing in his tailor made leather pants. But he had been waiting for the maniac to leave before calmly walking back to the car and defusing the C4. Marty was trying to remember what he had done with the car keys when the explosion shook the hotel at four minutes before midnight. Lilibeth screamed. Marty closed his eyes and grinned as he imagined the cigar-smoking bastard crapping in his britches.

CHAPTER 21

Room 702, Tuesday night, February 11

Steve and Amina returned to the Cebu Midway exhausted, sun baked and joyous. They had traveled by jeepney, motor-tricycle and a banca boat that they had hired to explore the islets around Olango Island east of Cebu. It had been a romantic outing, just the two of them. For lunch, they ate at a tiny outdoor restaurant with three tables—milkfish broiled with garlic and oil. Afterwards, while their boatman dozed beneath the canopy of his outrigger, they frolicked in the surf at a little secluded beach and then took a nap on the sand. Neither spoke of databases or password-protected files. No one mentioned Apex Fruits or the Moro insurgency. Their past had pleasant remembrances, the future beyond their control; they lived in a present of spontaneous exuberances—in the land of don't-give-a-shit, he said. Then they returned to room 702.

After they showered, he fired up his laptop. Amina came out toweling her hair and said she had to call Nashita.

"Where is Nashita?" he asked.

"She's with family here in the city. I stayed there Sunday night. They are devout Muslims." She looked at him and smiled. "One of those mumble situations, but I managed."

In that conversation at the Van Der Zee's house on the night they had met, Steve and Amina had shared anecdotes about having to mumble prayers. In their formative years, Amina had been a fervent Muslim and the Benedictines had reformed Steve. But by their early twenties, both had become disillusioned and had disassociated themselves from ritual. They talked about those awkward times, where for the sake of sociability or conformity, they had had to mumble through prayers they had forgotten. Isabela had experienced similar encounters. Gerrit, the atheist, listened to their petty mortifications with amusement and occasional snickers. As they sat down to dinner, Steve clasped his hands, bowed his head and prayed: "Mumble, mumble, mumble..." and everyone, including Gerrit, joined in— "mumble, mumble, mumble...amen."

Amina called Nashita, greeted her, and became silent, listening with a slack jaw. Her right hand pressed against the desk and her left shook in an effort to hold the phone. Her skin turned ashen, the sparkle in her eyes clouded. "Air Force!" she exclaimed, her body shaking. Then she spoke in Maranao, a question, then another and others in quick succession. She ended the call with a dejected murmur and *Insha Allah*.

"What happened?"

She held up her hand for him to wait. Her arm trembled. Fearing her collapse, he helped her stumble to the bed. She sat down on the edge. Again, she raised her hand and shook it. He went to the desk, sat down for an instant and then bolted to the mini-bar. He gave her a bottle of cool water. She gulped the water and then held the bottle to her temple. After several minutes, she set the water on the nightstand, knelt on the floor, pressed her forehead to the carpet, and prayed. She did not mumble.

He sat at the desk, clasped his hands and bowed his head, waiting in perplexed silence. When she stood, some color had returned to her face but her eyes remained dark. She sat on the bed, rubbed the tears from her cheeks and looked at him. It seemed she did not know what to say or where to begin, but after a minute, she spoke without inflection.

"The army attacked us today without provocation or warning. Thousands of soldiers swarmed into our camps near Pikit with tanks and artillery and planes. They are killing us. They intend to take the Liguasan Marsh. I'm sure of that."

"Where are these places? Are they near Marawi? Is your family safe?"

"No one is safe." She shot the words. Softer, she added, "No, not near my homeland. This is the south, Maguindanao and Lumad domains. My family is safe. But Nashita's father is a commander in the Buliok camp there." She stared at nothing for a moment and then scooted onto the center of the bed and tried to compose herself. "Again they broke the cease-fire agreement as President Estrada did when he declared all-out war and invaded Abubakar. We fought but lost. Abubakar had our camps, but also businesses, marketplaces and farms. The army drove out peaceful Moro communities of thousands. Many of those people fled to the Liguasan Marsh where we set up new camps to protect them. It's happening all over again," she said, her voice failing her. She squeezed her eyes tight, as if pinching desperation. A tear leaked down her cheek. She choked, sighed and resumed.

"After they impeached Estrada, Arroyo declared all-out *peace*. We renewed the cease-fire and started negotiations again. Then, today, Arroyo attacks without warning. Nashita's father says we're losing at Camp Buliok. We don't know what else we've lost yet." Amina threw up her hands. "It's all-out war again."

"Why? What reason did they give for the attack?"

She laughed—a sarcastic laugh. "Sweet Steve, this isn't the United States. This government doesn't need to orchestrate a media blitz about weapons of mass destruction before they attack. They will announce their excuse in a few days, probably something about the Pulangi dam project. Remember my stories about the dam? Here we go again." She tossed her hands and contemplated him. Then she slid off the bed. "You look like you need a beer."

"Yes, please. I want to go there, to the lake where your village was. I want to take pictures, try to document what happened."

She did not seem to hear him.

He had listened to her stories about the dam, but he had not felt them—not back then, not before he fell in love. The regulatory dam stabilized the river but destabilized the lake. It caused disaster. During heavy rains, the dam held back the water and flooded the farms, villages and mosques on the shores of the lake. During dry spells, it lowered the water level away from the wharves, which disrupted transportation between Marawi and the villages around the lake. It drained rice paddies and irrigation canals. Several species of birds and fish unique to the lake became extinct. The politicos of imperial Manila and the oligarchy of business interests issued "recommendations," which Hypocor ignored. The Maranao, without influence or a lobby, received neither compensation nor relief. They destroyed her village. She joined the insurgency.

She handed him a San Miguel and returned to the bed with a bottle of juice. "Okay," she said, "Hypocor is at it again. They want to dam the Pulangi River, which will drain seventy-five percent of the Liguasan Marsh, about 50,000 hectares I guess. This isn't just about electrical power. They want to drain the marsh so they can drill for oil and natural gas. Most of that land is ancestral domain. Thousands of farmers and fishermen live there. They depend on the marsh. Many live in houses built on stilts and raise ducks under their homes. They incubate the duck eggs and sell *baluts*. We have many camps there to protect them, but we can't protect them from the hoards of Philippine military. They will drive us out. Once they clear the marsh, Arroyo will apologize for the inconvenience and begin negotiating again."

"Where will the people go? What will they do?"

She shrugged and drained her juice. "Let's go to sleep. I'm weary and I need to rest. My ticklish family concern is now urgent Moro business." She smiled. "Our brothers will be itching to blow something up. We are at war again."

They turned off the lights and crawled into bed. He kissed her. In the dim light filtering through the drapes, her black eyes glittered again. No doubt, she was thinking about blowing something up. He rolled onto his back. He had ten days before he had to go back to work. If necessary, he felt certain he could get more vacation time. He pictured refugees fleeing from homes on stilts, in the background explosions reddening the night sky. He would capture the faces of frightened children and frantic mothers clutching their babies. He closed his eyes and chose the things he would carry.

CHAPTER 22

Pasigan Resort, early Wednesday morning, February 12

Terrified, Lilibeth stumbled out onto the balcony. Still drunk, she babbled in Visayan about demons and monsters, night and darkness. She alternated between clutching Marty and pounding him with her little fists. "Jew fuckin' Sammy bastard, why'd jew drag me to jungle." The startled guests shouted questions back and forth from their balconies, as if one might have more information than the other did. The younger Aussies and a Filipino man ventured out to investigate. Zorro, oddly wearing a raincoat, plodded toward the hotel and listlessly asked them to go back to their rooms. He ignored their questions, went into the hotel for a few minutes and trudged back to the restaurant. He looked bewildered and haggard, which delighted Marty. When the police arrived, and then soldiers, they ordered everyone back to their rooms and posted guards. No one learned anything, but from the swarm of uniforms they agreed that something serious had happened not far from the resort.

It took Marty a couple of anxious hours to coax Lilibeth back to sleep. He needed to prepare. The cops would soon be searching him and his personal effects. He inspected his soggy cargo pants and running shoes. Despite his sloshing in the ocean, the pants had dark stains and his shoes had faint speckles. He was frantic. With soldiers milling around the hotel, he could not ditch his clothes and burning them would be impossible. He had no choice but to scrub them while he took a long shower. After he used the last of the little soap bars, he opened the tequila bottle, doused his trousers with the liquor, rinsed them and draped them over the balcony.

The recorder did not work. He removed the disc, rinsed it with fresh water and put it in his toiletry kit with the two spares. Hefting the recorder, he shut off the lights and went to the balcony intent on heaving it over the perimeter fence. The shadows of cops or soldiers below changed his mind. The noise of something hitting the ground after his lights went out would be far more risky than keeping the recorder. He tossed it into his suitcase.

He deleted his pictures of the Toyota after memorizing the license plate number. The remaining photos of the Aussies and his companions were keepers, especially the provocative shots of Lilibeth. Then he poured some tequila into a tumbler, set it on the little table next to his bed, sprinkled a little on the floor and flushed most of what remained down the toilet.

Even though condensation fogged the crystal of his watch, it appeared to be working. About four in the morning seemed right. The seawater had not harmed his trusty Maglite. If it weren't for the soldiers, he would throw it over the perimeter fence along with the duct tape and airplane glue. The cops might think them curious things for a tourist to be carrying. At least he would not have to explain the sewing needles. He slipped them into Lilibeth's bag.

He sat on the balcony worrying about what he might have overlooked and how to explain the scratches and cuts on his arms. This set off the aftermath jitters. He wished he had returned to the room to listen to the recorder. If he had, he would be at the safehouse reporting to Nadine, sipping coffee perhaps, and she would unleash the mighty wheels of justice to crush Zorro and his cohorts. Instead, he had burst down the road in rage, thinking on the hoof. It seemed stupid now. Chopsticks could have reached for his Glock the instant he saw the barrier. The kid could have had a pistol, not on his person, not with those clothes, but in the back seat. So many things could have gone wrong. Maybe they had. Maybe someone had seen him on the access road or in the parking lot. *Maybe they've got the kid.* It had been a wild, idiotic and dangerous stunt. He had reacted with stupid plans hundreds of times in the past and gotten away with it. Regrets, yes, but the jitters were a recent affliction, an omen maybe. He was getting old. He might not be getting away with this one.

The eerie light on Chopsticks throat and his awful look of resignation bothered Marty. He regretted not having killed him the first time. The image of Chopsticks maimed and deteriorating seemed more tragic than death.

Better to kill a man than destroy him. Did I kill the kid or destroy him? You can't kill a doll. Should have saved Raggedy Ann for Perla.

After daybreak, he watched a helicopter arc over the ocean and sweep back toward the jungle. Three soldiers guarded the perimeter fence beside the hotel that ran from the backside of FerMar to the sea. The prospects for escape appeared bleak. He was wondering if his deceit would fail him when two uniformed cops marched toward the hotel. They strode with purpose. As they approached, he called down to them in English.

"What was that explosion last night?"

They stopped and looked up. "An accident," one of them said. "We want all the guests to assemble in the restaurant as soon as possible."

"Okay."

He woke Lilibeth. She moaned, blinked and cussed, but seemed happy with the sunlight. He dressed in knee length shorts, sport shirt, sandals and baseball cap to look as different from the previous night as he could. Although he had a long-sleeved shirt, hiding the cuts would arouse suspicion. Someone not guilty of anything more than stupidity would let the cuts air and scab over, not chafe them against sleeves.

As Marty and Lilibeth approached the restaurant, he saw the heads of two soldiers standing near the half-buried piling on the beach. Two more lounged at a patio table they had moved onto the walkway coming into the resort.

"Looks like they're not going to let anyone leave for a while," Marty said.

Lilibeth looked through the restaurant window and groaned. "Or let anyone in. None of the employees are here. I need coffee." She pressed the heels of her hands against her temples. "Oh, god, my head hurts."

Two soldiers stood by the restaurant door. One had a roster of guests by room number. He checked off their names and asked about Perla and Tata. Marty explained that they worked and could not stay over at night. The soldier nodded, made a note by their names and pointed to the coffee urn. Lilibeth stumbled toward it.

Marty looked past a bored cop into the reception office and saw Zorro slouched behind the desk. He did not look good. His arms dangled between his legs. *Handcuffs*, Marty thought, hiding his glee. He drew a mug of coffee and sat down with Lilibeth and the Aussies.

"Anybody know what's going on?" Marty asked.

"Seems someone blew up the access road," Christopher said. "They're not letting anyone in or out except cops and soldiers."

After the last of the hotel guests came in, one of the soldiers at the door left. He returned with two men in civilian clothes and an army captain. The captain spoke.

"Does anyone here *not* speak English?" He waited and looked around. Everyone, it seemed, spoke English. "Okay. I imagine you all heard an explosion last night. It blocked the road out to the highway. These two detectives will ask you a few questions. When they finish with you, please go to your rooms, pack your bags and wait there. Do not leave the hotel building until we tell you to do so. We are evacuating the resort. There will be trucks on the highway to transport you to Talisay or Cebu City as you wish. My soldiers will help you with your bags and lead you through the jungle. I suggest you wear walking shoes. Are there any questions?"

A chorus of voices asked what caused the explosion.

"We are investigating the cause. After we finish our investigation, we will have a press conference. You can read about it in the newspapers."

There were grumbles and more questions, which the captain refused to answer. He repeated what he had already said until the guests gave up trying to get something more out of him. Then one of the detectives spoke.

"Good morning. I am detective Sagapan. This soldier will call your name." He pointed to the soldier holding the roster. "When he does, someone will escort you to either detective Vitug or me. After we finish talking to you, go directly to the hotel. Do not attempt to return to the restaurant or the pool area. Is that clear?"

It was clear to Marty. They were not going to allow anyone they had interrogated to talk to someone who they had not yet questioned. When the detectives left, they walked toward the hotel. Marty guessed they would use the shelters by the small pools for their interviews. Sure enough, before the roster guy called the first name, the Captain stationed two soldiers on the walkway and dispatched two more to cover the pathway to the hotel. It seemed they worried someone might not follow directions. Then Marty noticed the cop sitting at Zorro's reserved table by the window. The cop was looking at him. Marty picked up his mug and went to the coffee urn. The cop's gaze followed him.

The first persons called were a Filipina woman and her teenage daughter. Marty noted the time. Twelve minutes after they left, a soldier escorted another

Filipina woman out. Her husband remained with their two young boys. Two minutes later, the soldier called for Patricia, the Aussie woman.

Marty thought about the detectives working separately. He hoped that meant they were looking for witnesses rather than suspects. But the length of the questioning concerned him. At nearly fifteen minutes per session, the questions were more than perfunctory.

As he waited, he wondered about the kid. The primary blast radius for twenty kilos of C4 in an open field would be around eighty yards; the secondary blast radius twice that. The range in thick jungle would be far less, but the pressure would blow over everything within forty yards or so. He imagined the kid had hid until he felt certain the madman with the knife had left. Marty could not remember throwing the car keys into the trunk and wondered if the kid had started to drive away.

Two policemen and a plainclothesman came in and led Zorro away. The soldier with the roster called for the Filipino man and his two boys, then about ten minutes later for Lilibeth and Patricia's husband, Peter. Marty had a bad feeling, which worsened as the restaurant emptied and he sat alone with the cop who looked as if he expected Marty to bolt. Marty kept glancing at his watch and feigned irritated boredom. The detectives had interviewed everyone but him. He imagined them comparing notes before they did.

Marty worried the kid might not have abandoned the car and had survived long enough to describe the assailant—a short lunatic covered with muck looming out of darkness. Not a damning description, but enough to hold Samuel Fuentes Mora until they checked him out. That was worrisome. Finally, the soldier interrupted his worries and marched him to the third shelter.

Sagapan sat on the bench, on the exact spot where Tata had. That helped Marty smile. He needed help. Vitug leaned against the rear of the shelter behind Sagapan. On the table, Sagapan had a notebook open to a blank page.

"Good morning," Marty said.

"Please sit." Sagapan gestured to the other side of the table. "Do you have a photo ID?"

"My passport is in the resort's safe with my other valuables." Marty pointed in the direction of the restaurant. "It's in the reception office."

Vitug shoved away from the wall and left.

"Where do you live, Mr. Fuentes?"

"I have a room at a boardinghouse in Intramuros. I stay there when I'm in Manila, but most of the time I'm traveling." The detective asked for the address. All of Marty's licenses had the address of the boarding house where he had lived when he had worked in Manila.

"What do you do?"

"I'm a freelance writer."

"What's a freelance writer?"

"I'm a self-employed writer. I write articles and sell them to different magazines under the by-line Harris Maxwell."

"Why not use your real name?"

"Some Americans don't trust authors with Hispanic names."

Sagapan wrote in the notebook and appeared to be framing another question when Vitug returned. He handed Sagapan a passport and a sealed envelope.

Sagapan felt the envelope. "What's this?"

"Cash."

"How much?"

Marty shrugged. "Around sixty thousand pesos, I think."

"You don't know? You hand over a bundle of money for strangers to keep without counting it?"

"I sealed the envelope with a filament of glue. I'd know if someone steamed it open."

Sagapan turned over the envelope. He had to tilt it back and forth before the light caught the thin line of glue. "Neat trick. Where'd you learn it?"

"I grew up in an orphanage."

Sagapan looked at Marty for a moment and then nodded. "Interesting. You would know if someone opened it, but not how much they took."

Marty could not tell Sagapan all his tricks. "Well, yes. You're right of course."

Sagapan handed the envelope over his shoulder to Vitug without taking his eyes off Marty. "We are going to count it for you."

Vitug sat down and slit open the envelope with his penknife. Sagapan started going through Marty's passport. He wrote the dates of entry, exit and visa extensions in columns.

"What's your date of birth?" Sagapan asked the question without looking up from his notebook.

"April 24, 1944."

The birth certificate for Samuel Fuentes Mora had that date, which was close enough. They had decided Marty was born on June 6, 1945, the day someone had found him in a washbasin at the bus terminal.

"When did you get this passport?"

"Three years ago, in April or May, I think. The cherry blossoms were in bloom."

"Where was that?"

"In Medellin," Marty said without hesitation. He often tested himself on the particulars of his various identities, including the date stamps in his passports, both the authentic and the forged. He was not sure of the consistency of the dates, though. The forger might have screwed up.

"Seventy-three thousand pesos," Vitug said.

Sagapan wrote in his notebook, a long note. His comments no doubt included a filament of glue and the owner miscalculating his cash reserve by over twenty percent.

Sagapan finished his table of dates and checked them. Marty watched Sagapan's eyes. The forger had not screwed up.

"I see you have been in and out of the Philippines several times during the past three years."

"Yes, my specialty is the Philippines."

"What do you mean by specialty?"

"I write articles about the Philippines."

Sagapan gave the passport to Vitug. He took the envelope and handed it to Marty. "Here's your money. We'll hang on to your passport for a little while."

Marty figured they suspected him enough to hold his passport, but not him, not yet. He hoped they might think he would stay in town until they returned his passport. He was fond of Samuel Fuentes Mora. Being Colombian had advantages. But he would be leaving

Sammy behind. The time to vamoose had caught up with him.

Sagapan probed Marty about his freelance writing. Marty tried to answer with enthusiasm. It was his primary cover story. He claimed to write under the pseudonym Harris Maxwell, the name used by actual writers hired by The House. Marty had a few magazines with articles written by Maxwell in his suitcase.

They asked about his staying at the resort with three women. He explained he was taking a holiday, met the women at the Monarch lounge and hired them to party for a week. He outlined their agreement.

"Tell us what you did from lunchtime yesterday up to the time of the explosion."

"Let's see. Lilibeth, Perla and I had lunch. Perla left and Tata arrived around one-thirty. We hung around the pool with the Aussies until just before sunset. Then I took Lilibeth and Tata to the room to party. We all got crocked and I snoozed for a while. Tata had to leave around ten-thirty or so. Shortly after she left, I went to the restaurant to get a book to read in the morning. I usually wake up quite early. I went to the beach, to get some air and clear my head. I was pretty drunk. Going back to the hotel, I stumbled into the surf and damn near drowned. Anyway, I managed to crawl out and get back to the room. A little while later, I was messing in Lilibeth's drawers when the explosion scared the shit out of us."

Sagapan wrote at length in his notebook. "What time did you go to the restaurant?"

"Around eleven, a little before or after, I'm not sure. They were closing."

"When you went from your room to the restaurant and back, did you see anyone?"

"Uh, yeah. I did. The waitress, the jeepney driver, and another guy, an older man with a pistol; the watchman I presume. All were in the restaurant."

"Did you see the owner?"

"No, I didn't see anyone else."

"Did you see or hear anything out of the ordinary while you were out of the room?"

"No." Marty thought for a moment. "I heard the Aussies out on their balcony, but that's normal."

Sagapan jotted something in his notebook. "Which ones?"

"I really didn't pay attention. All male voices, I think."

Sagapan made another note. "Did you see anyone out of the ordinary around here yesterday?"

Marty nodded his head. "Yeah, a Chinese looking man with a big scar on his neck. He arrived just before sunset and went into the restaurant. Before he went in, he leered at my friend Lilibeth in a creepy way. That's why I took the ladies to the room to party there. That guy looked like trouble."

While he scribbled something, Sagapan asked, "Did you speak with him?"

"No, I just thought it best to get Lilibeth elsewhere. I didn't want any trouble. You know what I mean?"

"Did this person come alone?"

Marty thought for a moment. "I think another man came at the same time, a young fellow, but I didn't pay attention to him. The creep looking at Lilibeth is what caught my eye." Marty raised his hand. "The Chinese guy sat at a table by himself. He wasn't with the other guy."

Looking at his notes, Sagapan added a few words. Marty figured he knew about Chopsticks, else he would have asked for more description. Marty hoped Lilibeth had said something about his leering. And he hoped she had been too drunk to notice that he had not opened the bottle of tequila.

"Where are you going from here, Mr. Fuentes?"

Marty shrugged. "I guess I'll find a room in Talisay City or maybe Cebu for a day or two. Then I'll go back to Davao."

"Davao, why Davao?"

"I'm working on a story there."

"Where will you stay in Davao?"

"Probably at the Palm Tree Hotel. I don't have reservations, though."

Sagapan looked at Vitug. Vitug nodded, stood and took a camera out of his pocket.

"Okay, Mr. Fuentes. Tell us about those cuts on your arms."

Marty extended his arms, twisted them and examined the scars. Most were fresh. A few older nicks came from handling the concertina wire and crawling on the hummock. "From fighting the surf. I floundered around drunk and disorientated for a while, then crawled out."

Sagapan gripped Marty's wrists and studied the cuts, all of them superficial. Vitug took pictures.

"Please take off your watch," Sagapan said.

Sagapan examined the watch and pulled on the expandable band, a detail Marty had not thought of. He tried not to show his exhilaration when Sagapan discovered grains of sand between the links. He had Vitug take pictures of the clouded crystal and held the watchband open for a shot of the sand.

Sagapan handed back the watch. "Where did you fall?"

Marty turned around. He shook his head a little. "I'm not sure, about there maybe." He pointed. "I swallowed some water and flailed around choking. I crawled out about there, I think," he said, pointing a little to the right. "I was drunk and it was dark, so I'm not sure where I was." Marty closed his eyes and shook his head without turning around. It was stupid to emphasize being drunk. Emphasis marks lies. He opened his eyes and imagined his struggle in the surf. He tried to remember details. Most lies require details, but not this one. He stared at the ocean, shook his head and then turned to Sagapan.

"I'm bullshitting. I have no idea where in the hell I fell or how I got out."

Sagapan smiled. He wrote a few lines and closed his notebook. "Okay." He pointed with his pen. "That soldier will escort you to the hotel. Pack your bags, but stay in your room. Please do not leave your room."

"What about my passport?"

"We'll be seeing you before you leave."

Marty walked back to the hotel thinking a few grains of sand might have saved his ass. They did not say they would return his passport, but that they would be seeing him before he left. Sagapan told the group to stay at the hotel, but told him to stay in the room. They were going to search him and keep his passport until they verified it.

The soldier escorting Marty did not leave him at the entrance to the hotel, but followed him up the stairs and stood outside the door to Marty's room. It appeared he intended to stay there.

"You're guarding me?"

"You must stay in room—no visitors. Those are my orders."

"No sweat. I'll make your job easy. I was a soldier once, American Special Forces, in Vietnam. The Cong took me prisoner." Marty pulled up his shirt and turned around to show his back. "But I got away."

"Ai!" the soldier exclaimed. Marty's back looked like a hockey rink after the game. "What happened?"

"Bamboo stakes," he said, pulling his shirt down.

The soldier straightened and stood at attention.

"Tell me, what happened last night?" Marty asked.

The soldier glanced at the stairwell. "A bomb blew up a vehicle. It's all over the place. Two men died. That is all I know, sir."

Marty nodded. "Thanks. Well, I better get packed."

He went into the room and walked to the balcony. He shut his eyes, bowed his head and sighed. *No witnesses.* After a few minutes, he started packing. Before he finished, someone knocked. He opened the door and faced detectives Sagapan and Vitug along with two uniformed cops.

CHAPTER 23

Pasigan Resort, Wednesday morning, February 12

Marty looked from Sagapan to Vitug to the two policemen and then back to Sagapan.

"May we come in?" Sagapan asked.

Sagapan and Vitug entered. The two cops remained outside. Lilibeth came out of the bathroom.

Sagapan smiled at Lilibeth. "Miss, the two policemen waiting outside are lonely. Please keep them company. We won't be long."

When Lilibeth shut the door, Sagapan said, "Mr. Fuentes, I would like your cooperation. We don't have a search warrant, but I could get one. Because of the difficult logistics at the moment, it might be tomorrow before I could present it to you. I can and will detain you for twenty-four hours. You can avoid this inconvenience if you give us permission to inspect your personal effects."

"Why me? Why are you harassing me?"

"Mr. Fuentes, we have a serious, inexplicable situation. I have to investigate anything out of the ordinary. To be frank, you do not fit the profile for guests at this resort. I am sorry that you feel harassed, but I'm obliged to check you out."

"My profile? Without me having to check the mirror, just what in the hell is wrong with my profile. I don't get it. This place doesn't care who I take to my room as long as I register and pay for them, and it's cheap. I'm self-employed. My paid holidays are paid by *me*." He tapped his chest. "I hoped to have some fun and at the same time write a travel article about a resort in the boondocks. What's wrong with that profile?"

Sagapan nodded. "That's a good story, Mr. Fuentes, but we've another view. You have seventy-three thousand pesos you don't bother to count, yet you stay at a cheap hotel. Ordinary folk don't use glue tricks. You are sixty-years old, which is a record age for guests at this dump, by about twenty years, I think. You wake up your neighbors doing calisthenics on your balcony. Despite your age, I wouldn't try to arrest you without backup. We have inexplicable violence and you have fresh scars. So now, Mr. Fuentes, do we search your room or do we lock your ass up?"

Marty thought for several moments. "I would think it a nuisance for you to have to hold me. Perhaps we can help each other. Give me a press pass with the same privileges as the local journalists. I don't do newspaper reporting, but there's surely a story here. I'd like to take some pictures. If you allow me that, then you can search as you wish. I can convince Lilibeth to give you permission to go through her stuff too."

Sagapan thought about it and smiled. "You're too old to be hiking through the jungle. I'll have someone escort you out by the road. You can take pictures, but don't bother asking questions. We do not speak to the press."

Marty chuckled and held out his hand. Sagapan shook it. Marty opened the door. "Lilibeth, these men are going to search you."

While Marty and Lilibeth watched from the balcony, the detectives searched the room and their bags. Marty smiled when Vitug took note of the liquor bottles, but his glee turned to cold sweat when Sagapan dug the three recorder chips out of his shaving kit. A few minutes later, he called Marty into the room. His tape recorder, camera and the memory cards for both were on his bed along with a magazine. Sagapan picked up the recorder.

"This is a pretty fancy gadget. What do you use it for?"

"When I interview people for the articles I write, I usually record the conversation. It's also handy for notes and ideas."

Sagapan pointed to the recording discs. "I suppose those are for the recorder. Please let us hear them."

Marty shrugged. "I'll try, but this morning it wasn't working." Marty fiddled with the recorder, removed and replaced the battery, but he could not get the recorder to power up. "I'm afraid I ruined it last night."

"When you fell into the water?"

Marty frowned and nodded.

Sagapan picked up the camera. "Does this work?"

"Yes."

"Show me how to play back the pictures."

Sagapan scrolled through the pictures, lingering over those of Lilibeth and Perla in bikinis, which he shared with Vitug. When he finished, he put down the camera and picked up the magazine. He opened it to a long article about *baluts*, from raising the ducks to consumption. The byline was Harris Maxwell.

"Did you write this?"

"Yes."

"Did you take the photographs too?"

"I took some, those without a credit." Marty pointed to a photograph. "Those with a credit line are stock photos added by the editor."

Sagapan dropped the magazine. He picked up the recorder and the three discs for it. "We will return these after we have examined them. I also need to photocopy your passport; the resort doesn't have a copier. I will have it returned to your hotel this evening."

Marty nodded.

"Okay," Sagapan said with a sigh. "I thank you for your cooperation. Stay here, even if the others leave. I'll send someone to escort you to the highway." He reached into his shirt pocket. "Here's my card. Call and tell my assistant where you are staying once you have a hotel room."

After the detectives and cops left, Marty sat on the bed and thought about his predicament. He cussed himself for not having flushed the recording chips down the toilet.

"Are you in trouble, Sammy?"

"No, no trouble at all. They're going to let me take pictures of the accident. Lilibeth, do me a favor. Take my suitcase to Tata's boarding house. I'll call as soon as I can to let you know where I'm staying."

Lilibeth caressed Marty's head. "Go to the Monarch, Sammy. I'll show you how much better I like it there."

"That sounds like fun."

Fun was not on Marty's agenda. He wanted to see the site of the explosion, but he could not linger. He would hustle to the safehouse and tell Nadine the good and bad news. Sagapan seemed reasonably convinced for the moment, but Marty knew he had to get out of the Philippines before they listened to the recording.

CHAPTER 24

Room 702, Wednesday morning, February 12

Steve eased out of sleep and stretched his arm to caress Amina but found her space empty, although still warm. He heard her come out of the bathroom and pick up the phone. Rolling onto his side, he saw her wrapped in the hotel robe, alert and anxious. He closed his eyes, knowing the cadence of her voice would decide his day.

He listened as she called Nashita. They spoke in Maranao. He did not understand the words, but inflections told the story—a stressful question, then *Allah Akbar* whispered with relief, and he presumed Nashita's father safe. She listened, interrupting with questions from time to time. An update, news from the front, he guessed. He heard "imperial *bleep* Manila," and wondered if she cursed in Maranao. The call ended with *Insha Allah.*

"Good morning, Tigress. Is Nashita's father okay?"

"Good morning, Sweet Steve." She smiled. "A few hours ago he was okay in a safe place, but it is chaos."

He swung his feet to the floor and sat on the edge of the bed. "How's the war going?"

"Too early to say about the war, but so far it appears we've lost all the battles." She turned on the TV and watched the news on a Manila channel. "Nothing from the government yet. They won't make a statement until they finish forcing the families out of the marsh."

He looked at his watch. It was six thirty. "I'll shower now." He shoved off the bed and went to the bathroom. When he came out, she was on the phone again, the TV muted. She spoke in English, her expression perplexed.

"I'm his niece. Where is my uncle?" Then, after a pause, she said, "Amina Taiba. I came from Davao to visit my uncle." As she listened, her face darkening with concern and then she jotted down a name and phone number. "Thank you. I will call in the morning."

"What's going on?"

"More problems," she said, holding up her hand. She got her address book, flipped through the pages and called a number. After a brief greeting, she spoke in Maranao for several minutes. When she replaced the phone, she looked at him, first with concern and then crinkled her brow. "I can't remember you feeding me last night. Order room service. I'm going to have a busy day. I want tea, mango juice, scrambled eggs, rice and *bulad*."

He winced. Filipinos loved *bulad*, a dried, salted fish that smelled rotten. He realized soldiers would carry them. She kissed him lightly, slipped out of the robe and let it plop softly onto the carpeted floor. He watched her naked bottom as she rummaged in the cutesy paper bag with pink flowers. She chose a yellow panty with tiny colored clusters that might have been berries, but he was not paying attention to those. She put the panty on. It had a wide pink belt of lace or something that hugged the curve of her tummy. With a naughty tug, she hefted the panty into the crack of her fanny. He grabbed her and tossed her onto the bed.

"Whoopee," she said.

After their love making, Amina called Nashita again and talked for a while. She turned to Steve. "Can you go to Talisay City with me today?"

"Sure, I'm going to go everyplace with you now."

"How about jail?"

He hesitated. "Can I answer that after breakfast?"

She smiled and finished the call. During breakfast, she watched the Manila news on the muted television.

"What's in Talisay City?" he asked.

"It's about that ticklish family concern."

"Tell me about it." He flipped his soft fried eggs upside down onto a heap of boiled white rice and mashed the yokes.

She caught his eyes. "Do you really want to know?"

He lifted the eggs with his knife to inspect the yellow stained rice. He looked up again. "Yes, it's about time I got involved."

She nodded. "Okay." She thought for a moment. "I have an uncle in Talisay City, they call him Zorro. He has a license to sell explosives. His legal customers are construction companies and miners, but he also sold bomb-making materials to an MILF renegade in Mindanao. Three people died in General Santos City, including the bomber." She paused to bite off the head of a *bulad*. "Zorro is married to my mother's oldest sister. Another aunt has a son in the Abu Sayyaf. Jemaah Islamiah trained him in explosives. He goes by the name Kule. Jiriki learned that our cousin made a deal with Zorro for a large quantity of C4 explosive. That is an unusual and hugely expensive transaction. For several reasons, we do not want that deal to go through." Amina popped the rest of the *bulad* into her mouth and glanced at the TV.

"Let me guess. You don't want the family name connected to a terrorist plot."

She washed the fish down with tea. "Yes, that is the ticklish family concern, a relative in the Abu Sayyaf who can handle C4. He's in my database of suspects." She watched the muted television news program. "I'm really curious to hear their excuse for the attack. The Liguasan Marsh and Pulangi Dam may be their goals, but I was wrong to think the Pulangi would be their excuse. The people have only protested the dam. Even Manila cannot use protests to justify such a massive attack."

"Tell me about the ticklish plot."

"Somehow, Zorro obtained over thirty kilos of C4." She looked at him and shook her head. "Thirty kilos is incredible. The only way to get C4 nowadays is to have connections in the army and a great deal of money. We couldn't imagine uncle Zorro having either, but he did. With thirty-some kilos, Kule is involved in something extraordinary. Whatever it is, it must be stopped." She looked at the TV.

"So where do you fit in?"

"We think Kule is Zorro's only contact in the Abu Sayyaf. Jiriki has Kule under house arrest so Zorro can't talk to him. We assume Zorro doesn't have another customer for such a large quantity of C4. My job is to squeeze Zorro and buy the C4 for the MILF at discount, maybe even less than he paid for it."

"What does the MILF want with the C4?" She looked at him as if her were a naïve jerk. "Oh, yeah, to stockpile in case Arroyo invades the Liguasan Marsh. So, how goes your negotiation?"

"Ah, it appears hoodlums have interrupted our talks. My eggs are getting cold. Let's eat and then I'll tell you what little I know."

He watched as she finished her breakfast with gusto. As always, she cleaned the last morsel from her plate. He called room service and they set the dishes outside the door. Amina sat by the desk.

"I opened negotiations with Zorro Monday morning. I was going to wait for him to contact me through Nashita, but this morning I decided to close the deal. Once Zorro learns about the attacks yesterday, his price will go way up. Zorro owns a resort just south of Talisay City. I called him there this morning and a detective from CIDG answered the phone."

"What's CIDG?"

"Ah, Criminal Investigation and Detection Group, something like that." She picked up her note. "When I called the Pasigan, this guy Ronny O'Campo told me there was an incident last night at the resort. They closed the resort and took my uncle for questioning. O'Campo told me to call him tomorrow morning. He said he would know then when I can talk to my uncle."

"Did he say what the incident was?"

"No, but I called my aunt, Zorro's wife. Around midnight last night, an explosion, shook the resort. Not at the resort, but somewhere on the road going to the resort."

"So what are you going to do?"

"*We*, Sweet Steve, are going south, to the Pasigan Beach Resort."

Amina wanted to see the eight o'clock newscast before leaving. There were no reports of the army invading MILF camps in central Mindanao, but the local news had a story about a vehicle explosion near the resort that had killed two unidentified persons. Video footage, taken from a distance, showed numerous trees blown over, a mangled chain-link fence and debris all over the place. Although the authorities had yet to determine the cause of the explosion, the announcer mentioned that FerMar, a company authorized to trade in explosives, was located nearby. Mr. Ferran Yuchengco de la Cruz, the owner of both FerMar and the Pasigan resort, was being held for questioning.

"They call *that* an incident," Steve said, pointing to the TV. "See if another channel has more pictures."

Amina, nodding, flipped back and forth through the channels until she found another report on the Pasigan explosion. They studied the video footage. She muted the TV and flopped back into the chair beside the desk. "Shit," she said.

"Tigress, it doesn't take an enormous amount of explosive to collapse a structure, but to knock over a forest of trees you need something more powerful than a few sacks of fertilizer. I think someone liquidated your ticklish family concern."

She shrugged. "Well, if it was the C4, then it seems there is nothing left for me to do here."

"Shall we go to the resort and see what we can learn?"

She shook her head. "Not yet. I have to think first. The police won't tell us anything. I have to talk to Zorro…somehow." She stared at the TV. "I have to make some phone calls. Please watch for news on the explosion. If they release the names of the persons who died, perhaps we can figure out what happened." She pointed to his computer. "They might be in my database."

Amina spent the remainder on the morning on the telephone and checking her email. Steve kept an eye on the TV while he went through his email as well. He opened a message Bipsy had sent the night before.

> Hey Blue Eyes,
>
> This morning, my wits not being as frazzled as usual, I came to work almost on time and discovered the slick-headed sleuth scrolling through my computer files. He asked the purpose of your visit on Sunday. I explained you came for more software before traveling. By the way, I was chatting with Grandma. She accidentally trashed the recipes you gave her, every last one. Shoot great pictures of the natives but keep your head down. They shoot back.
>
> Bipsy

Amina hung up the phone. "Well, that's all I can do for now."

He pointed to the TV with the remote control. "There's nothing new about the explosion. What have you learned?"

"Not much. I have to find out if there's any C4 left." With a suppressed grin she added, "We need it for a special mission." The CIDG have Zorro at their headquarters here in Cebu City. My aunt seems certain we can talk to him tomorrow morning. Jiriki wants me to stay until I either get the C4 or am sure there's none to be had." She smiled and mussed his hair. "He doesn't know about you yet. He assumes I'm staying with Nashita. What fun I'll have telling him about our romantic holiday." She looked at his watch. "It's lunchtime. Let's eat and then go to the Pasigan. Maybe we can find out something there."

"Okay. Look at this email from Bipsy."

"Grandma and recipes?"

"Old computer and your files. When I burned them to CDs, I forgot to delete them from memory. Bipsy did. The problem is Haradji somehow learned you used my computer and figures I had a backup of your files on diskettes. He guessed Bipsy and I transferred them to CDs. It seems he wants to prove the burglar came for your files, even after Stillwell told him to forget about the theft. I've no idea why he wants to do that. He's up to something. It worries me."

She stared at the email for a moment. "Don't worry about Haradji. He was never an NBI agent, as he likes people to think. He's just a perverted little cockroach without testicles." She tossed her chin at the computer screen. "Delete that and forget about him. He doesn't scare me."

Steve reread Bipsy's message and hovered over the delete button for a few moments before pressing it. The screen flipped the message into the trash bin. Steve had a feeling it might not be so easy to get rid of Haradji.

CHAPTER 25

Pasigan Beach, lunchtime Wednesday, February 12

Although Amina lamented the extravagance, she decided to hire a taxi to take them to Pasigan Beach and have it wait as long as necessary. If she discovered something of importance, she said, they would need rapid transport back to the hotel. They were at war. Room 702 was her communications center.

The area around Pasigan Beach was mostly jungle and scrub, sparsely populated with squatter's shacks, but the two-lane highway was a jam of vehicles creeping through a swarm of spectators. Frustrated cops and soldiers were trying to move vehicles and stubborn bystanders to clear a path so a backhoe and flatbed truck could enter the access road. In the confusion, a TV cameraman snuck under the perimeter of yellow tape. An alert soldier seized him, and after an intense argument, forced him to retreat. More onlookers gathered in the shade on the opposite side of the highway. They appeared bored, having been there awhile. Some struggled to get on an already overloaded jeepney headed for the city.

Two middle-aged women stood beneath a coconut tree. One of them, peering over eyeglasses perched low on her nose, nudged her companion. They watched the tall blond man walking with a woman wearing a silk-like scarf wrapped around her hair despite the heat. When Steve spotted them, he touched Amina on the arm and they went over to chat.

The soldiers seemed to assume that the man with the camera accompanied by a uniformed cop was another police photographer. They let Marty move around unhindered, some even helping him by pulling aside scrub and pointing out items that they thought worthy of photographing.

It appeared that the men investigating the site would soon be finished. A backhoe was pushing trees aside to clear a path for a flatbed trailer backing down the access road. Soldiers were scouring the jungle for overlooked parts of the car and toting them to the roadside. Marty hustled to take pictures of the twisted pieces of the Toyota before they hauled them away. One chunk of the body appeared to have been cut with a torch, perhaps to remove the charred remains of Chopsticks. From the stains and markings on the road and splintered trees, it appeared the kid had been standing near the car when it exploded. The arrogant snot had gotten what he had planned for others. Marty visualized him in the back seat barking cryptic orders at his chauffer, whining about every thump or jolt and threatening dire consequences should the careless clod scratch the car. Marty thought he might have given Chopsticks some satisfaction by having blown the little twerp to bits.

Two army men, ordinance technicians, huddled over a cardboard box containing charred bits of metal, poking them with pencils. Marty recognized a piece of one of the timers. He took a close up shot.

After taking a few more pictures, he thanked his escort and started toward the highway. The cop watched him, but did not follow. When Marty reached the yellow tape, onlookers and reporters hounded him for information. He gruffly shunned them, told them to get out of his way in rude Tagalog and looked for transportation. He had to get out of the Philippines before the cops listened to the recording. With his hand shading his eyes from the sun, he scanned the road in both directions. On the other side of the highway, he saw a jeepney driver trying to squeeze more customers into his fully loaded vehicle. Marty was planning to muscle in when he spotted Bracelets with a tall blond guy who had to be Steve Bryce. They were talking with two Filipinas. Marty hesitated, but he could not resist the challenge. *Gringo to Gringo*, he thought. He dashed across the highway and with a gregarious grin strode toward Steve and Amina. Steve looked like a photojournalist. A professional camera with motor drive dangled from his left shoulder.

"Hi, that's quite a mess, huh." He waved at the other side of the road and then extended his hand to Steve, ignoring the women. The feel of Steve's hand startled him. "I'm Max, Harris Maxwell. You American?"

"Yes, I'm Steve. This is my friend, Amina."

Marty looked at her and bowed slightly. "Say, didn't I see you at the resort the other day, having lunch with the owner?"

"Yes, he is my uncle. You came from the area of the explosion. Are you an investigator?"

"No, no, I'm a journalist. I was vacationing at the resort and talked the cops into letting me take a few pictures." Marty looked at the other two women and scowled. He turned his back to them and they drifted away. "Would you like to see the pictures I took?"

"Sure," Steve said.

Steve scrolled slowly through the photographs. Marty watched their eyes as they looked at the little screen together. They did not look at the pictures; they studied them. Bracelets' dark eyes gleamed. They fascinated Marty. *Cougar eyes— lovely and apt for a cunning feline. She wears the scarf to hide them.*

After they went through the pictures, Steve scrolled back and toggled between two frames. Marty peeked over his shoulder. He was examining the pictures of the two large chunks of the car's body, trying to figure what type of vehicle it had been. When Bracelets saw Marty eavesdropping, she took the camera from Steve and turned it off.

"Thank you," she said, returning the camera. "Do you know what happened?"

"Not much. Around midnight an explosion rattled the hotel. By daylight, there were cops and soldiers all over the place, even a helicopter. I heard two people died. Some detectives questioned all of us who were staying at the resort, but they wouldn't tell us anything. That's all I know."

"What about my uncle? Did you see him?"

Marty frowned. "I'm sorry, but I think your uncle is in trouble. I saw him in handcuffs this morning. He looked worried."

"In handcuffs!"

Marty nodded.

A commotion on the other side of the road drew their attention. The truck with the remains of the vehicle pulled up to the end of the access road and stopped. Steve whipped up his camera, darted about and took a dozen or more photographs of the wreckage. He returned to Amina's side.

Marty pointed to the camera dangling by Steve's side. "Are you a photojournalist?"

Steve chuckled. "I wish. It's a hobby. I'm a shutterbug."

Or shutter spy, Marty thought.

"Did you learn anything about the two people that died?" Steve asked.

"No, a soldier told me a bomb blew up a vehicle and two men died. That's it. The army officer in charge would only say there had been an accident and they were closing the resort. Say, maybe you can help me. I have to find another hotel. Can you recommend one?"

"We're staying in Cebu City, at the Cebu Midway Hotel. It's a nice place for fifty bucks a night. I'm sure they have rooms available."

"Sounds good to me."

Steve looked at Amina. "Do you want to see more or are you ready to go back?"

Amina smiled at Marty. "Thank you again. Your pictures satisfied my curiosity. We have a taxi waiting. Would you like to ride to the hotel with us?"

"I sure would. Thank *you*."

When they arrived at the Cebu Midway, Marty thanked Steve and Amina and said he hoped to see them around. He waved and smiled at them as the elevator doors closed. Then he turned to the waiting desk clerk and registered as Samuel Fuentes Mora, telling him he would return later with his luggage. He asked to use the phone, called Sagapan's office and told his secretary where he was staying.

Marty hurried out of the hotel and loitered on the shadowy side of the street a half-block away. He watched the lingering shoppers, the slow moving traffic, a tranquil Wednesday afternoon in Cebu. He eyed everyone—pedestrians, drivers, passengers—looking for a tail. *Sagapan thinks Fuentes awaits his passport. Secretary copies passport, sends courier to Midway, Fuentes not there, courier requires receipt, courier waits. How long does he wait before asking if there is luggage in the room? Okay, Sagapan keeps passport, sends tail to hotel. How long before tail discovers there is no luggage in room? So, put luggage in the room. How long do they watch luggage? How long before they shake the bushes and discover the rabbit vamoosed? Sagapan took the recorder because they don't have one. He sends it for repair or gets one from Manila. I've got time, but not much.*

Marty felt Bracelets pulling, her siren eyes luring fools. And her shutterbug boyfriend too, who carries a camera like a weapon, shoots it like a weapon, with hands like weapons. It takes years to get grotesquely oversized knuckles. And he is cozy with a subversive who is shopping for C4. That's not businesslike.

Marty blinked, focused on the street again. He had gotten the room next to Steve's. It would be fun to hang around, but he had made a mistake by not flushing the chip. *The rabbit has to run.* Not finding a tail, he hailed a taxi.

CHAPTER 26

The safehouse, Wednesday afternoon, February 12

Marty paused to examine the filament of glue and unlocked the door. Perhaps he would remember this safehouse as he did his last foster home, a place of change, this the place where he reinvented himself for the last time. They had his picture and a description by two pros. Before changing his appearance, drastic change required, he would settle with Tippy's wife. *No more mistakes, old man.*

While powering up the laptop he pressed the panic code on his phone and told Beacon to have Nadine contact him for an emergency report. Then he called Lilibeth. She was relieved to hear from him. He had not yet paid her in full, but she was hesitant and evasive. Just sleeping off her hangover, she said. It took precious time before she admitted she had a date to screw the Aussies again. He ordered her to take his suitcase to the Cebu Midway before she did.

He bought an e-ticket on the 10:30 PM flight to Manila for Eduardo Duarte, a solid Filipino identity. The earlier flight had been booked full. He wondered if he should risk hanging around on standby. After searching through possibilities, he decided on the 8:00 AM flight to Hong Kong and bought a ticket for Marty Santana. He would disappear there. While contemplating his disguise, his cell phone rang.

"Are natives revolting?"

"They smell bad. I'm pushing buttons."

He summarized how he had blown up two delinquents and put Zorro out of business. The recording he explained in detail, citing the exact words that had triggered his actions. He confessed his stupidity in not destroying it.

"Once they listen to that recording, they'll lock up this island and Manila airport. Whether they find me or not doesn't matter. I'm finished. I leave for Hong Kong at eight in the morning. If I'm lucky, I'll send my final report from there."

"No, do not move. Send report now. I will call again in two hours."

Marty held the dead phone to his ear. Nadine had warned him not to attempt to disassemble the phone; it would self-destruct. He waited for it to blow his head off. After a minute, he set the phone aside. He guessed it did not pack a charge sufficient to pulverize the room. What would they do? He had made a mistake. They could not risk him being caught. Although he did not know where The House was, or the names of the occupants aside from the so-called Nadine, he had knowledge of thirty-years of dirty tricks to trade for his freedom. Supposedly, The House knew within a hundred yards where the phone was. Nadine could not get the cavalry to it in two hours, yet his gut told him to wait for her call. He wondered what she had in mind.

Marty wrote his report and sent it to Beacon. He was daydreaming about Hong Kong and waiting for his photographs of the explosion to upload when Nadine called back.

"Leash, we are making arrangements. You stay at safehouse until we have confirmation and assurances. We should have them in couple hours."

Marty looked at his watch. It still worked. "At 7:15, I disappear."

"Calm down, Leash. Philippine authorities requested assistance from FBI Manila. Agent in Cebu will get recording discs and confirm validity of passport. Friends are preparing for extraction if necessary. Trust me."

"Let me go. I've done my job, a good job. I'm finished." And Marty thought he had done well until today. It was the first time he had been near caught, and he felt being caught near. Hong Kong would be nice. He liked Hong Kong. "Let me go, Nadine. I don't feel well. It's not fun anymore. My instinct is off. I should have flushed the recording. I'm too old for this."

"Leash, I understand. Age is currency. We both have spent much. But you are in. Job is not finished. Bracelets is collecting vital intelligence. We need you there. We will protect you. Trust me. But you must protect Bracelets. You must stay until I can replace you. We need you to keep Bracelets safe until my patrons can."

"Patrons! Who the fuck *are* your patrons? Who am I working for? Wait...don't answer that. I don't want to know. I'm done. I'm getting out. I don't need this. I'm done. I'm out, over and out. Goodbye, Nadine."

Marty drew back his arm intent on hurling the phone against the wall but he choked the throw. The thought of breaking the connection with Nadine was more terrifying than the dangers he imagined. He shouted. "Wait! Whip, are you still there?"

"Yes, Leash," she said, in her Slavic accented, patient-mother tone, the only voice he trusted. He did not want to be alone. He waited for his heart to stop pounding.

"Okay, okay, I'll wait. But please call before seven. Ciao."

"Ciao."

Marty examined the phone, an incredible gadget. He felt obsolete. His replacement would be some kid who grew up playing virtual war games with night-vision goggles. They would implant his head with a global positioning chip and a tiny charge that self-destructs intellect, no disassembly required. Push red button, ping signal off satellite. Poof! You're deniable. That's what The House sold: reliable, deniable, dirty tricksters.

He had put his spirit on a plane, flying away. He did not want to disembark. His mind wandered around Hong Kong, wondering if he had regrets, and he guessed it had to be done as he did it, except he wished he had salvaged Raggedy Ann. *I'm sorry, Mr. Santana, they canceled your flight.* Trust Nadine to get the recording, cover the blunder, and finish the job. *How tough could it be to keep Bracelets safe.*

Waiting for Nadine, Marty recharged his confidence. Maybe his instincts were still okay. The recording might have useful information, some clue to help unravel the plot for the C4. And his instinct had been right to get a room next to Shutterspy and Bracelets.

Shutterspy! Marty laughed. He wanted it to be hearty, to drain the stress, but giddy is all he could manage. He fell back on the bed and looked at the ceiling. It *did* sound like a caper. He saw himself in a dim bar, in Hong Kong, better a whorehouse in Tijuana, his own whorehouse, hanging on to his fifth shot of tequila and a jar of jalapeno peppers, telling the hookers, better gringos, young gringos, they humoring the old man, telling them about his last job, about how I took care of Bracelets and Shutterspy…and Chopsticks. He wondered if he could get a Dick Tracy watch somewhere.

He quieted and let his mind wander. Without grandchildren, to whom do you tell the stories. A doll maybe…maybe the doll was Chopsticks' legacy. Quitting seemed scary all of a sudden. Marty jumped out of the virtual plane and went back to work.

He thought of a couple of schemes to stay close to Bracelets. One he thought brilliant, although tricky. He called Lilibeth again. She was stuck in traffic not far from the hotel. He told her to stop by the department store to ask Perla to meet him in room 700 when she got off work. He told himself he was not making a commitment. His passport and suitcase were expendable. He did not cancel his tickets. If Nadine could not convince him he was safe, he would disappear. Marty tried hard to believe she could do it. To his relief, she did.

"You are in clear, Leash. Friends have physical control of all three chips. Detectives thought you were probably legit. They were covering their asses."

"Great." Marty slumped. He felt stupid for panicking. "So I can forget the whole thing."

"Not quite. You interrupted major terrorist plot and every agency in Philippines is trying to figure out what was going down. We are trading information on Zorro. The army found third magazine and CIDG is twisting Zorro's toes as we speak. Tomorrow, Camilo Mapandi will contact you. He is chief of CIDG for region seven. He wants to talk with you. We are giving him your reports on Zorro, but nothing about Bracelets. Mapandi wants absolute control over your information. He is having turf war with army and NBI. Discuss what you know about Zorro with Mapandi but not with his detectives. Do not tell him about Bracelets. She is ours."

Marty leaned into the phone. "Whip, do you trust this guy Mapandi? He could frame me for the whole mess, including the terrorist plot."

"Mapandi knows how much grief we can cause him. He will not bother you. I can guarantee that."

Marty sighed. "I've got the jitters. I hope it's not a premonition. Let's talk about Bracelets. Why does she need protection?"

"She is collecting useful information for database and this is making powerful people nervous. You protect her until she finishes her project and then steal her files again."

"And then am I done, finished, the Last Hurrah?"

It took Nadine several moments to respond. "Yes, Last Hurrah, Marty, maybe for both of us. I'm sixty-four. Time to retire, perhaps."

He could not remember the last time she called him Marty, or ever having mentioned her age.

"Whip, to stay close to a Muslim woman, I'll need an assistant, a female. I've someone in mind. I figure a budget of thirty-five grand should be more than enough for her salary and expenses."

"Leash, I do not authorize more than enough. Tell me what you need and why."

"I'm guessing twenty-five grand, but it might take more. I'll talk to her tonight. I need it now."

"Wait."

Nadine muted the line and came back on a few minutes later.

"Okay, Leash. Email Beacon with breakdown and particulars when you make deal. Also account number where you want money."

"Good. I'll be at the Cebu Midway as Sammy, but I'm using Harris Maxwell with Bracelets and her boyfriend. I expect we'll be going back to Davao soon."

"Okay, keep Beacon informed."

"Whip, are you telling me everything?"

"I tell you what you need to know."

"Damn it Nadine, don't blindfold me. Who's the boyfriend, Bryce?"

"Oh, yes, you met him. Talk to me."

Marty clenched his teeth. She withheld information. He still thought she knew Bracelets and Zorro were related. "He doesn't fit the businessman look. He handles a camera like a photojournalist. His knuckles are deformed, freakish. I've seen that before, in the orphanage. He was breaking boards before his bones matured. And if his work is in Davao, what's he doing in Cebu?"

"Good question. We think he was with Bracelets before she started database. He looked like lover until they showed in Cebu. I will have report on him soon. Trust me. I will inform you. Protect Bracelets and watch Bryce."

Marty groaned, "Alright."

"Ciao."

At eight o'clock Marty locked up his gear and sealed the room. As he took a circuitous route to the Cebu Midway, he wondered if Perla could get close to Bracelets. Then he thought of Mapandi and his stomach turned sour.

CHAPTER 27

Room 702, Wednesday afternoon, February 12

Steve closed the door to room 702. "There's something strange about this guy Max. He seems too coincidental, too friendly, like a con man."

"I agree," Amina said, taking off her scarf. "We'll talk about him later." She pointed to the blinking light on the telephone. "We have messages, and I want to check my email. Please turn on the TV and see what's on the news."

For the next few hours, they sought information—Manila's excuse for war, the cause of the explosion, the names of the victims and Zorro's whereabouts—but they learned nothing to help them decide what they ought to do. Then Amina received an urgent call from Nashita. After a brief conversation, Amina hung up and turned to Steve.

"You will soon meet the lovely Nashita. She has news, but not of war."

Nashita stunned Steve. He pictured her on the cover of Vogue. Her skin radiated with the sheen of polished marble, but she was too young for stone, more like a breathing porcelain doll. He fought the urge to touch her cheek to see if it were warm. She wore an ankle-length skirt, a *malong*, crimson with washed yellow flowers. Her black, long-sleeved top, miracle fabric from outer space, clung to her torso tighter than paint. The long tails of her *hijab*, golden with a luminescent green tinge, gathered in tucks of inscrutable geometry to sweep across her breasts and cascade over her shoulder. She tortured him. Whenever the hijab moved, he could not stop his eyes from looking for the nipple. She could not be the devout Muslim, conspirator and daughter of an MILF commander. Not her. But she was. He had to focus on that. Nashita held his ticket to the Liguasan Marsh.

They sat on the floor, the ladies composed and balanced in a kneeling, side-sitting posture. They spoke in Maranao. He rested his back against the bed with his arms around his knees. After a long day of partnering in Amina's intrigues, he felt shut out, pushed back into the corner of his once chosen role, his former self of the day before yesterday.

His mind raced to solve the photographic problems—use available light, 50mm lens, f2.8 maybe f2.0 to fuzz the background, $1/15^{th}$ or $1/30^{th}$ for slight blur of gestures, reposition desk lamp to soften shadows, move left to emphasize Nashita, put a scarf on Amina, devout Moro woman debates apparel choices with Muslim debutant, no matter the lie, get the picture, the telltale expression, the decisive moment.

Put down the camera, Bryce.

He wanted to jump in, wanted to say, "Hey, I'm in. Please speak a language I understand." But he knew his place as a foreigner not privy to Moro affairs. He was lucky to be as close as he was. He sensed Nashita's discomfort with his presence, tolerating him as Amina's folly because he did not speak Maranao. He vowed to learn their language. Until then, he could only eavesdrop on their intonation and gestures.

Nashita seemed excited, joyous. Amina looked doubtful. By the inflection of her voice, she was drilling down, asking questions within questions. Nashita, frustrated and impatient, leaned forward, battling logic with emotion. They bargained to a stalemate.

"Okay, ladies, what's going on?"

Amina turned. "We are being offered six kilos of C4 at a reasonable price. It seems Zorro has not yet learned that we are at war."

"How much did he have?"

"Kule arranged to purchase thirty. Zorro said he had a little more than that."

Steve thought for a minute. "It seems Jiriki was mistaken. Zorro had another contact in the Abu Sayyaf. That explosion was the thirty kilos. The six kilos are leftovers."

Nashita nodded.

"That is what Nashita thinks. But the Abu Sayyaf was not involved."

"What makes you so sure?"

"Abu Sayyaf could not get another of their bandits from Sulu to Cebu so soon. And if Zorro had another contact, he would have laughed at our proposal. It was not the Abu Sayyaf."

"Could it have been MILF?"

Amina shook her head. "No, we represent the MILF." She pointed to Nashita and herself. "And a renegade wouldn't want thirty kilos, couldn't afford it if he did. Jiriki worried that Zorro might have friends in the RSM, the Rajah Solaiman Movement, and would get them to bid against us." She shrugged. "So let's say the RSM bought it. That is not helpful. Knowing who bought what is gone does not tell us who is selling what is left. Look." With her index finger, Amina scratched lines in the pile of the carpet. "Here is the access road that goes to the resort, which is here, and then the ocean. FerMar, where the explosives are, is behind the resort, here." She retraced some lines. "FerMar and the resort are enclosed with fence topped with razor wire. If this offer is legitimate, someone had to take the C4 out of FerMar before the authorities arrived, but no vehicle could leave because the explosion blocked the road. Okay, where's the C4?"

"Let's see. Your uncle hustles the remaining C4 out of FerMar hoping to create doubt as to the cause of the explosion. He stashes it at the resort." Steve stared at the faint marks on the carpet. "But the police and army search the resort." He shook his head. "Okay, Zorro bought the C4 from the army, from an ordinance man. That man is going to be at the scene. He makes sure the C4 is not found during the search."

Amina frowned. "Possible, I suppose, but shaky."

"Your uncle sold thirty and has six left," Nashita said. "We need it."

"Wait a minute!" Steve exclaimed. "We're *assuming* he sold thirty kilos, the quantity the Abu Sayyaf wanted, yet we agree the Abu Sayyaf didn't buy it. And we're assuming the total is thirty-six."

Nashita shifted. Quantities interested the commander's daughter.

Amina nodded. "Go on."

"That blast wasn't an accident. Even if you throw C4 into a bonfire, it won't blow. You have to have a detonator. The buyer wouldn't knowingly drive around with a fused bomb, and Zorro didn't rig it to explode near his resort. A third party must have stopped the car, disabled the occupants and detonated the C4. What if the buyer bought *all* the C4 and third party took six kilos before blowing the rest. Six kilos fits into a satchel or knapsack, and if you're on the run, the weight is about right."

Amina sighed. "That makes more sense than Zorro hiding it, but that doesn't solve our puzzle as to who is offering it. This could be a trap."

"Why a trap?"

"Your third party would not know we're in the market or how to contact us. Only Zorro would know that," she raised a finger, "or the CIDG."

"How?"

"Remember when I called the resort? I gave that CIDG guy my name and told him I was Zorro's niece. Stupid, but I assumed the resort had a problem, not FerMar. The CIDG probably knows I work for the MILF. And maybe they know Nashita and I visited my uncle at the resort."

"But how could they? Zorro wouldn't tell them."

Amina smiled. "Max, our new friend with the camera, who we both think is phony. Isn't it strange that they allowed a foreign tourist to photograph a crime scene where Filipino journalists were not allowed?" She leaned back. "Max was sitting by the pool when Nashita and I went to talk to Zorro. He took pictures of us. Later, he moved inside and sat close by. He was eavesdropping. Max could be an undercover agent."

"I don't know," Steve said. "My gut feeling is Max is the opposite of cop. When we were in the taxi, he kept glancing behind us, checking the rearview mirror and studying the traffic. It seemed he worried he was being followed."

Amina nodded. "I noticed that too."

"And he talks and acts like an American, a Hispanic American. If he's Filipino, he's a damn good imposter."

"Or he's CIA," Amina said. "I agree he is not a Filipino agent. My uncle pays the police for protection. They would have warned him about an undercover cop snooping around. But they wouldn't know about a CIA rascal."

Nashita let out an exasperated sigh and glanced at the ceiling. "Zorro is offering us six kilos of C4, but we must respond to his offer by midnight tonight or he will sell it elsewhere. He has proved that he has other customers. We must get the C4. You are being too cautious, Amina."

Steve thought the midnight deadline could be a negotiating ploy to forestall haggling over price, but Amina had said the offer was reasonable. It could be that Zorro had to unload the C4 in a hurry, or it could be a trap.

They sat in silence for a while, Nashita irritated and impatient.

"Nashita, how did you get the offer?" Steve asked.

"Someone delivered an envelope to an address I *wrote* for Zorro," she said, her tone testy. "I did not speak, I was not overheard. This offer is legitimate. We are wasting time."

Steve thought her too brash and young to be careful. If it were a trap, it would be the end of Amina. He did not scold Nashita, though. He needed her. "Do you know the person who delivered the envelope?"

"No. I used an internet-café mailbox service. Someone leaves mail with the attendant. Anyone with the lock combination can pick it up."

"How do you accept the offer?"

"The same way. We deliver it to the mailbox. I gave Zorro the address of the café, the box number and the combination. I *wrote* that information. No one overheard it, not even Amina. Only Zorro and I have that information."

"Is that right, Amina? You don't know where the drop box is?"

"No, I don't, but my uncle does. The CIDG can be persuasive."

"But how would they know what to ask him?"

Amina smiled. "Our friend Max."

Nashita tossed her hands in the air. "We need to reply before Zorro sells to someone else. We are wasting time with this worrying over nothing."

Steve thought for a minute. "Amina, if Max were involved in trapping you, he wouldn't have introduced himself. He'd avoid you, at least until you took the bait. He's up to something else."

She considered that. "Yes, I agree."

Steve thought for a moment and turned to Nashita. "To deliver mail, does the courier need the combination to the mailbox?"

"No, he gives the envelope to the attendant. He does not know the combination."

"Okay, I'll deliver the envelope. We'll write the reply in English and make it read as if I'm agreeing to a date with a Filipina I recently met. If someone is watching, they won't be expecting an American. Even if I'm apprehended, I can say I must have gotten the girl's box number wrong."

Nashita smiled and looked at Amina,

Amina thought about his plan. "It's risky, Sweet Steve, but acting like an over-sexed American will be easy for you."

CHAPTER 28

Cebu Midway Hotel, Wednesday night, February 12

At the Cebu Midway, Marty made sure his suitcase had arrived and was in his room, got a second room key and went down to the department store. He found Perla in women's apparel.

"Hi, Sammy. What happened at the Pasigan?"

"We partied last night. Had a real blast. Here's your key, room 700."

Perla laughed. "Ah, a new lair, conveniently located. We're keeping an eye on Bracelets?"

"You want to be my daughter or my niece?"

"Hmmm, you're too dark for a daddy. Undercover Uncle Sammy sounds better."

"Okay, uncle it is, but I'm Uncle Max now. Com'on up to the room when you get off. I'll have a rum and cola waiting."

She wagged the key card. "Uncle whoever, you do know how to keep a girl interested."

Marty was relaxing in a white terrycloth bathrobe with a glass of tequila when Perla came in.

"Wow, nice room." she kicked off her shoes. "Is there another robe?"

He pulled down a bathrobe from the closet shelf. She shucked her uniform and bra and smiled as he mixed a rum and cola; he had gotten lime for her. The room had a sitting area with loveseat, armchair and coffee table. She curled into the loveseat. Marty added ice to his tequila and took the armchair.

"Okay, *Uncle*, what happened at the Pasigan?"

"First, I'll tell you what the cops know. Then you tell me what the cops are thinking."

Showing Perla his pictures, he described the appearance of the explosion, mentioned the two fatalities and then told her about his being interrogated in detail, the search of their room and CIDG taking the recorder, chips and passport. "That's what the detectives know. Forget about what you know. What does CIDG think?"

Perla thought for a while. "I've two questions. Is the passport legitimate and what is on the chips?"

"The passport is valid. The detectives will be told that the chips do not contain any pertinent information."

She popped her eyebrows. "My, my, the detectives *will be told*." She got up, took his glass and made fresh drinks. When she sat down again, she placed her glass on the coffee table and swirled the ice with her finger. At length she spoke.

"Besides Zorro, you were the only suspicious looking character at the hotel. The sand in your watchband supported your story, but that only proves you wore your watch to the beach. It helps, though. With the articles by Harris Maxwell, you're looking okay.

When they are told the chips are innocent, they forget about you unless they tie you to Zorro."

"Okay, now what do you think?"

"Who are the dead people?"

"Bad guys who bought cakes."

"Lucky you didn't kill innocent people."

He chuckled and leaned back. "I like the way you think."

She picked up her glass and stretched out on the loveseat. He propped up his head with his fist and watched her, waiting. She sipped her drink in silence, waiting. Marty could not believe her not asking questions, but then, he did not want to know about Nadine's patrons.

"I heard you talking to Christopher about college, the university, I mean."

Her jaw dropped a bit and she studied Marty's expression. She placed her glass on the coffee table and sat up sideways on the loveseat, drawing up her knees. "The Australian government has tuition assistance programs for Filipinos, but none that I can qualify for."

"How much is the tuition?"

"I'd need about 75,000 dollars U.S. for a bachelor of commerce at the University of Melbourne."

He whistled softly. "Sounds like you have a plan."

"No, I had a silly dream. I'll go to the university here when I've saved enough." Perla held his gaze for moments of silence. "Okay, Uncle Max, why am here?"

He shook his glass and took a gulp. "Alright, here's the deal. Someone wants to liquidate Bracelets. My job is to keep her safe for a while. I don't know how long, perhaps several months. A Moro woman half my age with a boyfriend is not going to let me hang around her. But as your dear uncle, I can be close to you. I need you to gain her confidence and tell me her routine so I can protect her. By the way, her name is Amina Taiba. She is associated with the MILF and is gathering sensitive information."

Perla swung her feet to the floor. "Why doesn't the MILF protect her? Why don't you just tell her she needs protection and offer your services?"

"My job is to keep her safe until she finishes collecting the information and then I copy her files."

She bobbed her head. "I see. Will you kill her when she finishes?"

"No. I want her files, nothing more."

Perla rested her head on the back of the loveseat and stared at the ceiling. After several minutes, she exhaled. "Okay. You blew up the booty and Zorro's in jail, so the bargaining over cakes is finished. Bracelets and boyfriend have nothing to do here. They will return to Davao soon, maybe tomorrow. I would have to quit my job, move to Davao and somehow get into Amina's confidence. That won't be easy. I might fail. Then what?"

He leaned forward. "Steve Bryce works in Davao for an American agribusiness. He and Amina live in a compound of four identical houses, big houses with three or four bedrooms. I'm sure Steve recently fired his maid and doubt he has replaced her yet. You get that job or we invent something else if you can't. You get five thousand dollars up front. If our best efforts fail, you keep the five grand. If we succeed, then it's another fifteen thousand when the job is done. I'll cover your travel expenses. Please don't haggle. I've already tried to get you more."

"Will I have to steal or harm anyone?"

"No. You are not to engage in any illegal activity other than deceit. That, my lovely, is a condition of the job. If you're involved in any wrongdoing, all you get is the five grand and maybe, just maybe, my best efforts to get you out of jail."

"That's reassuring. Deceit is not a big crime. But I don't want to be sucked into *your* illegal activity. You hired me to pose as your niece and tell you her routine. That is all I know, period. Hookers take the cash and don't ask questions. I don't want to know who you are or who you work for or what you are doing. You are not going to screw up my life."

"That suits me fine. Will you take the job?"

"Give me a few minutes."

She sipped her drink. When she finished it, he refilled her glass and his own. He opened a jar of jalapeno peppers, took one out and placed the open jar on the table. She plucked one, ate it, and nursed her drink. She had near finished it by the time she nodded, extended her glass and clinked it against Marty's.

"Tomorrow morning, I'll get a couple of suitcases at the department store. That's travel expenses isn't it?" Marty nodded. "I'll need a new wardrobe too. That's expense too." Marty smiled and shook his head. "Okay. It will take me all day to settle affairs. I should be back here around six. I'll leave a message if I'm delayed, but no matter, I'll be ready to travel Friday morning."

"Will Lilibeth be a problem?"

She shrugged. "We share expenses and a bed. She has bitching rights, but she's not part of my future." Perla smiled. "My future just started."

"Okay. Let's work out our history. I ran into Amina and Steve at the Pasigan this afternoon and introduced myself as Harris Maxwell. Steve will recognize you from the department store, and Bracelets no doubt saw us together at the resort. We'll build on that. Oh, what's your name?"

"Edna Armamento Serrano, but no one has called me Edna since my father ran off. I hate that name."

"Good. That's the sort of detail we need. Deceit depends on details. We have to move fast. When they go down for breakfast, we go down a few minutes later. The maid angle will be ideal, but if it doesn't work, I've a few other ideas. We'll fit our background for those too."

The air-conditioned chill woke Marty before daybreak. Perla lay by his side curled into a ball with the covers pulled up to her nose. She looked innocent, vulnerable. He slipped outside to jog, run and then race, trying to outdistance his anxieties. He had two women to protect and Cebu's number one cop on his tail. At the thought of Mapandi, he turned about and headed for the hotel to change the departure date on his ticket to Hong Kong.

CHAPTER 29

Cebu City, Wednesday night, February 12

Steve strolled along P del Rosario Street until he came to a motorcycle shop across from the internet café. The shop was closed, the windows covered by a steel curtain of interlocking rods. Peering through the gaps, he regretted having left his motorcycle in the States. Before leaving Apex, he would have to buy another, one with a storage compartment for his photo gear, but this was not the time for window-shopping. He turned and studied the mail drop.

A wood plank sign above the storefront heralded "Internet" in shocking-pink script squeezed at an angle in front of "Café Correo" in faded gray letters. Beneath it, placards taped to the inside of the display window and door offered UPS mail service, local and international phone calls, worldwide faxes, mail boxes, photocopying, book binding and internet connections for Php 24/hour, free coffee and popcorn included. A sign in the middle of the door announced they were open 24/7, 360 days a year, but did not mention which days they were closed. In the tiny spaces between the plastered notices, he saw shadowy movements interrupting bright lights. If a detective were staking out the place, he would have to be inside. Steve crossed the street.

Inside the store, two customers waited at the counter while an employee made copies of a pamphlet. A whiskered guy sitting at the cluttered table in the rear corner peered over his eyeglasses at the tall, blond foreigner, and then resumed reading his newspaper. On the right side of the room, a high partition of mailboxes separated the work area of office machines from a corridor that led to a spiral staircase. On the mezzanine overhead, Steve could see the tops of cubicles crammed along the walls but not the people using the computers.

The door opened and a dark skinned Filipina entered, a plain woman without jewelry or make up, wearing baggy slacks and a long-sleeved blouse buttoned to the neck. Whiskers scrutinized the new arrival. He seemed to think she were a stranger customer than Steve was.

While he waited, he considered handing over the envelope and leaving, but imagined the attendant glancing at the box number and nodding at Whiskers, who would summon a couple burly detectives from upstairs. He opted to buy some internet time and have a look around first. He asked for black coffee, accepted the small paper bag of popcorn and climbed the spiral stairs.

The upstairs customers were all young males. A group of five, four on adjacent computers and a floater, swapped information and checked out one another's screens. They were surfing porn sites. Steve chose a computer across the room from them, opened a search engine and typed "hot panties." He browsed until he found a juicy, full-screen image, turned around and waved to the floater.

"Hi," he said, picking up his paper bag. "You want this. I don't care for popcorn."

"Sure. Thanks." The floater came to his station and pointed to the screen. "That looks hot."

"Yeah, it's a neat site with a panty theme. You guys come here often?"

"Every once in a while. Most places don't want you looking at porn." He smiled. "They're family orientated. You live here?"

"No, passing through. Just came to check my email, but they have a one-hour minimum."

The floater munched popcorn and looked over Steve's shoulder as he browsed the hot panties website. They commented on the pictures. Steve wanted to ask about Whiskers, but could not think of how to shift the conversation. He lingered over a striking image of a sensual woman in an erotic pose. He saw Amina in the picture and a solution to his problem.

"I'd like to park my boots under her bed."

The floater chuckled. "Small breasts and long black hair, she looks like a Filipina. We like blondes with big boobs."

"Is there a printer?"

"Downstairs. They charge by the sheet."

"Good, I have to print one of my emails too." He opened a new browser and went to the Hotmail sign in page. He paused and looked at the floater.

"Well, thanks for the popcorn." He left to join his friends.

Steve went to his favorite site for photographic equipment, pulled up the specifications on a digital camera, sent them to the printer and went downstairs. He bought a manila envelope for the printed sheets and wrote the box number on it.

"Can you post this for me please?"

The clerk glanced at the number. "Sure."

Steve watched the attendant walk to the boxes and stick the envelope into a cubbyhole. Whiskers, still reading his newspaper, paid no attention.

"Oh," Steve said, reaching into his back pocket. "I forgot this." He handed over the plain white envelope. "Here's another one."

Whiskers looked up and stared at Steve. Steve's heart pounded. As he turned to leave, Whiskers sniffed and turned the page.

Steve crossed the street and staked out the internet café from the shadowy entrance of the motorcycle shop. While he watched, he wondered about the science of traps, his third-party theory and Max. His gut kept telling him Max was not a journalist.

Customers entered and left the café carrying purses, book bags or parcels, any one of which could contain the envelopes. The stakeout seemed pointless. Steve decided to peek through the spaces between the signs to see if his envelopes were still there. Then he would go back to the hotel and tell Amina about the cleverness of his first mission. As he was about to cross the street, the floater came out. Steve eased back into the shadows. He shook his head in disbelief. The floater had two envelopes in his hand, one manila and the other plain white. He sauntered down the street, his gait insouciant, as if he were fantasizing about a blonde with big boobs. Steve stared after him, feeling like an amateur who had just flunked his audition for imposter.

CHAPTER 30

Cebu Midway Hotel, Thursday morning, February 13

Amina, her hair covered by a scarf, examined her place setting while Steve asked the waitress to bring hot tea for his companion. Marty walked over to their table with Perla a few steps behind him.

"Good morning."

Steve looked at Marty, then at Perla and back to Marty again. "Good morning." He stood up.

Amina nodded, her face without expression.

Marty rested his hand on Perla's shoulder and eased her forward. "This is my niece, Perla." He looked at Perla. "Steve and his friend gave me a ride yesterday, from Pasigan Beach to the hotel."

Perla smiled at Steve. "Did you get your Visa receipt okay?"

"Yes, I did, thank you." He looked at Marty. "The other night I talked with your niece at the department store here. Is it a small world, or what?"

Perla smiled at Amina. "Hi. We saw you at the Pasigan Resort a few days ago. You were with another pretty young lady."

"Yes, it is a small world, isn't it?"

Steve pulled out a chair. "Please join us. We just sat down."

"Thank you," Marty said. He looked at Amina. "Have you talked to your uncle?"

"Not yet. Perhaps later this morning."

Over coffee and tea, Steve asked Marty about the night of the explosion. As he had never been to the resort, he had numerous questions about the layout and facilities. He was curious as to how soon the authorities responded, and fascinated by the roles of the army and police during the investigation. He learned that the army provided security while the police questioned everyone staying at the hotel. As far as Max knew, they had not searched any of the guests or their rooms. The conversation continued while they filled their plates at the buffet. By the time they sat down again, they had exhausted the subject of the explosion. Aside from Marty's pictures, no one knew more than the scant information given in the newscasts.

Perla asked Steve, "What do you do in Davao?"

"I work for Apex Fruits, an American company."

"Do you think I could get a job with them? I'm good with numbers, but I'll take any job—clerical work, cleaning lady, anything. Uncle Max is taking me to Davao. I need to find work there."

Steve shrugged. "You can check with the personnel office. I'll give you the name of the person to contact. They'll want your resume and references."

"Can I list you as a reference? Maybe you could recommend me." She touched his forearm and smiled. "But please, don't mention I forgot to give you your Visa receipt. I'm usually not so careless."

Steve looked at Marty. "Why are you going to Davao?"

"I've sold a proposal to do a series of articles on the mayor of Davao. He's quite the character, a human-interest story suitable for a variety of periodicals in the Americas and Europe. Great stuff."

He told a couple of anecdotes on the mayor, speaking with the authority of truth, as he would be updating his research if time permitted. Marty's routine work included collecting intelligence on the political underground for The House. Nadine skimmed the fascinating stuff for Maxwell Harris articles created by a ghostwriter.

Perla too spoke truthiness. She mentioned her intention to go to the university in Davao once she had saved enough money. Smiling at Max, she said her uncle had promised to help her. He was a blessing. She was alone. Her mother had recently died and her father had abandoned them long ago when she was a little girl, calamities that happened, and her voice crinkled with genuine sorrow and bitterness. Marty conjured authentic replicas of despise and disgust for his worthless brother who ran away from his wife and daughter. As they related their emotional tale, they attracted curious glances, except from the two men at the corner table who studiously ignored them.

Steve picked up his plate. "Perhaps we can help," he said to Perla. "Amina, let's get a little more to eat."

When they returned to the table, Steve hired Perla to be his live-in maid for nearly the wages she earned at the department store, and invited Uncle Max to stay in his home for a few days until he found suitable accommodations. He said they would be returning to Davao on the Saturday flight and asked if that would be too soon for Perla.

"Oh, not too soon for me," she said, with a fifteen-grand smile. "I'll be ready."

As soon as Steve closed the door to room 702, Amina snapped, "What are you doing? Are you out of your mind?"

"Take it easy, Tigress. Sit down and I'll explain." She sat in the armchair, scowling, he at the desk, close to her.

"Last night, I got to thinking Max must be an undercover somebody. Consider what happened. On Monday morning, he and Perla were at the resort, he took pictures of you and Nashita and they eavesdropped on the conversation with your uncle. Monday night, we encounter Perla in the department store. Then, yesterday afternoon, Max approaches us and asks about a hotel. Up until breakfast, that is everything we knew about Max and Perla. Correct?

She thought for a moment. "Okay, get to the point."

"No one except Jiriki and Nashita, not even me, knew you were going to visit your uncle Monday morning. I didn't reserve this room until a few hours before I left Davao. So, Max and Perla weren't sitting around waiting for you, Nashita or me. They were watching Zorro. Correct?"

"I agree."

"We go to the department store, a coincidence. Perla spots you. She's clever. She asks me questions, finds out who I am, where I'm staying and tells Max."

Amina interrupted. "I'll find out how long Perla has worked at the department store. I don't believe in coincidences. Go on."

"Okay. Max is a suspicious character, an imposter. Consider the possibilities." He ticked his fingers. "One, Max is your CIA rascal who was staking out Zorro. Two, he is Zorro's associate or bodyguard. Check with your uncle. As an associate, he's the one offering six kilos of C4, which he hid in his hotel room and carried out of the resort. Three, he's the third party who triggered the explosion. Four, he is in fact Maxwell Harris, a gregarious freelance writer. Five, he is Marty Santana."

"What?" Amina gawked.

Steve stood. "There were tasty morsels in that buffet of bullshit. Max admits to being in the Philippines for several years and that he's been in Davao lately. He's muscular, in great shape for a man his age. And he has the distinctive posture of an old soldier, perhaps a Special Forces soldier. He could pass as a Filipino. If he stole the hard drive, he knows your databases are incomplete and wants to steal them again. And," Steve tapped the desk, "if he stole the hard drive with Posey's help, he'd know I'd fired her and needed a maid. Last night I wondered if he could be Santana. That sham during breakfast has me near convinced."

Amina glared. "No! That's too farfetched. First, he's not my uncle's associate. If anything, he's CIA. He overheard me dealing with my uncle for the C4. He is planting Perla in our home because he thinks I'm a terrorist. Tell them you changed your mind. I don't want her near me. You are endangering us." She pushed out of the chair, started to pace and stopped. She turned and glared at Steve. "Get rid of her!" She snapped.

He waited for her to cool a little. "Tigress, you are trying to identify saboteurs and someone took your files. We have to find out who took them. Max could be Santana. I'll take his picture and we'll show it to Posey. If he's not Santana, I'll fire Perla."

Amina paced, stopped to get a bottle of juice from the minibar and looked out the window. After a few minutes, she turned. "I apologize for yelling. The thought of a maid going through my things....yuk." She nodded. "You did right. Even if it's farfetched, we have to find out who has my files. Take his picture and we'll have a chat with Posey." She smirked. "Meantime, let's hope she cooks better than Posey did."

He chuckled, stood up and patted her behind. "I'm glad that's over. Okay, should I go check the mailbox now?"

"I'll make some calls first, see if Nashita has found out anything about the guy who picked up our message, talk to my aunt and see what O'Campo has to say. Maybe you don't have to risk going to the drop again. Please keep an eye on the news. Manila can not keep the war quiet much longer."

Marty and Perla returned to their room elated. "You were perfect," Marty said. "Christ, you near had *me* crying. Okay, I'll give you cash to buy your airplane ticket. I don't want the cops to find out we're leaving on the same plane, not until we do, anyway. On Saturday, I'll make an excuse to leave early for the airport and get

Steve to take you with them. We ignore each other until we get on the plane. Understand?"

Perla flicked her eyebrows.

The blinking light on the telephone caught Marty's attention. He listened to the message. "Good morning Mr. Fuentes," a female voice said. "Mr. Camilo Mapandi would like to have lunch with you. An escort will pick you up at your hotel at 1:00 PM sharp. Please call 232-6700, extension 100 to confirm." Marty listened again, jotted down the number and deleted the message. His glee ebbed. He hoped the two cops in the restaurant were his tail. If they were tailing Bracelets, Mapandi would not let any of them leave Cebu.

CHAPTER 31

Cebu Midway, Thursday Morning, February 13

Steve lounged on the bed with a photo magazine while Amina spoke with her aunt. She hung up the phone and grinned at him. "You and Nashita were right. I was worrying over nothing. My aunt invited Nashita and me for tea and cakes tomorrow morning." She collapsed into the chair. By tomorrow night, we'll have the C4. Now I'll arrange for the couriers to take it to Central Mindanao."

He dropped the magazine. "I'm going with them."

"You what?" She gave him a puzzled look. "You *are* crazy."

"I'm going to photograph the invasion and the refugees. The world needs to know this is happening. I'll show them the pain, suffering and dislocation. I'll shoot it from the Moro point of view, not the whitewashed Manila version. It's been my dream. This is my opportunity, my chance of a lifetime. I'm going."

She stared at him. Then she shook her head. "They'll kill you."

"Who?"

She jabbed her finger. "*You* are an outsider. They don't want outsiders." She jabbed again. "*You* are American. They don't like Americans. In normal times, Central Mindanao is dangerous, ungoverned territory. Now it's chaotic—soldiers at war, lawless people with guns—anyone can shoot you, take your cameras and toss you into the swamp. You will be surrounded by adversaries with no place to hide and no authority to protect you."

He heard suppressed fury in her voice. "I'll take my chances. I'm going."

She leapt from the chair with the look of a mother disciplining her moronic child, her arms tense with an exasperated urge to thrash monumental stupidity. She was a sight he had not seen before. She never lost her cool in a confrontation. He had unglued her, but he would not retreat. He felt the pieces snap into place— photography and Amina—no more chicken soup. All he needed was for Amina to convince Nashita to convince her father, the links to his future. He waited and watched her pace a few steps, look into herself and then look at him as if he were nuts. She did it again. *What's the matter, Tigress? What are you plotting?* She stared out the window. He watched her, saw her preparing. He waited. She squared her shoulders and turned. He saw his inscrutable Tigress again. She sat down.

"You do not speak Maranao or Maguindanao, you are not familiar with the dangers or accustomed to the hardships. You would be vulnerable, extremely vulnerable."

"I'll not be wandering. I'll stick with Nashita's father and use his men as the basis for the story. I'll move with them and document their fate."

"And who will document your fate," she snapped. "You can't be serious. Think about this, Sweet Steve. What has happened to you, you the foreigner who didn't want to get involved. Now you want to go get yourself killed. And what about Apex, your job?"

"I took two weeks holiday. I've saved up vacation. I'll get another week, two if necessary. I can't quit Apex yet. I'm too dependent on the company—house, car, computer, residency. But I *will* quit as soon as I get an agency for my photographs, and this is my chance. Look at the opportunity." He pointed to the TV. "Still no news. The media is unaware of the war, or Manila muzzled them. I'll be the first photographer on the scene. I'll have a scoop." He let her think about that and then tried to close the deal. "I love you, Amina. I'm staying in the Philippines. I won't let Apex tear us apart."

He had broken their pact. If love happened, they were not to mention it, not to share the burden. He had fouled the debate, had hit below the belt. They sat in uncomfortable silence. He studied her face. She did not twitch. He could not read her, could not imagine what she might be thinking. He started counting backwards from 5000. She knew his trick. He worried she was counting too, forcing a stalemate.

At 3819, she slithered out of her chair, reached into her blouse and pinched her nipple. He stopped counting. Her right hand unbuttoned her blouse while her left fingered it out of the waistband of her jeans. He could see she was undressing, but he focused on her eyes, searching for an explanation. Her eyes were strangers. Something had happened. He did not know what. Fear came to mind, the instinctive wariness of the unknown. Who was this person? Had she gone mad? He studied her eyes. He watched for the flicker, that involuntary spasm before your opponent strikes that tells you to parry and avoid the cobra's bite, but he could not see where they were going. Well, yes, he did, but he could not figure why. His good sense told him to prepare, to be ready to feign, to circle, avoid and counterpunch but she was his lover, his partner, his best friend. He wanted to shout, "What are you doing?" But her eyes were hypnotic. It was not fair. She had changed context. He suspected revenge. She was going to hit him below the belt and he would be helpless, unable to defend.

The blouse opened and he lost it. He stared at the hard, brown nipples and then her belly. Her hand opening her jeans, teasing them down, shucking them off, taunting him with the sexy panties he had bought as she came closer. Her stance widened. His mouth went dry and for god's sake before his eyes she grasped the hem of the panty and tugged it and humped it until she soiled it before letting it loose. He stopped thinking. Panting, he gawked at the droopy fabric with the damp spot and inhaled the lusty aroma of erotic splendor.

"Okay, I'll arrange it," she croaked, uttering hoarse words between gasps.

She shoved his shoulders and he fell back on the bed, helpless. He let her straddle him and waited as she waddled toward his head. He had allowed the Tigress to get him right where she wanted him—ecstatic, speechless and mindless.

CHAPTER 32

Cebu Midway, Thursday Afternoon, February 13

At five minutes to one, the two plainclothesmen who had been sitting in the restaurant during breakfast knocked on Marty's hotel room door. Standing up, they were comical: one tall and skinny with a crew cut, the other short and chubby in a rumpled suit. *Mutt and Jeff,* Marty thought. Mutt asked if he were ready. When Marty nodded, they entered and shut the door. Mutt frisked him. Satisfied that he had no weapon or wire, they escorted him to a waiting sedan. Ten minutes later, they ushered him into a private room at an Italian restaurant. The sunny room had a large round table that could seat twenty or so, but not today. It had two opposing chairs, two meager place settings, each with a small plate, fork, tumbler and linen napkin. In the center of the table, they had placed an oval plate with antipasto and a pitcher of iced tea. As Marty looked around, someone jostled him. It was Jeff's turn to frisk.

"You queer son-bitch, you want to suck that?"

As Jeff twisted Marty's balls with one hand, he pointed to the chair facing the unshaded window with the other. "Please sit down and wait. Mr. Mapandi will join you shortly, *sir.*" Superficial politeness while they busted your nuts seemed to be the CIDG trademark. They left and shut the door.

Marty sat and squinted against the light. He too would be superficially polite and wait for Mapandi before pouring tea, but the antipasto plate had a couple of wimpy pepperoncini. He snatched one, chomped on it and regarded the stem. He flipped it into the corner and nestled into his chair. Expecting a long wait, he snoozed.

Shortly before two, the doorknob rattled. Marty turned. Mutt opened the door for a tall, trim man in suit without tie. He strode in. Marty guessed him sixty-something. When he started to stand, Mapandi signaled for him to stay seated. Mapandi stood beside him, poured a glass of now warm tea and gulped half of it as he examined Marty. Still holding his glass, he took a small tape recorder from his suit pocket, placed it next to Marty's plate and switched it on. He walked around the table and paused to look over Marty again before sitting down.

"All right, Mr. Fuentes, please tell me everything you have done since you arrived on this island. Leave nothing out."

Marty had prepared for what he had to leave out—Bracelets—and what he had to work around—Perla, Chopsticks and breakfast. While dribbling tea into his glass, he noticed Mapandi inventorying the antipasto plate. Marty reached to pick a slice of salami. Mapandi grabbed the plate and eased it away, enticing Marty's hand to chase it.

Mapandi leaned forward. "Cut the hogwashing. Talk…now."

Marty recounted his movements starting with his arriving in the storm. As he spoke, he realized the bright light in his face was an advantage. He squinted, blinked and then leaned back, crossed his arms and spoke to the ceiling. It felt natural to speak in a dry, boring monologue.

Mapandi interrupted occasionally to ask the time of day or duration of an activity or what Marty had eaten for lunch or dinner, testing for gaps or inconsistencies. Times and places did not concern Marty. People worried him. CIDG could not know about Bracelets visiting Zorro or Perla's conspiring with him, but he had failed to ask Nadine what she had told Mapandi about Chopsticks. Looking at the ceiling, Marty mentioned the Chinaman leering at Lilibeth, their going to the room and his hunch about the kid making a deal. Then he gave a vivid account of the explosion, skimmed over Sagapan's interrogation and looked at Mapandi.

Mapandi pushed the antipasto plate to the center of the table. Marty took a slice of salami, dropped it on his plate and ignored it.

"Then what?"

Marty expected accusations, at least questions about Chopsticks, and he had hoped for something specific about anything, some clue as to why Mapandi wanted to talk to him. Instead, he had to cross the minefield blindfolded. He assumed they had followed him from the Pasigan even though he had not spotted a tail. He shrugged and proceeded with factual indifference.

"I talked Sagapan into letting me take pictures of the explosion site. Afterwards, I looked for the trucks the army said they had provided for the Pasigan guests, but they had already left. The only transportation in sight was an overloaded jeepney and a taxi waiting for a gringo. I approached him, we talked and he gave me a ride back to his hotel. I checked in there, called Sagapan's office to let him know where I was staying and then went to the safehouse to report to Control. Control told me to talk to you. I returned to the hotel to wait for your call and my passport. Here I am."

"Why check into the Cebu Midway? Why not stay at the safehouse?"

"To get my passport back, I had to give Sagapan an address. I had told him I would find a hotel. I didn't want him to know I'd rented a room while staying at the Pasigan."

"Why the Cebu Midway?"

"I had thought about going to the Monarch, but since I was already at the Midway, I checked in there to save time. I was in a rush to call Control. Besides, I remembered that one of the girls I'd hired worked around there, in the same building as it turned out."

"Who's the American?"

"His name is Steve. I don't know his last name, but he works for Apex Fruits in Davao, which interested me. Control wants me in Davao. I figured any contact there might be helpful."

"Why Davao?"

Marty shook his head. "That's not in the deal."

Mapandi glared. Marty stared at the bridge of his nose until he relented.

"You had breakfast with Steve Bryce and two women. Who are the women?"

"I was with Perla, the girl who works in the department store there. She stayed with me last night. The other woman I assume is Steve's girlfriend. She's shy and prudish. I couldn't figure her."

Marty was prepared to explain he had introduced Perla as his niece so as not to shock Steve's prissy girlfriend. Mutt and Jeff might have heard the introductions, but they were too far away to monitor their breakfast conversation without a bug.

Mapandi crossed his arms and watched Marty as if he were giving his lamb one last chance to come clean before fleecing it naked. Marty imagined Mapandi might say *The Chinaman is Lee Chung Wan, whose boss you killed in Manila eight years ago. That prissy woman is Amina Taiba, MILF operative and Zorro's niece. Your girl Perla is Edna Armamento Serrano who Bryce hired this morning. Must I play the tape to refresh your memory?*

While he waited, Marty ate the piece of Salami with his fingers and then forked more antipasto onto his plate, including the other wimpy pepper. As he ate, he glanced at Mapandi from time to time, and each time he felt better. Mapandi was fishing without bait.

Mapandi sighed. "Okay." He reached across the table and switched off the recorder. "In your inventory of the third magazine, you reported thirty-two kilos of C4. Are you sure of that number?"

Marty nodded. "Yes, positive. Relative to the other stuff, the C4 and detonators screamed. The count is accurate."

"Are you sure the deal was for twenty kilos?"

"Yes, I played that part of the recording three or four times."

"Were there twenty kilos in the trunk?"

"Shit, I was in a bit of a hurry. I didn't count them, but I separated the blocks into three groups." Marty paused to think. "I can't be positive, but there were twenty or twenty-one."

"Could there have been twenty-six?"

Marty shook his head. "No, definitely not twenty-six." He frowned. "And not twenty-one either. One of the three stacks was smaller than the other two." Marty closed his eyes and worked his hands. He looked up. "Twenty, I rigged twenty kilos. Why, is there a shortage?"

"You don't ask the questions here, Mr. Fuentes, or whoever you are. Now get this. I don't give a damn what the terrorists do in Sulu or Mindanao or Luzon. This is my region, and nothing ever blew up here until you came around. If it weren't for your friends, I'd hang you upside down until Jesus comes back to town. I'll not put up with any more of your hellery. In two years, I retire. You get out of my region and stay out until I do. If I ever see or hear of you again, I'll bury your ass in concrete." He reached into his coat pocket and flipped a passport into Marty's plate. "Get lost."

Marty picked up the passport and wiped off the olive oil with his napkin. "I've booked the Saturday flight to Davao."

"Why not tomorrow?"

"Control is going to call me at noon tomorrow. I can't move until after that call. And I've got to square things with the couple who are renting me the safehouse.

By the way, that couple and the hookers think I'm a freelance writer. Let's keep it that way. If your detectives start asking them questions, the press will be right behind them and they'll soon be hounding me. That wouldn't be good for either of us. Agreed?"

"You think I'm stupid? I've taken care of that already." Mapandi stood and picked up his tape recorder.

"Another thing, my luggage cannot be searched again. Instruct your hoods to keep their paws off my stuff or else Control releases my report on Zorro."

"Now *you're* being stupid. Don't threaten me." He pointed to Marty. "Make damn sure you get on that flight." He walked out, leaving the door open. He spoke to Jeff and left.

Marty nibbled on the antipasto and thought about the farce of an interrogation. Neither Sagapan nor Mapandi had asked about Chopsticks or the kid, which meant they knew about them and were happy to have them blown away. Everything Mapandi had recorded that was worth knowing he had already gotten from his detectives or Nadine. He wanted what he did not record. Mapandi came to verify the inventory of the third magazine. There should have been twelve kilos left, but they only found six. Mapandi had to be sure six kilos of C4 were missing but, for whatever reasons, he did not want anyone else to know, not even his own detectives. That had been the sole purpose for their meeting.

"Okay, Mr. Fuentes," Jeff said. "You're our puppy until you leave Cebu. Be a good mutt and stay on the leash."

Marty laughed and turned. "Woof, woof." He strode out of the restaurant and jogged back to the Cebu Midway with Mutt on his tail.

CHAPTER 33

Cebu Midway Hotel, Room 700, Friday, February 14

Marty's bladder woke him. Procrastinating, he remained in the bed semi-conscious and argued with his body, tried to convince it sleeping was more important than pissing. While he debated, he started to remember the wasted hours after his meeting with Mapandi. Relieved by the outcome, he had gotten stupid drunk. The bottle of tequila had not helped him solve the riddle of the missing six kilos. He had ended up deciding it was not his concern, to let Mapandi figure out the puzzle. His orders were to protect Bracelets. Sober, it did not seem so simple.

Marty thought about Bryce's curious interest in how they had searched the resort. It seemed Bryce and Bracelets knew some C4 went missing and he was trying to figure out how that could happen with cops crawling all over Pasigan Beach. Going over the night of the explosion, Marty realized Zorro must have taken the six kilos out when they loaded the twenty kilos for the kid. After the blast, he hid the C4 under his raincoat and stashed it in one of the empty hotel rooms. Then someone, probably the night watchman, took it out of the resort before the cops got a search warrant for the hotel. The watchman delivered it to whoever is trying to sell it to Bracelets. Mapandi will figure that out and squeeze the watchman.

And I'd better get off my ass.

Halfway to the toilet, he stopped and looked at the bedside clock. It was past three in the morning and it took him a few seconds to realize that was important. He glanced at the bed where Perla should be. He had the strangest of feelings—his partner was missing.

The long piss did not relieve him. CIDG had a dossier on Samuel Fuentes Mora aka Harris Maxwell. They had his picture and the address of his safehouse in Intramuros. Nadine assumes they will eventually match Fuentes to their file on Santana. He could not operate as before, so she gave him a new job, his last job. He was a bodyguard, like Chopsticks had been, and if he let Mapandi catch Bracelets with the C4, he too would retire in disgrace.

He leaned against the bathroom doorframe and stared at the empty bed. As she had promised, Perla had taken care of her affairs and returned to the hotel with two large suitcases—old stuff for her new future, she had said. She had showered, plucked and powdered, borrowed his razor and afterwards pranced around showing off her new dress. She was going to party with her friends from the department store and others, and Christopher, of course. She would be going to the university and had to bid farewell to her past. Excited and giddy, she left with jaunty steps, her hair bouncing. She did not have time to sit and have a drink, no time to celebrate with Uncle Max. She had left him alone with his bottle of tequila.

He cussed the empty bed. He had always worked alone, been alone, and now he had a partner, an accomplice, a smart young woman who had not yet messed up her life. *What happened to her? Did Mapandi figure her out? Is she hanging upside down waiting for Jesus to come back to town?* He could not go back to sleep. He had two women to keep safe.

At dawn, Perla stumbled in, wasted, said "Whoopee," and flopped on the bed. Marty wanted to scream, "Why didn't you call me. I've been worried," but he sighed and smiled instead. He felt ridiculous, like a father determined to preserve his daughter's virginity. She was going to get a chill, though. She was not accustomed to air conditioning. She giggled and played being a limp corpse while he fumbled to remove her new dress, and then she groaned with contentment when he buried her under the covers. He pulled down the edge of the blanket to expose her nose. She yanked it back to hide from the light. He could not remember ever tucking someone in bed. He wondered if he had contracted some old-age affliction.

After getting dressed, he wrote a note to Perla, telling her to invite Tata and Lilibeth, and of course Christopher, for a party at the hotel that evening. He wanted to tell her he approved of Christopher, which made him chuckle. Instead, he wrote that he would be getting another room for himself under the name of Maxwell Harris and added a smiley face to the end of the sentence.

He went to the lobby on the forth floor, which was as far as the elevator went. Guests had to transfer to another lift to get to street level. When the doors opened, he faced two kids slouched in chairs near the reception desk. The half-awake one jabbed the sleeping one with his elbow. The rookies gaped at him with open mouths.

Marty stepped out of the elevator and considered his tail, uncertain whether he should feel insulted or glad that Mapandi did not consider him dangerous enough for someone with experience. Both wore rumpled slacks and polo shirts. One had a cell phone, neither appeared armed. Marty glanced at their laced black shoes and thought he would have some fun, but he had to take care of business first.

"Are one of you kids old enough to drive?"

One scowled. The other shut his mouth and glared.

"Good. I'll take that as a yes."

Marty strode to the vacant reception desk, scribbled the address of his safehouse on a scrap of paper and handed it to the more alert of the two. "Do you mind giving me a ride?" They looked at the paper, then at each other, stood and gestured toward the elevator to the street.

At the safehouse, Marty fired up his laptop and sent an email to Beacon asking Nadine to call at noon his time. He added that he would send an update report in an hour or so. After swiping a beer from Tippy's fridge, he ate a few jalapeno peppers and started typing.

He began with a long essay about his new associate, Perla Armamento Serrano, detailing how she had helped him at the Pasigan Resort, his recruiting her and then Bryce hiring her over breakfast. He chuckled, and wrote that Bryce invited him to stay in his house for a day or two.

He explained Mapandi wanted the meeting because it appeared six kilos of C4 were missing and he wanted to know if that were so. And to personally tell him to get out of Cebu, or else. From the breakfast conversation, it appeared Bracelets and Bryce knew some C4 had gotten loose, but since they intended to leave Saturday, they must have decided buying it too risky. In conclusion, he supposed Mapandi had already alerted CIDG Davao about a lawless element headed for their region and sent them his dossier. If Posey exposed him, he would have to vamoose the Philippines and leave Bracelets vulnerable.

After sending his report, he disassembled his Beretta and hid the pieces along with the flying knives in the false bottom of his bag, which so far had proven good enough for checked luggage. Maxwell Harris had a permit for the Beretta, but it was forged.

Marty looked at his watch and smiled. He had almost two hours before Nadine's call. He put on his running shoes and went outside. The rookies were gone. Jeff was leaning against the empty sedan. Marty sagged with feigned disappointment. "Ah shucks, what'd you do with the kids? We had planned a race. How about it. You up for a little exercise?"

Without waiting for an answer, he jogged down the street. He heard Jeff whistle for Mutt, who no doubt was staking out the rear of the house. When Marty reached the end of the block, he turned around and saw Mutt running after him and Jeff getting into the sedan. He turned the corner and picked up the pace, cut through a vacant lot, looped around and tailed his tail. He watched them get frustrated, angry and then panicky. He snuck ahead of them, stepped into the middle of the road and waved. They were not amused. Mutt collared him, slammed him against the car and cuffed him.

"What, you guys can't take a joke?"

"You son-of-a bitch," Jeff sputtered. "We're not playing hide and seek. We're going to lock you up until we drag your ass to the airport—in handcuffs."

"Whoa big boy. If I'm not back at that house in ten minutes to take a phone call, Mapandi's going to hang you by the balls until the next resurrection."

Jeff pursed his lips and took out his mobile. "Dogs don't get phone calls." He looked at Mutt. "I'll locate the nearest cage for this mongrel." He walked off.

Marty watched Jeff punch numbers, speak and wait. And he waited and waited. Marty sweated and cussed himself for playing games. Then Jeff turned his back. When he finished the call, he smiled and returned to the car.

"Found a nice doghouse for our puppy."

"Didn't you talk to Mapandi?"

"Shut up." Mutt punched Marty in the kidney and shoved him into the back seat of the sedan.

They had attracted a small group of bystanders. Some young boys peered into the car. Marty ignored them and watched Mutt and Jeff jabbering several yards away. When they returned to the car, they blindfolded him with a dirty rag and drove off. The blindfold made Marty think they would take him to a CIDG safehouse where he would have plenty of time to think about his stupidity. Meantime, he tracked direction, guessed at the time between turns and listened for noises that could be reference points. It became impossible. Mutt and Jeff were not amateurs. They made frequent turns, backed up and circled or zigzagged through what he guessed were parking lots. He lost all sense of direction and started to think through his predicament. He had to contact Perla. She would have to handle Bracelets and Bryce until he got to the airport. With luck, they might avoid disaster.

Marty ignored Jeff's taunts and concentrated on listening to the noises outside. When he heard an electric saw and hammers, he felt better. He had heard them early in their journey. Wherever they had gone, it seemed they had returned.

Jeff said in Visayan, "That's enough." They pulled to the curb. Jeff yanked Marty's hair and pulled off the blindfold. "You lied. Your phone call isn't until noon. It's eleven forty-five. Now let's see if you can find the house in time. Stick to the roads." He turned, opened the glove compartment and held up a revolver. "If you take a shortcut, the deal is off. You're dead." He lowered his chin and looked into Marty's eyes. "I have orders, Mr. Fuentes, no more games, *please*. I hate paperwork. Do you understand?" Marty nodded. "Good. If you need our help, just ask. We'll be glad to tie your balls to the bumper and lead you." He smiled. "We'll see how fast doggy runs."

Mutt opened the rear door and removed the handcuffs. Having jogged the neighborhood, Marty knew he was about nine blocks from the safehouse. He told Jeff the route he would take and ran off, making sure they were never more than a half-block behind him.

Nadine first interrogated Marty about Perla and then said, "Leash, for you this relationship is extraordinary experience. You will have emotional upsets that will affect your judgment. Be aware of changes and talk to me. Do you understand?"

Marty thought of tucking Perla into bed. "You're right. I'm fucking nuts. I need a shrink."

"Okay. Congratulations on clever thinking, but their hiring Perla so easy is suspicious."

"It is." He closed his eyes, saw Bryce coaxing Bracelets back to the buffet and pictured them talking. "Before Bryce hired Perla, he had a private chat with Bracelets. Her face was inscrutable, but my sense is she disagreed with his intention to hire Perla. We will be careful, but we're in a good position to protect Bracelets once we all get to Davao."

"Leash, about Posey. If she fingers you for stealing hard drive, lawyer it down to misdemeanor and buy your way out. Bryce had ton of information on fertilizer tender in computer. Say you stole it for that. We will figure out who hired you to swipe it and send particulars."

Marty sighed and shook his head. "Whip, CIDG now has a dossier on Samuel Fuentes. If I'm caught for anything, no telling where I'll end up. Let's spend the money up front and I'll pay Posey to get out of town. She'll go. Her husband is a certified asshole."

"That is fine. Now, Bracelets may buy missing C4, but we believe her role is to negotiate price. She will not take possession. We have identified her companion. She is daughter of MILF commander. She will take C4 for war."

"War, what war?"

"Manila broke cease-fire and is invading Moro camps with overwhelming firepower to deny MILF territorial base before continuing peace negotiations. They are creating havoc, dislocating thousands in Central Mindanao, which is Bracelets' homeland. Manila is suppressing news, but she must know. She may change plans. Be prepared."

"The MILF must have seen it coming. That's why they were after the C4."

"Yes, and they used Bracelets to get it. She surprised us. She may have other role in war. Prepare for more surprises."

Marty groaned. "I can't stay in Cebu. If I don't leave tomorrow, Mapandi will have me shot and cast in concrete. I've been warned, twice."

After a brief silence Nadine said, "Keep phone close. Contact Beacon immediately if Bracelets does anything odd. We will prepare contingency."

"No contingency with me on Cebu, do you understand?"

"Yes, Leash," she said in her motherly tone that ended discussions.

"Did you get the report on Bryce?"

Marty heard the rustling of papers as Nadine spoke. "His mother died after long illness when he was ten. They had Mexican servant who looked after mother and raised Bryce. His father owned several carpet stores. Seems he devoted time to business and let Bryce run wild. Bryce was angry kid, serious fights. Father's money held off juvenile justice until Bryce was thirteen when he near killed man with bare hands. No indictment, but they sent him to Benedictine military school in Georgia to finish high school. Monks tamed him. He went into army for few years before college and then went to work for Apex. Army record is interesting." Marty could hear paper shuffling. "Okay, army trained him in ordinance and assigned him to munitions depot in Korea. They gave him top-secret clearance. You know what that means."

"He was babysitting nukes."

"Two months later they transfer him to liaison intelligence unit."

"What was he doing?"

"It says 'to monitor trafficking in counterfeit goods.' North Korean mafia ships counterfeit dollars and pharmaceuticals to States. Bryce had girlfriend whose family is South Korean mafia. He probably had useful contacts. His army application lists fluency in Spanish and Korean, but father is American of British ancestry. He must have learned Spanish from Mexican nanny. Korean he probably learned from chum in military school."

"So he spoke Korean when he joined the army."

"Yes, and you were correct about hands. While in Korea, he won martial arts trophies, also sharpshooter awards. After army, he studied international business in Phoenix and graduated with honors. Apex recruited him on campus for their headquarters in San Francisco. He has no criminal record and good credit. That is all."

"Anything to suggest he might be employed by someone besides Apex?"

"If he is working with friends, they will not admit it. He is interesting. Ordinance, martial arts, marksman, and has propensity for languages and women with clandestine connections. He is our kind of guy. Check him out, but first priority is Bracelets. Watch her and call in any odd behavior."

"Okay. I'll clear out of the safehouse and get back to the hotel."

"Ciao."

Marty called the Cebu Midway and reserved a room for Harris Maxwell. Then he finished packing, dropped his bag on the front porch and went to settle accounts with Tippy's wife, who could not stop whining about how much they were going to miss him. By the time he went outside, Mutt was repacking his bag in the trunk of the sedan. Jeff held the rear car door open. Before Marty got in, Jeff stopped him.

"We are a playful people. We like to play games, *our* games, and we make up the rules. Understood?"

Marty nodded. "I'll raise my hand before going to the potty."

Jeff patted Marty's cheek. "Good puppy. You will be needing a new lock for your luggage. And this," he opened his other hand, "we'll return as you get on the plane—professional courtesy."

Marty stared at the firing pin for his Beretta.

CHAPTER 34

Cebu Midway Hotel, Friday, February 14

Before Amina left with Nashita to visit Zorro's wife, she had asked Steve to watch the news in case Manila announced their excuse for war. When he turned on the TV, he cried out, "Holy shit." He stared at the screen for a few moments and then dashed out to make amends. He shopped for a card with the perfect message, chose a bouquet of flowers that were predominately yellow, her favorite color, and bought a heart-shaped box of fine chocolates.

When he returned to the room, he had a new dread. President Gloria Macapagal Arroyo had released the official statement on the invasion and he feared he might have missed something. He surfed the channels and jotted down the highlights: 5000 soldiers, tanks, artillery, helicopter gun ships, planes, at least 140 guerrillas killed versus six soldiers, reason—lair of Pentagon Gang. He watched and waited, changed channels, but none had anything to add. Newscasters sitting in suits announced the same statistics. None had video footage of the action, no pictures of anything, not even a map, as if the

Liguasan Marsh was as inaccessible and inscrutable as the backside of Venus.

When Amina returned, he felt relieved by her surprise. Like he, she had been too preoccupied to realize it was Valentine's Day. He waited until after she read the card and hugged him. Then he handed her his notes.

"Manila has spoken. Who is the Pentagon Gang?"

"That's their excuse! Is that it?"

"Well, they said Pentagon Gang and other bandits."

She flopped down on the bed, mouth open, eyes wide. "Incredible, ridiculous, insulting." She licked her lips and swallowed. "Manila claims the Pentagon Gang has a hundred members. We can't count more than two dozen or so."

"Who are they?"

"Thieves, kidnappers for ransom. Some hide in the marsh."

"Are they Moros?"

"They're a gang of hoodlums."

"But they're in your camps, I mean, according to the newscast."

She frowned and sighed. "A few move in and out of the villages around Buliok. They have relatives there."

She got up, paced, pondered, stopped and tossed her hands in the air. "Aaaahhh!" She shook her head and gave him a forlorn look. "They'll get away with it. Imperial Manila controls the media. If a journalist dares to wonder why they sent the nation's arsenal after a handful of bandits, no one will publish the story." Her shoulders sagged. "We are stupid. Arroyo tricked us with her all-out peace. She dragged out the talks, quibbling over words. We demanded they recognize our camps in the marsh. They bickered for weeks, changed 'recognize' to 'acknowledge' and our sleepy-eyed negotiators agreed. Now the government can say they did not recognize our right to our land, but acknowledged we are squatters on public property."

She snatched up his notes and scowled. She read them aloud, her voice fierce and bitter. "Troops, 5000, tanks, artillery, helicopters, gun ships, planes." She crumpled the paper and hurled it at the window. "Hang on brothers," she screamed. "We're sending reinforcements." She collapsed in the chair, mumbled "Six kilos" and cried.

When Marty returned to the hotel, he checked in again using Harris Maxwell's credit card and took a regular room on the sixth floor. If the desk clerk recognized him as a guest already registered under another name, he did not think it worthy of comment. But Jeff, who had accompanied him to the lobby while Mutt parked the car, scribbled in his little notebook.

Marty left his bag in his new room and went upstairs to check on Perla. When he opened the door, he saw Christopher in briefs and Perla in a terrycloth bathrobe. It looked like a tornado had touched down on the bed. Perla appeared embarrassed but with a naughty smile.

Marty laughed. "I see you started the party early."

"Hey, I hope you're not pissed off, mate."

"Not at all. Actually, I've taken another room under my pen name for the occasion. Call me Max and you two can have this room for the night."

Christopher stepped forward with his hand extended. "G'day Mr. Max, nice to meet you. Thanks heaps."

"I think you know Perla, *my niece*."

Christopher looked at Perla. She winked. He turned back to Marty. "No worries, *Uncle* Max."

Marty looked at Perla. "Are Tata and Lilibeth coming?"

"They'll be here for happy hour, around five o'clock. Lilibeth's anxious to see you."

"Okay, help me pack up my stuff."

As they gathered things and packed, Marty asked in Tagalog, "Did you tell the ladies about your uncle?"

Perla flicked her eyebrows.

"Are our neighbors in?"

Perla nodded. "She's pissed. About half an hour ago we heard her fuming and shouting, in English, something about brothers and reinforcements."

"Okay. Let your boyfriend recharge. Come down to room 609. We need to talk about complications."

When Perla came down, Marty told her about the war, the missing C4 and the possibility of Bracelets changing plans. Perla thought Bracelets' shouting had sounded angry and sarcastic, and that maybe the "reinforcements" could be six kilos when thirty-two were expected. While they watched the newscast about the invasion, they speculated on what Bracelets might do.

Marty had Perla call room 702 to invite Amina and Steve to her uncle's party. Steve told her they would be happy to join them after he settled his travel plans. "Thank you, sir," Perla said. "Uncle Max will be pleased." She hung up the phone and flopped in the chair. She looked worried.

"What's the matter?"

"They will come, 'After *I* change *my* travel plans,' he said. He didn't say anything about Bracelets or me, not yet. If he's not going tomorrow, maybe he'll not hire me. Then what?"

Surprise! Marty thought. He stared out the window and considered calling Nadine, but he needed more information first. He looked at his watch. It was ten minutes to happy hour.

"I'm hungry. We'll go downstairs and wait for them."

Except for a couple of business types at the bar, happy hour would have been a bust if it were not for the somber group that had pushed three tables together. Marty, who had not had breakfast or lunch, concentrated on devouring an immense steak. Tata sat next to him, pouting. She wanted to party, but not at the bar. Lilibeth looked glum and hurt over Perla's departure, whether for the loss of her companionship or steady income did not seem to concern anyone, least of all Perla. Preoccupied, Perla kept glancing at the elevators in the lobby.

As Marty finished his steak, he heard elevator doors opening. He hoped it was Bracelets and Bryce, but the sound came from the lift to the street. Christopher strolled into the bar carrying an armful of red roses and a bottle of rum. He grinned at Perla.

"Happy Valentine's Day, love."

Perla squealed with delight, hugged Christopher and gave Lilibeth and Tata each a rose. She gave Uncle Max one too, with a kiss on the cheek. By the time Christopher got a drink and led a toast to Perla's future, she had resumed her anxious vigilance of the lobby elevators. She took a sip of her rum and cola, excused herself and went to the house phone in the lobby.

When she returned, she looked at Marty and mouthed "soon." About ten minutes later, Amina and Steve came in, he carrying an impressive looking camera with an external flash. After Perla introduced Lilibeth, Tata and Christopher as her friends, Amina ordered a lemonade and Steve a beer.

"That's quite a camera," Marty said. "Mind if I look at it?"

"Go ahead."

Marty marveled at the high-end Canon. It had a relatively new digital body and a well-used, professional-looking zoom lens. Looking through the viewfinder, Marty whistled. "Wow, big and bright. This baby has...clarity. You must be a pro."

Steve shrugged. "I like to take pictures."

"I take pictures to supplement the articles I write, but the editors reject most and use stock photos. If I were a better photographer, I'd be making a lot more money. Maybe we could go on a photo shoot and you could give me some tips."

Steve and Amina shared a look. "Sure, what camera do you use?"

"I just splurged on a ten-mega pixel Nikon with an 8X zoom, but the viewfinder sucks. Its menu has more choices than a Chinese restaurant's. I've been practicing, but I'm sort of lost."

"Well, eh, in a week or two—"

Amina touched Steve's arm. "Weren't you and Bipsy going picture taking this Sunday? I think Bipsy would prefer not going alone."

Steve studied Amina's face, nodding slowly. "That's a great idea." He turned to Marty. "I won't be going back to Davao right away. But that doesn't change anything. You stay at the house for a few days if you like."

Marty grinned. His eyes darted to Perla who had gone slack with relief. "Thank you, thank you very much." He looked at Amina. "I'm good a fixing things. I'd enjoy it if you have chores."

"No working around the house," Steve said. "You're our guest. I've a good friend, an excellent photographer. I ah…had promised to join him for some street photography on Sunday and regretted having to disappoint him. He would enjoy your company. And he's a good teacher. I'll send him an email tonight and ask him to pick you up at the house Sunday morning. Is that good for you?"

"That would be perfect, thank you." Marty lifted his glass. "Sounds great, I'll drink to that."

They touched glasses. Steve gulped some beer and stood. "Let's record the occasion." He photographed the entire group, then Perla and Christopher with the roses, Tata and Lilibeth, had Marty and Perla pose, and Marty alone. He passed the camera to Amina and sat down next to Marty. She took a picture of Steve in the group and a couple of him and Marty.

Mutt and Jeff had positioned themselves in the lobby where they could watch Marty and his friends through the open doors of the bar. Around six, two guys Marty had not seen before replaced them. While Steve was taking pictures, they wandered in, sat at the bar and ordered soft drinks. One took out his cell phone, snapped pictures of the group and grinned. In the morning, Marty imagined, they would report that Samuel Fuentes had drinks with his three prostitutes, Steve Bryce and his girlfriend, and one of the Aussies from the Pasigan. In the afternoon, Mapandi would learn that Fuentes, one of the hookers and Bryce's girlfriend boarded the plane to Davao, but not Bryce.

What will Mapandi think of that? What should I *think about that? Not Bracelets the insurgent, but Bryce the businessman stays behind. To do what? Deliver reinforcements to the war? Who are you Shutterspy? What were you doing with the Korean mafia? Whose side are you on?*

Marty accepted that Nadine never told him anything more than he needed to know. She had to have other operatives in the Philippines. She had had impeccable information on how and when to steal the hard drive. Who better to provide that information than Bryce? How better for Bryce to protect his cover than make himself the victim. He imagined Nadine reading Bryce's reports about the suspicious Maxwell Harris and Nadine telling him to go along, to find out for whom Maxwell works, and to invite him to stay at his house, but reminding Bryce that his first priority is to protect Bracelets. It seemed a crazy scenario, but it was a crazy business. You learned not to trust anyone, not even Nadine.

Marty watched Bracelets—polite, refined, educated, riveting eyes. She was his last job. Nadine paid him to take orders. He would call her, report Bryce's odd behavior and await further instructions. He frowned. *Like a good puppy.*

CHAPTER 35

Room 702, Friday night, February 14

"Did you notice those two jokers at the bar?" Steve asked after he closed the door.

"You mean the guys making eyes with Lilibeth?"

"Lilibeth was trolling and they used her as an excuse. They were watching Max, or maybe us." Steve pulled out his cell phone and scrolled through the memory for Bipsy's number.

"What's trolling mean?"

He sent the number and held the phone to his ear. "Trolling is a fishing technique. Tata is sleeping with Max, Perla is sleeping with Christopher and you're sleeping with me. Lonely working-girl Lilibeth was angling for a bony fish but they weren't biting." He raised his index finger. "They were working." He wagged the finger at the TV. "Hiya Bipsy. How's Grandma doing?" He went into the bathroom and closed the door while she surfed the channels for news. When he came out, she muted the TV and shook her head.

"Bipsy's okay with taking Max on a photo shoot. He'll be at the compound around eleven-o'clock Sunday. He's expecting Max to buy lunch and keep him happy with beer." Steve started up his laptop and removed the disc from the camera. "Bipsy will print Max's photo and try to be there when you talk to Posey. For the moment, he's respecting our suspicions that Max might be Santana, but he thinks we're a couple of, how'd he put it...paranoia maniacs with illusionary disillusions, or maybe he said hallucinatory contusions. Reception wasn't that great."

She smiled and looked at the bedside clock. "I should be back before midnight with final instructions. I'll call if I'll be later than that." She moved close, wrapped her arms around his waist and snuggled her head against his chest. He sniffed her hair.

"Take a taxi both ways—promise?" She nodded. "Pray for us. Mumble if you must." She purred. He pulled back. "Watch for those two goons from the bar. If they follow you, buy toothpaste or something and come back. Don't try to lose them."

"Oh, they can tag along." She grinned. "We're meeting at the mosque—ladies only section." She caressed his cheek, picked up her scarf and left.

After downloading his photos to the laptop, he formatted the chips. Mindful of the adage that you never can have too much film, he decided to buy more memory chips in the morning. He cleaned lenses, checked camera bodies and made sure his batteries were fully charged. The knapsack Amina had bought him looked too new. He stained it with beer and rubbed it with the soles of his shoes. Then he studied all the stuff he had spread out on the king-sized bed and began to pack.

Amina returned before midnight carrying a grocery bag and her scarf wrapped around something.

"Did they follow you?"

She shook her head. "They were in the lobby. I waited several minutes but they didn't come down."

"Are you sure?"

"The produce section at the supermarket has a window overlooking the entrance to the hotel elevator." She held up the bag. "You want a banana?"

"Please."

She sat on the bed, broke off a banana and handed it to him. As he peeled it, she unwrapped her scarf, revealing a prayer book. From its pages, she withdrew a sheet of paper with two paragraphs in neat Arabic writing and a third in Tagalog. He sat on the floor by her feet, attentive.

"If you leave the room tomorrow, don't forget your cell phone. Nashita will call if anything changes. Your cell phone is your lifeline so charge it whenever you can." She turned over the piece of paper and wrote two phone numbers, marking one "N" and the other "J." "If you cannot follow the plan, call Nashita first. If you can't contact her, call Jiriki."

"Jiriki is in on this?"

"Of course. Rest here until checkout time.. Go to the ferry port and hang out at the Valencia Café. Bring something to read because you won't be leaving until four o'clock. Sometime before four, two men will approach you. One, about our age, goes by the name Gerry. You are a tourist and Gerry is your tour guide. Speak English when you're in public places. The other man, Abdul, will probably ignore you. He is in charge."

He swallowed banana. "Who has the C4?"

"That's up to Abdul. You will be taking a small cargo vessel to Iligan. They carry passengers, but they don't cater to them. Bring food. The trip takes about twenty hours. You'll dock in Iligan around noon. Call me. Make sure you call me. I'll be worried. You'll be taking a jeepney to Marawi City. From there you will go to Cotabato and then on to the marsh, how and when and with whom has yet to be determined. Make peace with your God. The trip from Marawi to Cotabato is dangerous." She reached out, wiggled her fingers into his hair and frowned. "It's especially treacherous for foreigners with golden hair." She handed him the paper. "If you get separated from Gerry and Abdul, show this to any Moro with kind eyes. Do *not* trust anyone in a uniform."

He studied the paper and pointed to the Arabic script. "What does this say?"

She twisted his hair, looked into his eyes and sighed. "It's the same thing as the Tagalog. It says you're an idiot, in Maranao and Maguindanao. Call me before you leave Marawi and when you get to Cotabato. Your cell phone might work in the marsh, but it's useless anywhere between Marawi and Cotabato."

Steve lay on his back in the darkness. It was quiet except for Amina's soft breathing. They had checked his stuff again: A change of clothes, extra socks and briefs, toothbrush, toothpaste, soap, deodorant, nail clipper, band-aids, antibiotic salve, Imodium, sunglasses, pen, some sheets of paper, two paperback novels, plenty of cash in small bills, credit card taped under the innersole of his shoe, passport, cell phone with charger and photo gear. She had him switch to long-sleeved shirts because of insects. He would not be shaving. If his running shoes got wet, they would dry. A cap could not hide his blondness. He had a black nylon jacket, lightweight and water resistant with zippered pockets inside and out. They thought it most useful. His rucksack still had room for six kilos of C4. In the morning, he would buy a pocket-sized notebook, more photo chips and a spare battery for his cell. Cargo pants would be better than jeans, but he had little hope of finding his size.

He rolled onto his side, patted her naked rump and closed his eyes to sleep and gather strength. Neither had had the urge to make love. That felt natural. Lovemaking is celebration and confirmation, done during lulls in battle perhaps, certainly afterwards if you survive, but not before.

CHAPTER 36

Cebu to Davao, Saturday, February 15

Bewildered, Perla sat on the edge of the bed holding a bunch of pesos. Christopher had left her early in the morning to return to Australia. He had insisted for the fourth time that she call or write him once she settled in Davao. Doubting that she would ever hear from him again, Perla had been crying when her boss came with instructions. She was to check out of the hotel and pay for the room with the cash he had given her and then go to the airport with Bracelets and keep her occupied away from the gate until he got on the plane, saying he would bribe the attendant to go first, because he did not want Bracelets to spot the two goons tailing him. *What else did he say?* She was to ingratiate herself with Bracelets. Perla thought she could be ingratiating, but not with someone who suspected she was an imposter. Bracelets had questioned her supervisor at the department store, about her honesty and such, and about her uncle. Her boss told Bracelets that she had been an excellent and honest employee for two years, but that she had never mentioned an uncle.

Bewilderment, Perla discovered, is the state of having eyes open without seeing, mouth agape without speaking and mind racing through a maze of questions without a gate. She understood gate. Gate is like door, but outside. She was to go to the airport and keep Bracelets away from the gate until her boss got on the airplane. So the gate had to be between the airport and the airplane, but it seemed the gate was inside the airport. *Why don't they call it a door?* She could not ask her boss. She did not want to admit she had never been to an airport. She riffled the pesos. She had never checked out of a hotel either.

Strapped in the window seat, Perla clutched Magic Monkey to her chest. She was careful not to snag the frayed cuffs of his trousers. Rimparac had made the rag doll from remnants of red linen, orange cotton and blue denim when Perla was six or maybe seven, after her mother told her, with bitter exasperation, that her father had abandoned them. Then the suffocating plane with little windows and howling motors bucked, lurched and went up like an elevator.

Bracelets had told Perla to take the window seat so she could see the city from the air but Perla missed it. She had closed her eyes. Bracelets sat beside her with a book written in Arabic script. It looked like a prayer book, but Bracelets was reading, not praying. She seemed to be reminiscing, as if it were a story she had not read in a long time. Perla tightened her seat belt and looked down at the sea. She would think of something ingratiating to say if her feet touched the earth again.

Perla sat in the back of the taxi with Bracelets and watched her boss in the front. Like Sammy during their ride to the Pasigan, Max did not talk. He was somber and plotting again, and she was headed for unfamiliar territory again. Someone had to say something. She looked out the window and commented on things that were strange until they turned off the highway, went down a dirt road and waited for a woman guard to open a gate. Behind it were four huge houses. They stopped in front of the second one. As they got out of the taxi, a small woman with black hair ran out of the first house shouting in English with an unfamiliar accent.

"Where have you been hiding?" the woman with the accent asked. She hugged Bracelets. "Where's Steve?"

"He's gone on a photo safari. He'll be back in a week or so." Bracelets turned. "This is Perla, Steve's new cook and housekeeper. Isabela is our neighbor and my special girlfriend."

Perla smiled. "Pleased to meet you, ma'am."

A tall redheaded man carrying a gray and white cat came outside. Bracelets introduced them as Gerrit, Isabela's husband and Julius, Steve's cat.

Uncle Max stopped unloading suitcases. He came over. As Isabela introduced him, Julius squirmed, jumped out of Gerrit's arm and yowled. When Bracelets tried to pick him up, he scampered several yards away, crouched on the ground and glared at her.

"He's angry because we left him," she said.

Gerrit helped Perla and Uncle Max lug the bags up the outside stairs to the dining room. Max stared at the photograph of the carabao hanging on the wall.

"Damn, did Steve take that?"

"Gored him in the side of his belly," Gerrit said. "Steve got pissed because the beast kept running, couldn't get another picture." Gerrit chuckled. "Crazier than a crazy water buffalo, he is."

As soon as Bracelets showed Perla her room, Perla changed into jeans and T-shirt and went to clean the mess in the kitchen. After tidying up, she inventoried the pantry, refrigerator and freezer. She examined a package of frozen fish and mused, *this could be ingratiating.* She found Bracelets unpacking Steve's suitcase.

"Excuse me, ma'am. For lunch, I can make hamburgers but on bread or toast because the buns are moldy. You have bean sprouts and a wrinkled squash. If you can wait a bit, there's frozen fish. I've a great recipe for fish in sweet sour sauce. An old Maranao woman taught me how to make it years ago." Amina stopped unpacking. "But I'll have to go shopping for the proper vegetables."

Amina considered Perla for a moment. "Yes, I'd like to try your sweet sour fish. Make a list of what you need. We'll send your uncle in Steve's truck."

After Max returned with the groceries, Amina went into the kitchen. She watched Perla work for a few minutes. Perla pretended to ignore the uncomfortable silence.

"I see you like to cook."

"It's fun for hungry people but not to cook for myself. How about you, ma'am?"

"I'm better at eating than cooking. How did you meet the Maranao woman?"

"After my father disappeared, my mother had to work two jobs and it was difficult for her to find someone to watch over me. Then an old Maranao woman who lived in our neighborhood lost her home. The bank took it, I guess. Her name was Rimparac. My mother asked her to live with us and take care of me. I was six at the time. Rimparac looked ancient to me. She had arthritis." Perla stopped chopping and stared at the wall for a moment. "Rimparac taught me how to cook and make clothes and so many other things. And she told me stories in song. She used her face and her twisted hands to animate them." Perla put down the knife, distorted her fingers and moved her hands while she hummed. "It was beautiful. She'd chant the stories in the Maranao language and then explain them in Visayan. They were part of an ancient epic poem."

"The Darangen. You are fortunate. Too few remain who remember even a part of the Darangen."

Perla turned. "You're Maranao, ma'am?"

Amina nodded.

"Do you know the Darangen?"

"No, I have heard but a few of the stories. The Darangen *is* ancient, from before we embraced Islam. The stories tell the beliefs and traditions of the Maranao people since time immemorial—from our origins. It is our shame for losing the Darangen. Tell me, what became of Rimparac?"

"She died the day after my fourteenth birthday. I think she stayed alive to give me my birthday present, a dress she made for me. It must have been terribly painful for her to sew it." Perla rubbed her eye on her sleeve and pushed pineapple and onion pieces into a pot on the stove. "I still have that dress."

"So Max is your father's brother."

Perla choked on the abrupt switch. Rimparac had done that too—one of her tricks to get at the truth. Perla nodded and busied herself. It had been too long since she had thought about Rimparac and this first day of her future was filling with her. The Darangen had a story about courage and treachery, about confusing them.

"That's a lovely story, about Rimparac, I mean," Amina said.

She left the kitchen before Perla could scream that Rimparac was not a story, that only Max was her lie.

A Filipina homemaker would be horrified at the notion of eating with their maid or cook, yet Amina insisted that Perla eat with Uncle Max and her.

"This has got to be the best sweet sour fish I've ever tasted," Amina said, wiping the last speck of sauce off her plate with a piece of bread. "You must give me the recipe. As a Maranao, I'm invoking ancestral rights."

Perla laughed. "Thank you, ma'am." A loud knock stopped her from saying more. She hustled to the kitchen and opened the door.

"Oh, hello," Brenda said. "Are Steve and Amina here?"

"Miss Amina is. Whom should I say is calling, ma'am?"

"Brenda, I'm the neighbor." Brenda gestured at the house behind her.

Perla glanced over Brenda's shoulder and hesitated for a moment.

"Is that Miss or Mrs., ma'am?"

"Miss"

"One moment, please."

Perla stepped into the dining area, stood at attention and heralded. "Your neighbor..." she paused and darted a look at Marty, "*Miss* Brenda is here, ma'am."

Amina smiled. "Please show her in."

Brenda waltzed in. She wore a billowing summer dress, sandals and a pearl necklace. Marty stood up. While Amina introduced Brenda to Maxwell Harris, freelance writer, Perla, head bowed, raced to vacate her place next to Marty. She scooped up her unfinished plate, utensils and glass, rushed them to the kitchen and returned with clean dishes before Amina had finished explaining Steve's absence. Marty held the chair for Brenda and she sat down next to him. Marty grinned at Perla. She flipped her eyebrows and retired to the kitchen.

Brenda ranted about Amina's good fortune to find such a marvelous cook. Amina explained that she was Max's niece and that they had met on Cebu Island.

"So, you're close to your niece," Brenda said.

Marty chuckled. "She's ambitious and intelligent. Perla thinks I'm a promiscuous old bachelor, but she tolerates me. I've promised to help her out." Marty put down his fork and looked at Amina. "I expect Perla will be a fine employee, but we don't want to deceive you. She will be going to the university here, in June I think. Perhaps Steve could keep her working part time after that."

Amina nodded. "We'll see, but she's not going anyplace until she gives me this recipe."

Marty talked about how he hoped to write several articles on Apex International. He questioned Brenda about her position and projects, but their conversation kept sliding to the tribulations of being transient and unattached. Their body language recognized the temporary solution was at hand while they worked on being diplomatic about it.

When Brenda finished her meal, she leaned back and dabbed the corners of her mouth with her napkin. "Apex is transferring me to Mexico."

"What does Apex have in Mexico?" Amina asked.

"Nothing until now," Brenda grinned. "I'll going to participate in closing a joint venture deal with a huge vegetable grower, and then I stay on as the sole Apex representative in Mexico. I'll be liaison, financial consultant, marketing coordinator, mail clerk and chauffer."

"Where bouts?" Marty asked.

"In Culiacan, the valley there is a rich vegetable growing area, like Salinas Valley in California."

"It's also home to some of Mexico's drug kingpins," Marty said.

Brenda looked a bit startled. "Is it dangerous?"

"Not as long as you mind your business. The narcos have estate houses there where they go there to relax. They have an agreement to avoid confrontations in their playground. Now there's another great article. Female businesswoman travels to valley of vegetables and drugs for giant Multinational Corporation. I need to get your story before you leave. When can we get together?"

Brenda smiled. "How about this afternoon—I've nothing planned."

"Great."

"We can go to my place."

Around seven that night, Marty thanked Amina for her offer of hospitality but said he would be staying at Brenda's house. Grabbing one of Marty's suitcases, Perla followed him down the outside stairs. They stopped midway between the houses and Marty rested his hand on Perla's shoulder.

"You're doing a fantastic job. Bracelets is thrilled to have you. Now, tell me what you are to do."

"I'm to observe and tell you her habits. If someone is going to harm her, it'll happen during her habitual routine, probably outside the compound. I'm to let you know as soon as she plans to leave and go with her if I can. If there is trouble, I get out of the way and let you handle it."

"Good. Any word from Bryce yet?"

"No phone calls at all. Wherever he is, he's traveling light. She brought back a suitcase full of his clothes and his computer. I didn't see his camera."

"Okay. She's going to be collecting information and putting it into that computer. Her work routine is important."

"Max," Perla grasped his arm and frowned. "She doesn't believe you're my uncle."

They looked up at the sound of a door sliding open. Brenda stood in the doorway with a mischievous smile, the light behind her silhouetting her body in a kimono-like nightgown, her heavy breasts sulking without a bra. Marty stooped to pick up his bags and mumbled, "Time to pay the rent."

On Sunday, Bipsy took Marty on a photo shoot around Davao. Every hour or so they stopped in a bar to critique Marty's pictures and have a few beers. Around four, Bipsy had to leave. Marty said he was going to shoot more pictures and then take a jeepney back to the compound.

After Bipsy drove out of sight, Marty hailed a taxi and went to a bar in barrio Ingles. He dispatched the bar owner's son on a familiar mission. Two hours later, in return for a generous incentive, Posey promised Marty she would leave Davao. He thought she would.

CHAPTER 37

Bohol Sea, early Sunday morning, February 16

For breathless moments as the freighter arched up toward ninety-degrees, Steve thought they might flip bow over stern. He grasped the edge of the bench with both hands and clung to it, as resolute as a cowboy determined to stay on his steed.

"Whoa, Archippus, wrong direction old boy," he said, as if his ass were a good compass in storms. "Forward, Archippus. Complete the task that you have received in the Lord." *Or Allah,* he thought, but the screams of frightened passengers smothered his prayer. *I have to call Amina. She'll be worried about me, mumbling maybe.*

Rain and seawater seeped beneath the hatch-like doors. He heard more retching, behind him now. Someone new contributed color, stench and substance to the sloppy water swirling around their feet. The boat teetered, twisted, listed to port and then plunged. Mucky water sloshed forward and swooshed past his ankles. He listened to the angry roar of the engines cursing the waves and plowing on, unmindful of the old hull that creaked and complained. Still, even if they made it they were going to be late. Amina expected him to call at noon and he was going to be late.

The dangling light bulb swinging amidships alternatively cast shadows and highlights across Gerry's face. He appeared green. "Are these trips always this much fun," Steve asked?

"This my first ride in slave boat, already."

Steve chuckled longer than the quip deserved, but with humor, they might survive. He had to photograph those infidels plundering the marsh, get their mug shots and take down names.

"I'm an infidel, you know. I did not sign a martyrdom agreement."

He could not hear Gerry laugh, but squeezed together on the bench as they were, he felt him giggle. Their coffin-like, windowless box, three-fourths buried below the main deck, did seem like slave quarters. They sat on rows of backless benches bolted to the floor like hopeful kiddies in kindergarten or hopeless slaves without oars—no paddles to help in the hustle for shore.

They had let him keep his rucksack. He felt safer having his cameras, lenses, toothbrush and other goodies strapped to his back, along with the detonators for the C4. They had not made him put it up with the other luggage, lashed to the roof of the cabin under plastic tarps. Abdul had heaved a twenty-five kilo sack of *bulad* topside, or for the sake of precision and honesty, nineteen kilos of stinky rotten fish and six of C4. In theory, the bomb-sniffing dogs could not snoop it out. Still, they could not risk the SuperFerry. Their bucket of bilge was safe—only the rats smelled what they brought aboard. Steve figured the freighter's cargo was contraband, the voyagers being smugglers and subversives, and a voyeur, a foreign photojournalist for the Moro cause.

Thump, slap, thump, crash—they pitched and rolled. Steve thought kindly of the captain. At first, the turbulence had been disconcerting. Now the thrusting, surging and plunging comforted him. They were making progress. The tub had proven its seaworthiness, the captain too. They had weathered a wicked wave and until they hit another, he would doze.

The storm blew us off course, Bipsy. It slowed us. That storm made me late.

Late for what, Blue Eyes? What were you doing on your vacation?

Well, Bipsy, first off, I crossed the sea in a storm, which threw me off schedule.

What schedule? You were holidaying. Holidays have dates, not schedules. Spill the beans. Show me pictures.

Well, I can't, Bipsy. I was conserving, saving space on my chips.

Space for what, Blue Eyes?

For my new job. I'm shooting for the insurgency now. I'm staying in the Philippines. I'm staying with Amina. But we didn't make it, you see. I was supposed to call Amina around noon, but with the storm, well, I didn't make it. Tell her not to worry. Tell her I love her. No matter what, I'll keep my word. I'm staying in the Philippines.

The swill sloshed over Steve's running shoes. They would dry. He felt relieved that he had not brought another pair. Gerry and Abdul wore sandals. They probably did not own spares.

The boat heaved again. Steve clutched the bench, not bothering to open his eyes. His photo chips were empty, formatted, squeaky clean, ready and waiting to capture dislocation, pain and suffering. Still, he worried. He had to call Amina.

Giddy-up, Archippus.

CHAPTER 38

On the road to Marawi City, Sunday night, February 16

Three soldiers in uniform without insignia halted them. Steve expected them to reprimand the loony jeepney driver for not turning on the headlights, as if he feared Hypocor would send him an electricity bill if he did, but the leader just inspected his papers. The other two beamed flashlights on the faces of the silent passengers seated on opposing benches in the back of the vehicle. Steve thought of Nazis looking for Jews. One growled in Tagalog for him to step down. Steve stared in his best imitation of a moron until Gerry, his tour guide, nudged him a said. "Get out." As he began to pick his way between the passenger's feet and their parcels, the soldier ordered him to bring his baggage. Gerry picked up Steve's rucksack and handed it to him.

Before Steve jumped down, the soldier took his rucksack as if to assist him. He unclasped the flap. Steve's blood surged in momentary fright. How could he convince soldiers who could not afford cameras that C4 detonators were photography accessories? Then he remembered Abdul had them. He had put them in his sack of *bulad* with the C4 before disappearing into the night with a motor-tricycle man. Steve wondered why Abdul had him carry the detonators. The etiquette of insurgency, he supposed, a token gesture for the new recruit to feel involved.

The storm had subsided before daybreak and they had enjoyed a glorious sunrise on the deck while they gorged on fruit—mangos, mangosteen, sugar apples, guava and strange things with gooey seeds. Filipinos in sandals vied to share their fruit with the foreigner in shoes, as if he were the impartial judge in a contest of tribal tastes. Abdul observed Steve until the feeding frenzy subsided and then handed Steve some of his stinky little fish. He watched to make sure Steve ate them all without complaint.

By the time they docked, at three in the afternoon, they were starving again. They ordered fish and boiled rice at a small eatery near the pier in Iligan. While they waited for their food, Abdul borrowed Steve's cell phone and walked off to make some calls. When he returned, he whispered to Gerry before eating his meal in silence.

"What's going on?" Steve asked.

Gerry shrugged. "We wait here before taking jeepney to Marawi. Abdul will take the packages." Gerry pointed to Steve's rucksack.

"When do we go to the Marsh?"

Gerry shrugged again.

And so they had waited. Steve called Amina to report he had survived crossing the Bohol Sea in an angry storm and complained that they were still in Iligan waiting. She said delays are to be expected and then she asked how he was getting along with Abdul. He said okay, not mentioning that Abdul refused to speak to him except through Gerry.

The leader pulled the contents of Steve's rucksack out onto a rickety table leaning against the side of the checkpoint's shack. The other two soldiers gathered like kids around a Christmas tree. The leader frowned as he scrutinized a heavy, motorized body with zoom lens. Speaking in English in a helpful tone and moving slowly, Steve extracted the camera from his hands, took his picture and showed him the digital image. The other soldiers reveled. Although not as delighted as the others, the leader seemed satisfied. Steve took pictures of the soldiers, the guard shack and a couple of the jeepney. The soldiers thought it fun, but his fellow passengers became irritated over the delay.

Farther on, the MILF stopped them. Gerry said something and they ignored Steve. At the next checkpoint though, an army officer who spoke English took a keen interest in Steve and his cameras. Clearly, the officer did not believe Steve a tourist. He studied Steve's passport, twisting and turning it to decipher every blurry ink stamp in the dim light while the passengers in the jeepney fidgeted and grumbled. Unable to find evidence of malicious intent, the officer returned the passport and waved them on. As the jeepney pulled away, one of the passengers complained to Gerry that with his blond-haired friend riding along it would be daybreak before they got to Marawi. Without waiting for the translation, Steve pulled his black nylon jacket over his head and slouched like a tired old man. There were more checkpoints, whether army or MILF Steve could not see. They slowed to a crawl from time to time, but no one stopped them again.

Wrapped incognito in his cocoon, Steve fretted. They were to stay the night in Marawi City, the Islamic Capital of the Philippines, but Gerry could not or would not say where. What would happen in the morning, he did not know either. Steve had assumed they would be taking the C4 to the Liguasan Marsh but Abdul, after waiting hours for the motor-tricycle man, had slipped away with it in the night—destination unknown. Steve's vision of being a freelance photographer documenting the war for the Moro cause faded. Instead, he felt like he was back in the army, just a weary soldier awaiting further orders. And he stunk. Wherever they were going, they would not have terrycloth bathrobes and king-sized beds or even hot water. He hoped they had a shower. The jeepney hit a pothole, jolted and swayed. Steve peeked and saw lights in the distance.

"Are there more checkpoints?" Steve asked.

"That's all, already."

Steve eased the jacket off his head and looked around. They were speeding past dark pastures, some with shadowy stalks, corn perhaps or maybe cane, toward the lights. Soon they entered the outskirts, a jumbled clutter of low shabby buildings, which gradually became a story or two taller. The traffic congested, the pedestrians too—all men as far as Steve could tell—but the scraggly, uneven disarray of structures did not change. Disappointment weighed on him. He had expected the Philippine Capital of Islam would be splendorous with gilded domes shimmering atop majestic mosques and inscrutable signs in neat Arabic script, but instead the signs were scribbled in Tagalog, some with a line or two of misspelled English.

"Is *this* Marawi?" He asked.

Gerry blinked and looked around. "There," he said, pointing to a sprawling roof sheltering a confusion of vehicles and people. The open-sided terminal had a concave metallic roof supported by sturdy-looking columns of pipe, the roof's curve smooth and the uprights straight. It was jammed with transport vans and jeepneys parked under the eaves of the long sides. People scurried about in the wide central aisle between them. Two men stood outside staring at their jeepney. They gestured and nodded. One looked like Jiriki, but he was not he.

CHAPTER 39

Marawi City, Monday, February 17

Unfamiliar noises pulled Steve awake. They did not sound threatening. Still, he pretended to sleep while he tried to figure out where he was. *Children laughing and shouting.* That did not make sense. He could not recall ever sleeping in a place where children laughed, not even when he was a child. He listened. Boys with high-pitched voices shouting in a youthful dialect, some words familiar and the lilt unmistakable—*Maranao*. He opened one eye to reconnoiter.

Shit! Taiba House.

He rolled onto his back and noticed the rafters. He was in a small room in the attic of the Taiba clan's homestead, although all but two brothers had moved on. Turning, he saw the cot, rumpled but empty. *Gerry up and about, already.* He flipped away the sheet, sat on the edge of the bed and studied the cubical. It had been Amina's room, but he could find no trace of her. Musty odors had replaced her smell.

He pushed the shutter and propped it open. She had had a nice view of green grasses, some trees and fewer than a hundred yards beyond, Lake Lanao, although it looked more like the ocean than lake. On the far horizon, he saw the misty outline of hills, or perhaps clouds. Before Hypocor's regulatory dam had made her village uninhabitable, Amina had lived somewhere out there along the shores of the vast lake. He examined the clouds. In the afternoon, if a storm did not agitate the lake, Zab would take him to the remains of their birthplace, the place that had defined Amina. Steve felt an odd excitement, like a kid waking on Easter Sunday anticipating the hunt for colored eggs.

The night before, Daub and Zabiri, the two youngest of the Taiba brothers, had taken Steve and Gerry out of the cluttered city center to a residential area west of the Agus River. Off to the left, Steve could see the river's mouth, but not the bridge back into the city. Down below, three young boys kicked a soccer ball. They were no doubt all from the Taiba clan. Daub and Zab each had five children, and both their wives were pregnant again. The Maranao had large families. Amina had a zillion nieces and nephews, but no children of her own, not yet. Steve imagined her eggs colored brilliant with intricate filigree designs. Despite the clouds, he felt certain of a spectacular day.

The pump boat could have carried two dozen people, but Zab and Steve had chartered it for themselves. Steve felt relieved that Daub could not join them. Daub, a younger version of Jiriki in both appearance and attitude, was too severe for humor and although civil, Steve sensed that Daub abhorred his relationship with Amina. But Zab, the youngest brother, did not. Just thirteen months older than Amina, Zab could pass as her twin except for the eyes.

As children, they had been pals, partners in mischief, and anything Amina did was okay with Zab. Sitting on the bow of the boat, he told stories of their naughty childhood pranks. And they were still conspiring.

Zab poked Steve and grinned. "We will hit back soon."

"Hit back who?"

"Hypocor. They will cry in the wilderness." He laughed. "With your packages, we will put their lights out."

"I don't have them. Someone named Abdul took them."

Zab gave Steve a puzzled look. "You are unaware? Abdul Jamil is our brother, one of the twins."

Steve closed his eyes and shook his head. Now he understood why Abdul had been aloof and cold. In talking about her brothers, Amina had characterized Jamil as the brother who would never forgive her for shaming the family. Although his given name was Abdul Jamil, Amina called him Jamil with a harsh accent on the second syllable, as if it were the name of a bitter tea. *"Abdul will probably ignore you. He is in charge"—deceptive wench*, Steve thought. Jamil must have promised Amina he would not toss her infidel overboard—family hostilities suspended for the duration of the ticklish mission.

Ticklish family *mission—Amina, Jiriki, Jamil, Daub, Zab—Taiba clan versus Hypocor, Taiba clan plus one.*

Zab stood and squinted. "We are there almost."

While Zab talked with the captain, Steve scanned the shoreline. He could see scattered houses and huts on the hillside, but that was not their destination. They were heading toward a dried up marsh with a stark cement structure. The engine slowed, then idled. Jagged remains of walls poked out of the muck like tombstones, a cement building the only mausoleum in the weedy graveyard.

"What was that?" Steve asked.

"Our mosque."

Steve had noted the tiny dome, but had not thought such a humble building to be a place of worship—a cement roof with capstones and crenellations it's sole adornment. Grasses and weeds grew in cracks in the mortar, and in the corner of a decomposing windowsill, wildflowers. Then Steve spotted something. *There's the picture!*

"Can we go ashore?"

The captain lowered a small skiff. Zab and Steve paddled. After they landed, Steve stared at the wall of the mosque, which was twenty yards from the water. "Look, look at that." Steve pointed to the markings on the walls. "Those are watermarks. The mosque has been eight feet under water. There it is." He swept his hand from mosque to shoreline. "There's the picture that tells what the regulatory damn did to your village."

Zab eyed the wall. "When the rains were heavy, they closed the dam so the river would not rush. They drowned us. When it was dry, they drained from the lake to feed their river. Our rice and fish ponds died." He pointed to a rotted piling halfway between the mosque and the water. "See, there was the pier we used for ablutions."

Steve took pictures, panoramic views and close-ups. He shot Zab looking forlorn at the devastation and gazing at the clump of flowers on the windowsill, as though it were a wreath on a grave. He wished he had a little girl to pose, a young Moro about ten-years old, a tot with fierce black eyes. He would send her picture to Hypocor with a caption.

"Expect trouble."

CHAPTER 40

Taiba House, Tuesday Morning, February 18

Rat-ta-tat-ta-tat. The sound echoed over the lake. Steve and Gerry leapt out of bed. The shots came from below where the boys had been playing soccer the morning before. They looked outside. The cloudy sky, a shade lighter than night, hinted it would soon be daybreak. Men talking in Maranao approached the house, climbed the porch and went inside. Steve grasped enough of their conversation to guess their satisfaction with a weapon that apparently had not been used in a long time, but he hoped he misunderstood why they had tested it.

He whispered. "Did they say *rido?*"

"Yes, they prepare for trouble, already."

"Oh shit, a bloody family feud. What about?"

Gerry shrugged. "Land. Maranao always fight over land, fight Christians, fight Maguindanao, fight Maranao." He started getting dressed. "I will go ask. You stay. War is okay for you, but *rido* is family." Before leaving, Gerry paused and frowned. "You stay quiet. *Rido* is danger for you."

Steve lay back on the bed longing for a mug of espresso. Someone's *maratabat*, their pride and honor, had been offended. The clan would now gather to save face. The Maranao took their *maratabat* seriously, dead seriously. If not quickly resolved, the feud would erupt in killings and violence that might last a generation or longer, family against family, and every man in the Taiba clan would join in the defense of their honor, including Gerry, Steve's last slim hope for getting to the Liguasan Marsh.

The night before, Gerry had said, and Zab confirmed, the checkpoints on the way to Marawi were jokes compared to what they would encounter on the roads to Cotabato and the marsh. The delay at Iligan had been for a change in plans. They could not get the C4 past the army, nor an American with cameras either. Imperial Manila did not want foreigners photographing their treachery. Steve had insisted they try anyway and Gerry, wanting to join the battle, had been willing to help. Then Zab called Amina. Despite her vehement objections, Steve had thought he might still convince Gerry to take him. Now with *rido* stirring up the family, he wondered if he would get out of Marawi with his genitals intact.

By sleeping with him, Amina had shamed the family, no matter that she was a widow, no matter that they lived in a Christian community far from the Maranao traditions. The male takes the heat. If a love-struck boy defies tradition and elopes with a Maranao girl, the family would likely kill him to protect their *maratabat*. Amina had convinced Jamil to give him safe passage, else he would be floating in the Bohol Sea, and Daub had suppressed his resentment. But for sure, not all the family had agreed to a truce.

Steve thought Gerry was right about the danger of *rido*. The clan was amassing with weapons. The men would fight while wise and brave women of stature tried to mediate peace. Subaida, Amina's mother, would negotiate for the Taiba clan. Steve imagined what might happen when Subaida came around and discovered she had the infidel who was bonking her only daughter trapped in the attic of Taiba House.

Bryce, you best get your sweet ass out of town.

At the sound of a vehicle stopping, Steve rolled off the bed and looked out the window. An old truck had parked under a tree near the house. Three men got out. Two of them carried rifles. He took out his cell and punched his landline number.

"Mr. Bryce's house."

"Hi, Perla. Is Amina there?"

"Oh, Mr. Steve, just a minute, sir."

Outside, another vehicle stopped. Doors slammed, and then footfalls of men in a hurry.

"Good morning, Sweet Steve. How is life in Marawi?"

"Cloudy, literally and figuratively. How is the Uncle Max situation?"

"Ah…just a minute."

Steve listened and waited while Amina sent Perla on an errand.

"He came out early to jog around the compound and exercise. Now he's sitting on Brenda's porch. He's not writing. He hasn't left the compound since Sunday when Bipsy took him out to take pictures. Which reminds me, please call Bipsy and tell him to print Max's photograph."

"Okay. How's Perla doing?"

"She is fantastic. I'm getting fat. Listen, I'd like to move the office upstairs and Perla downstairs. I don't want her listening to us."

"Okay, that's a good idea. But you and Perla don't have to bust your butts moving furniture. I've got a surprise. Apex agreed to clear out the other spare bedroom and put in a desk. They should do it today or tomorrow. You'll have your own office. When they come with the desk, they can do the moving for you. I'll ask Bipsy to make sure they do."

"A desk for me—thank you, Sweet Steve. But what does Bipsy have to do with it?"

"Ah, he's handling it with Slick for me. Wait..." Still another car stopped outside. Steve watched an elderly woman walk briskly toward the house followed by someone who looked like another of the Taiba brothers. "Amina, I think your mother is here. The clan is gathering. There's trouble, *rido*."

"*Rido!* Shit."

Steve listened to the commotion downstairs. "It's your mother. I can hear the kids greeting their grandmother."

"What's the trouble? Who started this?"

More noise from below drew Steve to the window again. "I don't know. Gerry went to find out, but that was a couple of hours ago. We woke to gunshots, but they were just testing a weapon."

"Guns! Never have we used guns. We are on the defensive. We have offended someone. I have never seen our guns."

"I've seen three this—" Someone knocked. "Hang on, I think Gerry's back." Steve opened the door. Zab stepped in, frowning. Steve handed him the phone. "Talk to Amina."

While Zab spoke to Amina, another vehicle stopped in front of the house. Steve went to look out the window but Zab grabbed him. "You sit," he said. "Stay out of sight." The phone conversation continued and then Zab passed the cell to Steve.

"What's going on?" Steve asked.

"Someone raped one of my aunts."

"Then the offense is against your family."

"Yes, if it was rape and not an affair. But that's not the problem. My uncle cut off the man's testicles—"

"Sounds fair to me."

"…and fed them to his dog while the man watched."

Steve laughed. "That's *haram*, I suppose."

"*No joking Steve.* You have to get out of there. When there is an opportunity, Zab will sneak you out of the house. Go to the terminal and take the bus to Cagayan de Oro. You will have to fly to Manila first. There are no direct flights to Davao. Once you get out of Marawi, call me. Until then, I will be praying."

CHAPTER 41

Steve's house, Wednesday, February 19

Wednesday morning a squadron of workers from Apex Davao invaded Steve's house. They carted away the bunks from the unused upstairs bedroom, replaced them with a desk, chair and worktable, moved Perla's stuff downstairs and hauled the office up to the room that Perla had been using. Perla scurried after them, sweeping and mopping up the accumulated crud exposed by the displaced furniture. Julius followed her, watching her as if he were the Inspector General. Outside, technicians clamored up a ladder to connect the new offices to the internet, while Marty loitered around, his eyes darting from one laborer to the other as if he thought they might be planting a bomb. Amina, trying to be in three places at the same time, heard another truck enter the compound and then footfalls struggling up the outside stairs. She opened the kitchen door. Bipsy, sweating, stumbled in and placed an open carton on the kitchen counter.

"Whew! Where's wandering Blue Eyes? He owes me a case of beer."

"What's that?" Amina's eyes beamed. "Is that for me?"

Bipsy nodded. "It's a loan, courtesy of Apex, for as long as you need it."

Amina peered into the box. "Whoopee, my own computer."

"Complete with your wiggle squiggle scribbles." Bipsy reached in the box for an envelope and dug out a CD. He wagged it. "Arabic fonts, and…" he pulled out another envelope, "transparent Arabic stickers for the keyboard." He smiled. "Now you can go both ways."

"How? When?"

"Friday night, when Blue Eyes called and asked me to take Max on the photo shoot. We conspired to surprise you with these despicable and barefaced acts."

"Thank you, thank you. You guys are the greatest."

Bipsy pointed to another envelope in the box. "Those are Max's mug shots."

"Again, thank you."

"Okay, spill the beans. Where's Blue Eyes?"

"His plane lands at 12:30." Amina glanced at the kitchen clock. "Oh my, he'll be here in an hour."

Perla rushed into the kitchen, stopped short when she saw the computer, and then opened a cupboard. "Hello, Mr. Bipsy. Ma'am, the workers are almost finished. I'll be starting lunch now. Is seafood *pancit* okay? Is Mr. Gerrit coming? Is Mr. Steve on time?" She grabbed a pot and started filling it with water.

Amina laughed. "Let's see." She counted on her fingers. "First, good that the workers are done. Seafood *pancit* is perfect. Mr. Steve will arrive soon. Only

Isabela and Margreet are coming." She turned to Bipsy. "Can you stay for lunch?"

"With grave sadness, I must decline. Indeed, I must hustle to a meeting." He hefted the box with the computer. "Lead the way to your office. I'll set this up pronto."

By the time Steve traipsed through the gate, the workers had left, Bipsy too, Amina and Isabela had set the table, and Perla had almost finished preparing lunch. Amina hurried down the stairs to greet him on the front porch.

"For an escaped prisoner, you don't look so bad."

"Zab got me out without a scratch and the hotel in Cagayan de Oro had hot water, but my clothes stink."

"Sweet Steve, I'm going to show my deep felt gratitude for the computer and the office." With a naughty grin, she stroked the three-day stubble on his chin. "But you must shave first."

"Ah, it's good you moved Perla downstairs. I'm going to make you scream."

"We will have to wait. I invited Isabela for lunch. Gerrit couldn't make it."

Steve looked across to Brenda's porch. "Where are Brenda and Max?"

"Uncle Max just went back to Brenda's house. He was patrolling around here all morning watching the workers as if they were thieves. I didn't invite him. Brenda's in General Santos City today. She grasped his hand and led him several feet away from the door. "Last night, Brenda and I had a juicy conversation about Max. She said Haradji described Santana as being hung like a mule, which I understand to mean a monstrous lingam. Guess who fits that description?"

"Dear Uncle Max."

"And he's got scars all over his back. He told her he got them in Vietnam. He has a U.S. passport with the name Harris Maxwell, but she thinks he left it laying around hoping she would look at it. He has two suitcases, but one is unpacked and always locked."

"Did Bipsy print his picture?"

"Yes, he brought them a little while ago. Toots lives near Posey. I'll have Toots show Posey his pictures and ask if he was her lover."

Steve shook his head. "I think that would be a mistake. The guards report to Haradji and I don't want him involved in our business. Just tell Toots we want to talk to Posey. If Max is Santana, we'll deal with him ourselves."

Amina nodded. "I agree. We do not want that pervert nosing around. Okay." She pinched his shirt and wrinkled her nose. "Go change these smelly clothes. Let's have lunch."

"Que rico!" Isabela exclaimed for the third time. "Look at Margreet. Never has she eaten so much and she wants more noodles. Perla is an incredible cook, and she is so young."

"I think she started cooking when she was six." Amina raised her finger. "A *Maranao* woman taught her." She glanced at the time. "Oh, excuse me. It's almost time for imperial Manila to make a statement on the Liguasan invasion. I'll be downstairs watching TV. I don't want to miss a single lie."

Steve stood. "Come, Isabela. I'll take your plate. We can finish this downstairs."

They settled in front of the television just as President Gloria Macapagal Arroyo entered the State Dining Room in the Malacanang Palace. Eight days after the invasion, she had assembled the press corps to tell them about the successful military operations in Buliok, North Cotabato.

I'D LIKE TO COMMEND OUR ARMED FORCES FOR THEIR SHORT AND SWIFT OPERATION IN CAPTURING AND OCCUPYING THE BULIOK SANCTUARY IN THE LIGUASAN MARSH AREA. THIS HAS BEEN USED IN THE PAST SEVERAL YEARS BY THE PENTAGON KIDNAPPING GANG AND OTHER CRIMINAL GROUPS TO ESCAPE JUSTICE AND AS A LAUNCHING PAD FOR DESPICABLE ACTIVITIES.

A CRIMINAL LAIR HAS BEEN CLEANED UP AND WE ARE GOING FULL STEAM AHEAD IN RELIEF AND REHABILITATION OF THE AFFECTED COMMUNITIES. I'VE ORDERED THE SOCIAL WELFARE AND DEVELOPMENT DEPARTMENT TO ENSURE THE ORDERLY RETURN OF THE EVACUEES BACK TO THEIR HOMES AS OPERATIONS WIND DOWN. I'M SADDENED BY THE DISPLACEMENT OF PEACEFUL FAMILIES

FROM THEIR AREA, BUT SOMETIMES THIS IS THE PRICE WE HAVE TO PAY FOR LONG-TERM PEACE AND ORDER.

YESTERDAY, I ORDERED THREE OF MY CABINET MEMBERS TO PROCEED IMMEDIATELY TO THE LIGUASAN MARSH AREA. SECRETARIES DINKY SOLIMAN AND GING DELES WILL MAKE SURE THAT THE NEEDS OF THE RESIDENTS OF THE AREA, ESPECIALLY THE EVACUEES, ARE MET. THEY WILL RECOMMEND TO ME SHORT AND LONG TERM PLANS THAT WOULD ASSURE THE WELL-BEING AND LIVELIHOOD OF RESIDENTS OF THE AREA.

I'VE APPOINTED MY SECRETARY FOR THE PEACE PROCESS, SECRETARY ED ERMITA, TO BE MY ACTION OFFICER FOR MY COMPREHENSIVE PEACE AND DEVELOPMENT EFFORTS IN THE LIGUASAN MARSH AREA. I'VE INSTRUCTED HIM TO ACCELERATE TALKS WITH INVESTORS FROM THE MIDDLE EAST WHO ARE KEEN IN HELPING DEVELOP THIS FERTILE AREA.

THE LIGUASAN MARSH SHOULD BE TRANSFORMED FROM BANDIT LAIR INTO A PEACEFUL AND BUSTLING AGRICULTURAL COMMUNITY.

They listened in silence until the questions from the press corps began. Steve leaned forward with his forearms pressed against his thighs, waiting for someone to ask about the Pentagon Gang, but no one did. The questions seemed to be orchestrated prompts for Arroyo to brag. When asked about refugees, she deflected the question to the Social Welfare and Development Secretary.

The Honorable Corazon "Dinky" Juliano Soliman stepped forward to announce her department served 214,072 individuals from 40,163 families.

"Served, served what?" Steve exclaimed, "Eviction notices, subpoenas, band aids? Sounds like a census. What did she do, trip them while they ran so she could count heads?"

Another reporter asked about casualties. An army spokesman said they lost six soldiers, but killed 157 rebels. As he watched the choreographed farce, Steve's incredulity percolated up and brewed a pot of rage.

"I can't believe this. She displaces hundreds of thousands of people, ruins their livelihood and boasts about putting them on welfare. Then her what, her *comprehensive* peace plan, what the fuck's a *comprehensive* peace plan? One that's as democratic as a bomb. And those pansy-assed reporters let her get away with it. Pentagon Gang my butt. She admits it." He pointed at the TV screen. "She admits she invaded the marsh to clear out the people for foreign investors." He turned. "Look, look at Margreet scowl. The president of the nation just insulted her intelligence."

"No, Steve," Isabela said. "She scowls because she does not approve of shouting and foul language. But you are right. Arroyo mocks the intelligence of a half-witted *cretino*."

Amina sat quietly on the floor with her back against the sofa. When President Arroyo left, she muted the TV yet continued to stare at it. Steve leaned forward to look at her eyes. They were watery and their light had faded. The set of her jaw frightened him. It spoke not of anger, but despair.

"Tigress," he said.

She spoke to the TV. "They have won. We cannot save ourselves. We will become extinct like the birds and fishes when they built the dam. We will mutate into some ignorant Filipino subspecies." She dropped the remote and held her head. "We are too poor to educate ourselves. They drive us away and take our land. The land belongs to Allah. We failed Him." Her voice softened to a murmur. "They have it now. They have plundered us…pride is gone. We lost."

She covered her face with her hands, tightened into herself and wept. Steve rested his hand on her shoulder. Isabela hefted Margreet and shifted to soothe Amina's hair. Margreet reached out with her little hand, as if to console desperation.

CHAPTER 42

The compound, Thursday morning, February 20

Brenda scrambled eggs while Marty set the table. He looked up when he heard the metal door beside the gate open. He did not recognize her at first, and then his stomach riled when he spotted Posey's distinctive gait. *Stupid bitch*, he thought.

The early morning visitor caught Isabela's attention too. "*¿Qué es esto?* Gerrit, look, that's Posey."

Gerrit stood up from the breakfast table and peered out the window. "She's dressed like a peacock but walks like a duck. Her girdle's too tight."

"That's got to be a brand-new outfit. Look at her hair. Please finish feeding Margreet. I'm going next door."

As Perla came down the stairs with a tray of coffee for Isabela and the visitor, she spotted the photographs on the coffee table that Steve hurriedly turned over. He was not quick enough. She caught a glimpse of Max. As she set the tray on the table, she glanced at the stranger, sitting stiff and looking nervous.

"Would you like anything else, ma'am?"

"No thank you, Perla."

After Perla went back upstairs, Steve picked up the photographs. "Posey, are you certain this is not the man?"

Posey clasped her hands in her lap and pressed them against her groin. She stared at her hands with tight lips and shook her head.

"Does that mean no, you're not certain or no it's not the man you let into my house?"

Posey shook her head again. "I'm sorry for what I done."

Amina took one of the photographs from Steve and held it just above Posey's clenched hands. "Look at the picture. Speak to me. Have you ever seen this man before?"

"No ma'am."

Steve looked at Amina. Her expression told him she had nothing more to say. He took twenty pesos from his wallet. "Thank you for coming, Posey. This is for your transportation."

Posey seemed on the verge of crying. "I didn't mean to do you harm." She stood, took the money and turned to leave.

"Posey," Steve asked. "Do you have a new job?"

She shook her head and looked at him hopefully.

"Good luck, then."

"That was a waste of time," Steve said after Posey had left.

"Steve, what's this about?" Isabela asked.

"Because of some coincidences in Cebu, we've been wondering if Max could be Marty Santana, the burglar. Max fits what little description we have, but lots of people do. Then Brenda said he's hung like a mule and has scars he says he got in Vietnam. But Posey is the only one who can identify him. You saw." He held up the photograph. "She says Max is not the man, but I'm not convinced."

"She denied it," Isabela said.

"Yes, she did," Steve said, "but her face flushed a bit when she first looked at the photograph—a woman scorned, perhaps. And that could be her outfit for special occasions, maybe she was hoping to get her job back, but her hair looks like she's been to the beauty parlor. If you're poor and don't have a job, you don't go to the beauty parlor. I suspect Posey may have recently acquired a substantial amount of money—hush money."

"If Max is Santana," Isabela asked, "then who is Perla?"

"Perla is a blessing," Amina said. "This place has never been so clean, and she's a fabulous cook. I checked on her. She's a young woman who had been working at a department store in Cebu for nearly two years. She is determined to go to the university and Max promised to help her. Whoever Max is, he is quite proud of Perla. You can see it in his face every time he looks at her. He is going to help put Perla through the university, and for that, she'll not rat on him. If Max is Santana, Perla would never tell us."

Steve sighed and looked at Amina. "Posey's the only one who can ID him. Should we give Haradji the photos and let him work her over?"

"No, let's leave that degenerate out of this."

"Posey's not the only one who knows the burglar," Isabela said. Steve and Amina gave her puzzled looks. "Julius witnessed the burglary." She looked at Amina. "Remember Saturday, when Max got out of the taxi and Julius started yowling. You thought him complaining about your absence. Maybe he was trying to tell you something."

Steve smiled. "I should have let Julius interrogate Posey. He frightens her."

Isabela stood. "I have to get back to the house so Gerrit can go to work. See you later."

As Steve and Amina walked Isabela to the front door, Steve stopped short. "Jalapeno peppers! Haradji said Santana does some sexual thing with jalapeno peppers. I'll tell Brenda to buy some and see if Max gets kinky." He grinned. Amina looked at Isabela. They both snickered.

Perla tiptoed into the kitchen from her listening post near the top of the stairs and started washing dishes. *Sammy Fuentes, Uncle Max, and now Marty Santana.* She giggled.

CHAPTER 43

Brenda's house, Friday, February 21

During the first hours of Friday, while Brenda slept, Marty sent an encrypted email to Beacon. He reported the good news and the bad. He was shacked up inside the compound, but Posey, instead of getting out of town, had effectively given him up. The residents suspected he might be Santana, but weren't certain enough to confront him. He asked for information on Haradji, or Haraji, who he described as some type of investigator in Davao who Bracelets called a degenerate. Finally, he asked Nadine to call him at ten; he could not take the scheduled call on Saturday because Brenda would be home.

Within several seconds of 10:00 o'clock, Marty's cell phone rang. He and Nadine went through the preliminaries.

"Congratulations, Leash. Incredible, you are inside compound."

"It might not last long. I'm hoping that when they throw me out, I can convince them to keep Perla. But I don't think they're going to turn me over to this Haraji guy. Do you know who he is?"

"Umar Haradji—that is with 'd.' For years, he informed for NBI. He is too outdated for them now. He handles security for Apex Davao. Also handles thugs who kill drug dealers and other criminals to clean up city for mayor. Bracelets has him in her database. He has bomb experience. If necessary, liquidate him, but make damn sure looks like work of hoods. You do not want mayor after you."

"I understand."

"Any threats to Bracelets?"

Marty got up and looked out the window at Steve's house. "Her brother visited on Monday. Perla understood some of what they said, and from their tone and body language, her sense is he told Bracelets he is worried about her safety, but instead of being concerned, Bracelets got pissed off.

"Bracelets has not left the compound since we've been here. Bryce returned Wednesday. He and Perla do the shopping, and they act as couriers. Bracelets sent Perla to a Moro butcher with a note written in Arabic script. When he gave her the meat, he passed her another wrapped package. It contained papers—input for Bracelets' files, I'm sure. She has her own computer now, an old desktop, and an office upstairs. If she ever leaves the house, I'll copy her files."

"What about Bryce? Where was he?"

"From what Perla heard, we think he delivered the missing C4 to Bracelets' family in Marawi City, maybe to sabotage an electrical company. That's conjecture, but probably close enough. I'll try to use that to keep him from going to the authorities if he decides I'm Santana. For sure, he intended to go somewhere else from Marawi but aborted because of a family problem, which could be the threat to Bracelets that prompted her brother's visit." Marty turned from the window and tried not to sound anxious. "By the way, Perla says Steve is fluent in Tagalog, is learning Maranao and may speak Thai. He's on vacation now, but his job takes him to Thailand, Indonesia and Sri Lanka."

"He is looking more and more like our kind of guy. Find out what you can. Maybe we can use him."

"Okay." Marty grinned at what he had hoped to hear. If he could recruit Bryce, he could quit being a bodyguard and retire. "I'll be his new best friend."

"How safe is compound?"

Marty chuckled and went to the window again. "Well, since I broke in, they put concertina wire on the wall. They did a good job." He peered at two workmen near the gate. "The wire contains a low voltage circuit. If it's cut, an alarm sounds in the guard shack. They're testing it as we speak. And the guards now patrol the compound on an unpredictable schedule. If they throw me out, I'm going to have a tough time getting back in."

"Leash, you are right. Bryce is not going to turn you in for stealing hard drive. You know too much."

"Too much what," Marty snapped. "I don't even know what was on the hard drive."

"Because you did not need to know, but now you do. For long time, spooks listen to her brother Jiriki as person of interest. They learn he is collecting information on ties between MILF and Abu Sayyaf, but information is for sister. Packages of documents for

Amina Taiba arrive at boyfriend's house once,
sometimes twice week. They suspect she uses computer
for data, so you snatch it. We learned she is collecting
much more than connections to Abu Sayyaf. She has
profiles of suspicious characters and details of bombings
in sophisticated databases. She is trying to identify
saboteurs, probably to prove they are not MILF. We
think she is correct. It appears powerful interests hire
saboteurs to implicate MILF so President will declare
them terrorists and they can take Moro lands. These
people fear she will expose them. We fear they will kill
her.

"We think Bracelets is desperate to know who took
her files but not just databases. One of her files outlines
strategy for MILF negotiations with Philippine
government. It could be official, or it could be her
invention. It is hard to imagine how she got it, but if it is
authentic, she must be frantic. We sold databases, but
not negotiation strategy. That is valuable currency in
Philippines.

"If they confront you, tell her databases have kept
President from declaring MILF terrorist group. That is
true. U.S. wants to believe MILF is cleaning house.
Without enough resources to manage adventures in
Middle East, President does not want another front in
Asia, not yet.

"Tell her your job is to protect her and that if she
throws you out of compound, The House sells MILF
strategy to Manila. If she kicks you out, we know
document is phony. If she keeps you, we confirm
document is legitimate."

Marty paced, bobbing his head. "I like it. Bracelets is not going to forgive me for that mess with her uncle, and she'll expect me to steal her files again, but if that document is legit, she'll let Perla stay and me too. Whip, about Perla. If something happens to me, I want to be sure she gets the fifteen grand."

After a silence, Nadine said, "Leash, you are infatuated with this girl. It will affect your judgment."

"I made a deal," Marty snapped.

"Okay, set up account for her and send Beacon particulars. We will make transfer if something goes wrong. But Marty…take care. Our Last Hurrah. I have decided. I too am going to quit."

Marty stopped pacing and stared out the window. "Maybe that's why I've got the jitters. Quitting is scary. What happens then?"

"Ciao, Marty."

"Ciao, Nadine"

CHAPTER 44

Davao, Saturday, February 22

Early Saturday morning, Brenda hustled over to the Van Der Zee house and interrupted their breakfast. "Hey, have you guys made plans for tomorrow?"

"Not yet," Gerrit said.

"Let's see if we can rent the *banca* boat and go out to that little island in the gulf. Max wants to go."

Isabela looked at Gerrit. "Yes, let's go. It's been two months since we've gone out there. Call your banca man and see if he can take us tomorrow."

Gerrit stood. "Princess Isabela summons her chariot, she has."

After Gerrit left, Isabela asked, "How's it going with Uncle Max?"

"Oh, I don't know. He seems preoccupied. Whenever the gate opens or there is some noise outside, he jumps up to see what is going on, and he's a nut about staying in shape. If he's a freelance writer, he writes when I'm not around. He acts more like a boxer preparing for a fight. Besides eating and sex, the only thing we do together is exercise. He seems afraid to leave the compound. But when I told him about us all picnicking, he became enthusiastic. Maybe we can get him to loosen up."

"Is the sex still good?"

Brenda beamed. "That's his good part. Old Max has the body of an athlete and the libido of a teenager. He's rough, but I like it. He busted my butt, took my virginity, and damn, I like that too."

"Did he do anything with the jalapeno peppers?"

"Yipes, I haven't had a chance to buy them yet."

Gerrit came up the stairs. "Okay, the banca will take us out to the island at eight in the morning and will come back for us around four. Brenda, have you talked to Steve and Amina yet?"

"No, I'll go see them now. I'll be right back. Isabela and I have to go grocery shopping for the picnic. We need jalapeno peppers."

"You'll have to take Margreet with you. I'm going to work."

When Steve and Amina told Brenda they would not be going on the picnic but that Perla should go, Perla said she had to talk with her uncle first. She went next door and soon returned with Marty, who appeared concerned.

"Say Steve, I thought we'd all be going. I was hoping you'd give me some tips on picture taking. Why don't you and Amina come? Maybe Bipsy can join us."

Steve looked at Amina. "No, we've a lot to do here in the house. Amina wants to enjoy her new office."

"So you'll not be leaving the compound at all tomorrow?"

Steve, Amina and Brenda looked at Marty. Only Perla did not seem to think the question odd. "No, we'll be right here," Steve said.

"Max, you should go into town and get fins and snorkels for Perla and yourself," Brenda said. "The best part of the island is the coral. Oh, Gerrit went to the office and I'm going shopping with Isabela. Steve, can Max borrow your truck?"

"Sure. I know a good sporting goods store. I'll draw you a map. They sell disposable underwater cameras too. You should get one. The tropical fish are incredible."

As Marty and Perla drove out of the compound Perla said, "Uncle Max, while we're out, I need to buy Amina a present. Next Saturday is her birthday."

"I'll get her something too, or maybe we can get something from both of us. You have any ideas?"

"It's hard to figure. She doesn't use perfume or cosmetics except for hand cream. She refuses to wear any jewelry except for those bracelets. Her father gave them to her when she was a little girl, or some like them. She has two pairs of similar ones. Steve's going to give her clothes. I want to get her something really nice. I like her."

Marty pulled into the shopping mall, locked the truck and they started walking to the sporting goods store. "Perla, I'm setting up a numbered bank account for you in Singapore. I'll show you how to use it. If something happens to me, they'll wire your money to that account."

Perla stopped walking. "You expecting trouble?"

"Nah," he flapped his hand. "It's just that with all this rent paying, at my age, I'm liable to have a heart attack."

Perla laughed.

After they bought snorkels, fins and two disposable cameras, Marty pointed to a computer store. "Let's go in there."

While Marty talked with the salesman, Perla wandered around the store. She stopped to look at LCD screens. They had a promotion on a small one. Marty walked over. "What are you looking at?"

"Look at the price on this screen. Let's get one for Amina. She's using a dim old monitor. Hmmm, let's see, I'll pay twenty-five percent."

"Like hell, we'll go fifty-fifty. By the way, when's your birthday?"

"On August the fifteenth I'll be twenty-four."

"Well, in case I miss your party, happy birthday." He handed her an empty canvas computer bag.

Perla looked at the bag. It had the store's name and logo printed on it. "Thank you, Max. This'll make a nice book bag when I begin my studies."

"Oh, that's a gift from the store, and it's not for books. See that nice man over there." He pointed to the salesman he had been talking to. "He's got something for you to put in it."

Perla saw the salesman grinning at her, and then she saw the laptop computer on the counter in front of him. "Oh, your kidding, Omigod!" She covered her mouth with her hand, her eyes widened as she walked slowly toward the computer. "Omigod, Uncle Max." When she reached the counter, she turned and gave Marty a look he would always remember—the only time he would see her cry.

After Marty returned to the compound, he opened Brenda's refrigerator to get a beer. He spotted the jar of jalapeno peppers—whole peppers—the kind he liked. He ignored them.

CHAPTER 45

Steve's house, Sunday morning, February 23

Naked except for light gray sports briefs, Steve sipped espresso by the upstairs window and watched the picnickers leave. They had loaded Gerrit and Brenda's trucks with towels, blankets, coolers, snorkeling gear, toys and floaters for Margreet and a hefty basket stuffed with food. The main course for lunch would be *escabeche*, a fish dish that did not have to be heated to be tasty. Isabela and Perla had each made their secret recipes. They had left generous portions of both for Steve and Amina to judge whether the Peruvian or Filipina version was better, but without revealing which was which. Gerrit's opinion would not count because he would know Isabela's cooking, but Uncle Max could vote, Perla had said. Steve wondered about that. Toots pushed the gate closed and the compound settled down for its day of rest. In the quiet, Steve heard the echo of Amina's despair that had haunted him for days.

The land belongs to Allah. We failed Him.

"Home alone."

Startled, he turned. Amina, holding a cup of tea, was curling into his overstuffed chair with a mischievous smile. She wore a *malong* tied provocatively, and as she tucked her bare feet against her bottom, she let him glimpse her thighs. He imagined the beauty of her nakedness under there, no underwear. Blood surged to his groin. She was feeling frisky for the first time since Arroyo's speech. He adjusted his sudden bulge.

"Feeling better today?"

She smiled, sipped her tea and nodded. "I'm ready for a date."

"No more despair?"

She pursed her lips. "Oh, sometimes it seems hopeless, but the only choice is to struggle on."

He sat on the floor and leaned his back against the wall where he could watch the *malong* as they talked. From first sight, his long, sleek swimmer's muscles had turned her on. Certain of mutual lust, they would distract themselves with conversation interrupted by lewd looking and lascivious thoughts, knowing that the more they prolonged the foreplay the more insatiable their fucking would be.

"In the Benedictine military school, I had to take courses in theology. I learned that celibacy for priests, birth control, abstinence and more are strictures contrived by the Pope and his henchmen, and if you don't do as they say you must feel guilty, confess and repent. I decided priests and monks are not soldiers of God but policemen for a gigantic mind-control organization that has nothing to do with spirituality. I shucked my Catholic guilt and forgot about God. But when you said the land belongs to Allah and we failed him, I understood. God or Allah loaned us this world and we're trampling the flowers. I'm going to take pictures and take down names, expose the bastards who plunder the land."

She smiled. "My Sweet Steve, you *are* a romantic." They gazed at one another in silence. His erection returned. She watched his thumb stroke the front of his briefs. "I'm going to be sinful and have a beer. Do you want one?"

"Great idea. Home alone, we can be drunken dissidents today."

He watched the *malong* caress her fanny as she strolled to the kitchen and thought about how passionate and demanding she would be after a beer. When she handed him the bottle, she stooped for a wet kiss and fondling before returning to her chair.

"What's the news from Taiba House? Have they settled the *rido*?

She sipped her beer as if it were wine. "Ah, I like the taste of this stuff. No, it is much too early for a settlement. It would be bad manners to reconcile quickly, as if the matter were not serious. But there is a truce. They have agreed not to use weapons. It seems everyone accepts that it was not consensual, it was rape, and as you said, the mutilation is a reasonable response. But the dog thing...well, that was disrespectful, I suppose. For now, my mother has the situation under control."

"The way your mother walked into the house made me believe she's a tough character." Amina's face clouded and her posture closed. She did not want to talk about his visit to Taiba House.

"Tigress, when did you decide to go to Cebu?"

She shook her head. "I didn't decide. They told me that Friday afternoon after my flight returned to Manila."

"So you knew nothing before then?"

"During the conference, they mentioned I might be needed and asked about my plans for the next few days. I assumed they wanted me to do some legal research before leaving Manila. But I heard nothing more until shortly after I called you on Friday. That is when I learned about my cousin and the C4."

"So it wasn't Jiriki who created the ticklish family mission. The MILF had been planning the operation for at least a week before you knew about it."

Amina nodded. "It seems so. The key was for Jiriki to abduct my cousin without the Abu Sayyaf knowing we had him. They got him Friday sometime."

Steve gulped some beer. "Okay. Max might be Marty Santana, but he looks more like a CIA rascal as you suspected from the beginning. Let's suppose the CIA has an informant in the MILF or Abu Sayyaf and they learn about Zorro and the C4. They send Max to watch your uncle. When you and Nashita visit him, you become persons of interest. Then Perla sees us together at the department store and I too become a person of interest. When Max spots us at Pasigan Beach after the explosion, he ingratiates himself and I like a fool go along thinking he could be Santana. He's here to watch us."

Amina stiffened. "You are not a fool. I think your first suspicion is the correct one. Okay, he's probably CIA but you did right to hire Perla. If he is Santana, he knows who has my files and I have to learn who that is. I had more than those databases. We face constitutional issues that complicate the negotiations. My work involved legal research on those issues and a bargaining strategy to frustrate those who intend to make autonomy dependent upon a constitutional referendum. If imperial Manila has my files, the MILF must reconstruct its negotiating strategy."

"Is it possible they took the hard drive to get the strategy?"

She shook her head. "No. Only Nashita knew I had it, and no one would believe a woman would have such a document. But many people knew about the databases."

Steve thought for a few moments. "It's an interesting situation, isn't it? The United States wants to reestablish military bases in the Philippines for a possible confrontation with China, but the Philippine constitution precludes that. With an autonomous region, the MILF could authorize the bases independent of the constitution. If Max stole your files for the CIA, then we can be certain they won't give the negotiation strategy to anyone opposing autonomy."

"I agree."

"We can't wait longer. Already a week has passed and we don't know if Max is Santana. Our chat with Posey was too civilized. I'm going to interrogate her again, but not here, not with Perla around. That's another issue. What do you think about Perla?"

Amina sipped some beer as she raked her eyes over his torso to stare at his crotch. He massaged it to a generous size while he watched her forefinger twiddle the fabric of the *malong* between her thighs. Mouths open, they panted as they taunted one another. By the time Amina withdrew her finger, Steve's light gray briefs had a very dark spot.

"Two people at the department store said she had been working there for nearly two years, and confirmed that her mother had died of cancer a few months ago. She had never mentioned an uncle to the people I talked to, and they assumed her father was a Filipino. She rarely mentioned her father, and never kindly, although you'd think she'd say he was an American if he were. I can't fit Perla into any of this except that maybe she *is* his niece. Look at the computer he bought her. That thing is expensive."

Steve laughed. "You like her cooking. I think he planted Perla for her to steal your files again."

"No, if he took the files, he knows they're not finished. Planting Perla to take them doesn't make sense to me. He'd wait until he thinks I'm done and come over the wall again."

Steve flipped his thumb at the window. "It's going to be tough with that concertina wire."

"If Max is Santana, we should thank him for improving security."

"Do you believe what Jiriki said, that someone wants to kill you?"

She frowned. "That's why he wanted all my stuff. He wants me to quit the project and disappear. When he came last Monday, he insisted I leave, leave with him right then before you returned, as if you were holding me against my will. I thought that your being in Marawi stirred up the family and they put more pressure on Jiriki to break us apart. That angered me. But what if there is a credible threat? The databases are about renegades who make bombs. If the threat is real, I endanger anyone near me, you and the others in the compound, including Margreet." She raised her finger for emphasis. "If it is true, I must disappear, but I'll not quit the project."

"But you will not disappear from *me*." He looked hard at her. "Not from *me*, will you?"

She gulped her beer, slipped out of the chair and moved toward him. The alcohol had flushed her skin and her eyes glittered with carnal urgency.

CHAPTER 46

Steve's house, Sunday evening, February 23

The picnickers returned around five. Perla slid open the front door and greeted Steve and Amina, who were curled on the sofa watching TV. As Brenda handed Perla towels, clothes, food containers, a plastic bag of trash and snorkeling gear, Perla piled them inside the front door. She talked non-stop.

"We had a wonderful time. We went to this little island with a sandy beach and the water was so clear with zillions of colorful fish and corals and stuff. Uncle Max taught me how to snorkel properly and with the fins, I could go down really deep. Imagine, we had the whole Island just for ourselves. No one lives out there. It was pristine, *pristine* I tell you. After lunch, wasn't it great, we all went skinny dipping just to be naughty. Swimming naked is *sooo* nice. God, I wish I had Brenda's boobs and Isabela's butt, she's got two dimples up here on her behind." Perla turned around and used her index fingers to show them the secret of Isabela's dimples. "Ohhhh," she moaned, spinning back around, "it was fabulous. Thank you so very much for letting me go. How did you like lunch? Which one was tastier?"

"Split decision," Steve said, smiling at her exuberance.

"Yeah, Brenda and Max pulled the same stunt. Can't ever get the truth out of polite people. Anyway, I'll put this stuff away, take a shower and cook you guys something for supper." She rushed off to the laundry room with the towels before Steve could tell her that it was her day off.

Brenda stepped inside and jabbed her forefinger at the ceiling. "We need to talk."

Steve and Amina followed Brenda up the stairs. Brenda touched Steve's arm. "That paper with the strange stain you found after the burglary, do you still have it?"

Steve thought for a moment. "Yes."

"Good, please get it."

Steve went to his office and returned with a manila envelope. He pulled out several sheets of yellow legal paper and placed them on the dining room table. The top sheet, scribbled with absurd ideas on how he had hoped to convince Amina's family to accept him, had a splattered stain. Brenda took a doubled-over napkin out of her pocket, unfolded it and placed it beside the sheet of paper. The napkin had a similar stain. Steve looked from the napkin to the legal paper and back again. He grazed the tips of his fingers over the napkin. The blotch was not oily. "Where did this come from?"

Brenda sat down. "I took a jar of jalapeno peppers to the picnic. During lunch, I opened the jar and asked Max if he wanted one. He reached for the jar, hesitated, and then said he'd try one. He picked up this napkin and plucked a pepper from the jar. He ate it like this."

Brenda held the napkin under her chin while pinching the stem of an imaginary pepper between her thumb and forefinger. She stuck the pepper in her mouth and snapped her teeth shut, but kept her lips open. "He bit the pepper off its stem and splattered a little juice on the napkin. I suppose I gave him a curious look. He explained the trick was not to let the seeds touch the lips. That's what really burns, he said."

Steve touched his mouth with his fingers, then slid them down over his chin and pulled on the skin of his neck. "Santana," he said.

"I know it's circumstantial, but—."

"It's enough for me," Steve interrupted. "Let's take these next door," he pointed to the Van Der Zee's house. "Tigress, he took the hard drive. I've no doubts at all now. Let's find out who has your files. You lead the discussion and I'll observe for follow up questions. Then we'll talk to Perla and find out what she's doing here."

Marty was relaxing after having showered when Brenda called and asked him to please come over to Gerrit's house. When he slid open the door, he saw that everyone had gathered in the living room except Perla. Steve, Brenda and Isabela, holding Margreet, sat on the couch, their faces cheerless. Gerrit, looking as serious as a pissed-off cop, leaned against the wall. Amina stood beside a chair at the far end of the coffee table. A black scarf draped her hair, the ends dangling over her long-sleeved blouse. She had turned back the cuffs, exposing the pastel-colored bracelets. An empty chair at the other end of the coffee table, the hot seat, awaited him. On the table, he saw a napkin and a yellow sheet of paper. He glanced at somber faces and nodded.

"Please sit down," Amina said, gesturing to the empty chair. "Would you like something to drink?"

"No thank you." By the time he sat down, he had figured the paper and napkin. He could not help but to smile at them.

Amina sat. "Mr. Santana, tell us who has my files and why you have Perla in our home."

When she sat at Zorro's table, he had not seen her eyes. They were fierce now. Bracelets would be as tough an interrogator as she was a negotiator. "I stole the hard drive for a private company that does odd jobs for government organizations. That company sold *some,*" he wagged a finger, "but not all of your files to the United States government. They have your databases. I was told that your database, or more precisely, the fact that you are creating it, is a major factor in the President's decision not to declare the MILF a terrorist organization."

Isabela gasped; Bracelets did not even blink. "This company, where is it located? Who are their customers? Who do you represent?"

Marty shrugged. "I don't know, and I've worked for them for thirty years. I have an email address and a phone number. I know one person, my controller. I've heard the voices of a few other persons who maintain a 24-hour hotline. I do not know where these people are, although I presume their headquarters is in the United States. I have no badge, no credentials and no authority. I am deniable."

"This is a for-profit private organization employed by the American Government?"

Marty shifted in his chair. "I think so. Everything they have asked me to do seems favorable to the interests of the United States. But the company must have contacts with other governments, either directly or through the Americans."

"What were you doing at the Pasigan Beach Resort?"

Marty caught Steve's sharp glance at Bracelets and then at him and understood Steve did not want to discuss the Pasigan in front of the others. "That was another project not related to your files."

Amina nodded. "Very well. Tell me about Perla."

"I was told to keep you safe. It appears someone wants to kill you."

Amina did not flinch. Marty looked at the others. Gerrit had pushed away from the wall and stiffened. Isabela clutched Margreet. Brenda looked frightened. Steve scrutinized him like a doctor looking for symptoms, his gaze steady even when Bracelets glanced at him. He gave her the slightest of nods.

"Go on, Mr. Santana," Amina said.

Marty thought for a moment and chose his words. "If I wanted to kill you, I would first determine your routine. Knowing your routine, I could predict when you are vulnerable. To keep you safe, I need the same information. Perla is an observant young woman. She seems to have a near photographic memory. She knows what brand of hand cream you use, and can predict when you will use it. You put a dab about this size…" Marty made a small circle with his thumb and forefinger. "You put it in your left hand. Before you rub in the cream, you screw the top on the bottle with your right hand." Marty mimicked her actions.

"Does your agency know who wants to kill me?"

"Not yet. When they find out...." Marty expected Bracelets and Steve would guess the rest, or ask, but they gazed at him without expression, waiting. He admired them. He had said someone wanted her dead and neither had twitched—no hint as to what they might be thinking.

They sat in silence until Amina asked, "Is Perla your niece?"

"No, I met her, ah...let's see, about two weeks ago. She knows nothing other than what she observes and that my job is to keep you safe. She is in my employ to assist me in protecting you. She does not know about the company I work for and she doesn't ask questions. We both like that arrangement."

"The computer is payment for her services?"

Marty shook his head. "No, that's a gift."

"You met her two weeks ago and give her a two-thousand dollar computer?"

Marty shut his eyes. After a few moments, he spoke softly. "I've been trying to figure that out too."

The room was silent. Marty opened his eyes. Amina looked at Steve.

"One final question," he said. "Do you have any children or relatives?"

Marty shook his head. "I was an orphan. They told me Marty Santana was my name. I grew up alone, and kept it that way."

Steve nodded at Amina.

"You have been forthright, Mr. Santana. We appreciate that. We will discuss this matter amongst ourselves and inform you how we will proceed."

"Miss Taiba, I would like to remain here. My job is to protect you. You are my final assignment, my Last Hurrah."

"So you can steal my files again? I don't think so."

Marty pursed his lips. "Why don't you just give them to me from time to time? I'll get a bonus for being clever, and you, the MILF I mean, can tell the President of the United States whatever you want."

Gerrit laughed, Brenda chuckled and Steve grinned. Isabela said, "Bravo!" Bracelets just smiled, but Marty sensed she liked the idea and from Steve's devious smirk, Marty figured he had been thinking about doing just that.

Amina stood. "Thank you, Mr. Santana."

"Miss Taiba, may I speak to you in private for a moment before you discuss this matter with your friends."

Amina gestured to the front door and they walked outside.

Steve looked at Gerrit. "Can I get a beer?"

"There's some in the cooler on the kitchen floor. Wait, I'll go with you. We'll bring the cooler down here."

Margreet was sound asleep. Isabela stood and handed her to Brenda. "I'm going for *chicha*. Do you want red or white wine?"

"Red, please. Bring the bottle. This might be a long night."

Amina came in. She looked in the cooler, took out a bottle of water and drank quite a lot. "Okay guys, tomorrow I'm moving to Jiriki's house. When my brother insisted I was in danger, I thought he had another agenda. But when the President of the World sends over a bodyguard, there's no doubt. I'm endangering you."

Isabela set a tray with a bottle of wine, pitcher of *chicha* and glasses on the coffee table. She took Margreet from Brenda.

"This compound is a fortress," Steve said. "I say you stay here and let Marty Santana do his job." He looked at the front door. "Where did he go?"

"He went to Brenda's house to get something, a gun I think. Said he'd be walking the perimeter if we needed him. I wondered why he jogged several times a day instead of doing it all at once. Now we know." She drank more water and sighed. "He is relieved this is out in the open. So am I."

Brenda watched Isabela study Gerrit's face and then look at Margreet. Isabela hefted Margreet and pressed her cheek against her child's head. She closed her eyes.

"Steve, you may be right," Brenda said. "But this is for Isabela and Gerrit to decide. I vote with them."

Gerrit tipped his beer bottle toward Amina. "Do you have any idea who wants to kill you?"

"We are trying to identify saboteurs who plant bombs and try to blame the MILF for their treachery. Whoever hires the saboteurs is trying to frighten us into abandoning the project, and it seems they have chosen me as their target." She smiled. "They encourage me. They fear we will succeed."

"But do you know who they are?" Brenda asked.

Amina grinned and shuddered with excitement. "We must have them. I have many names in my database, like a fisherman with a heavy net. We must sort out the trash fish, but we now know that we snared some big ones. I am going to go into hiding and see what we have caught."

"You cannot go to your brother's house," Isabela said. "It is not safe there, not like here in the compound with walls and guards and electrified barbed wire." She kissed the top of Margreet's head and looked at her husband. "Isabela is my best girlfriend."

Gerrit considered his wife for a few moments before raising his bottle. "We say Amina stays...and Uncle Max too."

Isabela lifted Margreet off her shoulder and laid her in her lap. Margreet woke, yawned and stretched her little arms. Isabela laughed and tickled Margreet's belly. "Viva los Moros, aye."

Amina shook her head. "Thank you. You are all dear friends. But I must leave you. I'll stay only until Jiriki can arrange for my disappearance. I cannot hide in your homes. I cannot endanger you."

Steve's cell phone rang. He answered and handed the phone to Amina. "Zab," he said.

Amina walked outside. She returned a few minutes later with Marty. "Attention everyone, we all need to stock up on canned goods and start eating the stuff in the freezer. Steve, make sure we have plenty of gas for the barbecue. I think we should buy another spare tank or two. Please do it tomorrow. Soon we are going to have a power outage that will last for quite some time. Trust me."

CHAPTER 47

Steve's house, Monday morning, February 24

Steve listened to the hiss of his little espresso machine and welcomed the aroma. It was not authentic espresso, not the stuff in dainty cups made with shiny-copper contraptions, but he enjoyed the dark, bitter, pressure-cooked brew from his one-mug machine. He liked to start his day with two mugs full of high-octane caffeine; today they were vital.

"Our old enemy will soon pay," Zab had said when he called the night before. Amina was thrilled. They would put Hypocor's lights out. But the gleam in her eyes had had a sad fringe and her shoulders sagged. She had to *disappear*. Hushed by dread, they had not spoken of plotting a new course in the quiet before the impending storm.

Is this our end?

She had to disappear. She could not be where they knew her to be. Her presence endangered the compound, the residents vulnerable to collateral damage. If she stayed, the guards would question why a freelance writer spent his time exercising and patrolling the perimeter, wonder why the residents flinched at any untoward sound, and puzzle over the atmosphere of anxiety. They would mention this strange behavior to their employer. Haradji would come snooping. And the moment Stillwell got whiff of the situation, he would sweep the compound clean of delinquents—Maxwell Harris, Amina Taiba and Steve Bryce, too.

He could not leave with her, not yet. He had to find a photo agency, plan photo shoots, propose assignments, query magazines. He needed a place to stay, at least an address, a computer of his own, a motorcycle maybe, and above all, residency. As the spouse of a Filipina he could stay.

Will the Taiba clan accept me if I marry Amina? Will they even allow me to marry her? Maybe I'll have to become a Muslim first, and pass a test of sincerity. Amina does not want to talk about the aftermath of my visit to Taiba House. She and her brothers conspired to put me there. No, Amina conspired and her brothers accepted, and she knew they would. Without talking to her brothers first, or even Nashita, she agreed to arrange my trip to the marsh. She sent the lamb into the wolves den, unprepared. What was that all about? What had she hoped for? What happened? We agreed to be friends with benefits. Would she marry me now? Can she? What is it? Brenda said it transcends individuality. What's the trump card?

When the steam quieted, Steve heard low grunting sounds outside. He looked out the kitchen window. In the dim, predawn light, he saw a shape lurching on the ground in Brenda's carport. For an instant, he thought it might be someone writhing with pain from a fall but it was not. Sipping coffee, he watched Marty Santana, the man commissioned by the President of the World to protect the woman he loved. He did one-handed pushups, alternating hands between each stroke. He was getting ready.

The residents had agreed to continue calling him Max, the freelance writer, and that he should stay until Amina left. But Amina did not want Max and Perla to know she was leaving, that she would disappear, although she admitted that the all-observant Perla would figure it out soon enough.

The breaking day began to illuminate the compound as Marty finished his calisthenics. Steve watched him pick up what looked like an old cell phone and stuff it into his cargo pants. He stooped again for a pistol, checked it and slipped it into the pocket on his right leg. He flexed his fingers and looked at the gate, as if he dared someone to invade. Then he started walking toward the back of the compound, eyeing the concertina wire on top of the perimeter wall.

Steve thought cargo pants a good idea. Tucking his pistol into the belt of his jeans would be uncomfortable in the humid Philippine climate. After reloading the espresso maker for his second mug, he dressed in cargo pants, a pullover jersey and running shoes. In his office, he unwrapped the Walther PPK, inserted the magazine and riffled his desk drawer for the other cartridge. The 9 mm short still looked lethal after lying around for months. He had not fired the pistol since he moved to the Philippines. He, too, had to get ready. He started chamber the round, hesitated, and dropped it loose into his pocket along with the weapon. Back in the kitchen, he split the espresso between two mugs and went outside. He found Max strolling from the back of the compound toward Brenda's house. Max eyed the two mugs and smiled.

"Good morning, Max. Would you like a little coffee?"

"Thanks. I was just going to get something to drink." Marty took the mug and gulped some. "Ah, good stuff. Is this a peace offering?"

"Hell no, I'll bust your nose later. For the moment, we're allies. Tell me what you know about this threat against Amina."

Marty frowned. "My control told me someone wants to kill her, but they don't know who, not yet. It's reliable. In thirty years, their information has been remarkably accurate."

Steve pointed with his cup and they started to walk back toward the guesthouse. "If your company is based in the States, how did they learn about Amina's files?"

"I'm a foot soldier. The House, that's the codename for my company, The House does not tell me how they operate. They don't want me to know. But they did tell me a little about this job." Marty paused to take a sip of coffee.

Steve nodded. "Go ahead."

"The House gets contracts from government agencies to do something, mostly spy stuff. Some agency, I don't know which, probably CIA or Army Intel, got interested in Jiriki Taiba and starts eavesdropping on his communications. They notice he's gathering data on suspicious characters, maybe some of the same jokers they're watching. This agency learns he's sending this information to his sister. They hire The

House to copy her files. Posey told me Miss Taiba doesn't have a computer any more, but she's using yours. I didn't expect diskettes, so I took the drive."

Marty gulped some coffee. "I didn't know any of this until a couple of days ago. They wouldn't tell me what I'm doing here until you were about to ask me. At the time I swiped your hard drive, I knew nothing about you or Miss Taiba or why they wanted her files. They didn't want me to know. If you caught me, I could tell you only that someone hired me to copy the files from your computer."

They leaned against the rear wall near the guesthouse where they could watch the gate and the guard shack. The slanting morning sun reached beneath the long eves to light the fronts the houses. Soon they would be in shadow.

"Who told you where I live? How did you know about Posey?"

"They sent me a satellite photo of the compound. It was so sharp I could damn near count the blades of grass. They gave me the names of your maid and the guards and about where they lived. My guess is the government agency knew where you lived but The House got the names."

Steve pushed away from the wall and glared at Marty. "Where did they get those names? If someone in Timbuktu can get the name of my maid, why in the fuck can't they tell me who wants to kill my woman? Who are they? The politicians? The military? The land grabbers? Who's afraid of her?"

Marty raised his arms. "Hey man, don't shoot the messenger. They don't know yet. I'm not supposed to know how they got Posey's name." He jabbed his finger against Steve's shoulder. "For all I know, *you* told them. That's how I had it figured. How else could they get that information? You're cozy with the MILF. You and your girlfriend pop up at the Pasigan. You truck the C4 to Marawi. Who do *you* work for? Whose side are you on? Who has the C4?"

They glared at each other until Steve glanced at the guardhouse and saw that Toots and Boots had been watching the confrontation. They settled back against the wall.

Steve broke the silence with a chuckle. "Okay, I can see it looks like I'm working for the MILF, and in a way I am, indirectly, but that started *after* you stole my hard drive, *because* you stole it. The MILF is not a terrorist organization. They are a people trying to defend their land. If I knew who had the C4, I sure as hell wouldn't tell you."

"Will you tell me whether or not you are working for a government agency?"

Steve looked at Marty, puzzled. "No, I am not."

They watched the guards. Toots had replaced Boots at six in the morning, but Boots was just now leaving. They had talked for a while, occasionally glancing at Marty and Steve.

"Max, I saw you doing push ups this morning, and I saw you pick up your weapon." He nodded at the gate. "We don't want the guards knowing you're armed. You're Brenda's boyfriend. We don't want them thinking otherwise. We do not want the chief of security asking questions."

"I'll be more careful. So the guards report to Umar Haradji?"

Steve looked at Marty. "I've never heard his first name. So you know him?"

"Control told me his name. Maybe I know him. What does he look like?"

"Tall for a Filipino, bald headed with ugly, bloodshot eyes. I'll guess he's sixty-something. He comes from some obscure Moro clan."

"I know about him. He's not Moro. He's not even Filipino. His real name is Alimar Patek. He and his brothers were pirates and smugglers in the Sulu Sea until they caught them in Port Isabela loaded to the gills with contraband. They were going to hang Alimar for beheading one of his crew, but he cut a deal and became an informant for the NBI. That was in the mid-fifties. Back then, he knew all the pirates and contraband traders in Sulu and on the west coast of Mindanao. Later on, the NBI gave him new identities and moved him around, but eventually his goofy eyes would always blow his cover. Haradji must be the third or fourth identity he's had."

Steve smiled. "How many aliases do you have, *Uncle* Max?"

Marty groaned. "I've lost two of my best in as many weeks."

Steve shoved his hand in his pocket and withdrew the cartridge. He cupped it in the palm of his hand and showed it to Marty. "I need ammo. Do you have 9 mm shorts?"

"Sorry. I use Parabellums. What's your weapon?"

"Walther PPK. I'll have to buy a box of shorts and get in some target practice. It's been a while."

Marty watched Steve drop the cartridge back into his pocket and heard the faint clink as it bounced against metal.

"I'm retiring. Since you're not already working for an intelligence agency, The House might be interested in hiring you."

Steve stared at Marty.

"I'm serious," Marty said.

Steve shook his head. "No. I can accept killing as revenge, an eye for an eye sort of thing, but that's intensely personal. Killing someone under any conditions is tragedy. It would push my life onto some godforsaken path. It's not for me. I'm into tranquility."

Marty, with a wry smile, watched Steve stare into space. He chuckled. "Right, Mr. Tranquility who smuggled six kilos of C4 into Central Mindanao."

Steve's lips tightened. He folded his arms and gazed at the gate.

"Listen," Marty said. "The House is not about killing, not any more, anyway. I believe the army organized The House as a super-secret bunch of psychopaths during the Vietnam War, but then someone decided they weren't politically correct. So The House went private and reformed. I'm a spy, maybe a dirty tricks guy, but not an assassin. I gather information without a search warrant and disrupt illegal activities without the inconvenience of due process. You can refuse if the job doesn't make sense to you."

"What happened at the Pasigan?"

"Who has the six kilos?"

"Touché," Steve said, and grinned. He looked at Marty. "Brenda told me you have magazines with articles by Maxwell Harris. Did you write them?"

"I do drafts or outlines and send them to The House with research notes on topics of interest. Someone else cleans them up and tailors articles for various periodicals. Freelance writer has been a good cover. It provides a credible excuse to be snooping around."

"What about a freelance photographer? Can your company hook me up with a photo agency and query periodicals with my photojournalism proposals?"

Marty pushed away from the wall, regarded Steve for a moment and smiled. "I'll ask. Freelance photographer might work. Freelance writing is good because it's an excuse to ask questions and look around. How are you at doing interviews?"

Steve shrugged. "Okay, I suppose. Much of my work is negotiation. For fun, I like to get into people's heads, especially strangers. If you're curious but not judgmental, it's amazing what people will tell you about themselves."

"If they handle your photos, will you consider working for The House?"

"What happened at the Pasigan?"

Marty stared at the toes of his boots for several moments before looking at Steve. "I suspect you know more than I do. They told me to spy on Zorro because they thought he might supply explosives for a terrorist plot. That job might have been for the Philippine government. They needed an outsider, someone who could hang around the resort and identify Zorro's associates. Then your girlfriend shows up. I flipped when I found out who she was." Marty sighed and raised his eyebrows. "Then it got interesting."

"Tell me what happened."

"Zorro found another buyer and I saw him taking delivery. I could have told Control what I learned and sat back with a cool drink. I thought about doing just that." Marty stared into space. "Well, I didn't."

"Why not?"

Marty shook his head and contemplated the tips of his boots again. "I don't know. I made a reckless choice." He rocked back and forth. "Some of these jokers will toss a grenade into a crowded marketplace or theater. Twenty kilos of C4 were headed for God knows where." Marty looked at Steve. "I didn't bother to ask what they planned to do with it."

"Do you have regrets?"

Marty laughed. "I'd damn sure regret it if they caught me." His face shadowed. "I knew one of those men and he wanted me worse than dead. The other guy, the terrorist connection, he did us a favor by hanging around for the fireworks. No, I've no regrets."

"And what if they had caught you? What would The House do?"

"The promise is they send in the cavalry. The CIDG had me for the Pasigan explosion. In thirty years, it was the first time anyone caught me. The House pulled some strings and saved my ass, I think because they still needed me." Marty turned to Steve. "The House is interested in you. I don't give a shit if you get the job or want the job, but understand the set-up. I don't know who hires The House. The House pays well and the intelligence they provide is damn good, but they never tell me more than I must know to do the job. That's the deal. They pay me for not knowing. I figure that if I ever got into more trouble than they could handle, my cell phone would explode and I'd have no one to talk to. I don't believe in the cavalry."

Steve nodded slowly. "Thanks for leveling with me." He glanced at his watch. "Speaking of jobs, my vacation is over. Find out if they want to handle a freelance photographer. Then maybe we can talk some more." Steve smiled and pointed at Marty's face. "But look after that nose, Mr. Santana. I caught you too."

Marty smiled. "That eye for an eye sort of thing?"

"You upset my tranquility." Steve walked to his house.

"Hi," Steve said, opening the kitchen door.

Perla jumped. "Oh, good morning, Mr. Steve." She scrutinized Steve's face. "You're up and about early. I think Miss Amina is still sleeping. Do you want breakfast now or will you wait for her?" Her voice squeaked at an octave or two above normal.

"Just make me another espresso, please. I'll be in my office."

"Mr. Steve, do you have a problem with me fibbing, about being Uncle Max's niece, I mean? I really need this job."

"I've no quarrel with you. You were part of keeping Amina safe. That part of your job is over. We'll tell Max what he needs to know. But as for you," he smiled, "you're a keeper."

"Oh, thank you, Mr. Steve. Thank you so much." She appeared to stop herself from hugging him. "Do you want something with your coffee—toast or juice maybe?"

"Just coffee—I'll wait for Amina." He started for his office but turned back. "How's the new computer?"

Perla beamed. "Wonderful, but confusing. It's much more complicated than the one I used in school. I'll figure it out."

"I'll fix breakfast. You go get Uncle Max to help you with your computer. Take the morning off."

"Oh, I couldn't do that. I've got to make the bed, clean the house, prepare lunch."

"Perla, *get lost*." Steve wagged his finger. "Amina and I will be messing up the bed." He smiled. "Do you understand?"

She grinned and flicked her eyebrows.

"We'll have the leftover *escabeche* for lunch. We don't even have to heat it up. You eat with Max. Come back at one. You and I are going shopping this afternoon. We need gas for the grill and I want to stock up on canned goods."

"Okay, Mr. Steve, one o'clock it is."

Soon after Perla left, Steve and Amina began to quarrel. He wanted to talk, but she insisted on calling Jiriki. To stop her, Steve grabbed her forearm and unplugged the phone.

"Tigress, we have to talk first."

"Talk about what?"

"Talk about our future."

"What future," she snapped.

"A future like Olango Island and room 702, a future of being together and working together."

He still held her forearm. She tried to pull free from his grip. She would not look at him.

"Tigress, calm down. You're safe here, for a while anyway. Let's sit down and discuss alternatives. Someone wants to kill you. I've a stake in that. I love you."

They stood close together, silent and as somber as if they had just heard on the news that God had died. The tenseness in Amina's arm began to subside. Steve released his grip and held her hand.

"I apologize for being rough but there's something you should know before you talk to Jiriki. I had an interesting chat with Max this morning." He sat at the dining room table. Amina took the chair opposite his.

"I apologize for my terrible mood. I had a bad night. What did Max have to say?"

"We talked about several things that can wait, but one is important for right now. I believe he told us the truth last night, except for one minor detail. He is not here to protect you for the President of the World. He is protecting you for The House, that's the name of the company he works for."

"What's the difference?"

"It's the difference between politics and capitalism."

Which is?"

Steve smiled. "Capitalism is predictable."

Amina nodded. "Keep talking."

"Governments pay The House to do dirty little jobs like stealing your files, but not just the United States government. He mentioned the Philippines. My guess is The House markets intelligence to a group of allied governments. If they get some juicy information, they might sell it to two or three different entities."

"I agree." Amina leaned forward. "And I'm not guessing. Remember I had the MILF negotiation strategy on your computer. Last night, when Santana asked to speak with me privately, he said his company would withhold that information as long as I allowed him to protect me." She sat back. "Imperial Manila would pay well for that document."

Steve tossed his hands. "Beautiful, capitalism at work. Now we're sure, and we can use it to our advantage. As long as The House thinks you are gathering marketable information, they have a stake in keeping you alive."

Amina shook her head. "No, I don't trust Max. My family will keep me safe."

"Max and his employer are in the business of not having ethics. I understand they cannot be trusted. But as long as they think you are useful, they have an economic interest in your safety. The House is trying to find out who wants to do you harm. You believe they are already in your database. If they can identify which group, at least we know the color of the snake."

Amina nodded. "I agree that would be helpful. Do you think they can find out?"

"Max said The House told him about Posey and the names of the guards and where they all lived. He doesn't know how they obtained that information, but they must have a contact in Davao unknown to him. That contact might learn something. Max also said The House, or the agency that hired them, eavesdropped on Jiriki's conversations. They have electronic monitoring, which—"

"Jiriki loves that stupid cell phone. I told him not to use it."

"Tigress, they have resources we don't have. They can identify the threat."

"How long will it take them?"

"We should give them as long as we can before cutting the link to Max."

"Will Max tell us, or keep it to himself?"

"I'll know if he knows." Steve smiled. "I'm getting chummy with him. He says The House might be interested in my working for them."

Amina leaned forward, her expression a wry smile. "Imagine, Sweet Steve the CIA rascal. Who would think? It's perfect. Who do you have to kill to get the job? Me?"

He laughed. "It's something to think about. It could solve some problems. The House markets stories so Max can pose as a freelance writer. He's going to ask them if they can represent a freelance photographer. I suspect they can. If so, I could work through them until I'm established or until they ask me to kill someone. Maybe they can get me residency." He shrugged. "The important thing is to talk to them and figure out who intends to harm you. Maybe we can match their intelligence to someone in the database. We should not break the connection."

Amina shifted in her chair. "Fine," she snapped. "You connect. I'm leaving. I will stay until my birthday. I want a party to say goodbye to Isabela, Gerrit, Brenda and Bipsy, to say goodbye to a rich and wonderful part of my life." She sat back and toyed with the bracelet on her right wrist. The air conditioner screamed in Steve's ears as he waited for the other goodbye.

"I am Maranao," she continued, "and that defines me. My family is first above all, then the clan, the tribe and our land. You cannot understand that. You would suffocate in my world." She tapped to her chest. "*I* felt suffocated. I wanted what they gave Jiriki. He went to the University in Manila. He became a journalist in Davao. He got outside the cocoon. I, the girl, went to the university too, but in Marawi, inside the cocoon. After classes I came home to nest under my mother's wing." She twiddled her bracelet again. "I'm thirsty. Do you want something?"

"Get me some juice, please."

Amina returned with juice and a cup of tea.

"I came to Davao to escape the cocoon for a little while. I was lonely in Marawi. I wanted someone. When I saw you, I thought you perfect. You did not disappoint me. We shared a beautiful experience, an interlude. Now I must return."

"But we still have a future together, working together. We can do it."

Amina shook her head. "My family will never accept you. I had a stupid hope that morning in Cebu, that if my family witnessed your willingness to become involved we might have a chance. So I arranged for them to take you to Marawi. Except for Zab, the sight of you only hardened them. When my mother found out you had been in Taiba House, her thunder shook the city. I am sorry, Sweet Steve. I am Maranao. I cannot survive outside my family. The butterfly has had her flutter. She must return to the cocoon." She lowered her head and stared into her tea.

"Before you leave, I want a secure and sure method to contact you. Give me that much."

"I'll talk to Nashita. She is quite clever at making those kinds of arrangements."

"We need an alternative, a back up."

"Zab will always know where I am."

Steve took Amina's hands and looked into her eyes. "Do you love me?"

She smiled as if amused by a childish question. "Sweet Steve, you're such a romantic. I don't know what love is."

"You were married. What do you call the feelings you had for your husband?"

"My marriage was arranged. He was a good and strong man. I said okay. That was my feeling. He was okay."

"I'm okay. Marry me."

Expressionless, she held his gaze. But he knew her eyes. They crinkled, suppressing a boisterous, belly-busting guffaw. She couldn't hold it.

She snickered.

CHAPTER 48

The compound, Monday, February 24

"Green mangoes, you want this full of little green mangoes?" Perla held up the empty fertilizer sack Marty had found in Steve's storage shed. "It's going to weigh more than me."

"Take a taxi back. Get the driver to help you. Don't bring them into the compound. Hide them in the bushes outside the wall behind Steve's house. Get the smallest ones, no bigger than tennis balls."

Perla looked forlorn. "Max."

"Yes."

"I never played tennis."

"Oh, ah…about this big." He cupped his hands.

Perla flicked her eyebrows and left for the market.

Early that morning, Brenda had rushed off to the airport. She would be gone for three days to review a pineapple project in Thailand. "As if it's any of your business," she had said in a tone hung over with belligerence. After a sleepless night of raging, he welcomed the respite. A deceived woman, he discovered, can be an incomprehensible bitch. She had called him a thieving scumbag, two-faced hoodlum, synthetic asshole and worse, although his being a vile and loathsome four-lettered vermin had not bothered her libido. Quite the opposite. He needed a rest.

Home alone, Marty got to work on a long email to beacon. He had much to report. As he wrote, he felt like an unemployed actor. Being Marty Santana seemed strange and unsettling. He had never played himself. And as Brenda the bitch had made clear, he had better play nice or the residents would vote him out of the compound and turn him over to the authorities. Looking at what he had written about Bryce sparked another bout of introspection. Marty wondered why Nadine had picked him, questioned his own qualifications for the job. She had liked spontaneous and violent back then, but The House had grown into something else. He deleted "too clever to be a foot soldier" and wrote, "They welded his lid shut years ago, but his gut instinct looks good."

Marty recounted Bracelets receiving a phone call and then jubilantly announcing an imminent blackout. He speculated the MILF would soon use the missing C4 to sabotage the central Mindanao power grid. He wrote that when he threatened to release the MILF negotiation strategy if they tossed him out of compound, Bracelets seemed uninterested, even bored. No doubt, as Nadine had suspected, the document was her own invention and worthless. He closed with a request for more motion detectors like the one he had. After sending his report, Marty went out to inspect the perimeter while he waited for Perla to return. She came in plucking thorns from her jeans with one hand and carrying a plastic bag in the other.

"What's that," Marty asked, pointing to the bag.

"Bagoong."

"Ah, stinky little shrimp for sliced green mangoes, I should have guessed. But before your snack, we've work to do. Go tell your boss I'm going to throw mangoes at his house and not to worry. I'll replace any broken windows."

"I'd better not. He told me to get lost until after lunch. I think they're doing the mattress mambo."

Marty chuckled. "Now I wonder where a nice girl like you learned that expression. Never mind, we'll get their attention soon enough. Come with me. You're going to be an artillery spotter. Watch out for friendly fire."

Perla took her position behind Steve's house. The first mango came over the wall in a high arc. She caught it and shouted "In line but short." The next one thudded onto the roof out of sight until it rolled over the edge. Blinded by the sun, Perla did not see it until too late. It hit her nose. "Yow!" She screeched and fell on her butt. She heard another one clip the roof. As she scrambled under the protection of the eave, she heard the upstairs window open. She looked up to see a hand holding a pistol. "Cease fire, cease fire," she shouted.

Steve leaned out the window and pointed the gun at her. "What's going on?"

"It's just me. Don't shoot. I mean it's not me. It's Sammy. I mean Uncle Max. It's him." She jabbed her finger at the wall. "Just mangoes, see." She held up the mango she had caught. "Imitation hand grenades, a test," she explained. She lowered her voice, "testing, testing."

Toots peeked around the corner of the house, revolver in hand. "We're playing, we're playing," Perla shouted in Tagalog, dropped the mango, held up her hands and squeaked, "You want green mango and *bagoong*?"

After an awkward and disjointed conversation, they had fun. Marty tried to toss mangoes to Steve in the upstairs window while Perla, Toots and Amina competed to see who could catch the most. Julius refereed. If Toots thought the game strange, she soon got over it just as the others quickly forgot its macabre purpose.

The long eaves and the narrow corridor between the wall and the building made it impossible to hit the window or even the backside of the house. And without a rain gutter, all the mangoes tumbled down despite Marty's best efforts to lay one on the roof. After exhausting his sack of ammo, Marty fastened a motion sensor to the outside wall behind Steve's house and programmed his cell phone to receive its signal.

Marty and Perla settled in Brenda's living room for more computer lessons. Shortly before noon, a messenger came to the gate and Toots delivered an envelope to Steve's house. More input for Bracelets' database, Marty guessed. Then Steve came over to tell Perla he had to go out for a while and not to disturb Amina, that she was taking a nap. They watched Steve drive out of the compound.

"Bullshit," Marty muttered. "She's gone. Perla, go check the house."

Several minutes later, Perla hurried back. "She is gone, Max. Her jeans are on the bed and there's a *hijab* missing. She's wearing Muslim clothes. All her personal stuff is there as far as I can tell. Something else. There's an empty glass and a teacup on *opposite* sides of the dining room table. They weren't making love. He told me to get lost so they could talk."

Marty stared out the window for a while and then turned to Perla. "What do you think they're doing?"

Perla curled up in an easy chair and rested her chin on her knees. "Steve came in from outside the house early this morning. He was going to his office but stopped as if he had thought of something. That's when he told me to get lost. He wanted to talk to Bracelets in private."

"He came out to talk with me. He wanted to tell Bracelets about our conversation."

"Maybe, but I imagine them leaning over the table talking. I would think they were plotting something."

Marty thought for a minute. "They left after receiving an envelope. Did you find it?"

"It was on her work table—empty—a small envelope."

"A message, and then they leave," Marty mused. "Steve's no fool. He would not risk taking her out of the compound unless he had no choice. She's meeting with someone who can't come here, or can't be seen here."

"A Muslim, a cleric maybe, that's why she wore Muslim clothes."

"The *hijab* is to hide her face. But you're right. She's likely gone to meet someone in the Muslim community." Marty sighed. "There's nothing we can do for now. Go busy yourself at the house, maybe you'll spot something else. Just knowing she's in Muslim clothes tells us something. We'll talk again tonight after you're done with your chores."

Marty cussed Steve. Any idiot would know the mummy by his side is Bracelets. But Marty could not get angry. He understood Bryce would not trust a mercenary to look after his woman.

After sunset, as the heat of the day diminished, Marty relaxed on Brenda's front porch and thought about his defenses. They would not climb over the wall in the middle of the night like Ninja assassins, too precise and personal for them. They used bombs and grenades; that was their style. No one was going to get a bomb into the compound on his watch. Someone would toss a grenade over the wall; send a message for Bracelets to mind her business.

He gazed across the driveway. From where he sat, he could throw a stone over the wall, but it would be a tough shot to hit the porch from the other side. Still, the grenade would most likely come from there. He would tell Steve to keep Bracelets away from the front of the house, and in the morning, he would move the motion sensor. With more of them, he could surround the compound with an early warning system, and with luck, he would catch the bastard, some raggedy teenager desperate to earn a few pesos. For sure, they would send another grenadier, but they would not scare Bracelets. She would not flinch.

Marty heard the front door of Steve's house slide open and then the pitter-patter of Perla's flip-flops. She heaved herself up onto the porch railing as if she were heavy with information.

"What's up?"

"When they came back, Steve came in first and kept me in the kitchen while Bracelets snuck into their bedroom. We made believe I didn't know she had left. No clues as to where they were, but he ate lunch and she didn't, said she wasn't hungry."

Marty smiled. "The chauffer wasn't invited to the luncheon meeting. Anything else?"

"He took me grocery shopping and told me to pick out stuff that didn't require refrigeration. He bought flashlights and batteries, and then two tanks of gas for the barbecue. I asked him why. He said there might be a power failure. Then we went to that sporting goods store where you bought the snorkels and stuff. He told me to stay in the truck, but I saw what he bought."

"Let me guess—bullets."

Perla flicked her eyebrows. "Two boxes, 9 mm." She wiggled. "I mentioned we were getting Amina a LCD screen for her birthday. That troubled him. He apologized and said we should return it and get a refund because he would be buying her a laptop. A few days ago, he said he would be getting her clothes. When I mentioned that, he said Apex loaned her the computer she's using and they had to return it. But when the queer guy brought the computer, I'm sure he told Bracelets she could keep it as long as she wanted."

They exchanged silent stares.

"Did he buy the computer?"

Perla shook her head. "He didn't have time. He had gotten a phone call about his job and said he had to get back to the house."

"You look worried."

Perla clasped her hands and thought for a minute. "Max, if someone was out to kill me, I think I'd be too frightened to move. They're calm, too calm. He's on the phone talking business and she works at her computer like nothing's wrong. They act as if they don't believe someone is out to kill her, but when that mango hit the roof, he went nuts. I'll never forget that gun and his eyes." She held up her thumb and forefinger. "I was this close to dead. He's scary, Max. He's polite like dynamite. Even the cat knows something's wrong. Julius usually jumps on his lap to get his ears scratched, but he won't go near him now, just watches him from a safe distance. I'm afraid of him too, I'm afraid he's going to explode."

Marty leaned forward and grasped Perla's knee. "Don't worry, I understand him. He's okay. Just remember, if there's trouble, stay out of the way."

"I've picked my spot, already. I can squeeze under their bed. That's where I'll be if you need me."

Marty smiled. "Good."

"Max, they have a plan. She's going to leave. That's why he's buying the computer."

Marty nodded. "I'm afraid she's going to vanish, but not without her files. When he gets the computer, watch it. We need to know when she transfers files."

"What do we do then?"

"I'm not sure. For now, you're job is to figure out when she's going to leave and if Bryce is going with her. I've got to talk this over with Control, my boss." Marty sighed and thought for a minute. "You should know how to contact Control. I think you should talk to her. Can you come over here at noon tomorrow?"

Perla shook her head. "Not until after lunch, around three would be good."

"Okay, I'll set it up."

"What about the LCD screen? Do we return it?"

Marty smiled. "Talk to Bryce. Tell him we want to return it for credit against the cost of the laptop. You'll have to go with him when he buys it."

Perla giggled. "And I'll offer to hide it until her birthday."

He patted her leg. "My boss is going to like you."

Benjie had summoned Haradji for an urgent meeting. Still weak from a long bout with the flu, Haradji could not climb the stairs to Gretchen's Club for Girls with his usual vigor, but he beamed a healthy smile when he saw the two suits sitting at Benjie's table. They represented powerful elements with deep pockets. Benjie looked gleeful too. He would be taking fifteen percent.

CHAPTER 49

The compound, Tuesday afternoon, February 25

Shortly before three in the afternoon, as Marty paced the floor in Brenda's living room, Perla came in carrying her computer.

"I asked for an hour. Bracelets told me to come back in time to fix supper. I think they want to talk again."

"Anything new?"

"Steve told Mr. Gerrit they should get permission to use the guesthouse for Amina's birthday party on Saturday. I'm to bake the cake tonight. When I suggested we wait so that it would be fresh, Steve snapped at me, told me just do it, but a few minutes later he apologized. I think he's nervous about her leaving. Do you think she might leave before the party?"

Marty thought for a minute. "Maybe, we have to be ready for that, but he may expect a power outage tomorrow. You went out with him this morning. Did he buy the computer?"

"He bought *two* laptops." Perla smiled. "He told me to hide hers in my bathroom. They won't have the one he wants for a couple of weeks. He told the clerk he had no problem with that. Either she's not leaving for a while, or he's not going with her."

"What have they been doing? Is she packing?"

"No. There is some problem between them. Both are sad and they hardly talk to each other, at least when I'm around. Both are working hard. He's busy with Apex stuff and she's capturing data from a stack of papers. When she finishes one, she moves it to the bottom of the pile. I put a dot on the top sheet yesterday. I'll know when she's done."

Marty stopped pacing and kissed the top of her head. "My pearl."

"I put a tiny bit of tape on the computer box. If they open it, we'll know."

Marty chuckled. "After college, apply for NBI agent. Control will get you a letter of recommendation from the CIA. Control's name is Nadine. Tell her what you just told me and what you told me last night." He glanced at his watch. "Meantime, I'll show you something." He pulled out his cell, sat on the couch and patted the cushion beside him.

"This looks like an old contraption. It isn't. If something happens to me, get the phone—left side leg pocket. Press star-zero-number sign. You don't have to turn it on. Just press star-zero-number sign in that order. Got it?"

She flicked her eyebrows. Her fingers wiggled and waved a rhythm as if she memorized in melody. Marty thought he had seen her do that before.

"It's like a 911 call. Someone named Beacon will answer. You say, 'Uncle'".

"Uncle?"

"Yes, 'Uncle' means trouble. Tell what happened and give your exact location. They can track the phone but only within a hundred meters or so. Then keep the phone as close to Bracelets as you can. If you lose her or something bad happens, press star-zero-number sign and tell Beacon. Be careful what you say—the 911 line is not encrypted."

"Okay, but why are you telling me this? What's going to happen to you?"

"When Bracelets leaves, we're going to follow her. I'm vulnerable outside the compound. If CIDG Davao spots me, they'll want to know what I'm doing in their region. It could be a long discussion. Even if I'm not arrested, it's easier for a woman to stay close to Bracelets. Besides, you speak a little Maranao. That's an advantage."

She smiled and nudged him. "I'm learning more. I got Bracelets to agree we'll try to speak only Maranao. She doesn't mind. She seems happy about me wanting to learn her language."

"You are precious. I wonder if Bracelets might take you—" The cell phone rang.

"I'll take this upstairs in Brenda's office. I'll yell when Nadine is ready to talk to you." He wagged his finger. "No eavesdropping."

"Is your pecker twelve inches long?"

"It shrunk. I'm pushing buttons."

"We are clear," Nadine said. "So, you think Bracelets is leaving?"

"I'm sure, but probably not before Saturday night. Perla will copy her files before then. They lock up her office at night. I'll teach Perla to pick the lock. The problem is tracking Bracelets once she leaves. That'll be a bitch."

"We will send you GPS tracking chip for new laptop with instructions to wire direct to battery power. As soon as Bryce buys computer, send Beacon specs."

"He bought it this morning. It's in Perla's room. I'll send specs on Perla's computer too. Send a tracker for hers as well. It's a long shot, but Bracelets might accept Perla as a companion when she leaves."

"What about Bryce. Is he going with Bracelets?"

"It doesn't look that way, but I'll bet he'll know where she is. There's a chance he'll quit Apex and join her. Are you going to offer him a job?"

"Yes, we like his connection to Bracelets and MILF. The House has photo agency. Beacon is sending you particulars for Bryce to submit portfolio. Agency will love photographs if he agrees to accept assignments."

"Will they assign him to Bracelets?"

"No. He will help you protect her, but he will not give us files without her consent. Your job does not change. We want those files."

"I understand."

"Send computer specs quick. Manila store will deliver tracking chips and motion sensors. Do you have anything more?"

"No."

"Then let me talk to Wonder Woman."

Marty turned to the bedroom door. "Perla, you can come in now." She opened the door with a mischievous smile. "How long will it take you to get the specs on Bracelets laptop?"

Perla shrugged, "A few minutes."

Marty looked puzzled. "But you're not due back for an hour or more."

"I greased my bedroom window, done that since I was a teenager. Never know when a girl wants to slip out for some fun."

"Vamoose," he laughed.

With a flick of eyebrows, she was gone.

"Did you hear that?" Marty said into the phone.

"Yes, I will time her. Meantime, we talk of design for dungeon. I am going to build house."

While Perla talked to Nadine, Marty sent an email to Beacon with the specs for the computers. He was setting up an internet provider on Perla's computer when she came back to Brenda's office, bubbling.

"She's a crusty old bitch, but I think she likes me. I think she was hitting on me. Is she a dyke?"

Marty stared at the wall for a moment. "I may have told her about you and Lilibeth. Nadine goes both ways." He pushed away from the worktable. "Okay, we've a lot to do. Leave your computer here. I'm going to copy some programs from my laptop. Come back tonight and I'll show you how to send encrypted mail to Beacon, and you're going to learn how to pick these locks. I have to go into the city but I shouldn't' be gone long. Here's my phone number." He handed Perla a scrap of paper. "If anything happens, call me. Meantime, pack a travel bag with enough for a few days. We have to be ready to leave whenever Bracelets does. Plan to take your computer. I'm renting a room in the city for the rest of our stuff. I know the owner. Our things will be safe there."

Perla thought for several moments and then nodded before shuffling down the stairs. Marty understood her apprehension. They faced an uncertain journey, no doubt to an unwelcoming destination in ungoverned territory. He would not blame Perla if she quit. He too had misgivings.

CHAPTER 50

The compound, Wednesday, February 26

Alone in his office, Steve thought about Santana's reasoning. A grenade tossed over the wall—arbitrary, impersonal, cowardly—would be typical, and it seemed reasonable that they would first try to scare Amina into quitting her project, although Santana agreed that would only toughen her. She was a soldier, he had said. But Steve considered Santana's scenario as dangerously optimistic as his own folly in thinking the compound could be safe.

Amina was not an arbitrary and impersonal target. She threatened powerful men intent on seizing Moro lands as spoils in the war on terror. Amina menaced their scheme. They would not gamble on scare tactics or a whimsical grenade. Amina required specificity. They would hire an assassin, give him her address and agree on a price. Amina would not be safe as long as they knew where she lived. She had to disappear, whereabouts unknown.

Steve thumbed the sheaf of papers Santana had given him, a proposal from Anthony Somers at the "Boundless Image Bank," supposedly a stock photo agency. A web search revealed Boundless to be an exclusive agency representing seven photographers. They had no submission guidelines and no physical address, directing all inquires to their website.

Somers' letter opened with an enthusiastic welcome saying that based on the recommendation of Mr. Maxwell Harris, Boundless looked forward to representing Mr. Steve Bryce as one of their featured photographers. He asked Steve to accept the included agreement and email a portfolio of as many images as he wished. The cover letter contained an extraordinary offer. Upon acceptance of terms for their representation and completion of his first assignment, Boundless would pay a retainer of $5,000 a month plus eighty percent of sales revenues from the portfolio. Boundless would continue the retainer and promote his portfolio and photojournalism projects with vigor and determination, blah, blah, blah, provided he accepted assignments of interest to the agency. Somers mentioned three projects from which Steve must chose one for his first job: an Iranian NGO in Sri Lanka, a Saudi charitable institution in Jakarta and a group of Libyan investors on Mindanao. Somers would provide specifics and pay scale for the project of his choice. However, should participation in any of these projects not be to Steve's liking, Boundless wished him good fortune in finding another agency.

Clear enough, Steve thought. If he were up to a bit of spying, and no doubt some miscellaneous dirty tricks, send Boundless a bunch of photographs and accept an assignment. If he produced, they would pay him a generous amount to be wired to his numbered account in Timbuktu, his whereabouts being unknown.

Steve felt insulted. Boundless did not care about his photography. He could send them a dozen snapshots of Julius and he would become one of their featured photographers. He tossed Somers' proposal into the trash basket but it did not stay there long enough to settle. Boundless could help him keep Amina safe.

The contract was solid enough for Steve to claim he had representation, yet it was not exclusive; he could sell his photos through another agency. The House had articles published under the Maxwell Harris byline to provide a cover for Santana, so Boundless was a legitimate storefront that would peddle photographs credited to Steve Bryce, or the alias of his choosing. *Why not?* And the recent influx of Libyan businessmen sponsoring vague projects had many wondering as to their intentions, including Apex, who did not want another competitor in the Middle East markets for Philippine fruits.

Steve began to assemble a representative portfolio for Anthony Somers. He would ask Somers for specifics on the Libyan project, saying he would pursue it with vigor and determination, blah, blah, blah, *provided* he received all information related to, and authorization to collaborate in, the current project of Maxwell Harris, and should such participation not be to their liking, he wished Boundless good fortune in finding another featured photographer.

Marty leaned against Brenda's porch and scanned the coconut trees across the road that passed in front of the compound. He had spotted the foliage rustle, but not from the wind. The *tuba* collector, in stained white trousers, scampered down the tree. He tried to picture a sniper shimmying up, assembling his rifle, adjusting the scope and waiting for Bracelets to come out and jog. Not likely, he thought, too tough a shot, but it would make a nice perch for a spotter.

He heard a vehicle clatter down the road and stop in front of the gate. Toots opened the porthole in the metal door. Her expression told him she did not recognize the visitor. After a perfunctory greeting, a male voice announced, "Package for Mr. Maxwell Harris." Marty smiled and glanced at his watch. He had plenty of time to set the motion detectors before sunset, and then install the tracking devices. As he strolled toward the gate, he heard Toots refusing to sign for the package until she inspected the contents.

"Oh, it's okay," Marty said. "That's for me."

Toots stiffened to a position resembling attention. "Yes, sir, but I must record the contents. It is a new rule. Mr. Bryce told us to inspect all containers entering the compound except those brought in by residents."

"I *am* a resident." Marty stepped forward, elbowed Toots aside and spoke to the courier. "I'll sign for that."

Toots touched his arm and gave him a frightened but determined look. "Please, sir. I must inspect the package."

Marty shucked aside Toots' hand, scribbled his signature and gripped the package with both hands. With an irritable grin, he shook the parcel in front of Toots' nose. "Writing materials," he sneered, turned on his heel and walked away.

Late that night, the sharp click followed by a sound like crunching cellophane penetrated Marty's dozing. He heaved up from Brenda's couch, fumbled the Beretta out of his pocket and blinked at the faint phosphorescent outline of the TV screen. It disappeared. Remembering where he had been watching the news, he spun about and looked at the sliding front door. The dim glow of city lights reflecting off low clouds extinguished as the air conditioner fan squeaked to full stop. In the hush after all electrical things died, he heard the muffled, joyous yelps from the neighboring house. He smiled, pocketed the Beretta and pulled out his Maglite. Half-past eleven, he noted. It would be a long night patrolling the perimeter. There would be no better opportunity for an assassin to come over the wall. He and Bryce could work in shifts.

Marty felt his way along the perimeter wall behind the houses, stopping every dozen paces or so to listen. He did not use his Maglite. Boots wandered around the driveway in front of the houses with a flashlight. Marty heard the Van Der Zee's front door slide open and then Gerrit talking to Boots.

Bryce's kitchen door banged and footsteps plummeted down the outside stairs. Marty quick stepped from behind Brenda's house in time to see Bracelets twirling around on the lawn, yelping with glee, he guessed in Maranao, as she cast the beam of her lantern at the black sky. Boots and Gerrit rounded the front of the house, their torches focused on the dancing nymph. The Dutchman laughed and so did Marty. Her jet-black hair, for once not hidden beneath a scarf, whipped back and forth. She howled at the darkness like a dog wailing at the moon. In the wavering beams from the flashlights, it appeared as if naked elves were cavorting inside Bryce's long-sleeved shirt and the shirt could not maintain the pace. Marty shook his head. He could not believe the demur little Moro woman could make so much noise. For a finale, she flung her arms skyward, shouted, and then scrambled back up the stairs. The beam of her lantern swept up over the body standing in the doorway. Bryce's face turned from grin to consternation as she shoved him inside and slammed the door. Light slashed across the window before her lantern clattered to the floor. Marty heard the bang of dining room chairs, and then the thumps of bodies hitting the floor. Forlorn, he slipped away from the carnal sounds. Bryce would be too busy to help him walk the wall.

In the stairwell outside her bedroom door, Perla sat in T-shirt and panty huddled against the wall. She had to pee. That could wait. She knew she should get back into her room, close the door, take a whiz and try to go back to sleep. Through cautious listening, she had decided the ruckus that woke her was not the feared trouble that Uncle Max had told her to avoid, but merely Bracelets celebrating the blackout.

Perla held her breath. Propriety be damned. She might piss her knickers but she had to listen. The blackout seemed to be the insurgent's aphrodisiac. Bracelets demanded and commanded. The nice Moro lady spouting raunchy vulgarities shocked Perla, but picturing herself commanding Christopher to do those things aroused her.

She heard someone crawling. On the floor at the top of the stairs, she saw a figure, Bracelets on her knees silhouetted by light from the fallen lantern. Then the other shadow mounted her behind. Perla, imagining Bracelets' cheek pressed to the floor looking down at her, closed her eyes. As her fingers mimicked his rhythm, she fantasized they were having a ménage à trois.

Perla rested but not the two animals upstairs. After Bracelets tugged Steve by the hair to their sitting area, Perla slipped into her room but left the door open. She drifted toward sleep wondering if she would ever see Christopher again. The noises upstairs resumed. Bracelets demanded another kind of sex, her voice penetrating, and then unrestrained moans. Perla realized Bracelets *had* seen her at the bottom of the stairs but had been too ablaze to care, and it seemed that knowing Perla was listening flamed her more. Perla understood. Listening with permission turned her on, aroused her even more than before.

Some minutes after the crescendo died down, tiny feet padded to the kitchen, beer bottles clinked and they went to their bedroom.

Incredible, Perla thought, as she pondered what she had heard. Bracelets' appeared so prudish she had wondered if they ever had sex at all. Her voice sounded like another person, someone domineering and insatiable. She wanted to believe she had had an erotic dream, but she could not have fantasized anything so intense, so sexually exciting, and frightening. The guttural groans and rasping demands—\don't you *come...don't you dare come...fuck me 'till I never forget*—had sounded desperate, as if she feared this sex might be her last.

CHAPTER 51

The compound, Thursday, February 27

Violent, oblivious lovemaking is an unhealthy distraction if someone is out to kill your lover. Steve lingered until Amina slipped into satisfied slumber. He glanced at his watch. It was nearly two in the morning, a propitious time for someone to scale the wall. He stuffed the Walther PPK into his hip pocket and went outside.

"I didn't expect to see you tonight," Marty said.

"All quiet on the home front, I trust."

Marty snickered. "*Now* it is."

They walked to the rear of Steve's house and began to patrol the perimeter, both scanning the concertina wire, Marty with his Maglite, Steve with a lantern.

"The alarm is inoperative with the power out," Steve said. "There's no battery backup."

"I've motion sensors outside, on the back and side walls. My cell will vibrate if one triggers, but we can't tell which one." Marty jabbed Steve's shoulder. "You snookered me, telling the guards to inspect packages. Toots near opened the box of gadgets that Control sent me this afternoon. That would have been touchy to explain."

"Sorry, I should have warned you. Christ, Haradji called me on that yesterday, wanted to know what I was worried about. I gave him some malarkey about vendors sending me bribes, which he didn't believe. Can't blame him. It sounded ridiculous to me too."

"He'll be coming around."

"Not right away. The blackout will keep him busy over at the Apex complex."

Once they came around the guesthouse to the driveway, they stopped and leaned against the wall where they could keep an eye on the guard. Marty stifled a yawn.

"You need sleep," Steve said. "We should work out a schedule."

"I've nothing else to do. You're still working for Apex, aren't you?"

"That's the problem with cell phones. They can get to you anytime, anywhere. But I can do the graveyard shift, say midnight to six."

"Swell. Brenda should be back late today. I'll be paying the rent. You want to spar before I turn in?"

"Not tonight, Max. Wrestling with Amina was enough."

Marty chuckled. "Sounded like it. Here's the cell."

"How long's the battery good for?"

"About twenty hours. I've one spare." Marty walked away, giving Steve a tired wave.

"Sweet dreams, Uncle Max." Steve grinned.

At daybreak, Steve grabbed a warm beer, shed his clothes and flopped into his reading chair. He surveyed the disarray in the dining room and thought about getting a camera, but then decided he needed no pictures to remember the night they would never forget.

For those accustomed to electricity, a blackout teaches them there are an incredible number of otherwise dependable devices that don't work without it, like radios and TVs for news. "What in the hell happened," is the first inquiry. Gerrit went to the gate and asked Toots, who had replaced Boots at six in the morning. The blackout, she said, was widespread—the entire island of Mindanao.

Breakfast is the next concern, at least for those who like it hot. The compound shared the gas-fired barbecue grill in Steve's carport. Gerrit walked over and rang his doorbell. Perla slid open the door.

"Hi, Perla. Is Steve up? I'd like to use the grill to cook up some vittles."

"Good morning, Mr. Gerrit. You can take it, I'm sure." She smiled, pointing over her head. "They had a rough night. Mr. Steve is sound asleep in his reading chair." She did not mention the pistol lying on his lap. "I'll get a frying pan and some eggs."

"No, Isabela will provide. I'll set up the barbecue over there." He pointed to the strip of grass between the wall and the driveway. "It's not hot yet. The sun feels good."

"I'll go help Miss Isabela then."

"Right you are."

As Gerrit rolled the barbecue across the driveway, Marty strolled up.

"Good morning. You're cooking out, I see. But I think it's better to set up between the houses."

Gerrit looked puzzled for a moment. "Ah, right," he said, glancing at the wall. "Best we stay away from the mango tree."

Without the whir of the room air conditioners, the noise outside woke Steve. He pushed aside the bamboo shade and saw the gathering under the eave of Gerrit's house. Perla and Toots were cooking on the grill. He opened the window. The smoke smelled like bacon.

"Hey, you guys got coffee?"

"*Por supuesto*," Isabela shouted. "Com'on down, and bring the terrorist."

Steve, feeling aching muscles, went to the bedroom and discovered his terrorist had showered and dressed in a *malong*, one shoulder exposed. She rubbed her fanny.

"I was a bad girl."

"There's breakfast outside. I'll be down after I shower. Then I'm going to spank the bad girl."

She smiled. "Sweet Steve, I'm going to miss you."

He watched her walk away, brazen without a scarf. The blackout had lifted her spirits. Still, he did not know if she meant she would miss him until he could join her or miss him forever. She had Nashita find a third party who knew nothing about them to relay their emails, which they agreed never to send from their own computers. They had worked out a scheme of code words and names, but Amina avoided any discussion of their future beyond that.

By eight that night, Amina's mood had turned bitter and foul. "Shit!" she had screamed when the refrigerator had clicked on late in the morning, but she calmed when it quieted moments later. Throughout the afternoon, as power surged on and off, Steve disconnected Amina's computer, the air conditioners and appliances, but kept a lamp turned on so they could monitor the progress. Since shortly after sunset, the lights had not even blinked.

Perla, respectful and somber, opened the kitchen door. Brenda burst in, skirt billowing, with an armful of newspapers. She bubbled into the dining room and spotted Amina curled up and pouting in Steve's reading chair. "You did well, girl, wiped out ninety percent of Mindanao." Amina's forlorn look stopped her in mid stride. "What's the matter?"

Amina pointed to the lamp.

"So what? They're scurrying like rats. And no one hurt—no casualties at all. You got worldwide attention. I saw it on CNN in Bangkok. Look." She took one of the newspapers and placed it in Amina's lap. "Here, here, read all about it. Hot off the press. MILF blacks out Mindanao."

Amina looked at the paper. "They're blaming it on us. Those scoundrels."

Steve came out of his office. "Hi, Brenda, welcome home. How'd it go in Thailand?"

"The usual, they're over budget and overly optimistic. Here, read how smart people accomplish a great deal with very little. Apex should hire these guys."

They sat on the floor at Amina's feet, Brenda, Steve and Perla, each one with a newspaper. Julius curled up on top of an abandoned sports section. As they perused the articles, they read interesting snippets aloud.

"Amina, listen to this," Brenda said. "'Mindanao residents should expect more power interruptions...erratic and critical...diesel fired power barges in key ports…Davao has a power plant in Bajada but it won't be enough…unable to meet needs of customers throughout the day…plan to rotate brownouts.' Isn't that better than a blackout? Discomfort, inconvenience, aches and pains for seven to ten days before they get things fixed, but they have enough power for hospitals, water pumps and communications. That's perfect don't you think, to get their attention without really hurting anyone?"

"I don't get it," Perla blurted. "One guy says damage of power outage is millions of pesos and another says economic loss will reach billions of pesos. But everyone is going to save on their electricity bill, aren't they" She giggled.

"You're right. Those billions are Hypocor's lost revenues." Amina smiled for the first time since the lights came back on.

Steve read. "'The attacks are reprisals for the capture by government forces of an MILF stronghold in Pikit town.' Wonder what gave them that idea. 'General Abaya …has ordered troops to guard vital power facilities throughout Mindanao and sent soldiers to hunt down the terrorists led by an MILF rascal known only by his nom de guerre Commander Bravo.'" He looked at Amina. "Anyone we know?"

She smiled and mouthed "Jamil" as if it were a pleasant word and not the name of a bitter tea.

"They can't get their story straight," Steve continued, "whether it's five, seven or eleven electrical towers damaged or destroyed. But get this, "The Agus-5 substation was severely damaged, some say by 81 mm mortar rounds, but an army spokesman said the guerillas employed a more devastating explosive." Steve frowned and wrinkled his brow. "I wonder what that rascal Commander Bravo used."

Brenda set aside her newspaper. "Amina, I'm happy for you. I cannot imagine your feelings, but Steve told me about the lake, and your village, and that whenever you mentioned Hypocor, the walls shuddered. That stuck with me. Sitting in the Bangkok airport executive lounge, I heard 'Mindanao' and 'blackout' on CNN. I worried when the announcer mentioned explosions and terrorists. But when he said 'Hypocor,' I yelped with delight. I knew it was you. The other business types in the lounge looked at me as if I were demented or sadistic. A few months ago, I would have reacted as they had. Being here, knowing you, has changed me. Napoleon said you have to break a few eggs to make an omelet. I understand that now."

Julius opened one eye.

"Thank you, Brenda. I feel better. Let's celebrate. Perla, we must have some white wine for Brenda and beers for Steve and me. Please join us. What would you like?"

"A rum and cola with lime, Ma'am. I've got the rum Christopher bought me for Valentine's Day."

Shortly before midnight, Steve slipped outside to relieve Marty. They talked for a while. Until he had his own computer, Steve had to rely on Marty to handle his encrypted communications with Boundless. They would send Steve the particulars on the Libyan project once he "resolved his current partnership," which Steve thought a clever ambiguity. Marty asked Steve when Amina would vanish. Steve said he would not burn his bridges. They jogged around the perimeter like inmates in the exercise yard, talking until they parried to a stalemate. Then, behind the guesthouse, out of sight of the guard, they stripped to the waist. Marty put up a good defense, but Steve broke his nose.

CHAPTER 52

The Compound, Friday morning, February 28

Fingering his swollen nose, Marty sat on Brenda's front porch and wondered what else he could do. He had installed the tracking chips, Perla had copied Bracelets' files and they had stashed most of their belongings in the Davao safehouse. It appeared Bracelets' computer, the box now re-sealed with a filament of airplane glue, would stay in Perla's room until the birthday party. Bracelets would not leave before then, but she could vanish as early as Sunday morning, during Bryce's graveyard shift, no doubt. They would not leave together, though. He figured Bryce would stay and wait for The House to identify whoever wanted to kill his woman.

Bracelets came out of the house and started to jog the perimeter. Since Monday, she had exercised twice a day. *Getting in shape to run*, Marty thought. She paced herself, doing a fixed number of laps and then bursting at the end. Marty timed her. When she finished, she came over to chat.

"Hello, Uncle Max."

"Good morning, Miss Taiba. Fifty-two minutes, that's quite an improvement. When do you run away?"

She smiled, "When I get to thirty minutes, I'm gone."

"You're not even sweating—just moist. I've tried to beat your time. I'm getting old."

"Let's have a race tonight." She pointed to the bulging pockets of his cargo pants. "I'll let you take out the weights."

He chuckled. "You're on. That was a neat power outage, but it didn't last long. What happened?"

"We only had six kilos, but it worked. The army had to pull troops out of the conflict to guard electrical towers. By the way, how much C4 did you blow up at the Pasigan?"

Marty hesitated. "Twenty cakes. Speaking of cakes, when and where is your birthday party?"

"At the guesthouse. Steve will start the barbecue around noon." She chuckled. "We've plenty of gas."

"Before you leave, will you give me a copy of your files?"

She smiled. "So you can keep the President of the World up to date?" Marty did not smile. They considered one another. "I'm thinking about it," she said. "I'll let you know. How's six o'clock for our race?"

"Take Perla with you. She's quite fond of you, you know. Dress her up in Muslim clothes. Two women will be less conspicuous than one." Bracelets looked at him as if he had mumbled to himself in a foreign language. "Okay, six o'clock it is," he said. She smiled, nodded and strode across the lawn.

He watched her. She was his last job. He had worked thirty years for The House without a mistake until he neglected to flush the chip. That worried him. If CIDG Davao held him for questioning while Bracelets was on the run, he would likely lose her. He had to protect her. If he failed, he would waste all that he had accomplished. He would be more desolate than Chopsticks had been.

He wondered how it would end. He and Perla would wander after Bracelets until she settled down and wait for her to finish her databases—or Nadine sent a replacement. Bryce could not replace him. They would not trust him to give up Bracelets' files, not the authentic ones. Nadine had to have someone else on Mindanao for her to know about Posey and the guards. Bryce felt certain she got that information from Haradji. The House would not trust him either. No, there would be no replacement. He hoped Bracelets would finish her databases soon. Bodyguard was a boring crapshoot—the shield waiting to take the bullet.

Marty got up and stretched. After Bracelets, he had to find something to do—a holiday in Hong Kong, perhaps—until Nadine finished whatever she had to finish. Then he would meet her in some godforsaken burg in the Bitterroot Mountains. She was building a house there, with a dungeon in the cellar. Marty could not visualize Nadine living in the Montana boondocks, much less himself. He would go to Tijuana and buy a nice whorehouse, or have one built with a dungeon of his own. Nadine could visit. He would grow peppers on the patio.

CHAPTER 53

The Guesthouse, Saturday, March 1

In the guesthouse carport, Steve basted the last batch of pork ribs with chipotle-laden she-devil sauce. Amina liked his spicy ribs. For her birthday, she would suspend the dictate that pork is *haram,* prohibited and unlawful, and enjoy a rib or two while sipping her beer.

Gerrit, leaning against the carport post, gnawed the last speck of meat off a rib. "Steve, you look glummer than a Dutchman spending his own money. Cheer up. This is a party."

"That's right, loosen up." Marty pushed off the porch railing, tossed a bone into the trash and took another rib out of the pan. "Eat one of your ribs. They're better than sex. If Adam had had ribs like these, we wouldn't have women."

Steve smiled. Marty's swollen nose amused him. In a sense, he had punched his boss. As the new recruit for The House, he depended on Marty until they could provide him with a cell phone and encryption software of his own, supposedly in ten days or so.

Bipsy slid open the front door. "Hey fellas, pronto-pronto. There're four women upstairs with hot lips. I'm fearing for my sexuality."

"Okay," Steve said. "I'm almost done. Guys, please take up that pan of ribs. I'll be there in a few minutes with the rest."

Alone, Steve thought about his extracurricular job. In his Apex job, he negotiated unambiguous contracts because he did not always trust his adversaries. There would be no written agreement at all with The House. A contract for an unlawful endeavor is not enforceable. Their deal, like honor amongst thieves, depended on trust. If he got in a spot, The House promised to send in the cavalry. *Trust us.* Marty figured the cavalry did not exist. If caught, he was deniable.

Steve hoped to keep his relationship with The House, but he was going to anger them. Tomorrow around noontime, he would go to the Insular Hotel and swim laps, get back into his daily exercise routine. He guessed three days should be enough. On Wednesday, Isabela would invite them all to lunch, which she would ask Perla to help prepare. When he returned from his swim, he would say Amina could not make it, turn to Marty, mention that he too used glue strands, and drop the tracking chip onto his plate. He would promise to send The House a copy of the databases whenever Amina finished. Complete and unadulterated files for the President of the World, he would say. *Trust me.* He smiled. *Fun but stupid,* he thought. He would admit to smuggling Amina out of the compound but that he had no idea where she and her files had gone.

After everyone stuffed themselves with ribs, sweet sour fish and potato salad, they went down to the living room to watch Amina open her presents. Most were clothes, Christian clothes from Brenda, Isabela and Gerrit. Jiriki, who could not or would not attend, sent Amina Moro clothes with a billowy *hijab*. She held it at arm's length and gave it a sad look. Steve imagined her shuffling along, bent at her tilt, posing as an old Muslim woman. Nashita sent a prayer rug. Amina held it, examined it shamefaced and then rolled it up without comment. She opened other small gifts and cards from friends and coworkers. The last gift, the laptop, shocked Amina, or so it seemed. Steve told her it was a gift from Max, Perla and him. Max explained they had only contributed the cost of a little LCD screen.

While Amina sat on the sofa admiring her computer, Perla, Isabela with Margreet and Brenda went upstairs to clear the dining room table. Soon they called everyone up for cake. Steve lit thirty-three little candles. Perla had never had a birthday cake. Amina invited her to help blow out the flames and they all sang the happy birthday song. Brenda and Perla cut the cake.

Steve hustled to the bathroom to get rid of a couple beers. As he passed the window, he saw Toots carrying a large mosaic box tied with a blue ribbon. Moments later, Toots yelled up from the front porch—they still had not fixed the doorbell—"Another present, Miss Taiba." He heard the pitter-patter of Amina's bare feet on the stairs and she exclaimed, "Oh, what a beautiful box." Steve visualized the unwrapped box tied with ribbon. Panic struck like lighting, "Bomb!" He screamed.

Brenda was handing Marty a plate of cake when Bracelets called up "Come look at this gorgeous box," and then they heard Steve bellow the alarm. Marty dropped the plate, shoved Brenda out of his way and thundered down the stairs. He saw the mosaic box on the coffee table, the lid open, twanging a metallic tune. To his right, he glimpsed Bracelets heave open the sliding glass door and vault over the porch railing. He figured the box would blow the moment the music stopped. *Lousy choices*, he thought. Without breaking momentum, he planted his left foot and aimed to kick the box into the corner beside the sofa. The music stopped an instant before his foot connected. The box croaked, "Goodbye" in Tagalog before it exploded.

Marty bounced against the wall and landed face down. He did not feel much of anything as he rolled onto his back. Then he saw his smoldering leg twisted at an impossible angle. It had not rolled with him. A foreign object protruded from his bloody crotch. His ears rang, his head spun and he could not focus his eyes. His left leg seemed okay. He pulled out his cell phone and punched star-zero-number sign. Then he lay back, closed his eyes and prepared to challenge the pain. He felt content. Bracelets was safe. He had done his job.

Perla screamed, "Max!" She heaved aside a section of splintered railing and bounded to his side. A red light blinked on his cell phone. "Hello," she shouted as she picked it up.

A male voice said, "Beacon on, Beacon on."

"Uncle!" she screamed.

"Ma'am, did you say uncle?"

"Uncle Max, Uncle Marty, Uncle Sammy, uncle off your ass. Marty Santana is dying."

"Where is he?"

"Davao, Apex compound, guesthouse."

"Keep the phone as close to him as you can. Do you understand?"

"I understand," she said. The light stopped blinking.

When Steve exited the guest bathroom, he crashed into Gerrit who had picked up Margreet from the hallway above the stairwell. Gerrit stood with his hands, arms and hunched shoulders encircling his daughter. He glared at Steve. "Where's the bomb?"

Steve bent over, tackled Gerrit and shoved him away from the stairwell. Pressure from the explosion gave him a boost and dumped them into Steve's overstuffed reading chair. A bit stunned, Steve wobbled upright, hopped over Brenda who lay on the floor shielding her head with her arms and stumbled down the stairs after Perla. He stood motionless, astonished: Perla had already contacted The House; Amina was not in the wreckage; she stood by the perimeter wall looking terrified but unharmed.

Perla dropped the cell phone and pressed her little hands against Marty's groin and leg to slow the flow of blood. Steve pulled off his tee shirt. "Use this." He jerked off his belt and wrapped it around Marty's thigh. He called for Bipsy.

"Right here." Bipsy stood at the top of the stairs, cell phone in hand. "What do I tell them?"

"Life-threatening bleeding, leg near severed at knee, shrapnel in groin."

"How did that happen?"

"Jesus…good question. Let me think."

They needed an ambulance but not the cops, not until everyone at the party agreed what should not be said. Steve glanced around the room as if he might miraculously find a plausible cause for the destruction other than a bomb. The cracked sliding glass doors led his mind outside to the carport.

"Gas tank, Bipsy, propane tank exploded."

"Gotcha."

Bipsy worked his way down the stairs and answered the 911 operator's questions about Marty's wounds. When he finished, Steve had him manage the tourniquet while he exposed the ankle of Marty's mangled leg. He removed the sheath and throwing knife, got the spare cartridges out of Marty's pocket but could not find his Beretta. He spotted it under the debris of the coffee table.

"Perla, get that gun," Steve said. He took out his PPK and picked up the cell phone. "Hide all this stuff in my tool shed."

"Beacon told me to keep the cell close to Marty."

"The cops can't find it. We'll call Beacon with the name of the hospital."

Perla touched Steve's arm. "Look," she said. She jutted her chin at the scene outside.

Amina knelt by the wall, her forehead touching the grass. Toots squatted beside her.

"Okay, I'll get rid of Toots. When she's distracted, hide the weapons and get back here quick. Stay behind the houses and come in through the kitchen."

Steve went outside. "Toots, who delivered the Mosaic box?"

"A young woman in Muslim clothes, Sir. I had not seen her before." She moaned and began to weep convulsively. "The box looked so pretty with the bow."

Steve held her shoulder. "An ambulance is coming. Go open the gate. Wait in the road and send it to the guest house."

"Yes, Sir."

Amina stopped praying and sat up. "Ambulance? Who's injured?"

Steve lifted Amina and ran his hands over her ribs and back. "Are you okay?"

She shoved his hands away. "I'm fine. Who's injured?"

"The blast crushed Uncle Max's leg. Bipsy is stopping the bleeding. Max is tough. He'll be okay."

"It's my fault. I should have left days ago."

"It's not your fault," Steve said, trying to sound emphatic. But he saw in Amina's shocked, closed expression an irreversible conviction that she had caused a catastrophe. She had escaped a horrible death by seconds. It would be days before she could deal with the complications.

"Tigress, you've got to get out of here before the cops come."

Amina looked dumbfounded at first and then nodded.

"Here," he said, handing her the keys to his truck. "Go to Jiriki's house. Perla and I will pack your stuff and meet you there as soon as we can."

Amina took the keys with trepidation; she had barely learned to drive. "Not to Jiriki's. The mosque is closer. I have to pray."

"Okay, but it will be very late, maybe tomorrow, before we can get to you. We will wait there if you have to leave."

Steve hugged her. She stiffened, pulled away and hurried to the guesthouse. Two paces inside she covered her mouth to stifle a scream.

Bipsy, who had been whispering words of comfort to Marty, looked up. "The ambulance is coming urgently. Max is going to be fine."

Steve came in behind Amina and grasped her shoulders. She twisted and swatted his hands away. "I did this. It's my fault. This is Allah's punishment for my lusting." She bowed her head towards Marty. "I go now to pray for you."

Steve watched her hurry to the house where she had lived with him for eighteen months. He wondered if he would ever see her again.

The kitchen door slammed. Perla rushed down the inside stairs, knelt beside Marty and caressed his brow. Marty opened his eyes and tried to smile, but lost it in a surge of pain. He saw Steve, lifted his head a little and struggled to annunciate something.

Steve recognized the first syllable, which sounded like a groan. He held up his hand and mouthed the name. "I know. I'll take care of it."

Having said that, Steve felt the urgency of what he had to do. "Perla, Bipsy, listen to me. Amina is terrified. She ran away. We don't know where. We know nothing about threats against her. Maxwell Harris is a freelance writer living with Brenda. That's it."

"I'm blissfully ignorant, Blue Eyes. I just came for the ribs."

Perla gazed at Marty. Tears streaked down her cheeks. "You've been like the father I never had."

"Perla, he's a freelance writer. You never saw that cell phone."

Marty nodded. Perla looked at Steve and flicked her eyebrows.

"Good. Go to the house and help Amina gather some Muslim clothes. Get her out of here before the cops come."

Perla did not move until Marty's eyes signaled for her to leave. She stood, grabbed the *hijab* that Jiriki had given Amina and scampered away.

Steve looked up the stairwell. Gerrit and Brenda stood watching from the rail. "You guys okay?"

"No problem," Gerrit said.

"Where's Isabela?"

"She took Margreet home."

"Max is a freelance writer. We know nothing more. Say nothing about threats. We have no idea who sent the bomb."

"We have to tell what we know," Brenda said. "Maybe Hypocor sent the bomb. The police have to find out who did this?"

"No, that's not going to happen. Amina has tried for months to identify the bombers and failed. This is no different. We will never learn who sent the bomb."

"We have been violated," Brenda screamed. "I want justice. We have to help them."

Steve spoke in a quiet, emphatic tone. "Brenda, listen to me. This is about politics. The rules of law do not apply here. There will be justice, trust me, but we cannot involve Apex. We do not know why someone wanted to harm Amina. Max is a freelance writer. Tell them he's good in bed. You know nothing more."

'He's right," Gerrit said. "This is politics. We are foreigners. We are ignorant of politics."

A siren wailed in the distance. "Brenda, are you with us?"

"Christ, I don't know. I'll think about it."

"Gerrit, talk to her," Steve said as he dashed outside.

The siren, very close, stopped abruptly. Steve figured the ambulance had turned off the highway. In a minute, it would enter the compound. Amina had not yet left. Steve saw her come out the front door. Perla grabbed her sleeve, pulled her back inside and signaled for her to stay put. Steve smiled. Perla would wait until Toots followed the ambulance to the guesthouse and then send Amina on her way.

As soon as the ambulance left, Perla called Beacon to tell him the name of the hospital where they were taking Marty. Before leaving, the medics had called the police, but Haradji arrived first. When he learned Toots did not know Amina had left the compound, his fury over her incompetence frightened her speechless. A pair of cops on motorcycles came to investigate. They called for more cops and detectives.

Two NBI agents, no doubt summoned by Haradji, drove in and began bickering with the detectives over jurisdiction. About an hour after the medics left, a CIDG representative appeared. He spoke to the lead NBI agent, who suddenly yielded jurisdiction to the Davao police. The agents stayed with the CIDG guy to observe the investigation but did not participate.

When the detectives learned that the bomb had come as a gift for Amina Taiba, sister of the journalist Jiriki Taiba, they suspected the bomber intended to silence Jiriki's investigative reporting. Haradji argued that Miss Taiba, an MILF subversive, had detonated the bomb herself and ran away. That claim infuriated Brenda. When asked about her relationship with Maxwell Harris, she became hostile, saying her personal life was none of their business.

The detectives ignored Haradji's theory; clearly, the bomber meant to kill Amina Taiba. But they wondered what had caused her to run out in time to avoid the blast. No one had an explanation. They all claimed to have been upstairs. When the detectives asked why Maxwell Harris went downstairs just as the bomb exploded, no one could explain that either. "You'll have to ask him," Steve said.

The NBI and CIDG observers listened to the questioning without comment. Haradji badgered Steve as to where Miss Taiba had gone. The lead detective smirked, saying if someone sent him a bomb, he'd not be leaving a forwarding address. He was more interested in Maxwell Harris, who no one seemed to know much about, especially the smartass Brenda. He had two cops escort her home to pack a bag and then sealed her house. Brenda said she would be at the Insular Hotel and left.

By sundown, the compound was quiet. Two cops remained with orders not to let anyone near Brenda's house or the guesthouse. Isabela and Gerrit had long before retired to care for their frightened daughter. In Steve's dining room, Perla waited anxiously while Steve argued with someone at the hospital. He hung up the phone with a grumbled thank you that resonated like "fuck you."

"His condition is stable, so they say. There will be no phone calls, no visitors and no further comment. I had to talk to three people before they even acknowledged he's a patient." Steve stood up. "We'll try again later. Now we have to find a place for Amina to hide. She can't go to Jiriki's house. Both the cops and the bomber will be looking for her their. Do you have any ideas?"

"Yes, sir. Uncle Max rented a little apartment in town that he called his safehouse. Most of his things and lots of mine are there. We were going to follow Amina when she left."

"Bless you. Pack some of Amina's stuff but not too much. Leave her toothbrush. The cops will likely search the house tomorrow. I want them to think Amina will return. I'll call a taxi and go tell the cops we're going to look for Amina. While I distract them, get the stuff out of the tool shed."

It took Perla nearly an hour to coax Amina out of the mosque. Listless and depressed, she spoke to Steve only to ask about Marty. She scoffed when he had no more information than what Perla had already given her and refused to talk to him. Perla told her about the investigation, laughing when she said that Perla told them to mind their own business. Amina seemed not to be listening.

Perla directed Steve to an entryway between two stores, unlocked the door and led them up a flight of stairs to an apartment. Amina peered out the window overlooking the street to get her bearings, to determine the direction of Mecca. Steve stashed the weapons and cell phone in an overhead kitchen cabinet.

Perla pointed to the plastic trash bag she had placed on the sofa. "There are jeans, a *malong*, three blouses and underwear, Ma'am. What else do you need for the next few days?"

"I want the prayer rug that Nashita gave me."

Perla fidgeted. "Yes, Ma'am. I'll get some toiletries too."

Amina stood as stoic as an ice sculpture, her hands clasped in front of her groin. Still wearing the billowy *hijab*, she looked like a straight-laced nun. Steve moved to embrace her.

"No!" She snapped. Her hands tightened. "You are forbidden, *haram*. Please go." Her eyes—fearful, pleading, watery—held Steve's.

Steve froze. For moments, he stopped breathing. His temples throbbed. He gasped for air. The unbearable tension chilled him. He trembled. He stared at Amina until he could see only the blur of their memories swirling in a centrifuge out of control. His mind could not cope with her finality; it could not argue or hope. He exhaled a convulsive sob, opened the door and stepped into the hallway.

"I'll bring the prayer rug as soon as I can, Ma'am."

Perla eased the door shut as if she were closing a casket. The click of the latch jolted Steve's mind. He looked down the stairs. Dizzy, he pressed his hand against the wall. Perla held his arm.

"I'll be okay in a minute," he whispered.

Steve took a few deep breaths. Then he heard Amina weeping. The echoes of their ending drove him down the stairs.

Steve leaned against his truck. The normalcy of pedestrians hustling to destinations jostled his mind toward reality.

"Perla, walk with me...please."

After they circled the block, Steve glanced up at the dimly lit window of the safehouse. He quickened the pace. The neighborhood consisted of three and four-story buildings, apartments above stores, and a few warehouses. He noted a pharmacy, grocer, Chinese restaurant and small shops selling inexpensive clothes and household goods.

"We'll see how things go tomorrow. When it's safe, go shopping and cook some meals for her. Make sure you are not followed. I can't go back there. She should not leave the apartment until she's ready to disappear."

"I understand, sir."

After several minutes of walking in silence Perla said, "Toots didn't know the box contained a bomb. The ribbon and bow looked so pretty she didn't want to untie it. She liked Amina. All the guards liked Amina. They're not involved. Besides, they didn't know about the party until it happened."

"Apex security knew. Gerrit asked them for permission to use the guesthouse."

"So Apex knew about the party."

"Apex security did, and they knew the guards had orders to open all packages."

Perla stopped walking. "Omigod! You know who sent the bomb."

Steve cursed himself, turned around and stepped close to Perla. "Forget what I said. I'm distraught and babbling nonsense. We did not have this conversation."

Perla stared at him for several moments. "You should tell Nadine."

Steve briefly counted backwards. "Who's Nadine?"

"Uncle Max's boss."

"He told us you knew nothing about his employer."

"I didn't until a few days ago when he asked me to talk to Nadine. He taught me how to use his cell phone and told me to use the codeword 'Uncle' if anything happened. You should talk to Nadine soon, sir. She'll know what to do. I really like my Uncle Max."

"I know."

"Oh…you know I like Max…or you know what to do?"

Steve pulled out his keys. "Let's get back to the compound."

As Steve drove off, Perla seemed to reminisce. "When I was a little girl, an old Maranao woman took care of me while my mother worked. Her name was Rimparac."

"Yes, Amina told me she taught you how to cook."

"She taught me many things. And she told me about the Maranao people, about their beliefs. They do not believe the government is responsible for their justice. They do not call the police when someone harms them. They take care of it themselves. They call it *rido*. Do you know about *rido*?"

Steve pursed his lips and drove faster.

Perla did not look at Steve. She spoke as if she were thinking aloud. "That's why you didn't want the detectives to know about the threats or that Uncle Max's real job was to protect Amina. And you know who sent the bomb."

They rode in silence until they reached the dirt road leading to the compound.

"Mr. Steve, Uncle Max has been very good to me. I like him a lot. This *rido* belongs to me too. I'll help in any way I can."

Steve nodded slightly. "Perla, we never had this conversation."

"Sir, what conversation? I've been dizzy ever since that bomb went off. Maybe in the morning I'll remember something, but I doubt it."

The Davao police returned the following morning to search Brenda's home and process the guesthouse. The lead detective came but did little more than accuse Steve of withholding information and complain.

"We can't get near your friend Maxwell Harris. We had to step on toes just to talk to the dumb monkeys guarding his royal highass. Who is he?

"A freelance writer."

"Right, I've heard that. CIDG Davao says their Cebu region questioned him and decided he's a freelance writer, but they refuse to tell me why CIDG Cebu questioned him. Your guards here say that all he did was exercise and toss green mangoes at your house. Why did he do that?"

"For fun."

"Right. I think he was trying to see if someone could toss a grenade into your bedroom window and blow up your girlfriend. Where is she?"

Steve signed and looked away. "I don't know."

"Right. Bryce, I'd like to toss you in jail until you tell me what happened here, but I can't. I've orders to cold case this mess today.

Marty was taken to a hospital in Davao and guarded by the Philippine National Police. Notwithstanding his guards, FBI agents from the U.S. Embassy in Manila walked into the hospital two days after the explosion and took him. (Some reports claimed they were CIA agents.) They flew him on a chartered plane to the Makati Medical Center in the suburbs of Manila. A Philippine immigration official said men he identified as agents from the U.S. National Security Agency accompanied Harris on the plane. The U.S. Embassy appointed Marty's doctor. Reporters could not get near him; they could not even speak to the people who were watching over him. The U.S. Vice-council paid his medical bills in Davao. Once Marty was well enough to travel, the American military evacuated him to the U.S. Naval Air Station in San Diego. From there, he vanished.

EPILOGUE

Five days after the explosion, Amina disappeared from the safehouse. She left her little girl bracelets on a slip of paper with the words "Memories Forever." Instead of a signature, it had a blotch that might have been tears.

Brenda left for a short vacation in New Jersey before going on to her new assignment in Mexico. By then, Apex had leased another home for the Van Der Zees and moved Steve and Perla into a two-bedroom apartment. Steve kept the safehouse. Nadine called him there until she left for the Bitterroot Mountains and then a young man with a Texas accent became Steve's Control. Amina's cousin Kule stayed at the safehouse for a while. Steve and Perla had long discussions with him there.

Marty did not go to Tijuana. A whorehouse did not appeal to him anymore; he had nothing left to whore around with. But he has a nice prosthesis for his right leg. He is in the Bitterroot Mountains living in a house with a dungeon in the cellar.

One morning toward the end of June, Haradji started his truck and a small bomb blew away his legs.

Perla did not go to the University of Southeastern Philippines. On July 14, from 2-3 PM, she will attend a briefing and orientation for international students in the Economics and Commerce Building at the University of Melbourne. She is living with Christopher in an apartment near the campus. Her Aunt Nadine and Uncle Max are helping with the tuition.

END NOTE

If you think Santana's exodus from the Philippines is over the top, look up Michael Meiring, the inspiration for the character Marty, and read how he got out as reported by the Philippine media. On second thought, don't bother—you've already read it.

Meiring blew off his legs while tinkering with explosives at the Evergreen Hotel in Davao. Some think he orchestrated bombings to implicate the MILF so the President of the United States could declare them a terrorist organization and station U.S. troops on Mindanao. But we really don't know what men like Meiring are doing in the Philippines, or why President Arroyo invaded the Liguasan Marsh, or who blew up those electrical towers. Lawless elements abound.

Since time immemorial, the Moros have fought for their land and beliefs. They have all but lost. During the last four decades of hostilities in Moroland, over 100,000 persons have perished, another million or so became homeless and destitute, and perhaps 250,000 more fled their homeland to take refuge in Sabah. Maybe Steve is right. Whether or not the land belongs to Allah, we're trampling the flowers.